Dodging Africa

A Novel

D. Lou Raymond

Fourth edition published December 2020.

ISBN: 9781723942983
ISBN-13: 978-1543206487

PO Box 442 □ Neskowin, OR □ 97149

971-219-6869 □ pulayanapress@gmail.com

DEDICATION

For Charles

Ke a leboga.

Ke rata wena thata thota.

Prologue: The Attack

Kalahari Desert, Botswana
November 1968

When Lesole stumbled he realized he was still of this world. It was real. All the blood and the rifle shot were as real as the sand under his head.

He should run. No, first he needed to stand up. Could he do that?

Lesole pressed closed his eyes, tighter, tighter, hoping that time might return to where it was before the blood.

They had been laughing. Grandfather and father had been exchanging proverbs. It was a skill their clan was known for. Clever proverbs, some ancient and traditional, others new, played with different languages like Setswana, Shona, Afrikaans and English. Men and women alike joined in competitions during the holidays and at weddings and other celebrations to challenge their cleverness and poetry.

But the world had changed in a split second.

Lesole groaned and thrashed in the sand. Stumbling to his feet he reeled again when he saw the blood. "Old father!" Shouting, someone was shouting. Lesole suddenly realized the noises were coming from him. Hot water covered his face. It was tears from his eyes. He did not know he was sobbing and shouting. The buzz in his ears was too loud. *Oh, Modimo, please God turn back the time*, he shouted in his head. Then he would tell his grandfather not to walk under that tree. It was an evil tree to have agreed to hide the spotted devil.

It had happened so fast that Lesole did not immediately understand. He was lagging behind father and grandfather, who had both insisted he go hunting with them. But it was so early and his bed so perfect. Mother had felt sorry for him and made sweet tea and bread to take along. It had only been hours before. It seemed like it belonged to another day.

No sound had signaled the danger. Grandfather entered the small glade first, a patch of green amid the bland beiges that made up the savanna. Quiet, so quiet, that the game would not catch on.

But grandfather was the game.

Out of nowhere the leopard had sprung silently in ambush from the dark tree, slamming onto the old man's back, and throwing him heavily to the ground. Like the precise cutting of a surgeon, the leopard's limb arched over the old man's head, its claws piercing his black forehead. The creature tore backwards, lifting off grandfather's scalp and shredding his upper back as it reared up and then back down on the chief's back, preparing to make the final piercing snap of its razor jaw on the old man's neck.

Lesole's father, Dadi, had seen the leopard at the very moment it pushed off from the branch and leapt onto grandfather. Although his warning shout was too late, his reaction was instant, his aim precise. A bullet pierced through the ear and brain of the devil leopard just as it hit the ground. A warm wash of blood hit the old man and sprayed back in a thick, sticky mist onto Dadi.

The old man and the beast lay together, blood and matted hair making a wretched pile. A cicada made a tentative chirp, asking, "*Is it safe, is it safe*?"

It was then that Lesole had stumbled backwards, unable to move his feet in the direction of his father and grandfather.

"Lesole, *takwano*, I need you!" It was his father, but his voice seemed different, as though he were shouting in a tunnel, the sounds hollow and far away. Lesole straightened, his father's voice giving him a focus. *There was so much blood.*

Suddenly, Lesole knew that his world had changed completely. He met his father's eyes and ran towards him. Together the boy and his father dragged the dead leopard off of the old man.

"Don't grab near the *nkwe's* claws. They can still come alive and poison you," Dadi yelled at Lesole as he dragged the animal by its front limbs, his sweating hands trying hard to grip the animal just above its bloodied claws. Lesole reached in and under his father's hands, grabbing the spotted devil's right limb just below Dadi's grip.

Lesole watched fear and disbelief fight one another in his father's eyes. Dadi knelt down and gingerly lifted the old man as he would a newborn. Blood covered grandfather's face and body and ran down Dadi's arms as he half carried, half dragged him towards the shade of a mopani tree.

On the spot near the attack, his grandfather's worn hat lay in the sand. Lesole stared at it, fixated again on his heartache and wish that time could return to that morning. Wishing that someone had needed them to help plow a field, or grandfather's leg had hurt, or that mother refused to let the old man leave the compound.

A sudden wind picked up the hat and flipped it over. Lesole jumped back, realizing that a spirit had just passed by. Was it death itself?

Terrified, Lesole's head snapped back. His eyes frantically searched his grandfather's bloodied face for any signs of life that the *nkwe*-devil had failed to silence.

# # #

Chapter 1: Willa's Ways

Mother Mercy Clinic, Botswana

The electric omnipresent whine mostly went unnoticed. It was just part of the air. Cicadas took the temperature, the old men said. But today the veldt buzzed even louder of them, their twitching legs vibrating in the heat, their alarm swelling across the gritty plain.

The din forced Willa's eyes open. *I have to figure it out.* She raised her head and confronted a face she sometimes hated to see. Looking at it would force a decision. "Stop it," she spoke only to her own reflection.

Willa could hear Mma Cookie's rambling, melodic voice in her head. "*Don't start worryin' till you sure you got somethin' to worry 'bout.*"

Mma Cookie's practical advice never failed, helping Willa interpret and maneuver around her mother, the hospital nurses, short-tempered Peace Corps doctors, crying babies facing sharp needles and witch doctors complaining about western medicine while asking for headache powders.

Damn her for choosing this week to go to Cape Town. Willa scowled at herself in the mirror. She was in way over her head with no safely net in sight. When her mother had flown to South Africa with Johnny five days ago, things were relatively normal at the clinic. Out front were the usual lines of the sick, mostly women with children, a few *banna ba golo*, old men with old men ailments, sweating more than anyone else. They had seen more than anyone else. It was their history that they sweated. Their old eyes squinted against all the changes they had witnessed, the pain built upon those dark, endless years spent in the mines or bent over ancient farm tools. Willa loved these old men and always found a way to get them in sooner than anyone else.

Then there was the shortage of antibiotics. *Still there.* Persistent as the infection it was meant to kill. Jan was going to also use the holiday trip to Cape Town to barter with her colleagues at Somerset Hospital to get a big enough antibiotics supply to hold them off until the regular shipment arrived. That was three weeks away.

But then the terrible confluence of events began. Only the unusual presence of a vulture in the hospital compound waiting area had provided a warning.

A violent bus crash just outside Tatitown brought a scared, young doctor to the clinic begging for all the antibiotics and supplies he could get. A stray cow had smelled clover across the roadway, forcing its own deafness against the rumble in the earth that should have signaled danger. The speedometer read 120 kilometers when the bus hit the beast, shattering the windshield into the face of the driver. Then it rolled, twisting metal against innocent bodies, turning tins of condensed milk from shopping bags into dangerous projectiles. The sand around the bus was red from the blood of the passengers and the cow's mutilated carcass. Over twenty Batswana passengers were critically injured and another twenty had various broken bones and contusions. The unfortunate driver, three old women and two school children were killed instantly.

It was clear to Willa that the doctor, obviously fresh out of medical school, had seen something horrifying. He was a young Dutchman who had been in-country only a month and had not yet seen the devastating results of bus accidents in remote areas. There were no ambulances or emergency medical staff to help the victims. The injured were laid in any available vehicles and driven to the nearest hospital or clinic, with no medical help provided on route. Those who made it through the ordeal of the ride then faced a wait until the few available doctors and skilled nurses could assess and treat their injuries.

The intern had seen all of this, the senseless tragedy reflected in his panicked eyes as he stuttered and choked out his request for antibiotics and supplies. Willa smelled vomit on his clothes and fear-sweat glazed his forehead. He wished he had never come to Africa, to this desert land of Botswana. His disgust for any place so disorganized that innocent children, old women, and young men in their prime died for no reason was all there in his eyes. It certainly did not make sense that this bus load of victims had little chance to survive.

Willa wished she could help the young doctor understand that this bloody, twisted nightmare was just one of the heavy crosses borne by Africans. Much worse than this had been dealt to the proud Batswana by white traders, missionaries, colonialists and mining companies. Each had taken what they wanted and left their African victims alone to pull themselves back up and face life again. But they did not just merely survive. Somehow they survived with dignity. That was the blessing and the curse of the Batswana. Dignity was no antidote when a blood transfusion was needed. But it did help you go on.

There was nothing Willa could do but give the Dutch doctor almost the entire remaining supply of antibiotics. He had nowhere else to go. Part of his spirit had died with those on the bus and Willa did not want to see the rest of him collapse when those still alive needed him badly.

Two of Mother Mercy clinic's best nurses returned with the Dutchman to help. That left one Peace Corps doctor, one nurse and Willa to care for the in-patients and new arrivals.

But the events continued to storm.

Mid-afternoon the next day, two young herd boys dragged in a third on a makeshift litter. The hurt boy's sallow, drawn face told of the blood loss he had suffered after his upper thigh was caught by an ax blade that had slipped, cutting his leg clean to the bone.

There went the last of the antibiotics. Willa had stashed the few measures left in the potato cellar where it was cool and would not be found. Marvin, the Peace Corps doctor, snapped at Willa when she hesitated for a second before running to get it, while he started the long process of sewing together tendons and tissue in the boy's leg. Willa knew the herd boy needed the antibiotics badly, but the thought of having none left at the clinic until her mother returned made her belly ache with worry.

Yet it still did not end.

That night a message was radioed to the clinic that Dr. Marvin's father had suffered a heart attack and was not expected to make it. Marvin threw a change of clothes into his jeep and tore out of the clinic compound towards the Rhodesian border and the airport in Bulawayo.

Now Willa wished her mother had taught her to pray because that seemed the only recourse against the last few days' disasters. But faith wasn't a fallback position.

There was her face again in the mirror. *Think, damn it, think.* How could she contact her mother to get back to the clinic and come bearing antibiotics?

Heavy foot falls on the stairs told Willa that Mma Cookie was on her way up.

"Ah, ah, these stairs. Hey, why is this second floor even here, hummn?!" Mma Cookie's voice resounded loudly up the stairwell and Willa could not help but smile. Without fail, Mma Cookie complained about the stairs on a daily basis. "What you doing *mosetsana* Willa? Huh?" Mma Cookie sat her bulk down on Jan's bed and the old springs squeaked with age and the rust of thousands of humid nights.

Suddenly a force of tears threatened Willa's countenance. She was overwhelmed with these terrible days, the deaths, and her inability to do anything about it. Willa turned and faced Mma Cookie, her bottom lip trembling as she tried to swallow the knot in her throat.

"Oh, my baby, come here." Willa fell into Mma Cookie's embrace and the tears broke through with a sob. Outside the cicadas seemed to pick up with Willa's sobbing, and the buzzing din grew more intense.

Mma Cookie pulled Willa's head down on her lap and rubbed her back. *It is just like when she was a small one.* When Willa would run to her, not Jan, to kiss away a scraped knee or a snub from a playmate. Mma Cookie loved Willa as her own child. This was her reason for holding fast to the anger she still held against Jan for always choosing the patients' needs over Willa's. There had been many times in the last nineteen years when Willa needed her mother's hugs, not another one from Mma Cookie. Yet Jan had not been there, did not seem to know about the needs of her little girl. Jan's hugs were sporadic and awkward. But undeterred by any lack of warmth, Willa was constantly attached to Jan's hip as a child, following her around the surgery. Jan never talked down to Willa or any other child. Not knowing what else to say to this beautiful, attentive girl who trailed her throughout her daily rounds in the clinic, Jan told Willa everything she was doing. Rather than being scared of the sick old men, the blood, the cries of pain, Willa was fascinated.

During Jan's monologues on the symptoms and treatments of each patient, Willa would often ask questions about the procedures. At first the intelligent questioning had surprised Jan. But soon it became commonplace and Willa began to seem like a colleague, not a little kid.

By the time Willa was thirteen, she was a full nurses' aide, often surpassing the technique of those she was assisting. Willa was also invaluable as a translator. Jan had never had the patience or sensitivity to master Setswana or Sekalanga. Willa, having been born right in the clinic and raised among African children, served as an interpreter, helping Jan diagnose patients and gain the trust of those reluctant to visit a white doctor. Willa's way with patients balanced her mother's natural impatience to quickly diagnose and treat. The long lines of Batswana that formed outside the clinic each day were Jan's daily challenge. Getting to each of them was her single focus.

That left little time to raise a daughter. So instead she raised a nurse.

Willa had inherited her mother's desire to heal, but not Jan's no-nonsense, clinical approach to her patients. What Willa lacked in age and medical expertise, she made up for in her bedside manner. Whenever Jan's brevity or cultural faux pas angered or insulted her patients, Willa was there to make amends and soothe tempers. It was a partnership that neither of them spoke about, nor consciously acknowledged.

Willa, sniffling and embarrassed, pulled herself up off Mma Cookie's lap and wiped her eyes on her smock.

Mma Cookie lifted her "daughter's" chin. "Willa-we, go wash your face and I will fetch Sammie to help us find your mother."

Willa sniffled again and nodded as she stood up. She wanted to ask Mma Cookie what good Sammie could do, but held back. If Mma Cookie thought that Sammie could help, then there was a high likelihood that he could. It would also be very disrespectful to question Mma Cookie as though she were a child.

A half-hour later Sammie Po sat at Mma Cookie's table. Willa re-filled Sammie's teacup and pushed the creamer and sugar bowl towards him.

"Willa-we," Sammie spoke in Setswana, "do you know my brother, Leonard, who works in Francistown?"

"*Nna, Rre. Ga ke ga itse.*" *I do not know him, my father*, Willa answered.

"Leonard my brother works in Mr. Player's hardware store and knows him very much, so much that he can ask Mr. Player to call his cousin in South Africa."

Will power and respect held her back, but Willa wanted so badly to ask Sammie to hurry up and say how he planned to help find her mother and overcome the antibiotics crisis. What did Mr. Player's cousin have to do with anything? She recognized her mother coming out in her. Always wanting the answer fast and simply not caring about any cultural precedents. Jan thought those were a waste of precious time. Willa had once seen Mma Cookie's two nephews imitating Jan's body language when she was frustrated that her information gathering was being hampered by friendly conversation. The boys rolled their eyes, huffed and puffed, shrugged their shoulders again and again and generally looked disgusted. It was so exact, so like her mother that Willa had laughed until her stomach hurt. Mma Cookie was embarrassed that the boys' display had been seen, but she too began laughing so hard that the kitchen floor literally shook, causing the boys to laugh until they dropped onto the linoleum, rolling back and forth on their backs.

Sammie continued. "Mr. Player's cousin is chief of police in Cape Town. Certainly he can alert Dr. Gakelape. Where shall I tell Mr. Player's cousin to seek out your mother?"

Willa could barely contain her relief. "Oh, Sammie!" She wrapped her arms around his neck and hugged him hard. Sammie smiled broadly, happy to have helped Dr. Gakelape's daughter to become herself again. Willa was still a child, yet she had looked like a worried old woman only an hour before. Now she was a nineteen-year-old girl again.

"You are too happy now, Willa-we," Sammie said in Setswana. "Wait until we find Dr. Gakelape before you ululate, child." Almost everyone referred to Jan as Dr. Gakelape, except for the white people, consisting of the Player family, the administrators at the mine's office, and the Indian shopkeepers in Francistown. It meant, '*I'm never tired*' and referred to the endless hours Jan put in each day at the clinic. Some of her patients thought that Jan had been touched by a friendly spirit that had blessed her with special powers and attributes, allowing her to work nonstop and only care about the clinic.

Sammie Po agreed to drive the clinic lorry into Francistown right away and see if Mr. Player would call his cousin. Willa wanted to go with him to emphasize the urgency, but she was due to relieve one of the clinic nurses in an hour. She also wanted to spend some time with Padmore, the herd boy who had split his leg open with an axe. His companions had gone back to their village to tell Padmore's family about his accident and to bring them back to Mother Mercy Clinic. Being alone, scared and in pain, Padmore needed a friend to talk to more than even another painkiller.

"Willa-we, a written missive from you to Mr. Player explaining your problem is needed. Can you do that now-now?" Sammie looked into Willa's hopeful eyes.

"Eh, Rre." Willa went to her mother's office and found a sheet of the official looking clinic letterhead. Sammie knew well that it would take him, an African man, much longer to gain access to Mr. Player if he did not have a note from another white person. Those rules had not changed even with the country's independence from Britain two years before. And although Mr. Player's family had lived in Francistown for a good 80 years, they continued to treat their Tswana neighbors with an aggressive paternalism unique to white people in Africa. There was a power in that relationship that few were willing to relinquish. Even those whites new to the color bar hierarchy of apartheid and the dusty legacies of colonialism, fell easily to treating Africans as children to be chided and directed at all times.

Willa also knew this, and quickly penned a note to Mr. Player, respectfully seeking his help in Mother Mercy's time of need, while noting her mother's location in Cape Town, and the name of her companion's company, Johnny's Air Transport Service. Mr. Player knew Johnny well and had worked with him for years. He would respond to the letter. Willa quickly estimated the minimal amount of antibiotics Mother Mercy would need until the normal shipment arrived, and wrote Mr. Player to please, respectfully please, pass along that number to Cape Town police so they could tell her mother. Licking the envelope, Willa prayed that the letter was enough to do that.

Even though the crisis of the last few days more than warranted this action, still Willa felt guilty about calling her mother back. How long had it been since Jan had really gotten away? How long had Johnny been needling her, prodding Jan to take some time off, to rejuvenate herself? Suddenly remembering the pink stuffed elephant Jan brought her last time she took a holiday, Willa realized it had been more than six years.

She closed her eyes tightly against the strain of the tears that threatened her composure. Sammie Po would worry greatly if she cried in front of him. He always took on the pain of others, dissipating the ache. That type of distraction could delay his arrival in Francistown. Too costly for everyone and too much of a heart strain for Sammie. Dear Sammie.

Things were going to be okay now.

# # #

Chapter 2: Tom's Lorry

Chief Tau's Village, Bodiba

For a moment the smell of coffee fooled Tom and he thought he was in his mother's house on Cape Cod. The rustling sounds were really waves crashing on the Chatham shore. But no, a second later the waves became the swishes of a straw broom. Mma Lilli was consumed with her morning ritual of sweeping the dirt compound outside Tom's rondovel. Cape Cod dissolved and the morning sounds of the African village filled his hut.

Tom had over slept. Mma Lilli's heavy broom work was a sign of disapproval that Tom should sleep so late on a Saturday. He groaned as he sat up in bed, lamenting the previous night's sins and his African mother's deliberate sweeping punishment that intensified the throbbing behind his eyes.

Pulling on his khaki shorts, Tom tried not to bend over too far. Never again would he share in the local brew with the village elders. It was not made for white men. Not only did he have a hangover, his gut felt distended and rotten. For months he had refused to partake in the pasty-thick, sour brew but realized that it had become a credibility issue with some of the men. Was he in or out? Was he a *chumza* of the village men or a white boy who was just a helpful and temporary fixture? Maybe fixture status was not so bad after all. It would have to do.

Suddenly the visual of him quaffing down traditional *bojalwa* beer became too much. Tom fell out the door of his hut, just making it to the latrine where his stomach reared up in revenge, shooting the foul bile into the hole. Shit-smell made him retch again and he reeled backwards on his heels. Tom stumbled out of the latrine, pale and dazed, his sour, swollen tongue a foreign object in his mouth.

Mma Lilli watched Tom's discomfort, a smirk on her face and hands resting authoritatively on her hips. A cackle broke from her lips and she walked up to Tom with a towel and clucked her tongue. "Do not try to be a headman, Tommi. Your belly is white and soft, not black and experienced." She cackled again and carried her large body across the compound to the cooking fire.

"Very funny, Mmawe," Tom replied weakly. "You're slowly poisoning me. It's a conspiracy, right?" Mma Lilli cackled even harder.

"Yes, conspy-racy, you lie, you see." She laughed even harder in delight over her poem.

"You don't even know what conspiracy means, I'll bet." Tom's hangover was a source of obvious delight to Mma Lilli but he was not in the mood this morning. He had been in a shitty mood all week as a matter of fact.

"If you can speak English and not American, I understand you, *mosimane*." Tom scowled at Mma Lilli for calling him a boy and insulting his language. She pretended not to notice him any longer and walked around the side of the cooking hut.

Tom went to the washbasin on the table outside his hut. Every morning Mma Lilli heated a small tub of water for him to wash. Today he pined for his tiled shower back home which would have beat down on his cloudy head and pushed off the worst hangover of his life; or at least the worst since his arrival in Botswana almost a year before. It seemed longer sometimes. Maybe it was the distance from home.

He remembered how far away the states felt the day after he had arrived in Africa. When absolutely everything was suddenly different than it had been twenty-four hours before, a strange sense of time loss occurred. Nothing was familiar; there was no comforting context, no reference point that brought equilibrium. For a man who had always felt a certain degree of confidence, it was disconcerting to be suddenly naked and without the language and familiarity to clothe his discomfort.

Tom recalled his first morning in Botswana. The Peace Corps training site, where he was to spend ten weeks learning the language and culture of the Tswana, was on the grounds of a church that had certainly seen better days. It was a type of African Baptist branch, filled with severe pews made of black wood. An old, off-key pump organ sat in the rear, eventually becoming a practice area when his group had to learn the Botswana National

Anthem for their "swearing in" ceremony.

That first day "in-country" was surreal. Was he really here? Was the sympathy of his mother and the comfort of his girlfriend really thousands of miles away in another world and at least two years from his grasp? It was early November, summer's peak in Botswana. Heat wrapped itself around everything by seven in the morning, making sleep impossible. The crunchy straw mattress and squeaky springs on the cot did not help, nor did the weevil that had chewed noisily inside his foam pillow all night.

Everyone rose early in Africa. An endless cacophony of roosters and barking dogs served as a primitive alarm each morning. There simply was no way to sleep in. Although groggy from almost no sleep during the two-day trip from New York to Botswana and the training site, Tom felt restless his first day in-country. No set agenda had been provided to the trainees that first day, so the thirty volunteers roamed about the compound or quietly unpacked their bags, all in different stages of culture shock or separation anxiety. Having been abruptly ripped out of their safe zones, via a twenty-hour plane ride and eight more hours of buses and vans, the green volunteers looked to one another for that old feeling of cultural comfort. Relationships formed quickly and tightly among the group, the only link with what was and what they knew.

Tom decided to set out and explore the compound and surrounding village of Molepolole as everyone else was unpacking. Two other volunteers joined him, Sam from Idaho and Jill from Connecticut. The church compound was set back off the main road about a quarter mile. What struck Tom the most was both the brightness of the sun and the homogenous tan color that pervaded everything from the soil to the huts to the colors of the children's tattered khaki school shorts. His baseball cap and Ray Bans seemed to tame the heat. Sam's Stetson and the wide-brimmed straw hat that Jill wore did the same.

Idaho Sam was a cross between a cowboy and an environmentalist. Never without his bowie knife, he liked to whittle while he walked, crouching down every few yards to examine and identify a rock or lizard species, always verbally providing more detail than anyone cared to know. Jill was the youngest of the entire Peace Corps group. At twenty-one, she was still trying to figure out her thoughts and opinions on issues, and generally found it easier to adopt whatever theories and comments were provided by whomever she happened to be with. For obvious reasons, the Peace Corps boys liked sitting next to her at meals and on bus trips, her agreeable nature and California blond palette providing an attentive audience. Tom liked her too and as the weeks moved by quickly during training camp he sought Jill out at meals and for walks through the village hills.

While Molepolole did not have a true "center", the post office shared an open area with a bottle store selling warm beer and spirits and a general dealer grocer selling one of just about everything. Feeling curious this first day, the trio entered the general dealer to scope out its wares and see how they would spend their meager Peace Corps allowance of one pula a day in training camp, and which they were told would increase to P125 a month once on the job. Before they had left the training compound, Tom had asked the site director how to say "hello" in Setswana. With this one word literally in hand -- he had written it on his palm -- Tom took his first stab at greeting a Motswana woman in her own language. But after saying, "*dumela*," he did not know how to respond when the shopkeeper greeted him in return and then rattled off another sentence which seemed like a question.

Tom flushed red, shrugged his shoulders apologetically and said in English, "I'm really sorry but I don't know Setswana yet." He smiled broadly, his blue eyes flashing sincerity. The two Batswana women giggled and said they knew English and could teach Tom Setswana. As he was learning what to say after *dumela*, Idaho Sam was examining the enamel cookware collection and Jill the strange array of biscuits, sweets and chewing gum, all in packaging written in Afrikaans.

By the time they left the shop, Tom was happy. He had successfully communicated with Africans, purchased a faded black and white postcard to send to his girlfriend and found an African print shirt. He would wear it that night at dinner and impress the other volunteers. Tom also left the shop with his old confidence back. He could deal with being in Botswana. It was going to be okay.

That feeling lasted for a good five minutes until a green mamba crossed their path on the way back to the church compound, only a foot in front of Tom's shoe. Fortunately, the mamba had its own agenda and quickly slithered through the tufts of growth that grew in the dirt-sand and provided excellent snake cover. It took a good ten minutes before Tom could no longer hear his heart beating in his ears.

A year had passed since that first day's experience. To Tom it felt both like a long time ago and like it was just yesterday. He had not seen Idaho Sam or Jill since training had ended almost a year before. Both of them were stationed in the southeastern corner of Botswana, a two-day trip on dusty roads from where Tom was in the north. It would be nice to see Jill again. Tom knew that if he wanted more with Jill that she probably would not refuse. During their time at the training site, Tom and Jill quickly stumbled together, allowing the gin to let them do what they had wanted to since they met. They made clumsy love in the darkest of Kalahari nights, only seeing one another's outline but making every touch count.

Now the thought of Jill in his bed caused the heat to rise in his cheeks and shorts. But she was the type of young woman who picked out the color of her wedding trousseau even before a first date. Tom had wanted Jill in his bed many a night over the last year, but not the relationship that would have gone with it. For this reason, he had not gone down to the capitol city even once and never bothered to answer Jill's postcards and letters. He knew he was a shmuck. He also knew he would sleep with her again in a minute.

Suddenly a scream broke Tom's reverie. "Tommi, *Tommiwae, takwano, takwano*, come, come!" yelled Mma Lilli. Pushing aside the rondovel door, Tom ran into compound where Mma Lilli was pointing to a crowd of villagers running and shouting with purpose.

"*Wa reng, Mma Lilli*? What's going on?" Tom shouted back.

"*Ga ke itse, Tommi.*" She did not know either but the crowd of villagers was approaching their compound. Tom and Mma Lilli moved quickly out of the courtyard through the front garden, and met the crowd in the cart path in front of the main gate. An elder stepped forward, the chief's brother, and his entourage grew silent.

"Mr. Tommi, we are needing your lorry. Chief Tau is felled by a leopard." His brown, lined face suddenly fell, his bottom jaw quivering with the terrible knowledge of his brother's fate.

Mma Lilli grasped the old man's hands in hers and then turned the strength of her gaze on to Tom. "You must go *janong ka bonako*, Tommi. The life of our chief blows in the wind and he cannot be lost now." There was not a question to be asked. Tom nodded.

The chief's brother called Lesole's name, and he moved his way forward through the crowd. Still winded from his four mile run through the bush, Lesole's little chest heaved in an out and his face and neck glistened with sweat. A great fear also shone in Lesole's eyes. He had to show Mr. Tommi where his grandfather was, but he dreaded returning to the evil, bloody spot. But his father needed him to be strong. He had said that to Lesole before he started running. So much running, but now he could not remember any of it. Somehow his legs and his fear carried him back to the village. Now his memory and his dread would lead him back to the leopard tree.

"I will show you. Come quickly!" Lesole grabbed Tom's hand and began running with him towards the Land Rover parked in Mma Lilli's side yard.

Tom had no time to think. What did he need? What did he have? "Wait, I need the keys. And, Mma Lilli, get some blankets and water, please, *ka bonako*." Tom broke from Lesole's grasp and ran to his hut. He grabbed the keys, a shirt and reached under his bed for the Peace Corps-issue first aid kit. What he would do with it he did not know since he had no idea what shape the chief was in. If Tom could get the chief to the regional health post, he might at least have a chance. What direction was that from the attack site? "Jesus," he said to himself out loud. "I'm not ready for this."

Water, bread, blankets and towels were tossed into the back of the Land Rover. Tom pulled out slowly while the crowd parted, allowing him through. Lesole sat tall in the passenger seat ready to navigate. Suddenly there was more shouting in the crowd and a nursing sister in a white uniform appeared at Tom's window.

"Oh, yes, thank god, sister. Please get in." Tom's relief was great. Having the fate of the chief rest solely on his shoulders was not a situation he was relishing. Nurse Cloud was a thin, small woman whose unfortunate looks and terse demeanor had relinquished her to permanent spinster status. She was a government appointed village nurse who had completed two years in a secondary school, and then had two years of nursing training. While her medical knowledge was limited, she at least kept down incidences of diarrhea and infections in the village that arose from bad water and untreated cuts.

The crowd of villagers silently moved aside and watched the make shift ambulance gain speed as it left the village. Lesole shouted the first set of directions to Tom. He barely heard the small boy's voice above the roar of the Rover's engine and the fear of responsibility pounding in his ears.

# # #

Chapter 3: Nora's Trip

Boston

November 1968

It was such a feeling of wonderment and release to be naked and not care. Caring was not even a question. Nora looked at her hand again, and it continued to swim and swirl in front of her eyes. Her neck felt so good. Was someone touching it? Yes, Gary was there rubbing and pressing her neck gently. Nora did not know Gary that well, so she surprised herself that her nakedness did not bother her. Only feelings mattered. That was why she had swallowed the tab of acid. Gary said that she would feel different, feel that she understood everything.

Did she understand everything? Nora focused on her father, who she did not understand at all, to see if now she would. A smile crossed her face as all the memories of her with her father flashed by. There she was a little girl, following her daddy around, having him all to herself. All around her was a crowd. Oh, it was a baseball game. Fenway Park's green towering walls swirled around her. Suddenly a cheer, and Nora's father raised her onto his shoulders. "My little girl, my little angel." He always said that to her. It made her feel so special.

When had she stopped liking it, she wondered? When had it started, this anger and annoyance at whatever her father said or did, no matter what it was? Yet, Nora could no longer deny or ignore the overwhelming feeling that she was suffocating in her father's life. All the comforts that made him feel good and safe were allergens to her, slowly choking her and leaving her with an overwhelming feeling of emptiness, of sickness.

These small annoyances began to weigh heavily on her. When she started listening to music unacceptable to her father, seeing a new set of friends that he referred to as "hippies" and dressing in ways that "embarrassed him," Nora began to detach. Then the anger began. She hated her father's judgments of everything she did or said. He was trapped in the world of his perfect second wife, his perfect medical practice, his perfect house and country club memberships, and he was trying to trap her in that world along with him. *No! No! No!* banged away incessantly inside her head and she felt herself slowly awake.

But the acid made Nora not care anymore because now she understood it. Her father had never had the opportunity to see life from an alternative vantage point. Well, he had one chance, but he blew it. He could have stayed with mother in Africa, but he couldn't handle it. Couldn't hack being apart from his fellow Bostonians and their Harvard circle of influence. Her anger surged. Why had her father taken her away from mother?

The acid made Nora imagine it all a conspiracy against freedom of movement, freedom of speech, and freedom of desire. *What*? That was Gary's voice saying those words. How had he entered her mind and joined her soliloquy?

"Freedom of desire, baby. Freedom to feel, to see inside one another." It was Gary. But she had not been paying that much attention to him. Nora noticed she was still on Gary's bed, on a quilt he said his grandmother had made for him. She was back to the present.

Gary's face nuzzled her neck from behind and his hands moved down over her breasts and hips. It felt so good, with her senses opened up, awakened from a long sleep. Gary had been right when he said she would not be so uptight if she tried the acid.

Nora opened her eyes and was surprised that it was still light outside. So much time had seemed to pass. A wind blew past her face although the window was closed. How funny, she thought, when the wind turned out to be the music that had surged up and blown by her. Maybe it wanted her to follow? Nora tried to focus on the words to the song, but the sounds suddenly turned into colors that began moving towards her. A purple ribbon wrapped itself around her waist and pulled her down onto the bed. A white ribbon brushed back and forth across her face and Nora felt pure joy in the sensation of it as it wisped back and forth across her cheeks.

Music returned and the ribbons became Gary's hands and lips and body. He too was naked and his skin glowed against hers.

Fingers touched her, entered her, causing explosions so hot that she shivered and rocked back and forth. Nora began moving faster, her hips finding new rhythms, rolling back and forth, thrusting upwards. Gary's hands lifted her up and pushed the two of them tighter together. Tight, hard pleasure and the movement of two as one gushed through Nora. She heard her own voice echoing in the air, laughing, calling out to the sensations. A weightless joy stretched out the time as her orgasm peaked again and again. Gary gasped and moaned loudly as his own pleasure climaxed. He held his chest tightly to Nora's and rode the beautiful, hot wave inside her.

How much time had passed? Nora rose up on her elbow and leaned over Gary to see the clock. It was almost seven o'clock. Nora did not know why she was suddenly wide-awake. Probably just thirsty. She slowly climbed over Gary so she would not wake him up and walked to the kitchen. There was one more Coke in the fridge and Nora gulped down half of it before burping loudly and putting the rest back for Gary. The kitchen window had a view of one corner of Fenway Park, now dark and looming over the quiet winter streets. Eight stories down the colored lights on the small corner grocery blinked at no one, *except me,* thought Nora. *I'm here, I see you blinking Merry Christmas, little shop.*

It was cold in front of the kitchen window and it made Nora remember her nakedness. She tiptoed back to Gary's bedroom and gathered her clothes that were scattered all over the room. She giggled as she pulled her panties off of the black light that was fairly high on the wall. Small snores rose from Gary as he slept heavily under the quilt and the drugs. Nora looked at him but felt no affection. It was hard for her to believe that she had felt such pleasure from him, when prior to this day she had seen him as a rather dull boy from Washington, D.C. who grew up under the influence of academic parents at a Catholic college.

Nora still thought of Gary in the same way, but she was thankful for his tutorial in LSD. Just as Gary approached his studies at M.I.T. in a methodical and pragmatic fashion, he did the same with his drug experimentation. He had started out slow with low doses of LSD and kept diaries of his experiences, both physical and metaphysical. Gary shared this information sparingly with only his close friends, who all wanted to experience a trip, but were not looking to overdose or do anything really stupid. Since he had tracked his trips and developed recommended type and dosage levels for low-level tripping, his friends trusted his judgment. Gary called it a "suburban high", but his pragmatism also saw it as a reasonable way to turn on. Hence, Gary's reputation as a guru of safe trips.

Nora moved into the small living room and dressed quickly while standing next to the heating duct. *God, I'm still so high*, she thought, *and thirsty*. She tiptoed back to the kitchen, weaving slightly, and grabbed the Coke bottle. She reached for it but the neck of the bottle leaned away from her touch. Nora squeezed her eyes shut and swallowed hard. When she opened them the bottle had returned to its normal state. *Time to leave*, she thought.

Outside, Kenmore Square was alive in lights. Nora moved towards its movement, the lights from the shops, theaters and cars drawing her in. *It is so beautiful*, she thought. *Electricity is beautiful, and we were so smart to capture it in holiday lights and the headlights of cars*. Nora laughed out loud, suddenly so happy that she now understood an infinite amount more about what she had taken for granted just that morning. For a moment she played out telling her father about the clarity, the sudden knowledge from a simple little tab called LSD. He would *have* to understand her tonight. Everything was so clear. Even he would be able to see that.

The old clock above the marquee of the Odeon Theatre showed 7:26 pm. *Damn, what happened to the day*? Suddenly Nora was really hungry, but also just wanted to go somewhere she could think, focus on the questions that had occupied her to the point of total distraction. A feeling of boredom pervaded her life of late, as had annoyance at everyone she knew and everything that made up her existence. Everything seemed pointless, meaningless. What was the point of being in college? Why was she living with Daddy and Carol?

Until a few months before someone or something had always compelled Nora to think a certain way about everything, but where did those ideas come from, she wondered? Why hadn't she questioned her own actions before? Questioned the opinions and lifestyle of her father? *I'm so stupid, I cannot develop any thoughts of my own*, Nora thought as tears welled in her eyes. *Who am I except Dr. Michael Dodge's daughter? Spoiled Chestnut Hill brat.*

Nora started running down Beacon Street and towards the Back Bay. Faster, faster, it felt so good. Those negative thoughts were left behind with the lights. *I am free right now*, she thought. *I am whoever I want to be, not who I've been, a nothing.*

At the old Harvard Club, Nora turned right on to Massachusetts Avenue. She looked up and saw dusky yellow light in the window of the second floor dining room. "I hated being there," Nora spoke out loud. An elderly woman walking by glanced at her and then turned away quickly and uncertainly, pulling her purse closer to her. Nora stared at the woman's reaction in disbelief and then started laughing. *Am I so scary now?* A low clatter of silverware made Nora look up again at the Harvard Club dining room window. No other place that she had ever been in held such an aura of boredom and banal tradition.

Her father always took Nora there for dinner when he had to meet out-of-town alums in Boston, there to observe a new surgical procedure or for a convention. Her father hated facing an old classmate alone, and bringing Nora always provided an excuse for a short evening. Daddy never felt that comfortable around people, she realized, not even me. Not even mother. That must be why she chose not to come back to Boston when Daddy had returned after less than a year of helping to keep Africans alive and well. Michael Dodge's ability to freely practice his newly honed surgical skills could no longer overcome his aversion to being in Botswana.

But that was a million years ago. Nora did not remember returning to Boston with only her father. She was just two and expressed the ache she felt for her mother by crying frequently and continually searching the rooms of their home for her. Until she was eight, Nora remembered setting up elaborate tea parties with real cake and tea, hoping the event would be special enough to bring her mother back.

When her father had married Carol ten years before, Nora finally accepted that her parents would never reconcile. Carol was here to stay, the model hostess and perfect wife. If only she had a personality, she might not be so annoying, Nora thought cattily. Carol hated it when Nora referred to her as "stepmother" with her friends. "Honey, it always makes me think of the evil stepmother in Snow White. Call me Carol and introduce me as your father's wife, please, honey."

It was hard to completely despise Carol because she was so damn nice about everything. But what a wimp! Carol's only defined role in life seemed to be serving the needs of her famous surgeon-husband. Nora just hoped her father would not be too hurt when Carol finally woke up to the fact that she had no life of her own, and would either leave or change into something Daddy could not tolerate. Just like mother had done.

Nora was suddenly aware of guitar music somewhere in the distance. She crossed Massachusetts Avenue and turned onto Newbury Street. She found the music. Half a block down people were hanging out in front of a café, part of the spillage of warm, happy bodies inside.

The music. What was that music? Nora knew the song, but she could not place it. It was then she realized that being high could mean either great focus and attention to the minutest of details, or complete lack of concern and no associative memory.

Nora felt a sudden need to be closer to the music. She could feel the guitar strumming in her stomach. It was like she had eaten the music. Would her burps be sharps and flats, she giggled?

Pushing her way through the entrance, Nora managed to slowly squeeze through the tables and chairs and people sitting on the floor. It was an eclectic crowd. A few college students and a hip professor or two mingled with a crowd who were there to immerse themselves in the music. Her father would call them hippies. "They are either benign or belligerent, but either way have absolutely no purpose or value." Absolutes were Daddy's tonic, uncertainty his paranoia. Nora remembered how profound Carol had found her father's criticism of hippies. She had run to her desk, which she properly called her "secretary," to jot it down for quick reference, a quip for their next cocktail party.

Cigarette smoke weaved among the café tables and rose slowly into the dark rafters above. Mixed in Nora was sure she smelled marijuana smoke. Where was it? Twisting slowly around in her spot just behind the sitting hippies, Nora surveyed the crowd. Since her high was still directing, she could focus exclusively on each person in the room, hear their conversation, feel their love for the music, feel the sensuality of the kiss at the corner table, the man's strong hand caressing a sweet neck. Feelings streamed through her and she felt overwhelmed.

Nora sank to the floor with a soft plop and ended up sitting cross-legged. She rested her head against the wall. It felt cool. That was nice. Closing her eyes was even better. A surge of pleasure began to rise in Nora's feet and rushed through her legs, under her ribs and up the back of her neck. It could only be compared to a full body orgasm, but it did not subside but grew to a crescendo and held her. She was captive to it.

Guitars stopped strumming suddenly. The whole world must have stopped and is looking at me, Nora thought. *And I don't give a shit.* She laughed out loud and opened her eyes. How much time had passed? Minutes, hours?

No, the whole world was not looking at her. Just one guy. Nora's eyes met the guitar player's. She felt another surge but this time it was between her legs. Jesus, she thought, he was beautiful. Right there she understood that she would know him, sexually and otherwise, very well.

As Nora stood up, slowly sliding up the wall, the guitar player also rose. The space between them closed as he moved towards her. His right arm was outstretched and his hand, the only thing in Nora's world, moved in to seek hers. As their fingers and palms met, the guitar player smiled. "I'm Pete. You're beautiful. But you fell asleep during my solo." He smiled, teasingly. Nora smiled too and then her head fell back as she laughed at his mistake.

"I wasn't asleep. I became your song." Her honesty and purity were sobering.

"Damn it, girl, don’t do this to me." Pete let go of her hand and reached up to her cheek, brushing aside a strand of hair. "You're high as a damn kite, aren't you?"

Nora just sighed heavily, and kept looking in his eyes. Those eyes she could look at for a long time, she could lose her way, never come back and not care. "You're beautiful too, Pete." She knew she must be high because she would never have had the courage to say that to the best looking, sexiest guy in the place. *And he's paying attention to me*, Nora mused. What would her old high school buddies think of her tonight, especially those tight-assed Wellesley bitches. High on LSD and getting wet panties over a café guitar player. That would fill their Dear Diaries for a few days.

"Are you thirsty? Want to get something to eat?" Pete's voice seemed to come out of his eyes, which were more compelling than anything she had ever stared at. "It will help you come down easier if you eat, you know." Pete tilted his head in encouragement and smiled. *This girl is definitely a rookie*, Pete kept saying to himself. *I'm liking this*. He could tell that this high, young co-ed had not yet learned the power and significance of her beauty, an understanding that Pete had seen other women in his life use skillfully to their advantage. Maybe he could have the advantage for once.

Here is a man I can trust. Nora just knew this. He cared about her even though he did not know her. "Yes, I would. I'd love to eat something." She looked around the room for a table.

"No, not here. Let's go to Harry's Place. It'll be quieter and we'll get served faster. Do you like really greasy cheeseburgers?" Pete looked down at the young woman's face. Her skin was exquisite.

"Only when accompanied by really greasy fries. And ketchup." Nora laughed and Pete put his hand on her back, leading her through the maze of people and towards the front door. Pete yelled back to his buddy to take care of his guitar. He would be back for the ten o'clock set.

Out on the sidewalk the cold air was a relief and Nora breathed it in.

"What's your name by the way? I like to know that level of detail whenever someone becomes my music and we eat cheeseburgers together." Pete smiled so beautifully that Nora almost reached up and kissed him. She looked in his eyes.

"Nora."

"Nora, who?"

"Nora who just met Pete and now is going to eat and come down more slowly over cheeseburgers and fries."

Pete stared at her and smiled. He felt like grabbing her and squeezing her. He wanted that mouth. Later. "Come on, beautiful Nora. Let's get some all-American grease into you while you tell me your life story."

# # #

Chapter 4: Tommiwe's Trip

Kalahari Desert, Botswana

Every time the Land Rover hit a rock-hard rain gully in the worn track, Tom grimaced in guilt and fear for the old man. He knew that each bump and turn must be excruciating for Chief Tau. His head snapped around to ensure that the chief was still conscious, and then jerked back, all his concentration on the rutted track.

The jeep was filled with blood smell. Nurse Cloud and Dadi, the chief's son, sat on either side of the old man, supporting his weight and keeping him upright. The chief's grandson, Lesole, sat in the front of the Land Rover, every few seconds glancing back in fear and fascination at the blood red beacon of the chief's head.

Dadi had done a good job of stemming the blood flow from the leopard's scalping by holding his hand firmly on top of his father's head. Even after Nurse Cloud had arrived at the scene with bandages, Dadi had refused to remove his hand, insisting that his father's head would fall off if he did so. Frustrated after none of her admonitions worked, Nurse Cloud had bandaged over Dadi's hand and around the chief's head, sealing him into the gauze and medical tape.

After one particularly bad bump, Nurse Cloud yelled, "Damnation, *lekgoa*, you're killing the Chief!" Hearing the Christian nursing sister curse and use the derogatory term for a white person had raised a pained chuckle from the chief that was cut off quickly by a cough and a deep moan that seemed to rise from the very earth they sped over. Tom glanced back again and saw the ashen, drawn face of the chief under the rivulets of fresh and dried blood.

"*Go swaba, go swaba*, so sorry, so sorry, *Kgosi*," Tom grimaced again. He wanted to yell so badly at the top of his lungs to release the tension, help him concentrate harder. *Fucking Africa*, he thought loudly in his brain. Why does everything here have to be so hard? Why do the best chiefs have their heads taken off by leopards? Why do the most beautiful babies die of TB or dysentery? Why do the lovely wives of mine workers grow old alone while their husbands live among hundreds of other men in mine dormitories in South Africa? Fuck this place. Why did he come anyway?

Tom's father had berated him for throwing away a promising engineering career to build water catchments and fix borehole pumps for "a bunch of illiterate savages." Tom remembered just staring at his father when he had said that, wanting to laugh at the ignorance of the statement, but knowing it would only lead to a shouting match. He had been there too many times before. Too many times it had turned much uglier with Tom taking his father's abuse, even asking for it, hoping to deflect it away from his mother.

Tom had been nine when his father sliced open his head with the metal straight edge of a ruler. For some reason it had not even hurt. He had just stared at his father as a trickle of blood ran down his face and neck, then quickly grew to a stream. In the emergency room Tom lied and said he had been crawling under the house and hit his head on something metal. His mother did not correct the story. His father had not come with them. Most likely he had gone out drinking at Eddie's. That was the usual scenario after his father lashed out and physically abused him or his mother.

The ruler incident only temporarily stopped his father from using Tom as target practice whenever things were not going his way. As Tom got older and matched his father's size, the abuse became strictly verbal. And if he kept his mouth shut, that seemed to keep his father from also lashing out at his mother. Those times when his resentment and pain could not hold back his own tirade, Tom would get physically sick. He knew his mother would then have to take the screaming and the insults, punches, kicks and worse from his father. She even had special pancake make-up that she used the next day so that no questions would be asked by neighbors or acquaintances she passed in the grocery store. Tom knew that she knew that others knew, but everyone agreed with their silence to be silent.

There was the answer. Why he had come to Africa. It had just gotten too hard to look in his mother's eyes or hear her voice during his college years when he called from California. His guilt still found him 7,000 miles from home, but it was weary and reticent. At that distance it had not hurt as much. Most of the time.

Suddenly the lorry track got smoother and the land rover's engine quieted down. Lesole sat up higher in the front seat, searching the road ahead.

"Rra Tommi, the clinic is behind the thorn trees." Lesole pointed ahead to a thick stand of acacia trees and used his hand and arm to mimic the turns the precise turns that the jeep would take to get there. A white sign with blue lettering was suddenly visible ahead.

Tom slowed down and made a right towards *Mother Mercy Clinic*. This would have to do for now because the hospital in Francistown was another hour plus southeast. Chief Tau could not stand a minute more of the rutted track. He had all but passed out, the hand of his son holding on to his life as it pressed down on his scalp under the bandages.

Amazingly enough, the clinic compound had clear signage and a lot of it, leading patients in Setswana, Sekalanga, English and with pictures to where they needed to be. The compound, with its many buildings, was relatively big for a clinic, and very different from what Tom had seen of other village clinics in Botswana. It was also very orderly and clean. Although it was surrounded by the chalky sand-dust that covered virtually the entire country, it was marked by pathways lined with paving stones, trees and cactus. Each building looked freshly painted in a range of pastels and had shaded outdoor waiting areas for patients. It almost looked like a real hospital. Hadn't he heard about this place last time he was in Francistown? Something about an American doctor, a woman doctor? What was it? Tom could not think. The chief's pain had his concentration.

Tom pulled up in front of a pastel green building marked "Emergencies," getting as close to the entrance as possible. As soon as he stopped, Nurse Cloud and Lesole jumped out and ran into the building, both shouting loudly in Setswana. Tom slid into the back seat and took Nurse Cloud's position supporting the chief. Dadi was almost as ashen as his father.

"We're here now, *Kgosi*. Nurse Cloud is fetching the doctor." Tom put his hand on the chief's knee and squeezed lightly. He remembered how good it felt when his mother would squeeze his knee or shoulder after taking one of his father's beatings.

"Rra Tommi, *Kgosi* does not know English good." Dadi's words slurred slightly with the pain of seeing his father mauled by the leopard and the nauseating ache in his arm from holding *Kgosi's* head on.

"*Le kae*, Dadi? You okay?" Tom knew he was not, but knew as well that Dadi needed a distraction until the doctor came.

"*E siame*." Dadi answered weakly. Of course he was not fine. Fine was a long way away, left at the base of the tree where the leopard had changed all their lives.

Suddenly Nurse Cloud and Lesole ran out of the building followed by two other nurses, one Motswana and one white. Even in the surreal motions of helping the injured chief out of the jeep, his son bandaged to his head, Tom could not help staring at the white nurse. She looked so young, but she was a nurse. Tom knew she was not Peace Corps, but maybe British? Or what about the American woman doctor he heard about? No, too young. Whatever nationality, she spoke Setswana fluently. And she was beautiful.

The odd feeling of déjà vu washed over Tom. How strange, he thought. This scene is definitely something I have never experienced. Why the feeling that it has happened before?

In unison, Tom and Dadi slid across the jeep seat as they both held tight to the chief. Even before they got the injured man out, the white nurse began asking him questions. Weakly, the chief attempted answers. Dadi suddenly looked guilty. The Motswana nurse was asking about his hand. Nurse Cloud joined in explaining Dadi's refusal to let go of the chief. Dadi stared at the ground, shame on his face. White-nurse took pity and assured Dadi that she understood why he had done it. All of this was going on as they clustered around the chief like a protective nest, slowly moving him into the surgery.

Within minutes the bandage was off and white nurse had slowly detached Dadi's hand, which had welded to the scalp as the blood had dried under his palm and fingers. An awful sucking and squishing sound made Tom's gullet convulse.

Motswana nurse grabbed Tom's shoulder. "Who are you?" she shouted.

"Tom. I live in the *Kgosi's* village. Peace Corps."

"Okay, Peese Corpse, leave the surgery and take *Kgosi's* son and grandson away. We have work to do. *Tsamaya* to the waiting room out front. There is a washroom. You can all cleanse yourselves."

Until she said it, Tom had not looked down at his clothes and his hands. On his white tee shirt were macabre imprints and smears of the chief's blood. Looking over at Dadi, Tom realized that the chief's son was far worse. His shirt was saturated and his arm coated with his father's blood.

"Eh, Mme." On his way out of the surgery, Tom glanced back at white nurse. She looked stricken, like it was her own father that she was sticking a needle into. Something worried her gravely. It was then that Tom realized that the chief might die. That would be bad for the village. It would certainly be seen as a curse, a sign of worse to come. Starting at the thought, Tom wondered again where the doctor was. Surely the chief's wound would need intense surgery.

"Can I help fetch the doctor?" he blurted out louder than he meant to. Nerves.

White nurse paused for a second as she set up an I.V. stand next to the chief. "We're it, *lekgoa*. There is no doctor," she said bitterly, glancing up and meeting Tom's stare. "Stay nearby. We might need your jeep."

"All right," Tom replied flatly, not sure whether to be angry or embarrassed. He knew he had said something wrong, but he did not know what. “I'm a fucking idiot,” he said under his breath to himself. As he backed out of the surgery, he heard white nurse cooing gently to the chief as she inserted an I.V. into his arm. Motswana nurse was gently cleaning the chief's head wound, a look of hopelessness breaking through her professional mask for just a second.

# # #

Chapter 5: The Dingaka

Kalahari Desert

It was so hot that even the *Mokowe* birds had stopped their monotonous cawing of *go-away, go-away*. Cicadas whined like high-tension wires, the air so taut it could barely carry the buzz.

Tom opened the back of his jeep and pulled out a metal storage box. Inside he kept a few extra tee shirts, a pair of shorts and some tinned food. He grabbed two shirts and the shorts. Dadi, the chief's son, would need a clean shirt too.

"Tommiwe." Lesole was suddenly at his side, his always soundless approach still startling.

"Lesole-we. Where is your father? I think he needs this shirt, eh?" Tom handed Lesole a shirt and put the other one on, almost violently pulling it over his head. He caught himself trying to panic about the day's events and stopped. A big breath filled his lungs and he pushed it out along with the stress twisting his stomach. The tee shirt, smelling faintly of Omo and not so faintly of metal and grease, was at least clean and felt like a whole new skin. Bloodless skin.

"I can take it to my father," Lesole answered. "He is bathing now." The young boy ran off with the shirt towards a small grove of lemon trees where the staff and guest housing were and where Tom had also cleaned up. As he watched Lesole run off eagerly with the shirt, he noticed with familiarity the cloud of dust that swirled around the young boy's ankles. Tom laughed, Lesole looking like Pig Pen from the cartoons. African style.

Steeling himself, Tom opened the door of the jeep. The overwhelming smell of fear and wounded flesh made him instinctively back off. Blood was everywhere across the seat where the Chief had held himself throughout the painful trip across the veldt. There was nothing he could do but attempt to wash it out. They had to drive back to Bodiba in it. Tom felt his stomach begin to rise. Swallowing hard, he pushed the acid back down. Suddenly he had a flash of his dog, Joe-D, flayed open on the highway. Tom was nine when Joe-D's wanderlust clashed with a Boston attorney driving a little too fast on Route 6 towards Provincetown.

"*Dumela, Rra. Le kae*?" Tom turned and saw a large Motswana woman standing behind him, studying him. She was formidable in stature and presence.

"*Ke teng, Mme. Le kae*?" answered Tom, knowing that, in truth, he wasn't well at all that day.

"*Ke teng*," she replied and spoke in English. "*Lekgoa*, you cannot clean that alone, for sure."

Tom smiled at her. "I think you are correct, Mme. Do you know where I can seek help to clean the jeep? This is too much, eh?"

"*Eh*, too much, Rra, especially for a man and most especially for a white man." She laughed suddenly. "Oh, *lekgoa*." Mma Cookie clucked her tongue in the Tswana way, signaling agreement that this was a predicament with difficult options. "I will fetch my nieces." With that, Mma Cookie walked away towards a large two-story house, a rarity in Botswana. It looked more like it belonged in New England than in the Kalahari Desert. Not at all like the typical colonial-style outpost bungalow.

A few minutes later Mma Cookie returned with two teenage girls and Lesole in tow. They came with sponges and cloths, a pail of water, cleansers, and other bottled substances held in buckets balanced on their heads.

"I know that your name is Tom. *Leina lame ke Mma Cookie*."

Tom smiled and showed his embarrassment at not having formally introduced himself before. Sometimes his American showed through.

"Forgive me, Mma Cookie." Tom reached out to shake her hand in the Tswana way, his right hand extended to her and his left palm resting on his right forearm. Tom knew it was complete rudeness to stick out just one hand and leave the other hanging, as though one cared so little that devoting two hands was not worth it. A slight bow was also standard since Mma Cookie was considered an elder and had raised many children and probably grandchildren too.

"It's a pleasure to meet you, Mma Cookie. Do you live in the compound?"

Mma Cookie clucked again. "Oh, yes, Tommi." She then laughed loudly. The young girls, returning with more full buckets of water, joined in. As usual, Tom knew he was missing something. Maybe he needed to get a Motswana girlfriend. The local great white drunk hunter guide had told him with stern authority that bedding a local girl was the fastest way to master the Setswana language.

Three minutes later the great white man was passed out on the bar and two *me-nice* girls were going through his pockets.

The so-called Grand Hotel veranda could get like that late on Friday nights. Lots of drunk, old sweaty white and black men passing around a few drunk, young and bored black girls and an occasional slutty Peace Corps or foreign girl. Tom remembered the wave of depression that hit him then. What was he doing wasting his weekend driving two hours into Francistown to sit in a stuffy Colonial bar dodging spit and banter. He had even started smoking again that night. Why hadn't his will power been strong enough to keep him in the village helping the men fix the well pump? What drove him to seek out something that wasn't quiet, wasn't lit only by candles and kerosene lamps, wasn't just speaking Setswana? Probably that same nameless, unknown, senseless urge to move that had got him to Botswana in the first place.

"Mma Cookie, Mma Cookie!" Willa's voice clearly carried fear. Mma Cookie snapped around and quickly began walking towards Willa, framed against the beauty of the blue stucco kitchen wall against the almost duplicate blue of the vast, desert sky. Tom looked up as well. Mma Cookie's reaction meant something was seriously wrong. He began walking towards Willa and Mma Cookie. They were speaking quickly in Setswana.

"Tommi, come, come." Mma Cookie's face was intense. *It must be the chief.* A fear shiver hit between his shoulder blades. *If only today would never have started.*

"Is the chief okay?" Tom asked as he looked from Mma Cookie to Willa. *Damn it, she's beautiful.* It was hard to not lock onto her eyes. *What would her braid look like down?*

The chief could be dead and he was lusting after a clinic

outpost nurse who looked all of sixteen but acted forty.

Yet, it would be fun to sit with her on the porch of the two-story house and have her tell him her life story. The scene made Tom homesick. He had never sat with a girl on a porch swing before, but he remembered wanting so badly to know what that felt like. To have a normal father and mother who smiled warmly at their son and his first love on the porch.

Mma Cookie was asking him something.

"Yes, yes, I can drive you. The front seats are clean now," Tom said as he glanced back at the Land Rover, and then at Willa, who nodded at him.

"Thanks," Willa said as she gave Tom a worried look. "How much petrol do you have? It's a rough fifteen kilometers. Deep sand and ruts. You'll need your 4-wheel drive." Willa purposely pulled her eyes from Tom. She felt a growing unease towards him. "Do you have at least a half tank?" Willa again looked in Tom's eyes. Could he be trusted? Other questions were unasked.

"Yeah, we'll be fine. I also have an auxiliary tank. We could drive to Chobe if you wanted."

Willa offered a tentative smile. "Shashe will do."

"You lead the way." Tom gestured toward the truck.

Mma Cookie yelled something down to the young girls. "The back seat is okay too, for the Dingaka. The girls can clean the same again when you return."

"Is that where we're going? To fetch the witch doctor?" Tom looked from Mma Cookie to Willa as they hurried towards the Land Rover.

"We're going to talk with the Dingaka. We need his medicine." Willa entered the passenger side and threw a canvas bag in the back seat. She recognized the smell of the surgery: blood and disinfectant.

It was the hottest part of the day. Greasy ribbons of white and orange light distorted the distance. It was a desert mirage: tan nothingness dusted with an occasional thorn tree and or rock outcropping.

Tom knew these Botswana roads well now. He had been to more than twenty different villages within a one hundred kilometer radius of his own village, dissecting broken down borehole pumps, squeezing water from nothing, saving water, storing water, moving water. The real currency of the desert. It could be a hero's work.

Just keeping the truck in the ancient wheel ruts was challenge enough without the Kalahari glare, dust and the heat to go with it. Muscles in Tom's arms flexed with each pock in the trail, forcing the Land Rover to stay on the road grade and dodge sharp ruts that smacked against the tires and slammed the axles.

The driving din made conversation in the truck near impossible. The windows were down to help with the heat, so the engine's grind and the bang and whirl of the tires on the sand track filled the cab with noise and cloying dust. But Tom's curiosity made him shout a question to Willa.

"What kind of medicine does the Dingaka have that the clinic doesn't?"

Willa's face darkened. Tom wished he had not asked anything. He hoped she would not call him *Lekgoa* again. She looked down at her hands.

"We have no antibiotics. Neither does the Dingaka. But he has something that works to protect against infection that is organic."

"Organic?" Tom also looked at her hands. Her fingers were long and her nails short.

"As in a plant source." Willa looked at Tom's profile. His jaw was exactly like an ebony carving that sat on the lamp stand in her mother's room. She quickly turned and fixed her eyes on the road ahead.

"How good are the chief's chances?" Tom looked at Willa and their eyes met awkwardly. Willa saw that he did have a connection to the chief. Tom's concern was real.

Willa closed her eyes for a second. "Without antibiotics, he's got about a 20% chance. With Dingaka's medicine, about a 30% chance. It's a guess. I'm not God. I'm not even a nurse."

"What are you?" The question popped out before Tom could stop it.

Willa smiled and leaned her head back on the seat. "Good question." She closed her eyes. Tom did not want to shout another question at her. He was enjoying the free look while her eyes were shut.

"Short answer is I'm scared." Willa's eyes met Tom's, something certain exchanged. An acknowledgement of respect and uncomfortable attraction. And that they were both very much responsible for the chief's fate.

Tom broke their connection and focused his eyes on the road, swerving quickly to miss a rut that was at least a foot deep. Willa was thrown across the seat, her shoulder hitting Tom's.

"Shit, sorry, Willa."

Willa just looked at Tom and didn't say anything. She scooted back to her side of the seat.

"How much farther?" Tom stared ahead, raking the back of his hand across his forehead, the grit on his knuckles scraping his skin. His eyebrows and hair were stiff with dust and sweat and nerves. Just as he asked, Tom saw a sky blue rondovel and then another.

"This is the Shashe village border. Drive straight on this path until you pass that big cottonwood tree up ahead. Go left there. And hope the Dingaka is in."

She closed her eyes, conjuring all her will and hope to save the chief. *Please, Dingaka, please be there. Please have the healing herbs. Please help me explain all of this to mother when she gets back.* A sharp pain rolled through Willa's stomach. *I'll take that pain every day, three times a day if only it would save the chief.* How silly, she thought. I'm negotiating with Fate just like I did when I was seven. *Dear god of the wind, please save my baby calf from the lions' night stalking and I'll never secretly sass my mother again.*

"Here's the tree." Tom turned left and the path became narrower and lined with dense tree growth. There must be a water source of some kind feeding this grove, Tom thought, always preoccupied with water.

The trees opened up again to a compound of three huts surrounded by a mud-dung wall about waist high. It was painted with a white border of geometric shapes and lines. The pattern was repeated on two of the rondovels and the third was a much more complex pattern of geometric shapes and animal, plant and human totems that danced on the mud walls, shining in the heat.

Tom pulled up next to the cooking hut. From behind a plain rondovel a young boy appeared and walked towards them. He looked about fifteen and wore tattered khaki shorts and an old school uniform shirt, once white.

"*Dumela, mosimane. O tsogile jang*?" Willa spoke loudly as she walked toward the boy. He returned her greeting, shaking hands in the traditional way. In Setswana she inquired about his family and health, and he did the same, with Willa politely describing her own family and health. Tom let his impatience show in his shifting feet and frustrated expression. This only caused the boy to ask questions about Tom and his origins and family, further delaying the meeting with the witch doctor.

Willa and the boy's conversation had gone beyond Tom's comprehension level. Suddenly both of them laughed and looked at Tom. "Am I the butt of a joke again?" Tom asked looking impatiently at Willa.

"Kabelo was wondering if you have to relieve yourself because your legs and face are shifting so much." Willa gave a half smile and the boy Kabelo laughed nervously.

"No, I don't. I just wanted to find out if the Dingaka is here or if we've wasted a trip." Tom thrust his hands into his pockets, something he knew was considered rude in the Tswana culture. Willa stopped smiling and turned serious. She talked again with the boy Kabelo for another few minutes.

"Yes, the Dingaka is in his medicine hut. Kabelo will announce us." As she said this Willa looked right into Tom's eyes. He suddenly felt embarrassed about his white man behavior. Willa's eyes held a small lesson of patience in them. Would he ever learn to slow down enough to not act and feel like an outsider? Maybe on his good days.

Kabelo walked quickly to the most decorated hut and vanished behind a fabric curtain. Five minutes later he emerged and signaled to them to come into the compound. "*Dingaka will see you. He said to talk quickly because other spirits need him today.*" Kabelo spoke in Setswana. She turned to Tom after thanking the boy.

"Just greet the Dingaka, but don't look him in the eyes. Keep your eyes at his chest level. I'll tell him you saved the chief from death. He'll let you stay, I think." Willa hoped that he would, anyway. She needed Tom's physical support in the hut.

Tom nodded and followed Willa through the doorway. The thick curtain brushed his face as it closed, smelling of wood fires and something close to frankincense. Visions of long Sunday masses in church resurfaced. Tom could feel the hard wooden pew against his bony back and the soreness in his knees from the sparsely padded kneeler. He chewed on the side of his thumb, dreading the revelation of his little boy sins in the confessional. *Bless me father for I have sinned. It has been two months since my last confession. I had evil thoughts of my father again, wishing him dead.*

Tom followed Willa, keeping his eyes down, his shoulders bent. Willa spoke to the Dingaka in Setswana and Tom greeted him when he was cued. He tried to follow Willa's words but understood only about a quarter of what was said. Willa knelt on a straw mat four feet in front of the Dingaka. Tom placed himself beside and slightly behind her. Willa spoke first, continuing in the Dingaka's native tongue.

"We greet you most honorable and powerful Dingaka. We understand that we are not worthy to be kneeling in front of you today. Thank you for letting us intrude on your most honorable self." The Dingaka said nothing, his face a stone wall.

"I certainly would never waste your time with any trivial matter of Lekgoa such as ourselves. But today your powerful medicine is needed very badly to save the life of one of our great chiefs." Willa stopped for a moment in case the Dingaka wanted to speak. He just waved a cow's tail attached to a polished wood handle through the space between him and Willa. She continued.

"Today our brother the leopard became impatient hunting for his brethren beasts. He went against the rules of the desert and attacked Chief Tau of Bodiba, hoping to kill him and feed upon him. Because our brother leopard broke the rule, Chief's son was able to kill him with a fire stick. But before returning to his

ancestors, leopard took off the top of Chief's head." Again the Dingaka said nothing, but waved the tail between them, cleaning the air. Willa went on.

"The power of the Tswana tribe remains in the Chief. But he is at risk from germ devils who also want his head and his wisdom. Dingaka, we beg you to consider the Chief's wounds with your powerful medicine. Please help me bring him back to himself." Willa stopped talking and bowed her head at an angle so that she was looking at the Dingaka's chest. The cow's tail wand flashed close to her face. It smelled of hay and smoke.

"Bah! I see you my child!" Suddenly the Dingaka bellowed his first words. Tom had to throw his arm out to catch himself from falling over from his sitting position. Dingaka stared at him, really through him, and Tom felt a deep chill spear his chest, powerful but not evil.

In an instant Tom saw everything inside the hut. It was not dark any more. Old baby food jars were stacked along the base of the walls, filled with herbs, powders, and what looked like stones and matted hair clumps. Animal skins covered most of the wall surfaces. Hung from these were animal skulls, chains of fanged teeth, wisps of tails. And incongruently, also on the wall behind the Dingaka was an old framed color picture of Jesus and another of John F. Kennedy. The torn edges from where Jesus had been ripped out of a missal could be seen under the frame glass.

Tom also became aware of a cacophony of smells. So many odors competed, each making an entrance and then leaving for the next to float in. Acrid waves from drying plants chased away a smoke smell so ancient it surely held a millennium of lives and mysteries. Tom felt lightheaded, like he was high from reefer. He looked at Willa for reassurance but she was meeting the Dingaka's eyes with hers.

Willa focused her mind, willing the medicine man to see the chief and feel his pain. She had brought both the chief's fighting spirit and his dying spirit with her to give to the Dingaka. If he was a skilled traditional healer, as she believed him to be, he would have to help.

"Mosetsana, my daughter," the Dingaka began to laugh, but it

was a laugh of discovery not of derision. *"You have come to see me because of failure. I am seeing you, Mosetsana."*

"Eh, Ntati. I am happy we are seeing each other," Willa continued in Setswana.

"I have heard of you, child. Yes. You play at being a doctor but you yourself are still a child! But the chief is not a toy."

Willa could feel the nausea of truth churning in her gut. The desire to jump up and run away from the Dingaka's words were so strong that it was only the memory of the chief's hopeful eyes, those eyes that wanted so much to live, that kept her rooted to the straw mat. She would just have to beg and grovel even harder, and agree with everything the Dingaka said or the discussion would go nowhere. These were the rules, Willa knew, that her mother had never bothered to understand or learn.

"Your honor. Yes, I am a child who knows nothing. My mother is the skillful lekgoa doctor, but she is in South Africa. The devil leopard must have known this when he took off the chief's scalp, thinking that my silliness would kill the chief. But the leopard did not know that I am clever enough to seek out yourself, the most skilled Dingaka in healing the sick of so many villages. Helping the chief to return to this world of normality is only something a powerful Dingaka such as yourself can accomplish. I am a child. I have no father here. No mother to approach you. Instead I must waste your time and make you listen to my unworthy self."

Dingaka abruptly stopped swishing his elephant tail brush back and forth. His eyes locked onto Willa's. Knowing she dare not hold his stare, Willa made a final plea with her eyes before she dropped them to the straw mat.

"The chief is my clansman and his spirit resides next to my spirit." Dingaka twisted around and reached for a rusted biscuit tin behind him. He set it out between him and Willa, and took off the lid.

"Your spirit is strong my white daughter. You have learned many things well. It will not stop failure from finding you, but it will trip the devils up that work at you. You see two worlds, but these will fight." Dingaka reached into the tin and scooped up a

handful of the dried green leaves. *"The chief will see his grandson become chief if a poultice of this herb wraps around the devil leopard's mark on Kgosi's head while I beg the leopard's spirit to release its hold."*

Willa stopped staring at the herbs in Dingaka's hand and met his eyes again. She was excited. She could feel the chief's life buzzing in her ears. *"You will come to the clinic and help the chief?"*

"Eh, my daughter. It is my destiny to bring the chief back just as it is yours to love this Peese Corpse boy."

"What?" Willa could feel her cheeks redden.

Dingaka snorted and started to get up. *"You will switch homes but fate cannot be fooled."* The spirit man grinned as he stood up, his old teeth crooked but still white. *"Pick up that tin, my daughter."* The Dingaka pointed to the biscuit tin of green leaves. Willa did as she was told. *"Hold that close to your heart on the journey. It will relieve the chief's pain until I touch him."*

Willa pressed the tin closer to her chest and felt her heart flutter.

"You feel the chief inside you now, yes," stated the Dingaka. His eyes shone, a confident, reassuring fire. Willa nodded. She could not help but think how crowded it must be inside her chest. Between the chief's presence, her fear and nervousness and her racing heart, she would be lucky to make it through the day. Her longest day.

# # #

Chapter 6: Nora's Good-Bye

Boston
December 1968

Nora loved watching Pete sleep. It made her feel like she was getting away with something, stealing some of him, without having to give anything back. In the mornings the smell of him made her come awake tingling. She snuggled closer against him, her breast kissing his chest, a thief taking some of his warmth.

It was also in the mornings before Pete woke up that Nora could pretend that she possessed him. When Pete was awake, this was impossible. Pete was not possess-able.

Nora laughed softly. *You are mine, you are mine,* she repeated in her head as she pressed even closer to Pete's back. He was so warm, so hers in these moments before he took over. Yet, Nora wanted Pete to take over, to watch him. Everything he did was a fascination to her.

Nora remembered the morning after they made love for the first time in Pete's studio on Marlborough Street. It was only three weeks before, but it seemed like years had passed. Pete had risen in the morning to get a drink of water and brush his teeth. What had surprised Nora was how unembarrassed he was about walking around naked in front of her, as though it were no different from having clothes on. She was not sure where she was supposed to look. If she stared at his cock would he be flattered or think her priorities were screwed up? If she stared at his face would he be scared off by her infatuated, sex-laden eyes, or be disappointed that she was not checking out his cock? Was there a guide book on this stuff?

It wasn't as though she was a virgin, but her two prior sexual adventures were done in dark places and did not leave Nora with any lingering thoughts of wanting to do it again with either guy. There was Steve the football player in her first week at college. A quick fuck in the basement of his fraternity after he'd gotten her quickly drunk on Ever-clear spiked punch. It was unfeeling and uncomfortable. He looked at her like she had a disease when her virgin's blood stained his sophomoric dick.

Nora happily remained celibate after that until her experience with Gary the acid dealer, only a month before. Her life, her perspective had changed so much in that short time. How was that possible? It made Nora question the value, or lack thereof, of everything she had ever considered worthwhile, and anyone she had called a friend in the past.

Nora felt ten years older than she had a month ago. Pete's influence on her had been overwhelming. She learned so much from him about music, poetry, philosophy, patience and lovemaking. Sometimes she felt so silly around him. She tried to hide her youth. Pete and his friends would be talking about the nature of time or who Jesus really was, prophet or ancient hippie. Nora had never even contemplated that Jesus was anything other than the Jesus in the missal at church, like Moses and his plagues or Adam and Eve. Nora felt so stupid because she had never questioned the gold-embossed colored pictures of Jesus in her grandmother's mass book as anything but a historical truth.

All of these new perspectives were flooding her with excitement and the sense that she had wasted so much time on elementary thought and action before she met Pete. Would she have naturally made it to the place where Pete was at 28 when she reached that age? At 22, Nora felt like a child being tutored in the basics of life's mysteries and pleasures. What would have happened to her if she had not taken that tab of acid at Gary's and wandered into the café where Pete's band weaved their music around and into the heads of hippies, college kids, high school geeks who sneaked in with fake I.D. and a few hip older folks not yet settled into Henry Mancini?

Nora's stomach flip-flopped as she remembered the conversation she'd had with her father the day before. She had been doing her best to dodge him and Carol by coming home late, or sometimes not at all, and not coming downstairs until after her father had left for the hospital and Carol for her usual shopping and ladies' functions at her suburban clubs and tea-and-scone cafes.

Yesterday her father had returned home early before she had been able to escape the inevitable conflict that had been percolating for weeks. He trapped her in the formal living room.

"Nora, what's going on with you? The semester break started almost two weeks ago but you're never here. I haven't even had a chance to ask you how your exams went. And what about Christmas? We haven't been able to plan the holiday events with you. You even missed the tree trimming!" He said it as though accusing her of mistreating a pet or good friend. Nora's father didn't stop there.

"Honey, frankly, Carol and I are a little worried about you." Dr. Dodge indeed looked pained. Nora felt guilty. Maybe her father did truly care about her whereabouts and he wasn't just trying to annoy her. It wasn't often that he expended such energy in her direction. She suddenly felt like a little girl again. Like she had rejected a doll he gave her or turned up her nose at a special treat he had brought home from Hershel's Bakery.

Should she dare tell the truth? Tell the good Dr. that she had met the man of her dreams while tripping on acid? That she was a completely different person than she was a month ago? That she was learning more from Pete than she had in all her years of schooling?

"I'm sorry, Daddy." Nora looked down at her hands, hoping to find some direction as she studied her un-filed nails. "I've been really busy."

"Really busy? Doing what? Have you gotten a job or something?" He sat down on the embossed couch and patted the space next to him. Nora reluctantly joined him.

"I've met someone, Daddy." Nora looked up and met her father's blue eyes. "He's really smart and I've been learning so much from him and his friends." Then more quietly she said, "I think you would like him, Daddy." It was more of a question, and one she had really already answered. Dr. Dodge would not like Pete at all.

"Well, why didn't you tell us, sweetheart? Who is he, someone from school?" So far her father seemed just curious, not mad. He and Carol had actually discussed Nora's lack of boyfriends thus far in her college career, wondering why their beautiful girl seemed content with her girlfriends and a few boys who were "just friends."

Nora knew she had to choose her words carefully. A small lie was in order.

"I'd gone into a café to look into getting a part-time job and I met him there. His name is Pete."

"Pete? Does he own the place or is he a waiter or what?" An edge of misgiving had entered her father's voice.

"He's a musician, and an intellectual." Nora thought that a second title was appropriate for Pete, but she wasn't quite sure how to describe his readings and musings on the bible, Sartre, Gurdieff and Bob Dylan.

"Is he going to Berklee? Why's he at this café?" Nora could see that her father was still hoping for the best, but it was fading quickly in his tone.

Suddenly Nora no longer felt guilty. She loved Pete. He cared more about her than anyone ever had. He told her she was beautiful and smart and that the softness of her skin occupied his thoughts all day, even when she wasn't around. To be questioned by her father cheapened what she and Pete had. Anger and disappointment merged into defiance, instantly reddening her face and neck.

"Daddy, for the first time in my life I've found someone who really cares about me. Me! Not who my Dad is or where I go to school or where I vacationed on spring break. Why do you need to know where he works?" The pitch of her voice rose higher. "Pete makes me feel like I'm somebody important, Daddy."

"Sweetheart, how can you say that no one has ever made you feel important? You know how much Carol and I care about you. That's why we're concerned, honey. You're young and there are a lot of guys out there who would love to take advantage of you."

"Pete's not taking advantage of me, Daddy. For crissake, I'm 22 years old!" Nora's voice was angry now and she stood up and walked to the window. In her ears the pounding of her heart was an alarm. *I need to leave. Now.*

"I'm not saying he is. You didn't answer my question about

him, Nora."

"What? About his pedigree you mean? No, Daddy, he's not a Berklee student or a Harvard grad. He's 28 and leads a band of folk musicians who play in cafes. He's from Rhode Island, the poor part of Warwick. His dad works for the A&P and his mom works in a shoe factory. He never went to college but he's the smartest, most interesting person I've ever met." Nora's words streamed from her and she hadn't realized she was shouting until Carol rushed in the room, a look on her face like a referee attracted by a fight on the field.

"Oh, god, Nora." Her father spat out the words, exasperated, as though she was a child who had tracked dirt onto a white carpet. He then stood up and Carol joined him, wringing her hands on a kitchen towel strangely coordinated with her pantsuit. He started up again. "He's never been to college, right? But he's the smartest person you've ever met? God, Nora, what are you thinking about? What has he done to you? Hypnotized you into thinking he's an intellectual?" Dr. Dodge exchanged a concerned glance with Carol, an unspoken agreement that Nora was on a troubling path.

Nora grimaced and turned towards the window. A light coating of snow covered the fir trees in the side yard. Most of the snow on the lawn had melted, the grass turned to straw from the cold. Standing alone against the fence, the Russian Olive tree's winter-bare limbs looked like tired bones, shivering and brittle.

"Nora, dear," it was Carol suddenly standing close behind her. "Your father and I just want you to be safe and happy. Why don't you bring Pete over next week during the holidays? We want to meet him. Won't you share him with us?"

"Oh, please, Carol. Give me a break. Bring him here? Why? So you can eyeball him and pick out all his failings? No thanks. I respect Pete too much to throw him to the wolves."

"Nora, that's not fair!" Her father actually raised his voice beyond his usual controlled monotone.

"No, Daddy, it's not fair according to your rules." Nora wanted so badly not to cry. It was very hard to convince her father that she was old enough to deal with a relationship if she started bawling. Clenching her teeth, she swallowed hard and stared out at a string of blinking lights on the neighbor's side window. Mrs. Polawski's house. That was a wonderful house at Christmas. Nora remembered Mrs. Polawski's fourteen nativity scenes -- what she called crèches -- and mint cream cookies and 7-UP.

One Christmas when Nora was seven, she had stayed over at Mrs. Polawski's for three nights in a row. There had been a severe snowstorm and her father had been stuck at the hospital helping patients in an overcrowded emergency room, his relief unable to get to the hospital through the 25 inches of snow. Nora hardly noticed he was gone. Mrs. Polawski took her around to all of the nativity scenes and told engrossing stories about the angels and shepherds and Joseph that were never revealed in catechism classes. Mrs. Polawski's children were grown and living in California, so she had all the time in the world to show Nora how to cut out gingerbread men and ladies. Nora remembered the hours they spent dressing the gingerbread cookies in icing coats and pants and with sprinkles and jimmies for eyes, belts and boots. That year Nora really understood what it meant to feel the spirit of Christmas. She thought of the homemade eggnog and white coconut Christmas cake with a snowman on the top in red and green icing. She must go and see Mrs. Polawski today, Nora thought to herself.

"Do you know if Mrs. Polawski is home?" Nora turned from the window and looked at her father.

"Mrs. Polawski? Nora...!" he looked at her and let out an exasperated huff. "You want me to treat you like an adult, but you can't even carry on a conversation to any conclusion. Carol, help me here..." He threw his hands up, and closed his eyes, rubbing them with slightly shaking hands. Nora hated seeing him so hurt but at the same time his pain seemed very far away. He was a character now, not Daddy.

"Daddy," her voice came out softly and resigned. Couldn't she be gone and with Pete, wrapping her arms around his warm neck. "I like Pete too much to bring him over here. You're already scrutinizing him and judging him." Nora was perfectly calm now. Remembering Mrs. Polawski had helped her not be angry anymore. Everything was really simpler than it seemed most of the time. Pete always said that.

Nora walked up to her father and put her arms around his neck. He instinctively squeezed her. She had done it so many times when she was a little girl. *If only she could stay a little girl,* he thought. *I'm not in control of her anymore. She can say no.*

"Daddy, I've got some errands to run. After that I'll be back and we can plan for the holidays."

But Nora had already left. Her father could see that. He wanted so badly not to. Nora was saying something to him, but he couldn't hear her. The buzzing in his ears was too loud. It always started when a certain look would move across Nora's face and she would suddenly be Jan, her mother. This time the buzzing was even louder. It was the look that Jan had on her face the day she said she was staying in Africa. His ears roared.

The doctor watched his daughter smile. She said something. He only heard the roar. He watched her back. Nora's back. Jan's back twenty years before. Walking away from him. So easily walking away from everything she had known and been. Not caring what he wanted. Not caring that he couldn't stay, wouldn't stay.

Africa should have just been a stage for them. It was not the place to raise a daughter. Nora fighting one sickness after another. Jan not there for her own daughter, but saving a native with a staph infection, or a mother giving birth to her seventh child, another hungry African kid. What had happened to Jan? The doctor knew he had not changed.

"Goodbye, Michael. I'll be home as soon as our replacement gets here. Good-bye little Nora. Nora, Nora, how I adore ya. Remember our song, baby."

Flat, tan scrub desert raced away below the plane. She wanted to stay. Michael could understand Jan not caring that they would be separated. But Nora? How could Jan leave her daughter without a tear or a backward glance? What had happened to her?

Michael Dodge remembered meeting Jan for the first time. He had never met anyone like her, she was utterly compelling and he was instantly mesmerized. Even if she had been a man, she would have stood out in medical school. But the fact that she was a woman excelling in medical school in 1947 made her notoriety and novelty even greater. Jan had always been so sure of herself. That was her moniker. Ironically, Michael Dodge had fallen in love with the very same conviction that ultimately drove them apart. He grew to resent her need to go it alone in Africa. He still did, even as he hated himself for being that weak and petty.

All of the professors loved Jan too. Even when she did not have the right answer, she was not embarrassed to guess. A joke would follow and the whole class would rally around, enlivened by Jan's contagious curiosity. She could have had any man, professor or fellow student. Conventional beauty could not match Jan's looks. Long, wavy brown hair framed a face that was never at rest. Her mouth constantly questioning, digging, cursing, kissing. Michael knew he had not been Jan's first lover. She openly and without guilt had told him about Professor Wiley, Malcolm Brent and an Irish anarchist who hid at her Auntie's farm the winter before Jan started at Radcliff. None of that mattered, he convinced himself. Jan did not think of it as her dirty secret. He loved her now. Michael knew he could eventually get Jan to love him.

Michael never knew, but it was his hands that she loved. Jan could watch Michael for hours as he dissected animals and cadavers in med school labs, and later in his residency as he moved quickly to assisting in more complex operations. The movement of his hands was symphonic, smooth, and the scalpel light. Memorizing his technique was Jan's tutorial in evolving from a good surgeon to a great one. But never as good as Michael and his elegance with a scalpel.

Jan traded her understanding of blood systems and brain functions for Michael's clean surgical techniques. It was a successful barter that eventually led to trysts in an unused office in the basement of a Harvard science lab.

Three months later Jan started throwing up. She cursed her womanhood and fertility and told Michael, after they had made love at midnight on Truro beach and without any fanfare, that she was pregnant. It had been the first time they had gone away from the campus together. Michael had planned the trip to the Cape for over a month. His uncle's bungalow was a perfect retreat. Jan's news only made it more perfect. All he wanted was to marry her. She would always love him then.

But Jan was not so sure. She told Michael that she wanted to have an abortion. When he started crying she was too startled to pursue the conversation. He hoped that Jan didn't really want to destroy the life growing within her, a life they shared between them. Jan simply felt trapped, knowing her options were limited. Running away from Boston at that point would mean either the slowing or the end of her pursuit to be a surgeon. Damn it to hell if women weren't being punished for something, she thought. Jan did consider Michael a friend, she rationalized. And, there was nothing more important than finishing medical school.

A week later they were married at Cambridge City Hall, with Michael's roommate as his best man and Jan's eccentric Aunt Dix at her side. They ate steak and toasted one another with good scotch at the Parker House Hotel. Aunt Dix gave them two nights there in the bridal suite as her gift. She didn't fail to mention that if a girl baby had at least the middle name of Dixie that a nice inheritance would certainly bless the child. Aunt Dix laughed when she said it, but everyone knew she was serious. Michael liked Dix. He knew where he stood with her. Crazy or not, she was honest.

Jan had been raised by a collection of aunts, pseudo-aunts, kind neighbors and family friends. No one ever knew quite what to do with her after her parents died in a car accident when she was five. She floated from relative to relative, living mostly with Aunt Dix in a sort of literary commune in Concord. Jan's teachers were writers and artists, poets, monks, and revolutionaries from around the globe. She learned to read the bible and Jane Austin, Lenin and Lao-tzu. Aunt Dix's "guests" sometimes stayed years and other times only a day or two. The only rule at Dix's was that everyone had to contribute either to the dialogue, the meal or the milking of the cows. No theory or philosophy or religion was taboo, just inactivity.

Jan was smart and talkative, and she quickly charmed and was adopted by almost every guest. They all shared their stories of travels across the country and the world, of wars, of banned books, of spies and love affairs with dukes and ballerinas. Jan's mind created moving, color pictures that followed along with their tales. It was movement and exploration that led to knowledge and purpose. Interaction with people who questioned and fought made her question and fight. They held opinions firm like swords, battling with words in the smoke-filled parlor with Aunt Dix serving cheap red wine and salty ham biscuits. There was laughter and love too. Aunt Dix believed in using her power as a woman to further her entertainments with her guests. She did not flaunt her liaisons with her men, but she did not believe in hiding her sexuality from her guests or from her niece.

Michael suddenly smiled when he remembered Aunt Dix and her farmstead and her guests. That part of Concord no longer existed, but was now housing Boston's newest and oldest wealthy families in its suburbs.

Jan could have been a good mother to Nora, Michael thought. But Africa captured her and held a much stronger hold on her than he ever could.

The sound of the front door closing brought the doctor back. He could hear Nora's boot heels clicking on the brick walk. He could see Jan again in her twenties, waving goodbye, the Kalahari sun lighting her from behind.

# # #

Chapter 7: Good-bye Old Life

Boston

December 1968

Three days could really be three weeks or three years. Time was just perspective, history, the need for order where there wasn't any. Nora smiled. She loved these simple truths that revealed themselves when she got high. She took another draw on the joint and then gently snuffed it out so she could re-light it later when Pete finished his gig.

She looked over at the alarm clock next to the mattress. Eleven o'clock. Five days to Christmas. Nora's tummy fluttered when she thought of Pete and her.

Nora wished she had someone to share Pete with; someone to tell how smart he was and how much he was teaching her, making her think about. But there was no one. No friend who would understand. They were all like what she used to be. No father who could ever understand why she was dropping out of college. No mother who cared. She was saving the poor tubercular children of Africa. No sister. She was an unknown. The last time Nora had seen her sister, Willa was 11 and Nora 14. They shared nothing in common except their parentage. Willa had shown much more affinity for her African friends than for her own sister. Nora felt left out and feigned an illness during most of her visit in Botswana so she could hide in her mother's house. Despite the stifling heat of the upstairs, Nora lay on her mother's bed most of the day, losing herself in Jane Austin novels and her mother's collection of Graham Greene, which, although she did not understand all that well, she could at least clearly visualize the characters, tropical towns and dark, humid bars.

Nora stood up and looked in the mirror on the dresser. What had she been, what was she now if she could so quickly become someone else? The old Nora was gone and would never return. The new Nora had given up dependency on her father, on her father's "space", as Pete called it – his houses, cars, private clubs, and Christmas trees in every room. Finding out who she was and what she was meant to do would be her new college curriculum. She was high and contemplating higher education. Suddenly that term made sense. Education that was higher, more advanced than traditional education. Higher as in outside the realm of academics, beyond into the works of mystics and pacifists, lamas and modern poets who wrote music to move their words to the people. Names floated in her head – Camus, Ginsberg, Castaneda and Leary. She knew so little as yet about who they were and what they said and meant.

Nora listened more than she spoke these days. She no longer had to be the controller of every conversation. She couldn't be. Nora was in a new league and trying to absorb every tidbit of every conversation. She kept a notebook and wrote down all of the names of the artists and writers and thinkers that Pete and his friends talked about so she could look them up at the library. Above all else, she did not want to seem dumb. Nora wanted to be one of them, not just the pretty dumb one. She knew Pete had had some of those girls before.

The night before an old friend of Pete's, Benny, had stopped by the apartment. Nora could barely follow his conversation. Benny was aloof yet right on the ground; he was classically trained at Harvard as a pianist and Greek scholar, yet he loved Moby Grape and William Burroughs.

Nora liked Benny. A lot of Pete's other musician friends were so involved in their music that they barely acknowledged her existence. Benny was different. He had drawn Nora into a discussion of Catholicism and treated her as though her opinions had merit. She could not believe how good that made her feel. Benny validated her, that was it. Nora sighed through a crooked smile. If only she did not feel so young around them. Or maybe inexperienced was a better term. Maybe just paranoid? This was not her world yet. But becoming part of Pete's and Benny's world had its wonderful times and uncertain times. Scary sometimes. *But at least I don't always know what to expect.*

That had been the boring part. Knowing so clearly what everyone's expectations were and that fulfilling them was meaningless. Empty. Fucking nothing. So easy, but a predictable void.

Now important, older, intelligent people thought she had value. People she admired now admired her back. People were genuine. That was it. No bullshit. This group of people was open and honest, sometimes to the point of hurting each other. That part was not fun, but it was real.

The front door of the apartment rattled. Pete was home. Nora felt a flutter again in her tummy. She had never wanted to see anyone or spend so much time with anyone as she did with Pete. Whether this was what love felt like, Nora still was not sure. Never having loved a boyfriend before, she was not exactly sure what it felt like. It was with certainty, though, that she knew she was in severe like with Pete.

Nora saw the guitar case before Pete's head came around the door. She couldn't help beaming.

"Hi, angel. Don't you look good, even with my very tired eyes." Pete smiled at Nora, his eyes doing most of the work.

"Hey, Pete. How was the gig? Sit..." Nora patted the bed next to her. "I'll get you a beer."

Pete shed his coat and began recounting the night. It had been generally good, with a few minor interruptions, starting with amp problems and ending with a wasted co-ed trying to sit on Arnie's lap and grab his drumsticks. But the audience had connected with them. Pete's eyes danced as he spoke of the feeling in the room that night.

"It was like everybody suddenly understood that we all were the same and shared something. It was magnetic, Nora. I just can't explain it, but it took the music, the words and the live notes and made it a common experience." Pete reached for Nora's hand and kissed it. "I wish you were there tonight. But if it was for real tonight, then that spirit, that unity can happen again. It was religious, really." Nora wished there was something that she could believe in as strongly as Pete did in the power of music to move people in more positive directions. She leaned over and kissed her musician, lightly feathering his lips.

Nora wished she had been there too at the gig. But she had

gone on a mission that was necessary but not pleasant. Her father deserved some explanation about why she would not be with him and Carol over Christmas. If only she was not such a coward. Nora knew her father and stepmother would be at Aunt Minnie's house. It was a Dodge family tradition. The weekend before Christmas Aunt Minnie roasted a goose and prepared twenty side dishes and five desserts. Uncle Les always carved and told silly jokes that made everyone groan.

Nora had spent the entire afternoon trying to write a note to her father. She did not have the courage or the strength to stand up to him in person and tell him she was (a) dropping out of school, (b) living with a man, (c) not going to be around for Christmas, and (d) leaving the state.

Rocking back and forth on the Green Line to her father's house, Nora could only think about the note in her pocket. It made her nauseous and jumpy. She could hear her heart beat in her ears and her butt felt weird, like it was both getting numb and getting stabbed with a million pinpricks. Nora wished she didn't remember the note by heart.

Dear Daddy,

There are a lot of things I need to do right now to find out who I am and where I am going. I know it will be hard for you to understand but I'm not going back to B.U. in January. Please don't be too disappointed in me. I'll pay you back the tuition money once I get a job. I'm moving out of state for a while. Pete has work and I'll find something too. I need to be out with other people now and learn how to be a more complete and open person myself. I don't have an address yet, but I'll write when I do. Since we're leaving tomorrow, I won't be able to be here for Christmas. Don't be sad. I love you and I'm really okay. I just need to follow my star and open up my heart. I'll have more to give you when I find out how to do this. I'll write soon. Peace and Love – Nora.

At her father's back door Nora lifted up the milk box and retrieved the spare key. It was dark inside except for the lights on the Christmas tree that cast a glow from the living room onto the kitchen floor.

"What am I doing," Nora whispered to the house. She sighed heavily and headed upstairs to her father's study. Dark wood and the smell of leather and books overtook her. Her throat began to constrict. *Dammit*, she was not going to cry. Nora set the note to her father on the seat of his chair. As a child she had done the same thing with her kindergarten drawings and "A" papers in grade school. He would always check his chair when he got home from long days at the hospital, hoping to find a treasure from his daughter. "Forgive me, Daddy," she said aloud.

Running out of the room, Nora tripped on a hallway rug and fell to her hands and knees. Suddenly she was sobbing, all the memories and all the changes she was forcing on herself bore down on her.

"Damn you!" she yelled at herself and pushed hard off of the floor. *How am I going to move ahead if I cry and lose it leaving a note for my Dad?* Nora sobered as she thought what Pete would have done if he had seen her so out of control over leaving her Daddy.

After grabbing an old suitcase and filling it with her favorite jeans, sweaters and gauze tops, Nora washed her face, grabbed a coke from the fridge and took one last look at the Christmas tree. "Bye old life. Bye Daddy."

Head bowed, she walked quickly back to the T-stop, glad for the darkness that shaded her face from the weary Christmas shoppers. Nora squeezed her eyes tightly shut. A tear rolled down her cheek. *What a terrible gift I left.*

# # #

Chapter 8: The Poultice

Foley's Crossing, Botswana

Somewhere along the road of her raising, Jan had learned the sheer waste of worry. Her Aunt Dix had much to do with it. Dix's philosophy was "solve it, don't maul it." She reasoned that, time being better than money in the bank, wasting it worrying was spending money you did not have.

When Jan was a young girl, Aunt Dix's anti-worry philosophy seemed so natural and right to her that stewing over problems was not even considered an option. It had led Jan down a sometimes precarious path of making very quick decisions and only infrequently questioning whether they were the right ones.

That is why as Jan flew high above the Kalahari she was not worrying about the frantic message she had received from her daughter. Jan did not worry about Willa because there were so many people around her daughter who protected her and were part of her life. She did not worry about the lack of antibiotics either. Instead Jan had acted.

Johnny shook his head and swore under his breath, but he did not hesitate to cut short their rare vacation when Jan said she needed to fly back to Mother Mercy Health Post. First they detoured to Somerset Hospital in Cape Town. Jan had several contacts there and managed to round up enough antibiotics to last them several months. As the plane began its descent to the airfield abutting Mother Mercy, the familiar landscape elicited a determined, "Well, we're here," from Jan. Johnny touched her arm and smiled.

"You really missed this place, didn't you? Jan met his eyes and nodded. She needed Johnny's smile so much it sometimes hurt her to look at his face. She knew she did not always deserve the love his blue eyes reflected.

"It's my home. And I miss Willa. But don't you dare tell her that! She'll take advantage of me for weeks!" Johnny laughed knowingly at Jan trying to hide her sentimentality. As soon as her tough exterior was threatened by an outburst of feelings, she would recoil from her own softness and become Dr. Gakelape again.

Yet, Jan could not help but smile at the thought of her Willa. She could not be nineteen, Jan thought, because I just had her! *Poor kid. What has she been going through at the health post?* But Jan knew that Willa would be fine and everything that was wrong would be righted. That was the pragmatic New Englander in her rising up again, always the conqueror, never the victim, of a challenge.

Dismissing the worry that had briefly threatened, Jan looked out the side window of the five-seater Piper, watching the cattle trails and the rondovels get closer and closer as the plane descended. Unlike anything else in her life, Jan felt the health post was hers. It was her only possession, her best creation. And one she guarded like a pit bull.

In her raising at Aunt Dix's commune, no one had personal possessions; everything was shared and belonged to the whole group. Even toys that Jan received at Christmas or on her birthday would often be sent away by Aunt Dix to the New England Home for Little Wanderers. Jan was never asked if she would share or if she cared which toys were sent away. One day they just would not be there anymore. Jan learned quickly not to ask where her favorite doll had gone, or her favorite statue of St. Francis of Assisi that a wandering priest had given her when he stayed on the farm after being fired for welcoming Black parishioners into his Richmond, Virginia congregation. She knew Aunt Dix had sent St. Francis to a poor orphan, a little parentless wanderer. How could Jan covet a possession so strongly that she would deny it to a child without a family? When she once reminded Aunt Dix that she, too, was an orphan, the freethinking matron looked at her like she was simply the most spoiled, selfish child on earth.

"Jan, I'm surprised at you. Here you have a whole extended family that loves you and protects you. Can you deny a child who has none of this security a lifeless possession?"

Jan had hung her head, the guilt of all orphans making her neck limp with regret. She watched her favorite porcelain

Appaloosa stallion leave the room in Aunt Dix's always-moist hands, off to an orphan worthier than she.

By the time Jan was a teenager she had learned not to desire anything permanently. Nothing would belong to her forever. Whenever one of the transient commune members would give her a gift, Jan would thank them but never make it hers. It did not pay to get close to things, only to have them taken away.

# # #

The sound of the Piper overhead brought Willa out of her chair. She ran to the porch and looked up at Johnny's plane. A sudden shiver attempted to shake off the worry. But it stayed, her fear driven by Jan's likely reaction to the state of the health post.

It was not as Jan had left it. It was not as Jan would have done it.

Willa's belly constricted. Was it only yesterday that the chief arrived? That Tom drove her to the Dingaka's compound? *Tom*. It was possible for a world to change in a day. Just as Mma Cookie had imparted in the many fables she told and retold since Willa tumbled across the compound in diapers.

Willa glanced at her watch. It was time to relieve Sister Beli in the patients' ward. Willa would meet her mother there instead of driving with Sammie Po out to the airfield. That would also give her more time to figure out how to best explain bringing the Dingaka and his witch doctor medicine to the clinic.

"Willawe are you ready?" Mma Cookie stood on the other side of the porch screen door. Pushing it open she handed Willa a cup of milky sweet tea. The look on Willa's face gave Mma Cookie her answer.

"Oh, girlie." Mma Cookie wrapped her arm around Willa's waist and drew her close. "You have only done what was best for our chief. Dr. Gakelape will know that, Willawe."

"Maybe." Her face drawn tight, Willa stepped off the porch stairs and headed across the grounds to the clinic. Mma Cookie watched her walk away. It was not often that Willa's words were so few. The old woman clucked her tongue in worry. She knew that

Willa was probably right. Saving the chief's life might not be as important if it meant using herbs instead of needle drugs. Mma Cookie closed her eyes and shook her head. Poor Willa. Poor Chief. Sometimes it seemed a million miles between the order and the right of the Tswana and the order and right of Dr. Gakelape. And no bridge in between.

# # #

When Jan saw Willa's face, she knew the situation at the clinic was worse than she had imagined.

More than anything, Willa swore she would explain the chief's case medically to her mother and not let the cumulative worry and stress of the last week surface as tears or excuses. Through how many days and months and seasons had she tried to prove to her mother that she was a useful daughter, that she served a purpose as a competent health aid, maybe the best the post ever had? Did she notice? Did Jan really understand how Willa's translation helped her diagnose a patient? Or was it so natural that it was now just part of the rush and expectation in the examination room, expected and unheard?

Willa had meticulously kept up the daily patient logs and the general clinic log from the day Jan left. Her notes always included the fears, hopes and misgivings that the patients spoke of in their native Setswana tongue. Willa kept these written histories to help her understand how to best communicate with the patients about their illnesses and treatment. It had been something the chief had said that sent Willa to seek out the Dingaka for "bush" medicine.

"The devils can swim through this cloth to my brain. There is no barrier." Chief Tau's eyes were wide and weary in pain and fear of the death devil.

Willa was startled by his perception, known or unknown, that there were no antibiotics, western or traditional herbs, protecting the stitched wound. It was also stitched badly, the shredded skin at the tear making the repair beyond Willa's skill. The precision of her mother's surgical art would be needed to repair what was Willa's best, but admittedly novice, work.

Maybe she will understand that everything I did was in trying to save the chief's life.

Suddenly her mother was in the doorway and Willa could no longer hide the battles of the last week. Her smile quivered, but Jan's strong presence bolstered her for a moment. Her mother looked so beautiful standing there. Her legs were so long and tan and her arms glamorously thin but strong. Willa loved her mother's hair. It was straight and a beautiful light brown that was always shiny. Willa had inherited "curls and curves" from her father's family. The first time Jan had said that to her daughter, Willa had to stop and think who her father's family was. She was nine years old when her mother said that to her, the same year she had met her father for the first time. Memory snapshots would resurface at odd times: the big brick house, a distant older sister, a father who was rarely there and was reserved to the point of shyness around Willa.

"Willa," her mother spoke her name in such an assuring way that for a moment Willa had some hope.

Jan hugged her daughter and then held her chin in her hand. "What did I leave you with?" Jan could see the tears well in Willa's eyes and she used all of her will power to hold back the lump in her own throat.

Willa closed her eyes and sighed deeply, the stress rattling in her throat. She sat with Jan and methodically described the week that led to the telegram: Dr. Marvin leaving because of his father's illness, the bus accident that drained supplies and nurses, the herd boy who had been dragged 30 kilometers from the cattle-post with a mortal leg wound, and finally the chief. Willa covered everything. Everything but the Dingaka's visit to the health post.

Jan prioritized the cases Willa described in her head and asked to be taken to the chief. Within minutes Jan was scrubbed, had started an antibiotic IV and was running through the vitals. Her questions to the chief and to Willa involved the timing of the attack and the chief's arrival at the clinic. It was time.

As Jan unwound the head bandage Willa quickly described her desperate visit to the Dingaka and his agreement to treat the chief.

The end of Willa's story coincided exactly with the bandage

coming off and a poultice of green herbs, almost iridescent, becoming visible. *Obvious herbs.* Jan stopped abruptly and stared at the herb cap. Her face went from tan to white to a deepening red color.

"Bloody hell, Willa! What were you thinking?" Jan stared dumbfounded at her daughter. "Christ, it's not like I haven't tried for almost twenty years to get these people to stop going to the Dingaka when they're sick and coming here instead. You've been through this with me Willa. Why? Christ! This is a goddamn mess, not a medical treatment!"

Jan's eyes drilled into Willa's, her voice cutting away what little remained of Willa's resolve that she had done the right thing in trying to save the chief. "Help me clean him up. Get some hot water and sterile cloths."

Willa was surprised she could hear, her heart was beating so loudly in her ears: *failure, failure, failure.*

"Don't just stand there Willa, move it! For crissake!" Her mother did not finish her sentence. Willa ran for the water and cloths. Her face burned with shame.

When Willa came back the chief was saying something over and over again that Jan could not understand, so she was ignoring him. Willa set an enamel pan of warm water and the sterile cloths within Jan's reach.

Willa looked at the chief and his eyes locked on hers. Again he began speaking in Setswana. Willa translated as though she was on autopilot.

"The chief is upset that you are taking his shield," Willa translated to her mother.

Jan shot a quick look at Willa as she cleaned the wound. "What the hell does that mean?"

Willa took the chief's hand in both of hers. "It means he is afraid to have nothing on his head to ward off the infection."

"Well tell him I do have something but it provides a shield inside his head and is stronger medicine than what that kook in animal skins and claws plastered on his head. God, Willa, did the witch man even wash his hands before he touched the chief?" Jan's voice was beginning to pitch towards hysteria again.

"I applied the poultice myself. The Dingaka just chanted while I did it."

Jan's face looked as though she had swallowed poison. "Willa, my god. How many people witnessed this circus? Huh? Did you invite the whole village?" Jan looked incredulous. Willa leaned close into the chief and translated her mother's message about the antibiotics. He looked straight ahead not meeting Willa's eyes. She prayed to herself that the chief had not given up hope. It was the strength of the Tswana people's will that had helped them survive every setback they had ever faced, from drought to over-zealous missionaries to the living hell of the mines. Many who went south to help the oppressors find gold never came back to Botswana. *But the chief had to come back.*

Willa touched the chief's shoulder and spoke in Setswana. "*My chief, please do not lose your hope. You have been protected by the strongest medicines of both your people and the white man's. Disregard Dr. Gakelape's manner. You know that she was not born here and so cannot know the power of the Dingaka's medicine. But she does know the power of her own. She wants you to live a hundred days times a hundred times a hundred until you are so old you will pass easily to the ancestors.*" Jan broke in before Willa could continue.

"Willa, you just might not be ready for pre-med like I thought."

Willa's hope sank further into her chest as her mother's disappointment and anger wrapped around it, dragging it down to a dark, faraway place.

"Do you know what would happen if anyone in medical school ever heard about this fiasco? Huh? You'd be laughed out of town, out of med school, that's what."

Her mother's voice seemed very far away, filtered through cold liquid. It was drowning her.

Jan had speedily cleaned off the chief's head poultice and used her headlamp and magnifying glasses to examine the stitching. She ripped the glasses and light off her head, banging them down on the counter next to the chief's bed.

"I'll need your help prepping him for surgery and your assist during. I need him under while I re-do the stitches, but time will be critical." Jan's eyes pierced Willa's. "Just pay attention to what I say. Don't do anything unless I tell you to. Got it?"

Willa hoped her mother did not really want an answer to that question. It was insulting and clearly meant to be. It took all of Willa's will power not to turn her back and walk out of the clinic. It was the chief who kept her there, not her mother's tongue.

Just then two of the senior nursing sisters came through the door into the chief's room.

"Glory be to all gods. Nurse Gobe and Nurse Poni, thank god you're back. Scrub up and meet me in the surgery." Jan spoke quickly and the nurses, just back from treating victims of the bus accident, would now help her with the chief.

Both women were skilled nurses and had been with Jan for several years. Gobe's and Poni's desire to excel in nursing helped them put up with Jan's strict rules and harsh criticism when they did not meet her standards. But the training the two Batswana nurses had received under Jan had been of a quality and content that neither could have received in Botswana or South Africa.

Jan looked up from tending to the chief and looked at Willa. "I won't be needing you now."

Willa met her mother's eyes but could not hold them. The blame and distrust reflected there was overwhelming as both judgment and sentencing.

"Mother, I tried..." Willa began to defend herself unconvincingly. Jan interrupted.

"I said go away and get your head on straight. We'll discuss this later."

Dismissed. It was always clear when Jan was finished with you.

Willa touched the chief's arm and told him in Setswana that he would be fine but he still had to be strong and fight the leopard one more time as Dr. Gakelape stitched him up better.

"Ke a la boga, Doktoro Willawe. Thank you. We are now bonded in life and will always help each other. I will fight now, again, with you as my shield." The chief reached up and grabbed Willa's arm.

“*Ke itumetse, Chief Tau. Your words make me very happy.*” Willa put her hand over the chief's and managed a weak smile. “*I have already felt your strength today, Chief. Sala sentle. Stay well.*”

Willa turned and walked out of the surgery and the clinic compound. For the first time in her life she did not know where she was headed. Only that she no longer belonged at Mother Mercy.

# # #

Chapter 9: Mma Lilli's Feet

Bodiba, Botswana

"*Wiggle your toes for me now, that's right.*" Willa spoke in Setswana as she took Mma Lilli's left foot in both hands. As she slowly massaged it, Willa could feel with her fingertips the bone damage wrought by the old woman's arthritis.

"*Oh, daughter Willa, umh, umh, umh. My foot wants to marry your hand*!" Mma Lilli guffawed loudly and Willa joined her.

"No fair, ladies. Tell me what you're laughing about," Tom said in English.

"Oh, Tommiwe. We women have our own things that we speak about that don't include you, *monna*." Mma Lilli laughed again, enjoying her teasing of Tom, who feigned a hurt look. Willa glanced up from Mma Lilli's feet, smiled and shrugged her shoulders.

She is so beautiful, he thought, *and she doesn't even get it*. A woman as pretty as Willa back home would first work very hard at ignoring Tom, and then would make sure her beauty was recognized often and with appropriate veneration. Willa was clueless that a glance from her sent out a sensual, confident energy that penetrated a man's insides. Part of Willa's beauty was that she was comfortable in her skin. *She knows who she is and has made a spot for herself in the world she inhabits*. Tom was jealous and smitten at the same time.

Willa's pronouncement that she was returning to Bodiba with him was so sudden and assured that Tom could only nod and bite down on his lip to stop a wild grin from overtaking his face. Willa reminded Tom that he had mentioned his landlord's foot problems and asked if they could leave quickly. Tom sensed that it was not just Mma Lilli's feet that made Willa force a fast exit from Mother Mercy.

Even though she was trying hard to hide it, Tom could see the distress in Willa's eyes. Was it the chief she was so worried about?

But no, then she would not be so anxious to get away from the health post. It was almost like she was running away, sneaking out the back door when no one was looking. Mma Cookie had told Tom that Willa's mother had returned that day too. Wouldn't Willa want to visit with her? Tom had not met Dr. Jan yet, but Mma Cookie had talked of her with both reverence and trepidation.

Tom didn't consider when or how he could get Willa back to the clinic. Having her with him in the truck again was as far as his thinking progressed. '*What a selfish asshole I am,*' he admonished himself, a bit too weakly. Tom was not thinking about Mma Lilli's foot problem at all. Only about having Willa sit next to him in the jeep and then being there with him in Mma Lilli's compound. '*Be cool,*' Tom hissed at himself, even as he knew he would ignore his own advice.

"Is everything okay, Willa?" Tom had asked when she requested that they leave quickly.

"It's fine." Willa turned her face away from him and started towards the bungalow. "I just need to grab my knapsack. Can you meet me outside the main compound?"

Tom shouted back affirmatively as Willa's pace increased to a run. *She's as graceful as a springbok,* Tom thought as he watched her skirt sway back and forth, brushing her legs. *I want her,* banged around inside his head as he hurried over to the jeep. A broad, goofy grin was trying to take over his face again. Tom pinched his cheek hard. He shook his head and revved the motor of the jeep a lot harder than he needed to.

"*You may want to marry my hands, but they don't want to even date your feet,*" Willa said in Setswana. She smiled into Mma Lilli's face but her eyes were serious. "*Mme-we, you have arthritis or stiff foot sickness,*" Willa told her. Mma Lilli looked a little scared and a little sad, Tom thought. Maybe her foot pain was worse than she let on. He suddenly felt guilty for all the wood chopping and other labor he had seen Mma Lilli do, never admonishing her and only occasionally taking over the cutting or fire building.

Willa continued to massage Mma Lilli's foot while explaining the treatment over the old woman's moans and groans of happiness. Mma Lilli nodded when Willa described her condition, brought on after years of carrying heavy buckets of water, bundles of wood and bags of mealie meal on her head. She had overstressed her spine and feet, leading to Mma Lilli's chronic pain and bone deterioration. Anticipating the arthritis, Willa had brought medication with her. She described when and how to take the tablets and kept asking if Mma Lilli understood.

"*Willawe, I understand you, my daughter. But time is not remembered by me so often. Please have Tommiwe give me the medicine when I need it. He watches over me.*" She then clucked her tongue and shook her head. "*If only I were a young woman. I would steal Tommi from you!*" Mma Lilli laughed. Willa glanced nervously at Tom to see if he understood what Mma Lilli had said.

A burst of laughter came from deep in Mma Lilli's belly. She took Willa's face in both her hands. Tom looked confused.

"*My daughter, I can see the fire sparks playing between your eyes and his. There is a connection between the two of you. It is too obvious, daughter, that even a blind man could see it. Tommi likes you, too much. So much that he had forgotten his girlfriend in the U.S. and the skinny volunteer with white hair. I have never seen him so dazed. Even after drinking too many white man's beers.*" Mma Lilli laughed again heartily.

"*He is not dazed, mother. He is tired from saving the chief. He is also confused because I took him to the Dingaka's with me to fetch medicine for the chief. Dingaka took Tommi's tongue and used confusion powders to make him forget that he had been in the healing hut. That's all.*" Willa authoritatively handed a pill to Mma Lilli. "*Now stop exercising your mouth and take this medicine!*"

Tom interested in her? On the road to Bodiba Tom had talked to her about some of his favorite music. Willa had hardly heard any of it. When he talked about what it was like in the states, none of it sounded anything close to what she remembered from her brief trip to Boston ten years before. Mostly she recalled her father's house that had deep, white rugs on the floors; Yogi Bear cartoons on the television and chocolate profiteroles in a dark university club that smelled of dust and old men. Tom's America was much more than those scant, childhood recollections. Kids her age were protesting war, racism and poverty, testing the limits drawn by parental tradition. Depressions and world wars had swung the pendulum back to a love of sameness and no surprises. If everyone just followed the rules, then life ran like clockwork.

Tom's voice was tinged with old anger and new optimism as he described the atmosphere on college campuses and the perceptions and mores of the older generation that students and young people were pushing back against across the states. Willa listened, imagining the excitement of change trying to co-exist with stubborn traditionalism.

When Tom talked, Willa could feel her face burning underneath her skin. How could an isolated "African" white girl ever catchup? Her world was the clinic compound and the grounds of the boarding school she had attended in Francistown.

Could Mma Lilli be right that Tom was interested in her? Did he know she was only nineteen? *But twenty-six is not that much older. Not in Africa.* Willa sighed heavily, startling herself. Mma Lilli laughed and said in Setswana. "*I told you I'm right. You and Tommi. Yes. It's a good fit.*"

"*Oh, Mma Lilli*!" Willa continued to speak in Setswana knowing that Tom's proficiency was fairly low. "*I'm sighing because all of the ache in your feet has transferred to my hands. I must push it away by blowing it out. That's why I am sighing.*" Willa met Mma Lilli's eyes.

"*Whatever you want God to hear is fine with me. But he might not like a fib*!" The old woman laughed again deeply.

Willa clucked disapprovingly at Mma Lilli and stopped massaging her feet. "*If you are my mother-sister than do not embarrass me in front of Tom,*" Willa implored.

"*I won't,*" Mma Lilli answered. "*I won't say anything to your husband.*" She guffawed heartily and Willa could not help herself and joined her. Then Tom started laughing, seeing the joy in these two very different women of two cultures and two generations. Involuntarily the mantra played over again in his head: '*I want her.*'

# # #

Chapter 10: Jan Alone

Mother Mercy Clinic, Foley's Crossing, Botswana

Jan picked up her teacup and walked out to the screened porch. It was still so hot that it didn't matter whether she was outside or inside. *If only a breeze could blow.* Just a small, cool, little breeze. Would that be asking too much? Would a tiny breeze be too much to ask during a week when her daughter "ran away," her lover flew off without a goodbye, Mma Cookie was barely speaking to her, and Dr. Marvin was not due back to Mother Mercy for five more days. The telegram had stated in a succinct way that his father had indeed faced death but lived to tell the tale. Dr. Marvin would return for at least twelve months to complete his two-year tour.

Jan took another sip of tea and stared out across the compound, her eyes fixing on the thorn trees reaching across the veldt that nibbled at Mother Mercy's borders. Even though the air was thick with heat, the warmth of the milky, sweet tea cooled her off. Mma Cookie always told her it did. Jan always pretended she was skeptical. Was she skeptical? Was it not pretend anymore?

Ever since Jan had laid into Willa in the surgery, some part of the normal world as she knew it had gone away. Jan closed her eyes tightly, remembering her harsh words shot at Willa, point blank range. The words could not be taken back now. And worse, the bitterness behind the words would forever be floating about, out in the airwaves, tensing the trust between them a bit more. Jan was used to trust becoming so taut that it snapped. She had done it to Nora, her daughter. How many lovers had she done it to before Johnny?

Jan was glad for the loud din of the crickets. It helped tamp down the deep emptiness that she rarely allowed to surface, and even more rarely acknowledged.

"What the hell is wrong with me?" Jan asked out loud and startled herself. Suddenly it was just too much to stand. The teacup fell first, crashing loudly on the polished cement floor. Jan dropped less loudly onto the edge of the rocking chair, falling back into it, her feet rising like one side of a teeter-totter. When the chair hit the side of the bungalow it sounded like bones being crushed.

"Dr. Gakelape!" Mma Cookie shouted her name from inside the house and ran towards the crashing noises.

"I'm okay, Mma Cookie," Jan called out weakly. She was not okay, but did not want Mma Cookie worrying about her. She needed her back as an ally and advisor. Mma's silent treatment was almost more distressing than Willa leaving without even a note. *Damn it, I'm tired.*

Mma Cookie crashed through the screen door and it slammed against the porch wall with a crack. She saw Jan slumped awkwardly in the chair. She looked exactly like Willa's old raggedy girl doll, limp wrists and no expression left but two dollops of color on her cheeks.

"Dr. Gakelape! *Wa reng*? What is happening here?" Mma Cookie lifted Jan's hand and held it between the two of hers. Jan looked up at Mma Cookie.

"I was suddenly so tired. My cup slipped away." She said it matter-of-factly, like it always happened when she was tired.

"You need to bathe and sleep. Now, now. Just sit still, eh. I have to collect these shards, *janong*." Mma Cookie bent down and gathered the teacup pieces in her apron. She set her face firmly so that her worry would not show. Dr. Gakelape counted on her to always be the strong one.

Jan sat motionless, absorbed by Mma Cookie's bent head and the steadiness of her shoulders. Always working. *Working to clean up our messes. My messes.*

Jan was suddenly overwhelmed with what Mma Cookie had done for her over the years. This formidable African woman was really Willa's mother, not her. A real mother would not be so good at destroying her daughter's confidence and joy with a few choice, cutting words.

The surgery was an appropriate setting for Jan to yell at Willa. The precision and depth of her verbal cuts were clean and quick. *Was Willa somewhere right now bleeding from the surgical precision of my cruelty?*

"You have to stand now, Dr. Gakelape. Let us bathe you now." Mma Cookie helped Jan out of the rocker. It banged against the house. A dog barked in response from somewhere across the compound.

Their eyes met. The eyes of the mothers who both loved the daughter.

"Tomorrow you will go and fetch Willa," Mma Cookie announced.

"You know where Willa is?"

"Of course," Mma Cookie replied.

"Then I'll fetch her tomorrow." Jan leaned against Mma Cookie more than she needed to. But the African woman felt so good, so solid. So trusted. The way a mother must feel.

# # #

Chapter 11: Kopje Songs

Bodiba Village, Botswana
December 1968

The kopje was an easy climb despite the heat of the day that made the air thick with sage and mopani tree smells. Willa looked over her shoulder at Tom who was a few yards behind.

"You doing okay, *Mosadi*?" Tom asked as he reduced the space between him and Willa. The well-trodden path rose again even steeper ahead of them. Smooth, geometric shale pieces formed natural ochre steppingstones and made the trail look almost checkered. "The crest is right at the top of this incline. I promise," Tom laughed.

Willa turned around again and laughed with him. She unstrapped her canteen and passed it back to Tom.

"You know, water is now my favorite beverage? It used to be beer," Tom shook his head at the craziness of this notion.

"I think you are really becoming an African, Tom," Willa responded as she took the canteen back and then filled her mouth with the cool liquid. She liked the idea of Tom's lips having been on it before hers. It was intimate, sharing in him. "To us, I mean to the Batswana, water is everything. It's life, birth, hope, money and good cheer. It's also scarce in a lot of villages and thus all the more sacred."

Willa suddenly stopped and looked back at Tom in embarrassment. "I'm sorry. I forgot for a minute that you're a water engineer. I was just thinking you were a *Lekowa* and white folk aren't often aware of the Batswana obsession with water and rain."

Tom laughed and touched Willa's arm. "I forgive you. Amen. And we're here."

Tom moved ahead of Willa and offered his hand to help her navigate a large, slippery shale slab at the crest. Willa had trod a thousand such kopje paths in her life and could well manage it by herself. But reaching for Tom's hand and having him pull her close was a stronger urge than her independent will. Had anyone else reached to give her a hand she would probably have replied, 'I can do it myself.' That was certainly one of the few traits Willa had inherited from her mother: a strong independent will that made her determined but didn't always result in positive outcomes.

"Oh, Tom. It is beautiful up here!" Willa's eyes scanned the scene below. A forest glade hugged the east side of the kopje, a verdant apron holding back the tan, dry expanse of the Kalahari. The weakening afternoon sun bathed the vista in pink, hazy light.

"I almost expect fairies or hobbits to come wandering out of the trees some nights. It's magical isn't it?" Tom's eyes met Willa's. He took her hand in his. Willa's eyes answered his.

"Here, come and sit, Willa." Tom took a Peace Corps-issue blanket from his backpack and folded it into a soft seat. As Willa found a comfortable spot between the rocks, Tom pulled two LPs out of his pack, followed by a small battery-operated record player. Willa chuckled.

"What else do you have in your bag of tricks?"

"Ah, just you wait and see, young lady." Their eyes met again.

What was it with her? He had never been so polite in his life. Tom had only known Jill, one of the women in his Peace Corps group, for a few hours when he read her body signals as a go sign. They had set up a pup tent in the yard of the training site and exercised all their carnal instincts for about a week. Jill then got a really mushy, teary letter from her boyfriend in the states and cried while she told Tom that they would have to break it off. Tom had not realized that they had been on, but faked disappointment as she returned tearfully to celibacy until their last few days together. He had heard that the impact of the boyfriend's letter had fully worn off a month later, Jill's celibacy edict forgotten with a burley South African safari guide she met at the President's Hotel.

Chalking it up to a learning experience about women, Tom vowed to be a little more careful. Despite Jill's and some other women's outward, casual approach to having sex, after one week – the seeming magic number – they had to pin the relationship down to its current definition in time. As far as Tom could figure, this continuum began with lusty sex and ended with marriage. All relationships fell somewhere between the ends of that scale. It seemed that to women, it was natural to move from casual sex to quickly advancing towards the serious relationship stage. For men, casual sex led to more casual sex. There was no incremental relationship scale in the male picture.

Yet somehow with Willa it was different. She was not a casual-sex girl. She grew up in Botswana at a health post. How many casual sex options could she have had? But suddenly a vivid picture of Willa with muscled African princes, safari guides, and bush pilots flashed through his mind. Of course, Willa would be considered a precious commodity in northern Botswana. A young, beautiful, smart white woman. Not a lot of those around.

Tom found his usual flat spot to set up the turntable, his pride and joy. His mother and best friend both thought he was crazy to bring his LPs and player to Africa. But Tom's collection of music had been a blessing in Peace Corps training camp. At first he was laughed at for using his precious 94 pounds of baggage to bring 30 records and his player. But after the second week of training camp, all the volunteers we're pitching in with batteries and even having fights about which LP to play next. Tom suddenly took on a leadership role in each evening's entertainment, his player and LPs forming the centerpiece of any event. His mother's insistence on bringing at least one Christmas record had absolutely made their holiday celebration. Most of the volunteers had never spent Christmas overseas, so Nat King Cole had the dining room in tears before the velvet-voiced singer had even completed the first line of '*Chestnuts roasting on an open fire...*'

Even though the Christmas season was upon them, Tom had left Nat back with his other LPs. Tonight he needed *Love.*

"Have you ever heard the band *Love* before?" Tom asked.

Willa shook her head. "I'm beyond uninformed when it comes to mod music. Johnny, my mother's boyfriend, attempts to bring some of the new music to us when he flies up from Jo-berg or Cape Town or returns from Europe. But my knowledge is very thin. I did like two LPs he brought up last month. Bob Dylan and Donovan."

“Um, those are good ones. I have Dylan records and one by Donovan. I’ll play those for you later tonight. But now, please bear with me. There’s one *Love* song that I play as often as I can as a tribute to the sunset and the view of the desert from up here, and what it makes me think about. Listen closely.”

Tom carefully placed the record on the turntable and moved the needle to the third song. He pulled a joint out of his shirt pocket and lit it. “This helps with the magic. Want to share?”

Willa nodded as the song began. Tom moved closer to Willa on the blanket and put the joint up to her lips. As she inhaled, their eyes met and the song lyrics filled the space between them.

Orange skies, carnivals and cotton candy and you
And I love you too, you know I do.

Willa looked down first. She had no clear idea what that kind of look led to. But sex seemed the likely end point. Unlike the few times in the past when Willa had refused to move beyond petting and a boy with magical fingers who played her sweet spots to her complete physical joy, she now wanted Tom. Willa was a rare nineteen–year-old: a virgin. She was not even sure why she still was, except that no boy had yet seemed deserving of something that marked a major rite of passage in a girl’s life.

Nightingale, prettier than anything in the world
And I love you too, you know I do

Her mother had helped Willa understand the sanctity and beauty of her own body. Every lecture or talk had the same message: don’t disrespect your body or let anyone else either. This not only included lectures on sex, but also on food. Jan constantly preached Jethro Kloss, the natural medicine guru friend of her crazy aunts back in Concord. While Jan did not automatically accept all the beliefs and practices of Jethro or her aunt’s commune farm, Jan understood the link between diet and health. Mma Cookie had to finally cave in to Jan’s demands to lessen the mealie-meal that she fed Willa at least two times a day, and increase the vegetables, fruit and grains.

You make me happy, laughing glad and full of glee
And you don't have to try girl

Willa was thinking about how good Tom's arms looked in his tee-shirt, and then his lips were suddenly on hers, then on her eyes and cheeks. He steadied her face between his hands and held her eyes. 'Is this okay,' Tom's eyes asked. Willa's eyes answered back with a yes-blink. They lay back on the blanket and faced each other on their sides. Tom heard *Love* in the background along with cicadas and the last daylight sounds of nesting weaverbirds.

For you it comes so naturally
Like here in my arms

There was no way he was going to rush this. Tom knew that Willa needed to trust him. Plus, he had some type of deeper respect for her than he had ever felt for a woman. With Willa it just seemed more real, worthwhile.

Willa found new ways to kiss Tom and explore his face with her lips while he found her wet sweetness. Willa wanted only to get lost in the feelings that Tom had ignited in her body. She was engaged in the moment, that was it. Tom was different and special. Willa felt connected to him, the way that people bonded after sharing a life-changing event. She wanted him to like her, to try to see who she was. With the boys she had known before, she did not care whether they liked her or not. They were not worth it. With Tom, Willa felt like the most popular girl in school, the one who the most popular, good-looking boy goes after. She was beyond the questions of why Tom would be interested in her to now wanting to find out more, but in a slow, natural way that involved learning how to make love to a beautiful man.

Love sang another song and the cicadas accompanied with their twitching legs. Tom knew they had to stop now or he would take her on this hillock top. Although his lust was saying 'now' his mind wanted a quiet, safe place with Willa. He stopped kissing her and moved his face away. Stray strands of hair wisped across Willa's brow. Tom touched them gently with his fingertips.

"Willa, I want to make love to you. But not here." She looked relieved and then smiled. He had guessed right. "You are so beautiful I'm wondering if I deserve you." Willa laughed softly at the flattery.

"I was thinking the same thing about you. I guess we deserve each other then," Willa said as she leaned over and kissed Tom.

"Let's not start again, lady. I can't exercise that level of self-control more than once a night." Willa smiled shyly and conspiratorially. Together she and Tom hastily packed up the record player, LPs and blanket.

It was that quiet, magical time between the dusk and the deep darkness of the night in the Kalahari. Willa's eyesight was accustomed to navigating the African veldt at night so she led the way. Tom was grateful. He also loved watching her shape move as a shadow in front of him. He shook his head and thought what a lucky man he was. Dreams seemed to happen during waking hours in Africa, because reality was often oblique, sideways to him, the non-African. It was not the reality with the boundaries he was used to. Women like Willa did not exist on Cape Cod. She was a child in many ways but also a woman who could negotiate with a powerful bush doctor and sew up the head of a scalped chief. What had he done ever that matched the guts and gumption that Willa had displayed over the last week?

Willa was glad to have the path to focus on. She trembled, aching for Tom to be close to her, inside of her and outside of her. Having to navigate the path in the dark kept her steady and let her pound her nervous excitement into the trail.

As Tom and Willa approached Mma Lilli's compound it glowed with firelight and muted voices. "*Dumelang, lovers of the night,*" Mma Lilli's Setswana greeting broke the spell.

"She's got our number," Willa leaned over and whispered to Tom.

"What did she say," Tom whispered back.

"Just look incredulous," Willa laughed.

"Well, well, *bana,* I was just now ready to fetch the kgotla police to look for you. I was becoming sure you were eaten by dusk devils," Mma Lilli bellowed.

"Tsk, tsk, Mmawe, but devils do not disturb good boys and girls," Tom bent down and took Mma Lilli's hand. She cackled loudly.

"Oh, Tommiwe, you are so fresh tonight, isn't it?" Mma Lilli spoke to her friend, Joseph, who came often to the compound around supper to chat with his lady friend. Joseph had lost his wife the year before and Mma Lilli consoled him with meals and conversation, and probably more, Tom thought. Mma Lilli was a big woman but she was still attractive and always good company.

Willa said in Setswana, "*I hope we are not disturbing you.*" Mma Lilli laughed and shook her head.

"*No, no, no. Young people never disturb me. You help me stay young*!" Joseph laughed too at Lilli's words and his eyes glowed and met his woman's.

"*Are you wanting to eat? Let us share porridge and nama. Rra Joseph brought us some fresh kudu meat and it is so-ooo sweet*!" Mma Lilli stood up and went over to the cooking hut.

"*Ke itumetse, Mme,*" Willa answered for them. "It is kind of you to offer."

Even with Tom's limited Setswana, he understood Mma Lilli's question. "*Ke itumetse, Mma Lilli.* I am hungry, *thata thota*!"

Rra Joseph laughed suddenly and Mma Lilli joined him. "We can see that you are really, really hungry, Tommiwe!" Mma Lilli cackled loudly.

"Mma Lilli! If I didn't love you so much I might have to spank you sometimes!" Tom joked.

"Hah! You are the only *batho* here who needs to be spanked. Here, eat this sweet meat so you will be strong tonight." She tittered and made a funny whistling sound through her teeth. Rra Joseph just grinned.

Tom clucked his tongue against his teeth. It was the Tswana sign that he did not like her words.

Glad that the darkness hid her embarrassment, Willa changed the subject. "*Mma-we, how do your feet feel tonight*?"

Mma Lilli handed Willa a plate of sorghum porridge in gravy

with a large hunk of kudu on the side. In Setswana she said, "*Oh, my daughter, my poor feet are better but miss your rubbing fingers. First you save my chief then my feet. I wish you were my daughter so I could be proud of you in that way.*" Mma Lilli stopped serving and met Willa's eyes.

"*Mme Lilli, you are my Auntie now, and I am your daughter. Tomorrow I will treat your feet again. Tonight I am grateful for this food you have shared and for letting me stay in your compound.*"

"*You are special, Willawe*. Tommiwe, do you hear me?" Mma Lilli stood over Tom and squeezed his shoulder. "Willawe is my daughter now. Treat her with the respect you would give any of my children, or else I will come after you."

Tom's lip curled into a smile, but then he looked at Mma Lilli. She stared into his eyes, a very serious look on her face. Tom cut his smile. "Respect is the only thing I can give to Willa. She has all of it that I have, Mmawe."

Mma Lilli smiled. "I love my *lekgowa* children!" she laughed loudly. "Eat now and be strong, my white family. Tomorrow I expect much from both of you."

# # #

Chapter 12: Nora's Eyes

Philadelphia
January 1969

There was something about silk paisley shirts that Nora really liked. They definitely were not Pete's style, but the curly yet formal patterns and the feel of the fabric against her skin made her understand the attraction of the shirts to the men who frequented the shop.

Nora had only been working in the boutique for a month, but already felt like she belonged. Primarily serving a gay clientele, the small shop in the center of Philadelphia glowed in bright colored shirts, trousers, belts, shoes and suits. Nora felt an instant affinity with the clientele, quickly becoming a skilled saleswoman. When she was helping one of the customers pick out a coordinated shirt to go with a pair of pants, Nora knew exactly what would best suit the man's physique. Accessorizing was also a specialty of hers that the boutique's owner-manager, Max, greatly appreciated. Maybe she had learned something from Carol after all, Nora thought, picturing her father's wife in her highly coiffed housewifery. The clientele would not only walk out of the store with a suit, but also with several coordinating shirts, a snake belt, socks, loafers and a chain necklace or wrist band.

Nora was comfortable around her clients, loving the sense of humor and style and the focus on color and cloth texture that many of these beautiful men had. Most of the guys were so honest and open. And they trusted her. Almost every day she was invited to a party. 'And bring your cute boyfriend, sweetie,' which is what Max would always add with a chuckle.

As Nora re-stocked one of the shirt racks, she thought about her new replacement family and smiled. She had Pete and she had all her guys now. She did not have her father any more. It was too difficult to call him, too scary. "I don't have the guts," she said out loud and startled herself that it had come out of her mouth.

“Guts for what, Sweetheart?” It was Max, the owner. He walked up next to her and put his arm around her waist.

“I’m sorry, Max. That was supposed to stay in my head and it accidentally popped out.”

“Sweetie, nothing accidentally pops out,” Max cackled suddenly at his own private joke. “Oops, sorry. Nora, if you said it out loud it means you’re subconsciously seeking help. My shrink tells me that all the time. Your personality is trying to get you to go underground, but your mind wants help. Thus spake Nora. Tell Uncle Max, Love. It helps to get these things off that lovely chest of yours.”

Nora could not help but smile and hug her manager-friend. “You’re too good to me, Max. I hope I deserve it.”

“Honey, do you have one major self-esteem problem, or what?!” Max stared at her, his head dramatically moving up and down as though surveying her whole body. “Look at you!” He grabbed Nora by the arm and pulled her in front of the full-length mirror. “Look at you! You have a face and a body that 99 percent of the women in Philadelphia would kill for and still might if you give them a chance. You’ve got great hair, you smell good and you’re not a bitch. What?” Max threw his hands in the air in exasperation.

“Oh, Max. Thank you. I guess a lot has happened to me in the last few months and not all of it makes sense yet. God, I don’t even know if it’s supposed to make sense. I mean, does it need to in order to be worth doing?” Nora moved away from the mirror and went back to the paisley shirts. Max followed.

“But you still have not told me. Enough guts for what? I can’t stand unfinished conversations.” Nora stopped buttoning a shirt and looked at Max.

“To call my father.”

“Oh, the Dad thing,” Max clucked his tongue and put his hand under Nora’s chin, raising it up.

“I left kind of suddenly. Dropped out of college. Missed Christmas and never called. I did send a card, though.” Nora’s eyes were beginning to fill. “I was just thinking that you guys are my family now, and Pete. And it’s so weird. How long have I known you? A month? And I feel closer to you, feel like I could talk to you about almost anything, and I never felt that way with my father or step-mother, or even the girls I hung around with at B.U. Isn't that weird?"

"No, honey, it's not weird. It's normal. You've been reborn. You're the butterfly who left the old skanky cocoon behind. That wasn't you back there in your old life. That was you trying to get out. Your father and the others probably only tried to keep you in, right?" Nora nodded, a tear rolling down her cheek. Just then the bell on the door sounded and an attractive black man walked in.

"Nora, put it on hold, child. Suck it up for now and we'll wrestle this little dilemma in half an hour when we close. Will you join me at Rudy's after closing?"

Nora smiled. "I'd love to. Thanks, Max. Sorry for the bummer."

Max looked at her up and down again, incredulously. "I am going to spank you, Miss Nora. Don't make me, make me!"

Max walked up to the customer. "Oh, Larry! God, you look good! I hardly recognized you. You've lost weight!" Max bear hugged Larry and they began an animated conversation with lots of laughter and excuses to hug. Nora smiled.

This place really did make her feel better when she thought of her father worrying about her. Nora could see him in her head, wringing his hands the way he did when there was a problem to solve. She had been sending him short notes and postcards just so he would not worry too much about her or report her missing to the police. His perfect life was not perfect anymore and it was Nora's fault.

Forty-five minutes later Nora and Max walked arm in arm down Sansome Street to Rudy's, a café that specialized in strong coffee, imported beer and folk music. It was a people-watching Mecca that expanded Nora's 'common categories of people' list that she tallied in her head. And expanding was the right word.

Nora was still in awe of the new experiences and people she had been exposed to in the last few months. Never before would she have thought she could so totally rearrange her priorities and view of the world, and feel so comfortable.

When she was living on campus or in her father's house, it was typical of her to know in advance what each day would bring, where she was going, what she was doing and who she would see. Everything planned out. Everything ranked in importance based on its impact on her. *'Damn, I've been so selfish,'* Nora thought.

"Have you ever put yourself at the center of the universe, Max? Judged everything only on how it affected you?" Nora looked up into his blue eyes.

"Oh, yeah, Sweetie. That was my I-me-mine phase. Yes, have I ever been there. Could I tell you some stories! Boring stories because "I" appears every third word." Max laughed and put his hand over Nora's. "It cost me the equivalent of several years' salary and three really good lovers before my shrink managed to pull my head out of my ass!" he laughed again in his Max-self-deprecating way.

"Did seeing a shrink really help you?" Nora asked, remembering her step-mother's weekly visits, after which Carol would always be ultra-reflective about everything that Nora or her father would say for the next 24 hours. Nora always said she had a lot of "homework" on those nights and stayed behind her bedroom door.

"It helped only in the sense that he was paid to listen, so listen he did. Which is more than I can say for my own father, 95% of my former lovers and 80% of my employees. Of course you're not on that list, Sweetie. In fact, I get worried because you pay too close attention to what I say. It's getting near impossible to deny my misstatements and faux pas with you around."

Nora smiled. "I learn so much from you, Max. You're so good with people. You always know just the right thing to say. I used to just blurt out whatever came to mind, but now I don't. I can't because I do not know what the hell I'm doing half the time, most of the time really."

Max squeezed her arm and stopped them both on the sidewalk. Rudy's was just across the street. "There you go again. Knocking yourself without cause. Trust me. You're fine. Don't think you need to lock into everything with a full Nora analysis before you speak." Nora smiled and nodded in acknowledgement.

"I guess I don't want to make an ass out of myself either. I want people to think that I'm one of them; that I belong. Most of the time I feel like I stand out like a sore thumb."

"Sweetie, don't worry. It doesn't show. I've got to teach you the bitch mouth."

"What's the bitch mouth," Nora asked with a giggle as they started to cross the street.

"It's a certain way of pursing your lips, sucking in your cheekbones and narrowing your eyelids that gives a distinct impression that you know it all, have seen it all, have done it all, and sit in judgment of all thoughts and actions of others, despite the fact that you may be crumbling internally and festering in fear. Observe..." Max demonstrated the bitch mouth and Nora broke out with a cackling laugh and couldn't stop. She finally sought out the curb and put her head between her knees, tears of laughter popping out of her eyes.

"Stop, Max, you're killing me!" Nora groaned and laughed at the same time. Max rubbed her back.

"You need more than a coffee, Sweetie. Let's step into the alley, blow this joint, and then hope they're serving at least beer tonight." Max pulled a joint out of his shirt pocket and helped Nora stand. "Rudy's loses its liquor license about once a week. Let's hope good ole Rudy paid off the right cop tonight and the spirits are flowing."

And flowing they were. Max and Nora were lucky and grabbed a small booth just as a couple was getting up to leave. It had a good view of the stage and a panoramic view of the other tables and customers. The pot high helped the place look and feel more exotic than the smoky, dingy dungeon it actually was.

The clientele were a mixed crowd. Folk music lovers in fringed leather jackets and open sandals with thick wool socks; youngish professors from Temple whose wandering eyes betrayed their recent marijuana experimentation and their penchant for long-legged co-eds; the poet-philosophers who listened intently to the music, hoping to glean something they could call truth and then find a way to pass it on; and teenage white boys from the neighborhoods bordering Philly who knew that there was more to growing up than Friday night dances and crashing their older sisters' slumber parties.

Nora soaked it all up, observing but trying very hard not to judge. She had spent her whole life so far rating and ranking and berating anything that she did not understand or had not seen before. Nora squeezed her eyes shut tight when she thought about the cruel way she had treated some of her old classmates, talking behind their backs, rejecting them as friends if they did not stay on the well-defined path of the Chestnut Hill rich girls. And she had been brutal to little Willa when a combination of jealousy and puberty had materialized into pure meanness during her little sister's visit to Boston.

"What's that look on your face mean?" Max leaned in close to Nora. "You look sick all of a sudden. What?!"

Nora suddenly looked apologetic. "I'm sorry, Max. I was just thinking about some of my past transgressions and regretting them."

"Oh, stop, already! You are being such a martyr, I'm going to start calling you Joan. Max tisked at her.

"Joan?"

"Of Arc, silly. Girl-child, you *are* from the 'burbs. You need much more polluting than that boyfriend of yours is providing so that at least you have something worthy of your angst to stew about." Max's look of exasperation changed to a smile.

Nora smiled too. "I will lighten up if I can just keep hanging around with you and the rest of the guys. You can take a girl out of the suburbs, but you can't make her hip."

Nora and Max both started laughing hard at her pun.

"You are a doll, Nora. Does that Pete of yours understand what he has, huh?"

"Yes, Max. Pete treats me great. I'm learning a lot from him about music and art..."

"...and sex, admit it!"

"And sex, I admit it!" They both laughed again. "I really do feel like I'm shedding an old cocoon and testing out new wings," Nora said, pushing her bangs back off her face.

"Well, I'll try to be there for you Nora when your wings fail at work, but you're going to have to be strong enough to pull yourself up off the floor when you're at home. Promise me you won't crumple when you hit the next wall."

"I promise." Nora looked at Max and imagined that this must be what it was like to have a brother. "Thank you, Brother Max."

"At your service, Sister Nora. Now let's get serious and order something really greasy and salty before some folk prophet ruins our appetite."

"I thought you liked folk music?" Nora questioned, squinting her eyes against the glare of an isolated but potent hanging bulb.

"Well, I like it to the extent that many cute, gay guys like it who happen to frequent this place. *Capice*?"

"*Capice*." They both smiled conspiratorially and leaned back in their seats as a fragile looking blonde woman took the stage with her guitar. The club owner walked up to the stage mike and announced, "Ladies, gents and uncertains, please join me in welcoming the easy, breezy Miss Joni Mitchell."

# # #

Even though it was raining and cold, it felt like a balmy spring evening. There was something about that woman's music – Max had called it evocative – that made Nora warm and thoughtful. She remembered the Joni part, but not the soulful singer's last name. Mostly Nora was excited to be able to share a musical tidbit with Pete. It was always Pete telling Nora about the rhythms and attributes of different types of music, like jazz or R&B, and turning her on to the top musicians, names she had never heard before, like John Coltrane, Wilson Picket and Miles Davis.

Nora loved the idea of telling Pete about Joni, her "evocative" music, the lyrics that took Nora's mind into California canyons and the streets of Montreal and revealed the love and confusion between women and their men. Everyone in Rudy's kept talking about how mellow Joni was, how she was just on the brink of being big.

In front of Nora the streetlights reflected off the stone facades of the old buildings, dark and lumpy in the rain.

Pete and the guys were playing at the Electric Factory and

Nora thought she remembered that his set was done at about ten. It was ten-thirty so he would probably be done helping the other guys break down the set. Nora also remembered that a folk group from England was going to play the late set. Pete had seemed excited about seeing them. They had a really different sound, folk rock anthems he had called their music. Nora thought Pete would definitely stay to hear them.

Nora's heart felt fluttery and sentimental, but at the same time she felt strong. Something was happening to her. '*I must be getting my sea legs,*' she thought. '*Or is it my woman legs? Or my grownup legs*', she queried herself. '*City legs, sexy legs, legs with confidence, shaved legs, my legs, legs wrapped around Pete's legs, loving his legs and being consumed by them.*'

Nora reveled in the rain and the feeling of newness and freedom. Did some people feel this way every day, she thought? Could she keep feeling this way, keep discovering so that her eyes were always wide open and open wide for any and all things? And would Pete and her new friends continue to like her and let her be part of the crowd if they found out how un-hip she actually was? Could she continue to contribute very little to the musical conversations, the stories about folk festivals, the acid trip tales, the bus trips with Hari Krishna apostles and the nights in jail? Nora's worst fear was that Pete and everyone would discover her for the rich suburban girl she really was, or at least really had been.

But Nora refused to let the self-doubt take over. The night was too magical, too veiled in symbols and serendipity to ruin with the leftover doubts of her old self.

'Fuck it," Nora whispered. *If I don't open myself up more how can others let me in*, she thought.

A block ahead Nora saw the Electric Company sign. It flickered slightly, dulling down and brightening up again, smearing color across the wet sidewalk. She stopped for a second and crossed her eyes, purposely blurring the sign into a neon rainbow. It was an old habit from childhood. Nora remembered kneeling in front of her bedroom window and being able to see some of the lights from the tall buildings in Boston. Crossing her eyes transformed the yellow office beehives into a firestorm of color. Nora would then imagine she was in Africa with her mother, the blurred lights became the desert and the sun beating down warming her small hand as it nestled in her mother's cool palm, so safe, so sure and solid. What she did not know was that on those same nights her father would find her asleep beneath the window, the street light illuminating her beautiful child's face. Dr. Dodge's heart would break a little each time he found her and gently settled her back in bed. He knew she was searching for something she did not have. He knew it was her mother.

At first Michael Dodge's habit was to tamp down his anger at Jan by leaving Nora's bedside and tossing back a few scotches. But the fiery hangovers soon stopped that. Dodge was too dedicated a surgeon to let anger and alcohol make him less than prepared for seeing a patient or performing a surgical procedure. Slowly his anger at Jan's abandonment turned into a singular focus on his work and making sure that Nora had the best of everything, from nannies to boarding schools to toys and summer camps.

Eventually Nora stopped going to the window and Dr. Dodge slowly forgot that he had ever been worried about her.

Nora uncrossed her eyes and the Electric Factory sign came back into focus. And so did Pete. He must have just stepped out, thought Nora, congratulated herself on such great timing.

Pete lit a cigarette as the club door opened again. A slender woman with long, straight, black hair came through the door. It was instantly clear that she was with Pete, because their eyes locked and they both smiled in a way that Nora had seen before: the night she met Pete.

Nora chided herself not to jump to conclusions. She was just about to start towards Pete when he took the black-haired girl's hand and they pressed against each other and started walking away from the club and from Nora. She watched them in disbelief as they stopped under the first street light and kissed each other hungrily. They shared a few whispered words and then began to laugh in the way that anticipating lovers do, hushed with an edge of sex and excitement.

Nora lost her balance and stumbled a little. She had not been breathing, she realized. The pounding of her heart roared in her ears. A prickling heat washed up from her butt and through her belly, a spasm of betrayal that was making her physically sick.

A low moan released itself from her heart and she sat on the curb to steady her legs. *Think, think*, Nora chided herself. What should she do now? Her first thought of violence against Pete fell away to the reality of her choices. One thing that Nora did have to credit her stepmother with was the training Carol gave her in assessing options before making a rash move. But Carol had taken this assessment system to an extreme that left little room for change and none for uncertainty.

"I need to get away," Nora said out loud but it barely surfaced as a whisper. *Flight. Flee. Escape.* It was what she now did when an outcome did not work as expected. Just leave. Start over. Leave the past behind.

Nora suddenly thought of her mother and wondered if that was what she had done when she stayed in Africa. For the first time Nora considered that maybe her mother did have a good reason for staying, even though that had meant abandoning her oldest daughter. *Flight. Flee. Escape.*

# # #

Chapter 13: Chances

Bodiba Village, Botswana
December 1968

The sound of an approaching lorry in the village was unmistakable from its noise and rumble. A distinct feeling of movement in the ground beneath the village often preceded even the noise of the engine and the axle banging against the chassis. Then some unique feature of the Kalahari sand turned it into a transmitter of faraway movement and sound. Only the bushmen of the Kalahari had mastered being able to sneak up on man or beast without being detected through the radio grains.

Both Willa and Mma Lilli looked up at the same time at the sound of the approaching lorry. Since very few people in the area had a lorry, it could only be one of a few possibilities.

Willa focused again on Mma Lilli's feet. "*This foot seems much better, Mmawe, much less tight,*" Willa said in Setswana.

"Oh, I'm telling you, my daughter, I think it is a whole different foot from that nasty old sore foot that was there before you treated me." Mma Lilli looked up at Willa from the blanket she was sitting on. Willa had Mma Lilli's feet in a towel on her lap and was rubbing in an ointment made with aloe and hot pepper.

Willa smiled at her new adopted auntie and looked up again as the lorry approached their compound. Even without standing, Willa could see that it was the health post lorry because it was painted a bright white with red crosses in several places. Sammie Po was driving but Willa could not yet make out the passenger.

"What's all the racket? Mornin' ladies." Tom appeared, pushing the hut door aside and walked towards the blanket where Willa was working away at the old woman's feet. Just then the lorry stopped in front of Mma Lilli's compound entrance.

Willa stood up as she saw her mother getting out of the vehicle. The sinking feeling in her chest returned, anticipating an eminent reprimand from Jan. But what had her mother thought she did this time? Unless Jan had become a seer, she could not yet know about her and Tom. Willa swallowed and walked towards her mother.

When Jan's eyes met Willa's she suddenly saw her daughter as a little girl again. Standing there in the compound with her arms hanging at her sides, an uncertain look in her eyes, the beautiful innocence in her face. Jan wondered where that had come from. Not from her that was for sure.

"Willa," Jan stuttered and shifted her weight. Suddenly a tear slid down the doctor's cheek. Willa watched it fall onto the road, instantly absorbed by the baked dust. She wanted to reach down and save the tear because it was so rare. Jan's arms rose in apology and need toward Willa.

"Willa, I'm so sorry, baby. I'm so sorry." Jan's tears fell onto Willa's shoulder as they held one another, hugging away the hurt and the guilt that had tested the trust and respect they felt for one another.

Despite their almost opposite temperaments, Jan and Willa were teammates. They were constantly surprised and awed by each other's behavior, so different from their own, but always a lesson to be learned from observing the other's skills and perceptions. It was almost as though they needed the other to fill in their underdeveloped parts, to offset Willa's blind trust in others and Jan's blatant skepticism of tribal custom and beliefs.

As mother held daughter and all of this was shared between them, Jan wondered how she would ever survive without Willa. In reality, Dr. Jan knew that she had to learn to survive alone because in only a matter of months, Willa would go to medical school in the states. As selfish as she really wanted to be, Jan knew that Willa's destiny lay in her skilled hands and heart. Egotistically, Jan also loved the idea of a second-generation doctor in the family. In this she knew she shared at least one thing with Willa's father. Maybe Michael Dodge would forgive Jan just a little bit when he saw who Willa had become as an engaging, responsible woman and as a skilled healer.

Tom stood just inside the compound, giving Jan and Willa their space to make up while still keeping a protective eye on

Willa.

After they had made love for the first time the night before, Tom and Willa had lain together and talked about their families. Tom had learned in full detail about the events leading up to the antibiotics shortage at the health post, Willa's disbelief when the chief came in needing medicine they did not have, and Jan's blow up when she saw the Dingaka's poultice on the chief's head. To cheer Willa up, Tom confessed how scared and displaced he had felt in the African healer's hut and it made both of them laugh so hard that they had to bury their heads in the pillows and muffle their guffaws. This led to another round of lovemaking and discovery of each other's young bodies and minds.

Willa had the most beautiful body that Tom had ever seen. Her white breasts were capped with the palest of pink nipples. A small waist led to surprisingly broad hips and sculpted hipbones that guarded the sweetest joy he had ever tasted. She was so hot inside, like she had stored up all of her passion for him for a long time and now it flowed unguarded.

Tom told Willa about his beloved mother, his father who hit and hurt them both, his small town on Cape Cod where memories of long winters were erased by idyllic summers of salty, warm air, midnight swims in the cool tides and dripping ice cream cones. And tourists, of course. But Tom never complained about the tourists like his father and most of the townies did. Tom loved anything new, anything different than the reality of his father's moods and his fists. Seeing the summer people come in and take over the town was the distraction Tom waited for all winter, and held close in his mind when his father came home drunk and looking for an easy target.

As Tom grew older and saw his mother deteriorate from the verbal and physical battering, he would purposely put himself out in front of his father's moods and madness. Mostly Tom succeeded in deflecting his father's attention from his mother, taking a fist or a belt in the face or on his back so she could be spared. More often than not his father would pass out after beating Tom, before he had a chance to move on to his wife. Tom's mother would find him once she heard his defeated footfalls in the hallway moving towards his bedroom. She would cry if Tom had a new welt or bleeding cut on his boyish, innocent body. She would silently clean him up, exhausted by the sickening routine. Sometimes they would quietly cry together. Never would Tom ask why she stayed, but his eyes always squinted in fearful wonder at his mother's ability to endure it.

By the time he was in high school, all Tom wanted to do was leave. He was just biding his time until he graduated and turned eighteen. But how would his mother get out? It was then that Tom would picture himself pointing a pistol at his father's head. One click and he would be gone. That was when Tom knew he had to leave quickly. Taking his father's life was not worth losing his own.

Three days after he graduated from high school, Tom bought a plane ticket to California, the farthest state away from his father that he could come up with. His dream over the prior two years had been to attend the University of California in Santa Barbara. With the help of a sympathetic guidance counselor, Tom had started a letter writing campaign to the admissions, financial aid and Engineering departments, using all his prose talents to convince them to accept him, and offer him a scholarship. Either out of awe or exhaustion from reading his letters that detailed Tom's academic and athletic ability, UC not only accepted him, but gave him a tuition scholarship and enough other financial aid that Tom could manage with no help from his father. With the money he made every summer as a custodian at the Ancient Mariner Inn and his winters at his uncle's auto repair shop, Tom had saved enough money to make his break and never have to return to Cape Cod.

Tom would never have asked his old man in a million years if he would help pay for college. The sarcastic answer that his father would certainly scream was, "Hell no, you arrogant shit. I never had to go to college to support my family. You think you're better than me, don't you, you pretty boy. You mama's boy. I want you out of this house. And I'm not supporting your wussy ass."

Tom had heard this tirade enough whenever report cards came in filled with A's and B's; or a teacher would see Tom's father in a store and say how smart Tom was and how far he could go. As soon as his father got home, he would corner Tom and accuse him of feeling superior. In truth, Tom felt inferior to the few friends he had in high school. Their personalities were not damaged with thoughts of hatred for a father and intense pity and hopelessness for a battered mother. Tom's thoughts were often so consumed by his anger and dread, that he had little space to let in close friends.

It was with a sense of relief and recovery that he could finally make and keep close friends once he was in California. By leaving his old life behind with a space of 3,000 miles in between, Tom could finally put his anger towards his father away in storage. Finally his thoughts had room for another topic. It was in thanks that Tom prayed to the ocean every day when he awoke in Santa Barbara. He had escaped. He did not have to descend into that daily hell with its terrible monotony of pain.

"I escaped," Tom chanted every morning when he ran out to the beach as the sun rose. He knew he was one of the lucky ones. By leaving he had left his personal history behind and was free, at least for a while. The ocean had become his daily balm and the Pacific's blue energy slowly healed his spirit. Tom thought of it as running towards hope. Hope in a future that was not yelling and despising, not the cracking of skin as knuckles broke open his face and smashed into muscle and bone in his arms and back, not the taste of blood in his mouth. And not the anger at his mother for her passivity. The guilt when he felt this way. The fear when thoughts of getting rid of his father began to seem like a plan.

Jan and Willa's laughter brought Tom back and he smiled involuntarily. There was a joy in it. Hope in it.

After Jan and Willa made peace, Tom introduced himself to the mother of the young woman he had deflowered the previous night. Jan was unusually gracious and polite, even attentive. Willa was astounded. Maybe she should run away more often.

Worried that her eyes might signal to her mother that she had lost her virginity the night before, Willa directed her mother's attention to Mma Lilli. Jan confirmed Willa's diagnosis that Mma Lilli had arthritis in her feet, but also took a blood sample, seeing a few other signs that could point to diabetes or even a heart ailment. Jan's authority made Mma Lilli suddenly dead serious. So when Jan said she wanted to see Mma Lilli in the clinic, the old woman nodded, in awe that the important doctor would want to see her, special, at the big surgery.

Willa smiled at the thought that her mother could tame Mma Lilli and elicit such respect. She worked it out with Tom and Mma Lilli that they would travel to the clinic in five days' time for Mma's appointment and to check on the progress of the chief as well.

When Willa went into Tom's hut to get her travel bag, Tom followed her in.

"Hey, Lady."

"Hey, Tommiwe." The two held each other, loving one another's smells and the still simmering heat and excitement from the night before. Tom pulled back and held Willa at arm's length.

"You are something else, Willa. Thank you for last night. You've sort of left me speechless," Tom laughed and Willa joined him.

"I'm speechless too, Tom. All I know is that I feel very comfortable with you. Like you've been a friend for longer than you have. It's funny. I've only known you for a week, but it seems a million years ago that we visited the Dingaka."

"Damn, you're right. That was a million years ago. I wish you weren't going yet," Tom whispered as he nuzzled into Willa's neck.

"Me too. But Jan needs me. Duty calls and all that," Willa whispered back. The un-paned windows made most conversation public, so Willa and Tom whispered for privacy and to have an excuse to be closer together.

"Now you sound colonial British!" Tom laughed.

"Oh, no! Anything but that!" Willa responded with a smile in her voice. Tom leaned forward and they kissed in the way that new lovers do, in uncertain yet passionate exploration.

Willa heard the clinic lorry's engine rev. "Gotta go." Her eyes were innocent ones and bared all that she was feeling. Tom would usually have been scared off by the intensity of feeling in her eyes, but this time he reveled in it. '*Damn*,' he thought, '*I think I love this kid*."

Tom grabbed Willa's bag off the floor and followed her to the lorry.

“It was nice meeting you Dr. Jan. Thanks for helping Mma Lilli. Thank you Willa for coming out and helping her too. She’ll probably have me rubbing her feet before the day is out!” All four of them laughed, Mma Lilli the hardest.

“*Ke itumetse*, my daughter, *tsamaya sentle*, go well,” yelled Mma Lilli in thanks as the lorry sped away. A little flutter in Tom’s belly told him he would miss Willa during the next five days until he went to the health post.

Willa was feeling the same flutter. Today was different than yesterday. *Damn. Today I’m a woman.*

Her reverie was broken when, from the back seat, Jan rattled off the status of the chief in great detail, and then each of the other patients in the surgery. Suddenly Willa was back in her life again. The surgery was her life. Jan was a big part of that. How could Willa ever leave to go to medical school? Who would smooth over Jan’s cultural faux pas and interpret for the non-English speakers?

Willa sighed and her mother reached over and squeezed her shoulders. Sammie Po simultaneously reached over and patted Willa’s knee as he laughed.

“Mma Cookie will be glad to see you, Willa, but watch out because you did not tell her you were going away,” Sammie Po warned.

Willa smiled. “I’ll be careful, Sammie. Mma Cookie always knows where I am. But I won’t ruin her fun,” Willa laughed. Sammie joined her.

Jan sank back in the seat and closed her eyes. She had not realized how much she relied on Willa’s laugh to revitalize her soul and energy. One of Aunt Dix’s sayings popped into her head: ‘Stop and smell the roses or their thorns will prick you.’ For the first time, Jan really understood what that meant.

“Touché, Aunt Dix,” Jan mouthed silently. It was surely time for her to take stock of what she had and what she had lost due to her choices through the years, and her single mindedness. ‘*Damn*,’ she said to herself when she thought of the way that she sometimes treated Johnny, her lover and companion for the last five years.

Jan squeezed her eyes tight again, trying to push away the

feeling of remorse for the times she had been downright rude to Johnny. For the times he went out of his way to make Willa's childhood birthdays special with rides in his plane to towns in neighboring countries with barely an acknowledgement from Jan. She would already be off in the surgery tending to her patients with no time to waste. Johnny always forgave Jan when she was short tempered, overwrought and never available to go on holiday even for a few days. And then the one time that she did agree to a vacation, all hell broke loose at the health post and Johnny had to fly her back, ruining his time off.

'*Why does he bother with me*?' Jan wondered. How could any man put up with her schedule and her singular focus on the health post? Jan realized then that one of the roses she needed to stop and smell was Johnny. She did love him but did he know that? Had she ever expressed it out loud? The way Johnny looked at her made Jan love him. He made her feel smarter than she was, more beautiful, more reasonable, more of a woman. And he asked for so little in return.

It was probably a blessing that Johnny was not around all the time. Jan knew that she wore men out quickly. She had done it since she was a teenager, in medical school with her husband, and with the other lovers that followed after she and Michael divorced.

Johnny's life as a bush pilot had him flying long distances across Botswana, South Africa, Rhodesia and Mozambique. Primarily shunting rich white men to remote hunting grounds, Johnny made a good living and enjoyed meeting men and women of means. He always had tales of these adventures with the rich and famous for Willa and her Batswana school friends when they were around during term breaks. Jan would hear them all laughing and the girls asking silly questions about the eating habits of a Hollywood star. But then his serious side would emerge and he would have the girls, and sometimes Jan, join him in reading James Joyce out loud and using special voices for the many characters and states of mind.

"The only way to really understand *Ulysses* is to read it out loud," Johnny always said. Jan had to agree because she had never had the patience to wade through Joyce's prose and disentangle

Bloom's and Molly's interminable day. But led by Johnny, Jan and Willa would close their eyes and let the characters come alive. With the help of Johnny's many voices and sound effects, *Ulysses* suddenly became a decipherable story, bringing Dublin into a living room in a home in the Kalahari Desert.

The night that Jan read aloud Molly's Soliloquy, Johnny had tears running down his face. Willa had run to him and held his hand while curled up at his feet. He later explained that Molly was his mother and aunt and sister and his first love in Belfast where he grew up. Molly's pain was the same as all the women he had ever known before he escaped Ireland as a deckhand on a ship when he was seventeen. Willa had asked him once if he wanted to go back to Belfast to visit his family. After hesitating for a minute Johnny just said, "I can't go home again, me sweet. The memories are pain enough for me heart. Seeing it all again would crumble me spirit for sure. Plus I'd miss you too much Willa nilla, my girl." Then he smiled grandly and scooped up Willa in his arms, twirling her around the living room of Jan's bungalow.

That was when Jan loved him most. When he would take a sad or awkward or scary moment and turn it into a smile or a song. Johnny was a comforter in so many ways and seemed to accomplish it effortlessly. He never went into great detail about his childhood, but Jan knew it contained poverty, the tyranny of the Catholic Church, and the constant threat of violence in the air between the Irish and the British.

Docked in Cape Town after two years as a stevedore, Johnny struck up a friendship with a man starting an air transport business. Johnny had always loved airplanes and anything to do with flight. Since he could remember he had dreamed of being a pilot and simply flying away from the gritty life of Belfast that held little comfort and even less hope for Johnny. The businessman he met on the docks needed a hard worker to help him build the company up from scratch and manage the logistics of tracking and transporting people and cargo. Johnny had been wise enough to barter some of his pay for flying lessons. Within a year he had his license. Within five he had helped his boss create a lucrative business flying great white hunters into the bush to shoot game.

Within ten years Johnny had his own air transport business, focusing exclusively on taking tourists to remote areas of southern Africa so they could live out their dreams of bagging a lion or an elephant.

It was 1963, the year of Elizabeth Taylor's Cleopatra and Capri pants when Johnny flew Hollywood's leading man, Matt Fox, and his secret mistress, Lacie, to Savuti so he could kill a lion in the Kalahari and prove his manhood. Fox thought that Africa was probably the one place in the world that he could visit with Lacie and not have their affair discovered by snoopy paparazzi and printed in the papers, particularly the *LA Times*, which his church-going wife religiously read over breakfast every day. Johnny was known for his discretion and had been recommended by a director on Fox's last picture. The director was rowdy and lived in extremes with drink and women when he was not shooting. Johnny remembered that trip too well.

On the third night of the lovers' safari, Lacie became violently ill. When she was not vomiting she was curled into a fetal position, moaning and shaking from the pain. Johnny quickly made a comfortable bed in the plane by taking out two of the six seats and he and Fox gently laid Lacie in the rear of the piper. By then her pulse was slow and erratic and her eyes had rolled back in her head. Johnny did not think she would make it to Johannesburg or Bulawayo in time to stem whatever illness it was that had felled her. Phiri, the Motswana game guide, also saw death hanging over Lacie and told Johnny about the health post outside Francistown. "It is run by a very skilled Lekowa doctor. We must hurry there or skinny lady will surely die."

Fox had visibly stiffened at Phiri's bluntness. He was scared. More scared than he had ever been before, for himself or another person. Scared that Lacie would die and make world headlines. Scared that his secret safari would become part of the public domain, part of the paper his wife read over coffee and jam toast in the morning. It would ruin him with his public as well. Fox was perceived as the handsome family man, made even sexier by his loyalty to his wife of fifteen years and their spoiled pre-teen daughter. If Lacie died he was facing humiliation and years of celebrity destroyed by a woman who was only supposed to be a refreshing fuck in an exotic locale.

Johnny had grown very savvy at reading these Hollywood types and realized fairly quickly that the bulk of Fox's fear was for himself, not Lacie. For a second he daydreamed it had been Fox that had been felled by illness, and that Johnny's plane had suddenly become disabled so that he could not fly the movie star to medical care. Fox would die in the wilderness and Lacie and Johnny would fly off into the sunset, the plane miraculously having repaired itself.

Phiri the guide knew the exact location of the health post as his home village was only ten kilometers south of it. Within 45 minutes Johnny was landing on the rough airstrip, separated from the health post compound by a small kopje. Just as he pulled to a complete stop and shut down the engines, a white lorry with red crosses on the doors pulled alongside the plane. Johnny could not have been more surprised by this level of emergency response out in the middle of nowhere. Then a beautiful woman jumped out of the passenger side of the ambulance with a medical bag in tow.

"Do you have an injured passenger, pilot?" Jan had asked him urgently. For a second he was too stunned to answer. Fox did it for him.

"Yes, yes. Oh, thank you. It's Lacie. She's really sick. Are you a doctor?"

Jan nodded as she crawled into the back of the plane and checked Lacie's vitals. Thirty seconds later she was shouting at Phiri to help Sammie Po, the ambulance driver, bring the stretcher. Johnny helped Phiri and Sammie maneuver the stretcher so that they did not jostle Lacie too badly. Fox stood back and watched nervously, biting the side of his thumb and murmuring to himself.

Johnny watched Jan read off Lacie's vital signs and Sammie wrote them down in a steno pad. As Sammie pulled away in the lorry, Jan started an IV on Lacie and began prodding the sick woman to regain consciousness.

Jan shouted at Johnny, "What's her name?"

"It's Lacie. Lacie," Johnny shouted, realizing he did not know her last name.

"Lacie, doll, hang in there. You're going to be fine. You'll be fine. But I need you to open your eyes, Lacie. Come on Lacie. I know you can do it. Just open your eyes. Yes, try hard, Lacie. Don't quit on me, kid. Come on, damn it. You're not trying hard enough. Fight, damn it." Jan looked up at Johnny and Fox who were both in the back of the ambulance.

"She's in some type of toxic shock. Tell me what you boys have been doing with her."

Jan looked accusingly at Johnny and Fox. The movie star's lips began moving but no words came out. Johnny looked at Fox's pathetic face and then at Jan.

"Doctor, I'm a bush pilot and have been ferrying these two around for three days. Poor Lacie began taking ill last night. We all ate the same food, so I don't think it was that. As far as I know she hasn't stepped on anything or cut herself. We weren't out long enough for any bush sickness to have grabbed her so fast. She only drank the potable water we carried in. I'm sorry, that's all I can offer."

Jan glanced up at Johnny just as they pulled up to the surgery. Her eyes told him just how serious Lacie's condition was. When she looked up at Fox his head was buried in his hands. Jan thought, '*What a loser*,' and knew he probably had more information about Lacie than he had offered up to that point.

Eighteen hours later Lacie was out of danger. Jan had fought hard with all of her skill and the medicines at hand at Mother Mercy to combat the toxins raging through the frail woman. When she had discovered vaginal bleeding in the early minutes of her ministrations, Fox broke down and began sobbing. Jan walked over to him and lifted his chin with her gloved hand. Then she did something that Johnny wished he had done two days before. She peeled off her glove and smacked him across the face so hard that he fell off his chair.

"Get the fuck up and talk to me. She just had an abortion didn't she? She's dying and you're feeling sorry for yourself." Jan pulled him up by his hair, as though he were a small boy who had just been caught writing curse words on the schoolyard wall.

Fox sobered quickly and admitted that Lacie had told him she was pregnant the week before they were supposed to go on the trip to Africa. He had given her the address of an abortionist he knew about; this had not been his first foray into philandering that had produced an unwanted child.

"You're slime, Fox. Get the fuck out of my surgery." She looked at Johnny. "You can stay. I might need your help." He simply nodded.

"Thank you, Doctor. She's a good gal. Far too good for the sly Fox, there. She deserves a second shot at it, she does. Thank god you were here to help the poor girl."

For the next two days Johnny was either in the surgery watching over Lacie or walking the compound, occasionally going out to his plane to check the engine prop or tires to ensure its readiness to leave as soon as Jan gave the signal that Lacie could handle the trip. Under Jan's orders, Sammie Po had driven Fox into Francistown and found another pilot to take him back to Jo'burg and from there, back to the states. Jan could not stand the sight of Fox and she knew he was not going to help out Lacie's situation in any way.

Before Fox climbed into the health post jeep to leave, Jan had handed him a bill for $5,000. She instructed him where to wire the money immediately when he got to Jo'burg or the international press would be given a doozy of a headline. The fear on Fox's face gave Jan the joy of payback for the terror and suffering he had caused Lacie.

A week later, Lacie was smiling again, having been adopted by Willa and Mma Cookie's daughter, JoJo. The two girls were in awe of Lacie and her mod clothes. JoJo would brush and braid Lacie's blond hair several times a day while Willa would paint Lacie's toenails or try on her collection of silk scarves. In exchange, Lacie told the girls what it was like on a Hollywood set, from the daunting heat of the lights to the arrogance of some of the screen's elite. JoJo was especially in awe of movies and tales of celebrity. Willa just liked talking with an American so she could pretend to know what her sister might be hearing and seeing in Boston.

Johnny also did his best to keep Lacie's spirits up with insider tales of his celebrity clients, but only the funny antics that would make her crack a smile.

Jan observed the bush pilot during this week and thought that he was probably the nicest person she had ever met. Johnny fell in love with Willa and JoJo, and created an extravagant scavenger hunt that kept the girls enthralled for two days while he flew back to Jo'burg to tend to another client. Johnny seemed so safe, Jan thought. He was the kind of person that you knew would fix anything that was broken, while also seeking equilibrium in every situation. Jan found herself attracted to Johnny. He was everything that she was not and could not be with Willa: a playmate and confidant; a parent that could toss a ball or play a game of cards.

But Jan did not show her attraction. She had seen Johnny look at Lacie in a way that probably meant he was falling for the young actress. What man wouldn't? Lacie was every man's vision of a twenty-two-year-old dream girl. Jan was a very real woman who had recently knocked on and entered forty's door. Still, she could have Johnny as a friend. He was another who thrived in Africa so it would not be necessary to explain why she had come or why she stayed. It was an unspoken knowledge and agreement. That felt safe to her, and just plain nice. Jan rarely liked just plain nice or even slowed down long enough to notice it.

When Johnny flew back in to pick up Lacie, Willa and JoJo threw her a going-away party, complete with nut cup party favors, homemade paper hats and a vanilla cake that was Mma Cookie's most famous dessert. Lacie laughed and cried. Jan handed her an envelope with three thousand dollars in it. Lacie tried to refuse, but Jan insisted she had purposely added it on to Fox's bill with Lacie's future in mind. Jan knew the starlet would need some money to tide her over until she decided whether to try Hollywood again or seek solace in her hometown of Bakersfield.

As Jan and the girls watched Johnny's plane take off, they all knew that Lacie's time at the compound would be a vivid memory. A time when an unexpected visitor added color and intrigue and a Hollywood glow to their simple health post. And, Jan thought, a time when she may have found the best man she ever met, but lost him to a beautiful and fragile California girl.

But a month later Johnny's plane unexpectedly circled Mother Mercy's compound and landed on the dusty strip. Sammie Po drove Johnny to Jan's bungalow where he waited in the cool darkness of the sitting room. Willa discovered him before Jan and engaged Johnny in a game of gin rummy with wagers of peanuts and raisins.

Sammie Po found Jan making the rounds in the surgery. When he told her of Johnny's arrival, her eyebrows rose with a start, the memory returning of his smile and his heart that he had been so willing to share with strangers.

That evening Mma Cookie made all her special dishes and giggled and grinned when Johnny moaned with pleasure at almost every bite. Willa and JoJo barely stopped talking long enough for Johnny to answer all of their questions about his adventures with movie stars and close calls in the plane. Jan was strangely quiet, but joined in the laughter and looked at Johnny as much as she could without attracting attention.

One of Mma Cookie's talents was her ability to read Jan's moods even better than Willa could. She had seen the Doctor's face become more beautiful and open when she had greeted the bush pilot in the sitting room. Jan even apologized for keeping him waiting as she fussed with the wisps of hair around her face and kept putting her hands in her smock pockets and then immediately pulling them out again. Mma Cookie's jaw would have dropped at this uncharacteristic feminine behavior from Jan but she did not want Johnny to think this was out of the ordinary for the Doctor. He would discover all of Jan's many moods in good time if he stayed around long enough.

Johnny began reading *Cry the Beloved Country* to Willa that evening after dinner was cleared. Jan sat on the porch swing on one side of Johnny while Willa and JoJo happily squeezed together on the other. After a half hour Johnny yawned and asked the girls if he could pick up the story again the next day. Willa and JoJo groaned in disappointment but hugged Johnny before Mma Cookie came out and shooed them both up to bed.

That night on the porch Johnny and Jan each shared their

personal histories and how they had ended up in Africa. Johnny seemed concerned that Jan had rarely seen her daughter Nora, and in his Irish bluntness asked her how she coped with it. Jan was honest with him. She explained the painful guilt cramps in her abdomen that she experienced whenever she focused her mind on Nora. Jan allotted herself rare periods of time to think about Nora and what the little girl must have experienced growing up without a mother. But she was also honest in saying that she would do it again – leave her daughter – for she was truly driven to practice medicine in Botswana. Something had to be sacrificed in order to establish the clinic and provide a level of sophisticated medical services that could not be matched in the country.

Unfortunately for Nora, she was the biggest loser: one child sacrificed for hundreds of Africans to live better and longer lives. It was the kind of math equation that Jan understood and could live with.

Johnny knew about tough choices; he had made some himself. While Jan's honesty about Nora surprised him and made him uneasy, he admired her for not trying to sugarcoat it or make excuses. It was the type of personal information that many people would not share at this stage of a friendship.

Jan told Johnny about Nora and Willa's father, a well-known surgeon whose lifestyle in Boston could not be more different than hers in Botswana. "If it wasn't for Sammie Po and some of the other men who have adopted Willa, I guess I'd be more concerned about her not seeing her father," Jan confessed. "But Willa has many fathers here and, god bless her, she loves them all and they adore her." For a moment Jan paused, began to speak and then stopped again.

"What is it, Jan?" Johnny questioned. He could tell by her face that she had wanted to say something but she had stopped. Johnny was intuitive enough to know that Jan needed to say it or it would continue to gnaw at her. He put his hand over hers where it rested on the swing.

"I wasn't ready for Nora when I got pregnant. She was unexpected and unwanted, at least by me. Michael was so upset when I talked about an abortion that I went against my better instincts and kept the baby, and then married him. I was young and at the time the future was only a few months in the distance for me. I didn't really think beyond that in terms of the consequences of the choices I made. Getting married and pregnant had seemed like temporary things to me that would go away somewhere down the road. To Michael, marriage and the baby were forever kinds of things."

Jan stopped again and looked at Johnny. Her face was quizzical as though she also had a hard time understanding why she could not stay attached to Nora. "The concept of forever is really hard for me, except with Willa and the health post. She's my little piece of forever, I guess. When Nora visited a few years ago, I was at first shocked by our utter lack of connection. And then I just wanted her to go away. It's horrible, I know, but I found myself actually disliking her. She was only thirteen and probably both homesick and in culture shock. But I couldn't do anything or say anything to make a connection. It just wasn't there. And that's my fault."

Jan closed her eyes tight and ran her hand down her face, pushing hard against her skin. Johnny squeezed her hand. Jan continued.

"I actually started resenting that she was here, especially after she faked being sick every day so she wouldn't have to play with Willa and JoJo. Now when I think about it I just feel sick. Nora could no more settle into this health post than I could feel comfortable at one of my husband's family get-togethers." Jan laughed. "You should have seen Michael's parents' reaction to me. They didn't know whether to spit or slam the door but they smiled because they had to and let me in. It was like the clash of the Brahmins and the Bohemians. Not a pretty sight." Johnny joined in Jan's laughter.

"The bottom line is, I make a better doctor than a mother. I've learned to live with that because it's who I am."

"Who you are is an incredible and real woman," Johnny looked at her and took both her hands in his. "Mistakes are what remind us that we're human. My grand-mum used to say that we all get a chance to right our mistakes at some point in our lives.

And if we don't have our eyes open to see when that opportunity arises, then we wander around on the earth after we're dead, always trying to find the opportunity again, but never getting there in time. Damn, she used to scare the living daylights out of me with her tales of the unhappy wandering souls seeking forgiveness and redemption. But now I understand what she was saying. It's not a crime to make a mistake, it's a crime not to fix it if the chance to make good comes around again. Your time with Nora will come again, Jan."

Johnny lifted up Jan's chin and kissed her softly on the lips. A tear slid over her eyelashes and then onto Johnny's smooth cheek as their faces met one another for the first time. Already she adored his lips and the lines around his eyes. This was a man's face. A face that had seen sorrow and pain early in its life and traveled far in search of something more hopeful.

Jan's life choices had scared away most of the men she had known. Mainly because she refused to be anything but honest about what she wanted and what she had done to get there. In her past, men had described her as cold and calculating. Jan remembered the words that Michael had used in his last letter to her. He had said that in Jan's world everything was disposable and nothing sacred, including the child they created and whom she had carried inside her. Jan remembered reading Michael's words and sensing his disbelief that staying in Botswana rated higher than Nora's health and welfare. If only Jan could have told him that Nora was really only his child, not hers. That she had helped make his dream of fatherhood a reality, but it was one that she could not share.

What Jan did not know was the extent to which she had broken Michael's heart. His dream included being her husband. But that was something that Jan could not provide to him for very long.

Johnny knew that there would be both joys and challenges if he let himself fall in love with Jan. But he was a pragmatist in matters of the heart. Jan could only give Johnny so much of herself. But Johnny could also only open his heart so far. It had been damaged long ago by a mother who cried out her love as she beat him until he bled for hundreds of exaggerated misdemeanors. That door to his heart could never be fully opened again. There was simply too much emotional scar tissue that had permanently rusted its hinges. Jan and Willa and Mma Cookie and the rest of Mother Mercy's family could become a home for him. His heart needed that as much as it needed to soar above the clouds in his plane. Maybe another door could be opened, or a secret passage built to his heart that would allow him to bypass the one that had been sealed shut.

# # #

Suddenly a strong jolt pulled Jan out of her reverie and she was back in the clinic lorry. Willa and Sammie Po were talking a mile a minute in Setswana. They had to shout across the front seat to be heard above the engine's noise and the banging of the axle against the Kalahari's ruts and stones. Seeing her daughter in profile made Jan realize that Willa had somehow changed into a woman when she wasn't looking. *'And soon she will be gone and finding her own path,'* Jan thought. She also knew that she had to start exercising her strength now. It was only a few months until Willa would begin packing and saying her goodbyes. The mother in her felt proud that Willa was headed to pre-med at Harvard, but also jealous that she would be living with her father and joining his elite world along the Charles River. The doctor in her felt cheated and selfish at losing a talented nurse and interpreter. Willa's involvement with each patient was a talent that could not be taught. Her dream of becoming a physician came from her love of people and a nurturing spirit that Jan knew was as rare as it was powerful in treating patients.

Jan watched the Kalahari roll by the lorry windows and began a mental list of warnings for Willa about medical school and Boston. But suddenly she stopped herself. Willa's Harvard and Willa's Boston would not be the one that Jan had experienced. It was almost the 1970s. That put Jan's time in medical school a quarter century in the past. It would be selfish and inappropriate to burden Willa with Jan's historical memory of a time that was a world apart from Mother Mercy and the Boston of the 1940s when she was there. *'I'll let her see it through her own intelligent eyes,'* Jan thought.

"Sammie, Sammie," Jan yelled from the back seat. "Didn't I tell you to take the Long Island Expressway back to the compound?!"

Willa laughed and turned to face the back seat. "You cahn't get theah from heah," she mimicked, in the New England accent her mother had taught her years before when they played word games and spoke in different dialects.

"That was good, Willa! You definitely have some Yankee running through your blood stream!" Jan started laughing and touched Willa's shoulder. She suddenly became serious.

"Willa, please forget what I said in the surgery. You are more qualified for pre-med than I'll bet any Harvard undergrad ever was." Jan paused and took a deep breath. Willa's eyes were closed but Jan knew she was listening. "I can be a pure shit sometimes, you know that?"

Willa's mouth curved into the slightest smile. "That's a rhetorical question isn't it?" Willa teasingly asked as she turned her head and met her mother's eyes.

"I'm sorry, baby. You won't see me that bad again. I know now what you went through the whole time I was gone. Sammie and Mma Cookie locked me in the cooking hut and made sure I would finally listen. I did."

Willa turned fully around in the front seat to face Jan. This was an altered mother who was talking to her. She had to see this full on. Jan very rarely showed such vulnerability. Her mother finally trusting her was an intimate connection that for the first time felt true and unshakable to Willa.

"Thanks, Mme-we. You always told me to just do my best. And that's what I tried really hard to do." Willa swallowed hard as she reached back and took her mother's hand. "There's no replacing you, mama, even when you are a pure shit." Jan and Willa began laughing so hard that their voices began reverberating, bouncing off the metal frame of the lorry and getting sucked out the open windows. Sammie smirked, satisfied that Dr. Gakelape and Willa had made up. Tomorrow would be like the old yesterdays again. He was an old man now. Fighting with the uncertainty that his tomorrows would lose out to the comfort of his predictable yesterdays. Sammie would let Willa tackle all the tomorrows for him.

A song suddenly formed in Sammie's head:

'*Yesterdays are the best of days,*
tomorrows can only be borrowed
are only a dream,
so seemingly demure
a stalking leopard,
a life blurred
regained,
eyes opened after pain
makes the worth
acknowledged,
never the same.'

# # #

Chapter 14: Beautiful for Spacious Skies

Midwest U.S.
March 1969

Because the road was a corridor of thick trees interspersed with farmhouses, the car seemed to be going a lot faster than it actually was. Green leaves flashed by Nora's face so quickly that she was starting to get queasy. She inhaled a deep breath and exhaled shakily.

"You okay?" Tunney glanced over at Nora and she nodded.

"Yeah, fine. Thanks. Maybe a little carsick, is all."

"I'll stop at the next gas station. They'll have a Coke machine. Burping helps."

Nora glanced at Tunney. "Getting out of all these trees would help even more than a Coke. I'm suffocating."

Tunney did not say anything. He just shrugged and kept his eyes focused on the road.

Nora leaned her head back on the seat and closed her eyes. That seemed to help a little bit. She breathed in deep again, trying to blow out the nausea that had built up in her stomach.

Was it just the blurry trees making her sick or the knowledge that she had no idea what she was doing? America the beautiful had been rolling past the window for two days now. Rolling away from Philadelphia, from betrayal, even farther from Boston, from her friends, and farther and farther from her father and the person she used to be.

After the night that she had seen Pete with the black haired woman under the street light, Nora had run back to Max's with a broken heart and a very confused mind. Max had taken her in his arms and rocked her, his shoulder soon wet from her sobbing.

"I can't say I told you so because I only thought this, I was never rude enough to say it. But, Honey, Pete is afraid of the Big C. Commitment. I saw it in his eyes the first time I met him." Max lifted Nora off his shoulder and brushed the hair off her forehead, sticky from her tear-stained face.

"Pete's a slut. Forget him, Nora. Just focus on the good time you had and chock the rest up to learnings in the book of life."

Nora sniffled and blew her nose in a paper towel. "I'm so fucking naïve. What an idiot," Nora chided herself.

"You're 22 years old, lady. You're not supposed to get it all yet. Then you'd be jaded. You're too young to be jaded. Now me, I can smell a slut like Pete a mile away. But does that always stop me from diving in dick first, hell no! And I'm 40, honey."

Nora broke a smile through her tears. "You always know the right thing to say," Nora said in a voice choked with the pain of a lost lover.

Max shrugged. "I've been dumped enough times to have written three volumes on the art of crashing and burning over useless men. The only thing I can guarantee is that you will feel better in time, and that this isn't the last time that your lover will walk in a different direction than you're heading."

Max opened his liquor cabinet and took out a bottle of B&B and two brandy snifters. "I've been saving this for just the right occasion. I received this lovely amber fluid from a former lover as his going away present." He poured the brandy and handed Nora the glass.

"To jilted lovers and the demise of all two-timing sluts! Cheers!" The two clinked glasses and gulped down large sips.

"Whoa, Max!" Nora coughed and cleared her throat. "This stuff is strong."

"The better to numb you with, my dear. You need serious lubricating tonight, Nora. That way your head will feel worse than your heart in the morning. It's a backasswards way to begin getting over a former lover. One hundred percent foolproof."

Nora smiled and wiped her eyes again. "To all sluts, then. May they never find true happiness." She clinked her glass against Max's and slugged down the rest of the liquor. "Fill her up, Max."

"Yes, señorita. But let's set you down on the couch so you'll at least have a soft landing."

"But I will land okay won't I?" Nora looked up at Max and his heart broke for her. There was such a real innocence in this Brahmin girl from Boston. Max wondered what rich parents taught their kids in the absence of all threat and hardship. In Nora's case, it certainly was not how to handle an errant boyfriend afraid of the Big C. Nora did not seem to possess any defense mechanisms when it came to surviving a relationship. Pete's infraction had hit her head on.

Indeed, the next morning Nora's head was hot and throbbing and her stomach alternately burned and shivered. Max made her drink tomato juice and eat dry toast. By that afternoon she was back on her feet and weighing her options.

"I don't think I have the energy to confront Pete," Nora said as she stared down at the silver ring that Pete had given her for Christmas. He had told her then that it was a friendship ring and that the round shape signified the sturdiness of true friends.

"Oh, you're no fun. I was hoping you'd go for entrapment or surprising him at an inopportune time."

"I just don't have the strength for that, Max. I feel like someone dropped me and a few of my limbs broke off."

"That's the B&B debauching still haunting you, dear."

"Okay, so I'm a wimp. If I see Pete I'll get all upset and start crying."

"So, then he'll feel guilty. At least it's something."

"Oh, you don't know Pete, Max. He won't feel guilty at all. It will just verify how right he was to cheat on me since I'm such an emotional child who cries instead of confronts. Guilt is not an emotion that you'll see in Pete. That would be 'too uptight' for him. I bet that's how he justified fucking around on me. I bet he kept saying to himself how uptight I am."

"Oh my god..." Max looked Nora straight in the eye.

"What, what..." Nora moved closer to Max. She could tell by the look on his face that he had a brilliant idea.

"Turn the table, girl."

"What do you mean, turn the table, tell me!" By now Nora was shaking Max's arm like a child who wants a pack of gum in the grocery store.

"You were the one out all night. You are the one who decided you two won't work out; you can cite various reasons, I can help you with that."

“Max, you are one genius,” Nora began laughing and hugged her friend hard.

“I agree! But are you a good enough actress to look like you don’t care that much?”

“I can do it. I’m so mad that he fucked around on me that I don’t think I do care anymore.”

“You care, honey. But I’m happy to see that your survival instinct has kicked in,” Max touched Nora’s cheek and smiled.

“Go over and get your stuff out of the apartment. Here’s ten bucks for a cab. If he’s there, kiss him and say, thanks for the memories, and no hard feelings, bub. If he’s not, take your shit out and leave him a nostalgic but blunt note signed with an imprint of your lips.”

Nora laughed. “What! Where do you come up with this stuff?” Max joined her in laughter.

“Too many 1930s movies I’m afraid. All my best moves are rip offs from Garbo, Clara and Marlena, of course.” Max grinned.

Suddenly Nora was serious. “So instead of saying that my father was right all along and Pete is a useless jerk, instead I’ll say that it was a four month lesson well learned and it was in the cards all along.” Nora walked over to the window. She could see the outline of her reflection. It looked as lost as she felt.

“Now I see why a lot of my friends just want the same old thing: the neat wedding after graduation, the house and kids, the clubs, the clothes. It’s somehow easier. This is hard, Max. There’s no model to follow.” Nora sighed heavily. “Is the only way to learn a lesson through pain?”

Max walked over to where Nora was leaning against the wall and staring out the window and rested his chin on her head. “No, you don’t need pain, but the extremes definitely stick with you most.”

# # #

And now here she was driving across the states with a man she hardly knew. Tunney was not easily defined. All of the adjectives used to describe him seemed contradictory. Last fall, Tunney finished his three-year stint in the Marines, the last 14 months of which he carried an M-16 in Viet Nam. His buzz cut had grown out quickly in six months and he looked more like a hippy than a Marine.

Tunney was not gay but for some reason had applied for a sales job at Max's boutique. Once Nora saw him with the clientele, she knew right away why Max had hired him. All the gay men loved Tunney. He was cute in the way the shoppers liked: deep blue eyes, honey brown hair, small lips that were quick to smile, not too tall, and a nice firm ass that looked great in a pair of jeans. Tunney knew the gay men liked him and he flirted with them in a way that sold a lot of paisley shirts, but that also told them that he was unavailable.

Max and Tunney got along really well. Tunney served the dual role of sales clerk and security guard. When Max suspected someone was shoplifting or casing the store for a possible robbery, he would alert Tunney who would flip his own switch and turn back into a Marine, handling all ne'er-do-wells first with a firm voice, and if that did not work, he would use the arm twisting "come along" MP lock that disabled even the largest of perpetrators.

Tunney's intellect was also contradictory. Like Pete, he had never gone to college. But unlike Pete, Tunney was intelligent. Also unlike Pete, Tunney did not bring up topics just to impress people with some random cool topic he knew about. Tunney was interested in dialogue, in the act of two or more people discussing a concept or a book or the pros and cons of war protests, and really trying to figure out the answers to serious questions.

When Tunney announced that he would have to leave the boutique because he was moving to the west coast, it was a sad day for Max. Between Tunney, Nora and his three other sales staff, his business was booming. Nora had even attracted straight guys to come in and look around. They mostly bought belts. Tunney attracted gay men and women shopping for gay brothers or friends, and the occasional musician or actor doing a gig in Philly.

As soon as Tunney had said the west coast, Nora knew that she had to go with him. California had always seemed like such an exotic, faraway place to her, and one that held the promise that all searchers sought to unravel, that mysterious and elusive "enlightenment." Nora did not know what others thought enlightenment was. But to her, it was clarity. She longed to wake up in the morning with some clarity of purpose, some focus, seeing some point to it all. Did one grow out of this haze phase? How long would she be the one standing in the background and listening; waiting for a few opportune moments to add a pithy remark, practiced in her head four times before she would say it?

Nora both respected and was in awe of Tunney's confidence. He had no fear of speaking up or out. When Tunney stated his opinions they did not seem like opinions. They seemed like axioms. Part of that was Tunney's confidence. He knew who he was. There was not any shyness or hesitancy about him; no games.

Although, Nora and Max had both discovered that he did have a temper and a mouth when he thought he or someone else was being treated disrespectfully.

A wealthy Philadelphia matron accidentally wandered into the shop one afternoon. She had admired the window display that Nora had designed with clothing and accessories that were all various shades of blue. After about four minutes of browsing she figured out that all the men in the shop were gay when Max asked if she was looking for anything in particular.

"Oh, mother of god. You're a homo!" She had said to Max in a shocked voice lined with disgust.

This was not a new phenomenon to Max. He had been called homo and fag and much worse by boys and men and women since he was a teenager.

"You're such a quick study, Mrs. ---," Max paused as though waiting for her to fill in her name.

"I will not disclose my name to you, you fresh faggot." Mrs. Nondisclosure huffed, turned on her heels and headed quickly towards the door. But she was not quicker than Tunney.

"Excuse me, ma'am. Before you leave I think you forgot something." Tunney stood in front of the door blocking the woman's escape route.

"What did I forget?" By this time there was a tinge of panic and fear in her voice. Tunney took note of that. “I haven’t forgotten anything. Now get out of my way!” She glanced nervously around and grew more frightened as she saw the eyes of several gay men looking unsympathetically at the scene.

“You forgot to apologize to Mr. Max here. That was really rude and uncalled for what you said to him.” Tunney barely raised his voice. It was steady and clear.

“I’m calling the police! Let-me-out,” she screamed as she tried to push past Tunney.

“Apologize first.” Tunney stood his ground and continued to stare down the rich woman. Her nervousness released a puff of lavender perfume overlaid with fear sweat.

“Why should I apologize? You homos are ruining this city. You’re sick, sick people. Now let me through!” She started lamely punching Tunney on the arms.

“Mrs. Addison, you apologize now to Mr. Max or I’ll make sure that a picture of your husband’s latest lunch fuck will be sent to the *Inquirer*.”

The red color of Mrs. Addison’s face drained to white. In a split second Mrs. Addison realized that she had only one option. She let out a frustrated sob and choked out, “I’m sorry.”

“That’s good enough for me, Tunney.” Max started moving towards them and the door. “I’m satisfied, Mr. Tunney. Please allow Mrs. Addison to pass.” Max’s voice belied the nervousness he felt. All he needed was one of Philadelphia’s elite being held captive in his store. A shiver ran through him as he thought of a SWAT team shooting up his spring suit collection. Max’s eyes met Tunney’s and the Marine stepped aside and held the door open for her.

“Have a nice day, Mrs. Addison. Say hi to Larry for me.” Tunney smiled his best altar boy smile as Mrs. Addison clop-clopped away quickly in her pumps, never once glancing back.

Suddenly all the customers and sales staff we’re clapping and cheering. It wasn’t often that gay men won any of their battles.

Nora had watched the whole scene from the doorway of the stock room. She had been afraid for Max, thinking that a rich woman who was hassled in a gay men’s clothing store would certainly call the police. The vision of Max being dragged out of the store in handcuffs made her close her eyes quickly and try to banish the thought. Philadelphia's finest were not what one would call sympathetic to homosexuals.

When the clapping and cheering stopped, Max asked Tunney how he knew Mrs. Addison's name.

"I have a rich aunt who has a townhouse in Rittenhouse Square. The Addison's are her neighbors. I remember as a kid, my aunt gossiping about the dalliances of Mr. Addison when they didn't think I was within earshot. But I was an observant kid. I had read far too many James Bond books by that point. I fancied myself a Bond protégé, gathering secret information for Her Majesty's Secret Service."

"Tunney, I didn't know you were a blue blood," Max said with surprise.

"I'm not. I grew up in East Lansdowne in a cramped little lower middle class house. My aunt was really my great aunt and had married into money. She certainly never shared much with us. Once in a while she'd call my father and ask to see us. Not sure why. The last time I was there I threw up on her rug. I was eleven. It was all the grape juice she had been giving me that morning. I wasn't used to it. Puke from an eleven-year-old is no longer cute. We were never asked back."

Max, Nora and the rest of the sales staff started laughing. Poor Max could not stop.

"Max, stop! *You're* going to throw up," Nora laughed at him.

"I can't help it. I just keep picturing this stream of grape juice flying out of Tunney's mouth and soiling Auntie's rug!" His laughing became even louder and he bent over in pain, but still could not stop.

"It was a white rug. Did I mention that?" Tunney added.

"Stop! You've already killed me!" Max ran laughing into the back room and fell face down on the couch. Half laughs, half moans could be heard from his office for the next ten minutes.

That was Tunney's temper. Well meaning, but sometimes bordering close to trouble.

For the next few days, Max kept nervously glancing out to the street waiting for Mayor Rizzo's men in blue to come visiting with their billy clubs. But it never happened. Tunney's quip about the indiscretions of Mr. Addison must have been threatening enough to keep the Mrs. from alerting the cops about her afternoon adventure in the "homo" boutique.

Nora was glad she had seen Tunney in action. On the one hand, it made her feel safe that he could protect her on their road trip to California. On the other hand, his adversaries might not always be as easy to handle as Mrs. Addison.

Now, as Nora looked over at Tunney, she wondered what he would be looking for in California. What had chased him out of Philadelphia? His family? His time in Viet Nam? A relationship gone wrong? Nora realized that in all her conversations with Tunney, he rarely said anything about his family or his tour in Viet Nam.

"Ah, here we are. Let's see the man with the Texaco smile. This is your burp stop, kid." Tunney turned and smiled sympathetically at Nora. "How's the stomach feeling?"

"A little better. I've been trying to think about funny things to take my mind off of it."

"Just holler if you run out of funny scenarios. I have a few in storage that I can dust off and share," Tunney called as he got out and walked to the Coke machine. Nora watched him put the money in the slot. He saw the attendant and asked him to fill up the tank.

Suddenly, Nora's stomach reared up again. She ran to the bathroom and just made it to the toilet. The smell of industrial strength air freshener, vomit and urine combined with the freezing cold floor and toilet made Nora reel. Fumbling with the toilet paper roll she finally managed to tear off enough sheets to wipe her mouth. When she reached up to wipe her lips, Nora realized that the low moans she heard were coming from her.

"You don't look so good, kid," Tunney observed after Nora got back to the car. She had cleaned up in the bathroom and rinsed her mouth out in the sink. Facing the rust stain in the basin had almost caused her to throw up again.

Nora did not answer. She just folded herself back in the car and breathed in as much cold air as she could. Tunney handed her a Coke.

"You want some aspirin? Let me get you some aspirin." Tunney reached behind the passenger seat and pulled out a battered first aid kit. He handed two pills to Nora. She nodded thanks and took them with several quick sips.

"I gotta stand up." Nora opened the door and started walking to a stretch of grass next to the gas station. Tunney paid the attendant and pulled the car to the edge of the paved lot. Then he waited.

When Nora finally burped after pacing the grassy spot for five minutes, it felt so good she almost started laughing. How could she have felt so lousy a minute before and now be fine after a few rumbling belches?

"Sorry, I'm fine now." Nora slid into the front seat of the Mustang.

"You should be. They heard those burps all the way back in Philly!" Tunney laughed and Nora joined him.

"Don't be mean, Tunney," Nora playfully slugged him on the arm.

"I'm not being mean!" He held up his fists in equally playful self-defense. "Are you okay now?"

"Yeah, I'm fine. Too much motion for someone who has been working and living in the same building. My life for four months has been lived in about a square block! I haven't seen this much scenery since summer camp in 7th grade."

"Are you sure it's just car sickness? Maybe you've got the flu or something." Tunney pulled back on the Interstate. "Anyhow, we're just about in Iowa and then the rest of the plains states. You won't be getting carsick from trees flashing by the window in these states. Get used to flat and brown. Just flat and brown for a couple days here."

Tunney glanced at Nora. To him, she looked just like all his sisters had a few days before they told the whole family they were pregnant. Tunney had five sisters, and he was the youngest. All but one started having babies within a year of getting married and made sure to bring a new child into the world every 12 to 36 months. Tunney had 14 nieces and nephews already. Grey skin and puking had preceded almost every family announcement. Nora's condition was way too familiar.

Shit, Tunney thought, *I hope she doesn't screw up this trip for me. I just want to get to California. And I'm letting her loose as soon as we hit the Haight.*

Nora's offer of sharing the gas, food and expenses had come at an opportune moment. Tunney had reassessed his meager savings and decided he would have to work another month or so before he left Philly. Nora's eagerness to go to California and her ante into the gas and food kitty put him back on course.

So far they had spent two nights on the road. Each night Tunney had set up a pup tent and arranged in it his supply of sleeping bags and Marine issue blankets. The cold did not seem to bother him even as Nora shivered under her sleeping bag in the Mustang's bucket seat that was reclined as flat as it would go. All night she would bump up against the foggy, wet window or a piece of cold chrome would hit her bare skin and startle her awake. During those restless nights she even imagined the hook-arm murderer of her childhood camp stories crashing through the front window.

"I've got a buddy in Iowa that we can stay with tonight I think. He's outside Dubuque right off the Interstate. I'll call him when we get close. Even sleeping on his floor would be better than the bucket seat, yeah?" Tunney looked over at Nora. He could not believe that he knew she was pregnant before she did. *Shit*, he thought to himself. *I'm starting to feel sorry for her. Damn it if I'm getting sucked up into her problems.*

Tunney sighed loudly.

"What?" Nora asked. "Is this friend of yours hard to deal with?"

"Oh, no," Tunney realized his sigh was misinterpreted as a comment on his buddy. "He's a good guy. A fellow Marine. He'd give you the shirt off his back if he likes you. Or take your shirt if he doesn't." Tunney laughed.

Nora laughed too. "Any advice on how I make him like me? I'd like to keep my shirt on."

"Hum...like or dislike, when Hammersley sees you he is going to want to take your shirt off." Tunney tried to look serious but the corners of his mouth started turning up.

"Tunney!" Nora slugged him in the arm. "You are being so mean!" She tried to pretend to be hurt but started laughing.

"I'm not! I'm being truthful. Hammerhead, that's what we called Hammersley, is a chick magnet. Somehow he always ended up with the girl at the end of any adventure. I never quite figured out the attraction. You can tell me after you meet him."

"Oh, I don't think I'll be one of his victories. The thought of dealing with another guy right now makes me nauseated."

"But Hammerhead loves nauseated chicks! He considers them his greatest challenge." Tunney smiled, feigning sympathy and resignation. Nora stuck out her tongue. "Okay, just do that and you'll turn him off enough to stay away."

"What, my tongue is unattractive?" Nora laughed half-heartedly.

"Damn right ugly, sis. Sorry to tell you."

"So I'll be saved by my ugly tongue. A new weapon in my arsenal against the unwanted advances of males."

"Yeah, you're probably rusty in defending yourself. Working with Max and his entourage must have made your male fending off skills pretty stale."

Nora chuckled. "I miss Max."

"So do I. He gave me work when I really needed it. And he was always so appreciative about the sales I made."

"He liked your ass, Tunney. Don't kid yourself about your sales skills." Nora smiled at Tunney like the Cheshire Cat.

"I *was* a good salesman!" Tunney pushed his hand behind Nora and pinched her butt.

"Ow, ouch, you cruel beast!" Nora laughed between ouches and pinched Tunney back on his arm.

"Careful, passenger. You're not in the driver's seat, Miss Princess." Tunney faked seriousness but a chuckle slipped out at the end.

"Miss Princess!" Nora mocked. "You just wait, Mr. Chauffer. Just wait!"

They drove in silence then for almost an hour. Nora nodded off a few times but always awoke with a start when her head would drop against her chest. *Another sign of pregnancy*, Tunney thought. He remembered his sleepy sisters in their first trimesters. Between the puking, tiredness, grumpiness and lack of skin color on her face, Tunney was ready to supply the verdict to his naïve travel-mate. Nora was used to Max's directness about sex, money and everything else he talked about. Maybe she would appreciate Tunney being just as direct in presenting his pregnancy hypothesis.

But the timing would have to be right. He would bide his time. He had waited weeks in a foxhole for VC to climb out of tunnel entrances. He could wait a little time for Nora to be at her most receptive.

Tunney looked over at Nora as she slept. Suddenly he frowned. *Why the hell am I contemplating this*? Tunney thought. *What a fucking idiot.* If he told her now Nora would be alternately teary, brooding and probably freaked out. There was no way that Tunney wanted to deal with that while being stuck in the car for another 2,000 miles. If he had the chance when he dropped her off in San Francisco, he would bring it up. Nora was no obligation to him. She was just gas money and company.

Tunney knew that he had to shut off that valve in his mouth that always proved to be his worst enemy. Lost sheep, hurt kittens, and any other sad sacks who gravitated to him, his mouth valve would open and almost involuntarily say, 'You can stay with me; I'll give you a lift; I can give you a few bucks; I'll keep an eye on your girlfriend' – that one in particular had proven almost fatal in fact.

Tunney had almost lost his face once after he had driven home a friend of a friend's girlfriend. The "friend," Jerry, ended up blind drunk at a bar where Tunney and a few buddies were hanging out, and could not take his girlfriend home. She had to get to work early the next day and was pissed that Jerry was too smashed to drive her home. Tunney volunteered to give her a lift to her place, which was on the way to his apartment.

Mistake number one. The girlfriend jumped Tunney as soon as

he pulled up in front of her apartment complex. For a minute he succumbed until Jerry's crazed, drunk face flashed across his mind. Tunney pulled away and put his hands up.

"Whoa, honey. You're Jerry's lady. I can't do this."

"What's your trip, Tunney? I see the way you look at me. You've wanted to fuck me since you met me."

"Not true. I don't mess around with my friends' women. It's just a rule I follow."

"Rule! I've heard about you and Jerry's escapades with chicks. He fucks around all the time. Why can't I?"

"Honey, you can do whatever you want. But I ain't doin' it with you."

"Why, you limp dicked jerk. What?! I'm not good enough for you? Do you only fuck college chicks now? Yeah, that's what I heard about you, right?"

Tunney could see then that no matter what he did this scene with Jerry's girlfriend was not going to turn out well.

"Fine. I'm a limp dicked jerk. Now get out."

"Nobody tells me what to do."

"I just did. Get out or I'll take you back to Jerry and you can sleep in the bar."

"All you jerk-offs are the same. You use women. You use me. You treat me like dirt." She glared at Tunney and her bottom lip began to shake. "You'll pay for treating me like shit."

"Just get the fuck out. Now."

"You asked for it dick head," she screamed as she fumbled with the door handle and stumbled onto the sidewalk. "I'm telling Jerry what you did and you'll be sorry!"

Tunney could not even respond to her. He was just happy to have her out of the car so he could get back to his apartment.

The next night Jerry banged on his door.

"Let me in mother fucker. I'm coming through this door whether it's open or shut!"

Tunney closed his eyes. *Why me,* he thought. *The only guy who gets shoved around for not screwing his friend's girl.* Tunney opened the door. As soon as he did Jerry grabbed him by the throat.

"We're going for a walk asshole."

"Jerry, what is your fucking problem?"

"My problem is you, asshole. I trust you to take my girl home and you try to rape her in your car."

"What! For crissake, Jerry. She jumped *me*. I told her no way would I fuck my buddy's girl and she goes ballistic."

"Don't fuck with me, Tunney. I know what happened."

Tunney groaned. That stupid chick had made up some kind of story to pay Tunney back for rejecting her. Now he wished he had fucked her. He would have had a better chance at not being dragged out of his apartment, kidnapped by a crazed idiot.

Jerry pushed Tunney towards his front door. He smelled so strongly of booze that it made Tunney's eyes water. Jerry held Tunney by his neck and began pushing him down the street. He was working himself into a frenzy of even greater anger as he yelled in Tunney's ear all of his alleged indiscretions.

Suddenly Jerry pulled Tunney through the gate of a chain-linked fence and into a schoolyard playground.

"Sit on that fuckin' swing, dick face," Jerry slurred and pushed Tunney into the rubber seat. Jerry stood in front of him and grabbed onto the top of Tunney's head, yanking his hair into a five-fingered vice grip. Tunney cried out involuntarily.

"Shut up fuck face." Suddenly Tunney's head snapped back as he was hit across the mouth with something hard and cold. That was when he realized that Jerry had a gun.

Tunney's first thought was to laugh at the irony. *I survived Viet Nam and now I'm going to be killed for no reason by a goddamn American idiot.*

For the next hour, Jerry yelled and cried and hit Tunney again and again with the butt of the pistol every time he remembered that Tunney was still sitting there. Tunney heard every bad thing that had ever happened in Jerry's childhood through his drunken slur. He simply prayed to get through the night as he tasted the blood in his mouth and blinked it out of his eyes from the cuts on his forehead and the pistol-whipping across his mouth.

As luck would have it, Jerry finally passed out and Tunney stumbled back to his car and drove himself to the emergency room.

That was the last time he ever did a favor for anyone's girlfriend again.

And not this time either, Tunney admonished himself. *I'm not embroiling myself in Nora's problem. It's her problem. If I'm feeling especially groovy when I leave her in Frisco and am beginning to drive away, I'll yell back that she's one pregnant chick.*

Right then, all Tunney wanted was a place to sleep that was inside of a house and did not drop to 30 degrees at night. He was tired of waking up with a cold, pup tent face every morning.

Tunney looked over at Nora again. She was asleep and her lovely chest rose and fell like a bellows nurturing a fire. *Or a belly nurturing a baby*, he thought.

"This ought to be fun," he said out loud and then flinched as he realized the words had not stayed in his head. But Nora remained asleep, continuing to breathe her pregnancy breaths that fed the new life that was yet to be acknowledged by its owner.

A U.S. route sign flashed by the car. Dubuque was 60 miles away. The reunion with Hammersley was getting closer. *It will only be cool*, Tunney whispered to himself. *A cool, friendly reunion of Jarheads.*

"Semper Fi," Tunney said out loud. And still Nora did not stir.

# # #

Chapter 15: The Gift

Kgotla at Bodiba Village, Botswana
March 1969

Willa had never heard her name called so many times. Where was she to look? Her wide grin and darting eyes returned the waves and wishes of the Batswana as she entered chief Tau's village of Bodiba. *I'm home.*

As Sammie Po slowly drove the clinic lorry along the main road through the village, women ululated and young children ran alongside the vehicle trying to touch Willa's hand. She laughed and called out greetings to them. They laughed back and shouted in excitement, knowing that the day's event would include fresh meat, mealie meal and oranges. Unbeknownst to them, Sammie Po had a metal cooler in the lorry filled with ice cream flown up all the way from South Africa by Johnny.

Sammie Po joined in the laughter. "Willawe, you are too popular today! This would be a good day to seek favors from the chief's clan."

Willa laughed in return. "*If only I could think of something I need, Sammie. The happiness on this road is such a gift,*" she replied in Setswana.

For a moment Sammie Po got serious. "Oh, you still need to learn much, Willa. You must know how to ask and how to take. If you only give people will become suspicious of you. Be sure not to refuse anything that you might be given today. That would be the utmost insult to the chief."

"Sammiwe, I'm not a *lekgoa*! I know how to be humble and gracious!"

"Willawe, you are a *white person,* but you are also a Motswana. Just don't give anything back today when you are rewarded. You must only take today. Do you hear my words?"

"*Eh, Sammie, ke ultwa*. I will only give thanks, nothing else."

"Are you sure you don't have gifts or treats stuffed in your pockets?" Sammie asked, only half joking.

“Eh, *monna*. I’m sure. I have just myself, *hela*.”

As the last group of villagers parted in front of the lorry, the kgotla came into view. From the time Willa was old enough to be taken to the kgotla, she remembered being acutely aware of its stark power and mystery. The village meeting area and the chief’s sacred court, the kgotla was the grounds upon which all-important events were held. Whether marriage blessings or punishments for wrong doers, within the fencing of the kgotla, all decisions of the chief were final.

The enclosure was fenced with ironwood stakes the height of a tall man and pounded into the ground snug against one another. No mortar or rope held the strangely curved wood together. Just the precision of the village builders who knew how to construct these fences solidly and to last, always an honor to the chief who ruled over the ethics and activities of the village.

When Sammie Po stopped the vehicle, young children and ululating elder women surrounded Willa as she jumped down from the truck. Together they laughed and moved as a joyful protective pod towards the chief’s throne area.

As Willa approached the chief, the crowd suddenly went quiet. Willa was startled by the sudden change. A shiver ran from the back of her legs up and through her neck. *This is even more of an important day than I knew*, Willa thought to herself as her eyes met the chief’s. She clasped her hands together to stop them from shaking.

A kgotla lieutenant moved in between Willa and the chief.

“Dumelang, baigetso. You are in the kgotla of Chief Tau, son of Chief Moeti and son of the people of Bodiba, the people most loved by Modimo in the heavens and always protected against the evils of drought and cattle sickness. In Chief Tau’s honor, please greet him and let him greet his honored guest, daughter of Dr. Gakelape and young nurse to the sick of this land.”

A great roar of greeting slammed against Willa and took her breath away. Chief Tau was so highly regarded that each member of the tribe, from the very youngest to the most ancient, pushed their voices to a crescendo of joy that mimicked religious ecstasy.

As Willa’s eyes met the chief’s again, he beckoned her forward by holding out his hands and raising his palms to the sky. Willa put her hands together as though in prayer and knelt in front of the man who only a few months ago had the top of his head taken off by a devil leopard.

As was the custom for a Tswana youth to honor an elder, Willa offered her "praying" hands up to the chief. He enclosed them with his own and lightly touched her fingers to his lips.

"*Dumela, my daughter. You honor me by coming here today. I now have both the joy that an old man knows, and the joy that a man owns after he has faced death down and returned to the living. Ke itumetse. Yes, I am happy, very happy that you honor this village by coming here today.*"

"*Ke itumetse, great father. I am happy too, for the great honor of coming here today and being your guest in this magnificent kgotla.*" It was important protocol that Willa not speak longer than the chief, so she stopped and waited for Chief Tau to speak again.

"*Willawe, please rest here in this seat of honor.*" The chief motioned to the seat next to his throne. Only when Willa moved to her seat did she see that Tom, Sammie Po, Mma Cookie, and Johnny were seated in the area to the side of the chief's platform amid the kgotla lieutenants, important village elders and clan leaders.

And then suddenly Willa sucked in her breath. As one of the village leaders moved in his seat to the right, Jan's face appeared and their eyes met. *She came*!

Willa thought that her mother looked uncomfortable but resigned to her spot on a hard little stool in the Kalahari sun. *She's trying so hard for me. For me.*

Jan had railed loudly against the use of traditional medicine since arriving in Botswana almost two decades before. She would unapologetically and with no cultural sensitivity whatsoever, scold the Batswana patients against whom she had evidence of traditional medicine use. Many times, especially with the elders, men and women would come to Mother Mercy clinic only after repeated visits to the traditional doctor had failed to help them. Dr. Gakelape was their last hope.

Jan had seen festering infections turned to gangrene and old fractures lead to amputation when the patient had waited a few days or a few weeks too long to seek out Western medicine. It was after Jan lost two such patients in a single day, ravaged by infection and comatose when she finally got to them, that her verbal attacks on traditional doctors and their "phantom" medicine became even more frequent.

Because Jan did not speak Setswana she expected Willa or one of the nurses to translate her rants verbatim to patients who were already frightened just being at the clinic. Jan's tone, terse and reminiscent of the colonial white men who preceded her ire and tenure in Botswana, was well understood even before the translation. Of course, Willa and the nurses would soften Jan's language and her tone, stressing the importance of coming to the clinic next time before they were so ill, and before seeing the traditional doctor.

Today, Willa hid her surprise at seeing Jan at the kgotla, smiling broadly at her, hoping for that spark of connection.

Under normal circumstances Jan would have considered attendance at an event like this an endorsement of traditional medicine. Even though the chief had been treated both with the Dingaka's herbs and with Jan's antibiotics, he made it known that it was Willa's fast work with the traditional medicine that had truly saved him from a death walk to the dark world, with the leopard as his companion. A leopard with a bullet hole in its head and an old man with no head. Chief Tau had shivered violently when that image raided his mind as he lay recovering in his village compound.

Even Jan had heard about the chief's dismissal of her second surgery on his head. A hot anger drove through her when Nurse Cloud had told her this. How dare he disregard her surgeon's skill at turning his raggedy, torn scalp back into a normal looking head. A head fit for a chief, no less. And even worse, how dare he poison all his villagers against Western medicine just at the point when visiting the clinic had become routine for pregnant women and their young children. That had taken almost twenty years of effort on Jan's part, including continually training health "ambassadors" to act as information resources in the village, helping their tribesmen understand when it was time to seek the white man's medicine.

When the chief's top lieutenant delivered the news of an event to honor Willa's saving of the chief, Jan, Mma Cookie and Willa were finishing their breakfast of tea and sorghum porridge. Speaking in English, the lieutenant announced the invitation in a way that reminded Jan of the toga-clad bearers of Roman scrolls in old films about Caesar and his warring legions. He stood straight and stiff, his English robotic in annunciation, his chin raised proudly, aware that his words carried the chief's will.

For a moment Jan looked at the lieutenant through eyes squinting with curiosity and struggling to grasp the import of the invitation. But then she understood. Dr. Gakelape's chin dropped to her chest and she squeezed her eyes shut for a second.

Luckily, Mma Cookie thought, Willa was fully attentive to the messenger, also trying to understand the significance of the announcement. Mma Cookie was on the verge of kicking Jan under the table, a rebuke that would also take the disappointed look off her face. If Willa saw the resentment in Jan's eyes, she would first wither and then go through the self-analysis and guilt she always did when reacting to Jan's powerful will. Mma Cookie had seen her through enough of those painful scenes to know that Willa's reaction this time might be to leave for good. And it would not be out of anger at Jan. It would be out of sheer fatigue at being hurt and confused for the thousandth time. Wanting to please Jan but also recognizing how different they were. Always struggling with what she should do to gain Jan's favor but also knowing that it was impossible to do so just by willing it.

Sammie Po always said that Jan was a rock, solid and immovable, and Willa a cloud, full of lightness and movement. While almost opposites in temperament and preferences, in the surgery they were tight and cohesive. Willa acted as case assistant, as Jan named her, the mother and daughter hardly needing words to communicate as doctor and nurse. An instrument, ointment or pill, Willa was most always a step ahead of her. *She'll be a damn good doctor*, Jan mused in pride.

Their wills are surely at an impasse, Mma Cookie thought, as she weighed whether or not to kick Jan under the table. Jan's last rout with Willa over the chief's treatment had almost been the last straw for the old woman. There was only so much pain and forgiveness and pain again that Willa could absorb. The young girl was a woman now. The time was close when Willa would realize the power of her own will and resent Jan's rash words and criticisms of her decisions.

Mma Cookie looked hard at Jan, willing her to look up and smile. Willa needed a smile.

Praise the lord, Modimo, Mma Cookie almost shouted. Jan rose and gave Willa a hug.

"My African girl," she said softly in Willa's ear. Then she held Willa at arm's length. "Now get the details. I must relieve Nursing Sister Belli so she can go home."

Jan moved toward the door quickly, sporting a happy smile and blank eyes, before her real feelings could eat through the mask. She wanted to be happy for Willa but she could not. All she could think about was the many years she had struggled to get the clinic established as a safe and good place for the Batswana to visit. How much of that would be eroded by the chief's gesture of thanks to Willa? A gesture that would certainly be seen as an endorsement of traditional medicine.

Jan began to fume as she walked to the clinic compound. She could just see the smarmy look on the Dingaka's face as the chief praised traditional medicine. An 'I told you so' from the stalwart of bush medicine, the Dingaka himself, who had never been to the clinic until he crowned the chief with the horrid herbal slop the day of the leopard attack.

As soon as Jan left the room, Willa and Mma Cookie looked at each other and began to laugh.

"Willawe, Willawe, you have taken this village by storm!" Mma Cookie loved using English expressions that she had heard her own children or Willa use, or heard on *Voice of America.*

Willa laughed. "Mma Cookie, it was not me who saved the chief. It was so many things, so many people involved."

"What so many things?" Mma Cookie gestured to the

messenger to sit and put a teacup in front of him.

But Willa was already on another track. She expressed her gratitude to the messenger that a kgotla meeting was being called for the purpose of thanking her for saving Chief Tau's life. In Setswana she continued.

"Please tell Chief Tau that I am humbled and honored. I will attend with the others who also helped the chief that day."

The messenger nodded. *"The chief knows of all who helped that day. But you were the bull elephant, Mma Willa. Of course all will be recognized. But the chief's life was surely in your hands, Doctora Willa.*

Willa swallowed hard. The fear she had felt that day when she first realized the extent of the chief's wounds came surging back and hit her stomach like a twisting, sharp fist. Willa took a deep breath. It was then that she realized how far away she had pushed the incident with the chief. Besides the memory of chief's bloody, torn scalp, there was also the residual hurt and resentment of Jan's tirade.

Willa possessed the Tswana trait of forgiveness, letting go of resentments quickly. If a man had a fight with his neighbor one day, the next day they started over anew. Everyone simply agreed that holding grudges was not an effective practice if the village was to operate as a real community.

So for Willa to continue to feel anger and hurt over Jan's dismissal was not her usual reaction. Willa knew the pattern well, but could never seem to shake herself loose from it. Jan would get mad at her for something and Willa would go sulking to Mma Cookie, who in turn would tell Willa to shake it off and move on. At the same time, Mma Cookie would always spend extra time with Willa, spinning a folk tale or teaching her how to make a raggedy doll out of an old apron, with shiny buttons torn off a discarded coat for the doll's eyes and nose. By the time Jan would come home from the clinic for a dinner break, Willa would have forgotten she was mad at her mother. Holding a grudge, pouting or "wearing her heart on her sleeve," a frequent Aunt Dix saying that Jan was fond of quoting, were not options for Willa as she grew up at Mother Mercy.

And maybe Tom had something to do with it. Her whole world had seemed to change in the last few months, including meeting Tom. *This must be what if feels like being a woman and learning to love*, Willa thought. Tom was like no one she had ever met. Everything felt more intense when Tom was around. Music was richer and more melodic, food more savory, perfume from the frangipani headier, and the sunsets more breathtaking as they overtook the horizon with a flood of brilliant color.

On the nights that she could spend with Tom, Willa would wake up feeling giddy with the closeness of his body and the affect that his touch and nearness had on her heart rate. Would her stomach always do a flip-flop when she saw his Land Rover pull into Mother Mercy compound? Would her cheeks always turn red when anyone else mentioned his name?

And now Tom was here with her today as she received the thanks of an entire village which had not been ready to bury their best leader in many turns of the calendar.

Yet Tom himself was a hero, as was little Lesole, Chief Tau's grandson, and his son Dadi as well. Willa suddenly remembered the son's hand secured tightly under the bandages that Tom and the village nurse had wrapped around Chief Tau's head to secure his scalp. It was the hope that the chief would live that made the son refuse to let go of his father's head in order for Nurse Cloud to bandage it. Hope is what saved the chief. Hope against all odds and the claws and jaws of the leopard.

Willa had recognized it in the son's eyes, in Lesole's cracking voice as he told what happened when the leopard sprang from its hiding place in the tree, and in Tom's shaking hands as he drove her to the Dingaka's compound in hopes that a long shot treatment would save the chief.

Tom caught Willa's eye and he gave her the thumbs up. Her smile back was a lighthouse beam, so strong it prompted the women closest to the chief to begin ululating again.

Just then the chief stood up and the kgotla became silent.

"*Dumelang baigetso*! *And welcome to this day of happiness and recognition.*"

The chief paused and the kgotla exploded in claps, cheers,

ululating and stomping feet. For the benefit of all of the white people in the audience, the chief had his daughter, Bontle, translate his words into English after every sentence.

"*You know me as a man of action and few words. But today I must speak more than a few. Why? Because I can speak more than a few.*" Loud claps and shouts answered the chief's recognition that he was almost not there with them because of the leopard.

"*My life was given back to me a few months back. Why? Because God has something he wants me to do.*"

Every eye was on the chief. What had God told him to do? They waited in silence for the chief to continue.

"*I am here because many people put their hands together to pull me back from the arms of the devil Death. Lesole, my grandson, ran as fast as a jack hare to this village to seek help for me. My son, Dadi, held my head together with his strong hands and his strong spirit that willed me to survive the lorry ride. Tommiwe Peese Corpse drove his Rover to fetch me and had the courage not to stop as I began to die in the lorry.*" A few frightened shouts and moans from distressed women punctuated the chief's words.

"*And then Dr. Willawe refused to give up when the Lekowa medicine was not there to stop the devil from entering my head and taking me to the dark world. She defied her own mother to fetch the Dingaka to use his herbs to shield my head from the devil.*"

As the chief said this, gasps rose in the kgotla and all eyes went back and forth from Jan to Willa and back to the chief. Willa gulped and wondered what was next. Johnny, who was seated behind Jan, put his hand on her shoulder, knowing her first reaction to the chief's words would be to rise up, and that would not be good.

Jan felt Johnny's hand. It reminded her that she had promised Mma Cookie that, no matter what, she would attend the ceremony at the kgotla, and she would not leave until it was over. Mma Cookie had used her sternest, most serious tone with Jan that morning. "No matter what, do not leave the kgotla during the ceremony or stand if the chief is speaking. That is too rude Doctor Jan. I won't be nice to you for many years if you don't show respect to our chief."

The chief had everyone's attention and they waited in silence for his next words. In the distance the buzzing of the cicadas stopped abruptly.

"*Dr. Willawe showed her trust in the Dingaka and he used all of his knowledge of medicines and devil shields to help her protect my life.*" At these words the crowd's eyes shifted to the Dingaka who sat erect and proud, a slight but satisfied smile turning up one side of his mouth.

"*Dr. Willawe did not learn how to save my life from the Dingaka. She learned this from Dr. Gakelape, her respected mother.*" There were again gasps from the crowd. Even the translator paused before she spoke the chief's words in English.

Jan's back straightened up and she lifted her eyes so that they met the chief's. He looked out at Jan, respect and recognition passing from his eyes to hers.

"*Dr. Gakelape taught her daughter how to save lives. Dr. Gakelape dropped her holiday and flew back when she heard that all medicine was gone. Dr. Gakelape gave me back my beautiful head with her precise sewing.*" Chief Tau pointed to his scar and everyone laughed in joy. Willa's smile became a grin, and she looked over at her mother who was also smiling.

"*God wanted this to happen so that he could show us the way.*" Again, the chief had the rapt attention of everyone in the court.

"*Our Willa knows the way. Our white daughter who is also a Motswana, one of us, knows the way. The way is not only Western medicine. The way is not only traditional medicine. The way is the best of both of those worlds together. Sometimes you need one, sometimes the other. But to dismiss one or the other of these worlds is to be ignorant.*" By this time the chief was shaking his knobkerrie high in the air for emphasis.

For one moment there was complete silence. The only noise the dust-sand rising and falling against the leather skin capes of the elders. Then suddenly the loudest shouts and claps that had been heard yet rose from the crowd.

Jan felt the crowd vibrating in her bones. Emotion from them poured over her and into her and she was no longer in control. First she laughed deep and with a release that made her feel euphoric. Then Jan was shocked when she realized that the wetness on her face was her own tears. So many tears that had waited so many years to flow forth. Years of frustration in establishing the clinic. Years of worry that she would fail after all. Years of refusing to remember she had two daughters, and only barely remembering Willa during the crazy, busy years at the clinic when she was the only doctor. Years of regret. Years of toil. Years of accomplishment. Years of Johnny's love. Years of Mma Cookie's lessons. And years of Willa's innocence and probing mind.

All of these were blessings, Jan suddenly realized, because they all added up to something worthwhile. The clinic really had changed lives for the better in the area, and everyone in her life had enabled Mother Mercy to reach its place of respect and understanding in the community.

And most of all, Jan realized, was that she, too, felt a part of this community. She was welcomed here. She had become a part of their lives. Half the children under the age of eighteen had come into the world with the help of Jan's steady hands when the local midwife was not near. Her face had caught the breath of fresh life and she had listened in anticipation of so many infants' cries. So many trusting souls had shed their bodies when her treatment was not enough to save them. All of their lives were intertwined into a labyrinth of survival, pulled taut by the constant entrance and exit of life.

Jan rubbed her glazed eyes and sought out Willa. Involuntary laughter again escaped her control when she saw the pure joy on Willa's face, lit up like a haloed saint in a missal.

Chief Tau began stabbing his knobkerrie into the air again and the shouting and cheers quickly died down so he could speak again.

"Today we are learning something that only a fight with death can teach. Know who you can trust by their actions not by their skin or their birthplace or by pressure from others. Do you

hear my words, Baigetso?"

Chants of "*Pula*" and "*Eh, Kgosi*" rose from the villagers.

"*Willawe, can you please come and join me here.*"

Her grin turned into a nervous half smile as she rose and joined the chief.

"*Willawe, my daughter.*" The chief put his hands on Willa's head. Their power and warmth made her feel protected and calmed. It gave her a kind of comfort that she imagined a father would give through a single touch to a daughter whom he loved dearly.

"*What gift does a man give to his daughter who has given him back his life?" There is nothing of comparable value. But what I can give are tokens of regard for you.*"

One of the chief's granddaughters appeared at his side holding a package wrapped in white shiny paper and bound with twine. He motioned to her to give the package to Willa.

The chief nodded to Willa to open it.

It was soft and the twine slipped off easily. As the paper fell aside Willa saw her gift and her mouth fell open. Inside was a beautiful jacket made of rare albino karakul wool. Hand-tooled leather straps met ivory buttons to close the front of the coat. The coat was lined with White satin that must have come from South Africa. Willa could tell that the tailoring of the jacket was flawless.

Chief Tau smiled broadly at Willa's obvious surprise and delight. There were appreciative oohs and aahs from the villagers and a few clucks from the jealous women who knew how good they would look in the jacket too.

"*Try it on my child*," the chief urged, beaming with a gift-giver's anticipation.

As Willa slipped her arms into the karakul and the satin, a short, awed silence was quickly followed by clapping and ululating. Willa's smile turned to gleeful laughter and she clasped the chief's hands in thanks.

Tom stared in awe at Willa. He had never seen anyone look so beautiful in his life. It was not just the jacket but also the joy that shone from Willa's eyes and mouth, her whole body in fact. She was radiant.

And then suddenly he startled himself when he realized that he loved Willa. He had been so afraid to even think it, to risk it. Willa was proof that love did not have to lead ultimately to pain, or to a black eye and excuses to the neighbors. Love can be without physical abuse and chronic distrust. He could control that here. He would never control it in his father's house.

But then, Tom had decided the day he boarded the plane to Africa that he would never cross the threshold of his father's house again. Even if that meant losing his mother, it was the only option. His only because any other involved his father dying by his only child's hand.

But today was Love Day. *The day I realized what love is,* thought Tom. A red letter day. A Zen day. The day the world changed. The day that hope stopped drowning in the pool of his father's hate. He loathed the taint of self-pity that never left him. Tom saw his little boy-self mumbling: *Why can't my Dad be like their Dads, like anybody's Dad, but mine.*

Willa was glorious in her white jacket. Giggling Tswana girls came up to congratulate her and touch the coat. It was surely unlike anything anyone had seen before.

Tom laughed at the girls' admiration of Willa. He turned and Jan was right behind him. She was laughing as well and surprised Tom with a strong hug and a kiss on the cheek. He was speechless, but saved by the Chief who began to speak again.

"*It is time that Willawe and Dr. Gakelape are shown that they are also part of our village. Doktoro, please come forward.*"

Jan was surprised but her elation carried her through the crowd and up to the chief. Bontle the granddaughter appeared again, this time with a rolled scroll.

"Unlike the white men, we Tswana do not believe that the land can be owned by a mere person. We cannot presume to own what is not ours but is our God's and Mother Earth's. For many years Dr. Gakelape has come to us to ask over and over to use our land for the clinic. Because you are not of our people we made you ask every year to use this land.

"But now we know you and you know us. This scroll is a 100 year gifting of the clinic land for Mother Mercy, plus additional lands around the clinic totaling 200 hectares for any other uses by you and your family."

Jan's hand covered her mouth in surprise and then she spontaneously hugged the chief. With that the crowd went wild and began singing the Botswana national anthem. Willa was laughing and crying so hard that she had to sit down on the chief's vacant chair.

Suddenly Tom's arms were around her. She stood and faced him, and it seemed like it must be happening to someone else and not her.

"I love you Dr. Willa." Tom hugged her so hard that she gladly gave him all her breath.

# # #

Chapter 16: Tripping

Iowa

March 1969

Hammersley's house was a yellow, country box, its quaint still stronger than its shabby. Nora could not help but sigh in relief as they pulled up the long dirt driveway. Flowerbeds resting fallow in March's chill cut out brown swatches in the tall grasses lining the car path. Then the lane suddenly opened up and the house appeared in full.

"This has Iowa written all over it," Nora observed.

"This explains a lot," Tunney answered. "Hammersley was always smart and a brother Marine. But deep down he was also a fuckin' hick. I'm just waiting for Dorothy and Auntie Em to walk out," Tunney laughed.

"That's Kansas," Nora chided. "Be nice."

"I'm nice! He's my partner, you know. But he's still a fuckin' hick!"

An hour before, Tunney had pulled over at a truck stop and called Hammersley, so he was expecting them.

As he pulled the Mustang into the gravel parking area to the side of the porch, the front door flung open.

"Tonnage! Hey, man!" Hammersley ran toward the car, his grin hiding none of his joy at seeing his brother Marine.

Tunney started whooping in response to Hammersley's excitement. He jumped out of the car and the two Marines crashed into one another and held tight, as only men who had shared war could.

Nora watched the two men cling to each other. It was clear that much had passed between them. Things that they needed one another to remember and to forget.

"Look at you, mother fucker!" Hammersley held Tunney at arm's length. "How the fuck did you grow your hair so long?" He tugged on Tunney's locks.

"I'm a healthy boy, Hammerhead! You're just jealous 'cause

you still look like a jarhead and I don't!" Tunney laughed and slapped the back of Hammersley's head.

"I'm not jealous, man. I'm just afraid for you. One of these dumb farm boys is gonna think you're a chick and try to jump you!"

"You're still a sick-o, Hammerhead!" They both laughed.

It was like the old laughs in Nam. Being scared to death, exhausted and always on edge somehow brought out the comedian in at least a few of the guys and dark humor in just about everyone. It was always enough to break the tension for a while and get one another to skirt the fear for a few minutes. There was a kind of amnesia-joy in that, when a Marine could forget his dread for a precious few moments. Forget that the enemy may be sighting in on your head or laying a trip wire with your name on it.

Nora tried to unobtrusively slip out of her side of the car. She wanted Tunney to have his initial reunion with his buddy free from having to introduce her. It also gave her a chance to check out Hammersley.

He looked like an all-American, corn-fed kid, all grown up: blond hair and bright green eyes that sucked up everything in their path. And Hammersley's height was impressive. He towered over Tunney at six foot five as he wrapped him in another bear hug. *Gentle Giant*, Nora thought, but heavier on the bad boy side. She could see why he attracted all the women he did.

"Oh, Hammer, this is Nora, my traveling companion. Nora, this is Hammersley, better known as Hammerhead."

As Tunney introduced them, Nora walked around the car and held out her hand.

"Nora! Thank god you're here!" Hammersley took her hand and held it. "Having Tunney here brings a whole lot of ugly into this house, but your whole lot of pretty will balance it out."

Hammersley looked at Tunney with a message in his eyes saying, 'You're a lucky son-of-a-bitch 'cause she's a beautiful woman.'

Tunney groaned. "How little have ye changed, Hambone. Get thee out of the toilet long enough to find me a beer." Tunney turned to Nora and pulled her hand out of Hammersley's. "Watch out for farm boy here. All this fresh air does something to their brains. A little slow, you know." Tunney tried hard not to smile but the sides of his mouth began to curl up.

"I'm happy to meet you, Hammersley. Oh, what's your first name"?

Hammersley moved up next to Nora and put his arm around her waist, and began to guide her toward the yellow farmhouse.

"You can call me Hank, short for Henry, as you please, Nora." Hammersley smiled and Nora involuntarily moved closer into his arm hold on her. There was something very magnetic about Hammersley, Nora realized, as she willingly let herself be escorted into the house.

Tunney watched them flirt with each other from behind and took a deep breath. Why did he always have to notice the fatal flaws in everyone he met? He swore under his breath as Nora laughed at something Hammersley said.

Screw her, he thought. *She's learning she's pregnant tonight.*

# # #

From where she was in the kitchen, Nora could hear Tunney and Hammersley laughing and then talking seriously in the front room. Sensing that they needed time to catch up, Nora had insisted on doing the dinner dishes and cleaning up the kitchen.

Hammersley had cooked up a giant pot of spaghetti sauce and meatballs, simmering it all day. Red spots of sauce dotted the stovetop and the wall behind like a Seurat painting. Nora smiled.

"Girl bathing in spaghetti sauce," she said aloud and shook her head. She filled a bucket with hot water and Mr. Clean and removed the sauce's history from the yellow walls and stovetop. In a burst of sudden energy, Nora attacked the kitchen floor with a string mop she found in the mudroom. It felt like an accomplishment to make Hank's kitchen cleaner than it was before. It would leave it with the definite mark of a woman's touch.

He will remember me for a few days. But why do I care? Nora admonished herself. I do care. She admitted reluctantly to herself that it was fun to be flattered by Hank. Her foray with Pete had been an ego-bruiser. Hank made her feel like a woman who was attractive again. *Not that I'm attracted to Hank*, Nora thought. *But he makes me feel the power again.*

"Woman, what are you doing?" Hank yelled from the living room.

"I'm determining what color your walls were before they turned spaghetti red," Nora laughed as she yelled back.

"Oh no! I did that on purpose!" Hank yelled back and Nora heard his heavy footsteps approaching.

"Holy shit!" Hank exclaimed when he saw the kitchen. "Do I live here? This place looks great!"

Nora was suddenly in his arms and he led her, dancing across the kitchen floor. They both started laughing so hard the dance turned very freestyle.

Then she saw the look. She had seen it before. It was frightening. It was exhilarating. Without a doubt, the look shouted, 'I want you.'

There was power in that recognition of a man wanting her. Power to manipulate or capitulate. Power from having a level of control over another person through purely physical means. The last time that happened she got mixed up with Pete. Nora shook her head.

But why shouldn't she just be with Hank because they like each other and are having fun? Like men and women did naturally. That's all. Screw commitment. There was no longer a religious conviction or a rule from Daddy or some phony girl's school ethic keeping her from practicing her womanhood and learning more about these strange, wonderful creatures called men. *Screw those old rules.*

Pete was indeed a learning experience as Max had said he would be. There was no way she was jumping into a long-term live-in relationship again. That mistake was sheer inexperience, Nora realized. There's value in a kind of detachment until time and trust open the door for a greater investment in one another, slowly, incrementally.

Hank could be her intentional short-timer. Lying next to his large body and strength would probably be a lot of fun.

But what should she do now to respond to the look? The frightening, exhilarating look.

The ringing telephone suddenly over-ruled any action on Nora's part. Hank smiled at Nora and his eyes held her for another moment.

"I gotta get that, 'scuse me kid." Hank ran to the hallway phone.

Tunney walked in at the same time. Nora could not quite read his look. *Always a mystery*, she thought.

"Hey, Nora. Wow, this place looks great. Hammersley doesn't deserve it, of course. He'll never let you leave now, you know," Tunney said, sounding serious and coy.

Nora laughed. "I'm a big girl, Tunney, and I've recently learned the importance of a free will."

"That's good. I'll try to remember the big girl part too." Tunney leaned over the sink and shook out the last few drops in his beer can.

"What's that supposed to mean?" Nora put her hands on her hips.

Tunney bent his head and laughed. "Want to go for a walk?"

"Yes, let's go for a walk." Nora crossed her arms and followed Tunney into the back yard.

"I guess it's sort of cold for a walk," Tunney said. Nora thought he looked resigned and unsettled at the same time.

"You seem like you want to say something, Tunney. Are you mad at me or something?" Suddenly Nora felt like she would start crying. *Where the hell did that come from*?

Tunney looked at her with only half his face. "How do you feel by the way? I mean, with the car sick thing?"

Nora chuckled. "Out with it Tunney. You're lousy at being phony. In fact, you're exasperatingly real. It makes me feel smaller..." Nora was cut off by Tunney.

"...when in fact you're getting bigger," he blurted out and could not help but laugh. Nora looked confused and half pissed off.

"Nora, honey..." Tunney stumbled and lowered his head.

"What, for crissake, Tunney! It's friggin cold out here!" Nora looked so cold and had so many questions in her eyes. Tunney slipped his arm around her waist.

"You're pregnant kiddo."

"What!" Nora jerked out of Tunney's grasp and stepped back.

"It's a terrible expertise I have, Nora, because of all of my sisters. I can tell when a woman is pregnant. I know the signs, I guess." Tunney lifted his head and looked at Nora. Her mouth opened to say something but no words came. Tunney could tell she was weighing his statement against what her body had begun whispering to her of late.

"Have you ever been wrong," Nora asked, her hollow voice almost carried away on the winter wind. Her face had suddenly gone very white. Tunney took Nora's hand and held it in both of his.

"No, never wrong yet. But you see a doctor to be sure."

Nora looked away from Tunney. Her new future was already running away so fast, pulling at her so hard. The realization that she was pregnant had been lying in wait for a few weeks in her head, stumbling around her logic, ducking and hiding and trying not to be seen. As she turned back to Tunney a shooting star flickered over her head.

A beautiful fear, Tunney thought as Nora's face took on all the remaining light in the sky. *I hope I'm wrong*.

"I think I'm sure, Tunney. The signs were there. I just didn't want to see them, face them, I guess." Nora's face fell, her resignation so strong that Tunney felt it in his chest.

It was Tunney's sharp eyesight, specially trained in Nam to see in the dark and any other impossible situation, that saw Nora's eyes spill over onto her cheek. A hundred whys, admonishments, fears, and vendettas in those drops. The drop of uncertainty that escaped before her backbone stiffened up again. *That a girl*, Tunney thought. *Push it off, walk it off, kid*. Tunney wished he could say it out loud. But he did not think Nora would respond well to those words just at this moment.

"Tunney?" Nora looked directly in his eyes. Whatever she asked now he would have to tell the truth.

"Yah, kiddo? You okay?"

"Tunney, I just want you to know that this won't interfere with the trip. I'm not going to go weird on you or anything. I'll just be trying to figure out what the next step will be. But I won't bother you with it. That would be a bummer. I won't do that. If I do, you have permission to slug me."

"I never hit women, and particularly steer clear of pregnant women and their celebrated moods." Tunney looked at Nora and they both laughed.

"No, but you take them out in the freezing weather and torture them!" Nora stood still again, her voice softening. "Hey, Tunney. Thanks for being honest. But don't say anything to Hank, okay? I don't want to be a bummer on him when he's been nice enough to let me stay, no questions asked."

"Okay. If I can I will."

"Tunney, you can lie every now and again you know, or just say nothing."

"I've tried that and it never works for me. I prefer the consequences of honesty to those of treachery. I get tangled up too easily as it is."

"Well, then, let's honestly go inside before I honestly freeze to death." Nora rushed for the door and fell into the warmth.

"Hey, polar bears, what's going on in the back yard that I don't know about?" Hank shut the door behind Tunney and shivered involuntarily from the cold.

"Just grabbing a lungful of your clean Iowa air, Hams," Tunney said as he glanced at Nora. But she had her back to them both, standing at the sink pretending to rinse a dish. Pretending for a few more minutes that her life had not changed into something that she could not yet recognize.

Nora turned off the water and dried her hands. She could feel Hank approaching her.

"Nora, thanks again for cleaning up. I owe you one."

"No you don't, Hank." Nora didn't want to turn around yet. She just could not be sure what her face was showing. Could she make it neutral? Hank did not know her well enough to be able to characterize all of her faces, so of course she could hide anything she wanted from him. He did not seem like the perceptive type, either, not like Tunney who could tell a woman's hang ups by the way she said hello and held her drink at a party.

"I'm grateful that you opened your door to me, gave me a place to stay when you don't even know me."

"If Tonnage thinks you're okay, honey, so do I. No need to wash dishes for your room and board. But you sure do it nice. Gotta invite somebody over here quick that I want to impress!" Nora smiled and Hank grinned.

"I'm totally impressed, Hammerhead. But I'd be more fucking impressed if you rolled another joint and put on some Dylan or something. I haven't spent this much time discussing clean floors since I lived next door to Beaver and Wally." Tunney loved sparring with Hammersley and knew his mouth would move them all out of the kitchen and give Nora a chance to get some breathing room.

"Yah, well fuck Mrs. Cleaver, let's get stoned, General Tonnage!" Hammersley did an about face and marched like a wooden soldier to the living room. He yelled back to the kitchen, "Hey, I forgot. My buddy Krypto is coming over. Fasten your seat belts. That was him that called."

Tunney glanced back at Nora and she smiled sadly at him, the questions running through her mind reflected across her porcelain face. She looked so tired all of a sudden, he thought. Nora's shoulders drooped slightly, making her look like a little girl who had lost her most precious doll. The doll that made the girl feel like a mommy. The doll that seemed so real, that the pain of losing it was real too. *Little lost girl, lovely Nora.*

At least she is trying to figure it out, Tunney thought. A lot of rich girls just went with the flow of daddy's money and parties and influence. Still getting high and maybe even fucking the troops, but smiling in their navy pumps in the receiving line when called upon. But Tunney had to hand it to Nora. She had known that there was more to the world than daddy's circle. And even though she did not know what that *more* was she had the guts and curiosity to at least try and seek out some answers. Now all her answers had an asterisk next to them. A flashing blaring asterisk that shouted, 'Now you've got to factor the baby in!'

Tunney reached out his hand to Nora. "Let's go keep

Hammersley out of trouble." Nora took his hand and fell into him.

"Hey, do you want to go lay down for a while?"

Nora loved Tunney's voice. It always sounded so sure of itself. So safe and certain. She would do anything that Tunney suggested right now because he knew what he was talking about.

"Maybe I will for just a bit. Is that rude to Hank, though?"

"No way, Nora. He already showed me where you're sleeping. Let me lead you to your bucolic chamber."

Nora let herself be led to the stairway. Tunney held her waist from behind and guided her up. Blue flowered wallpaper moved by her eyes interrupted by grandpa and grandma photographs, an old farmhouse and a church steeple in a painting that glowed and looked holy to Nora, like the pictures in the family bible that rested on her father's side table all during her youth.

Why were her ears buzzing? Nora hoped that Tunney was not saying anything because she could not hear him. Time was not moving as it should either. All sound seemed filtered through a chamber. It was far away and hollow sounding. It was Tunney's voice, steady, sure. Tunney was here with her and his touch felt so good as he guided her to a warm, safe place.

For a second Nora believed that she could return to the place she had been in before being pregnant had entered the scene and redirected the whole program.

Tunney noticed that Nora's breathing was suddenly louder and faster. Too many flashes of truth were hitting her at once.

Pregnant and Pete and still running from Daddy, and pregnant and abortion and tiny hands floating in her womb, forming into a whole tiny body, mad because it might have to live in Philadelphia. But no, California and it's always sunny, didn't Tunney say so? Doesn't Tunney need to say more to her so she can follow his voice? Follow his voice to safety. Not the safety of her father's house. It had become scary and the walls closed in, shutting off her breath. That was her name being called.

Nora saw her third grade classroom and Sister Theophilus at the chalkboard. Nora knows that she can answer the question. Why doesn't Sister ever call on her when she knows the answer? Nora felt herself getting angrier and angrier. Damn, that Sister

Theophilus. It's not fair that I'm not getting a chance!

But wait. Her name was being called. I know who that is. It's Tunney.

Nora felt her face being stroked. Her forehead felt cool, like a soft ice cube was caressing it.

"Nora, open your eyes. Come on. Open your eyes, kid," Tunney whispered just to her. So she did.

"Hey, you're back." Tunney took the cloth off Nora's forehead and set it aside.

"Did I go somewhere?" Nora started to raise herself on her elbows.

"Whoa, kiddo. Take it slow. I don't think I can catch you twice in one evening." Tunney smiled at her and gently pushed her shoulders back onto the bed.

"Oh, god! Did I pass out on you? Oh, Tunney, I'm sorry..." Nora's eyes teared up and Tunney saw her lower lip quiver.

"I wish the catch was on film, Nora. We were both graceful in our offensive and defensive positions. You especially. Very smooth. Nothing to worry about, kid."

Nora laughed weakly as she rubbed her eyes. Tunney handed her the cool cloth.

"Thanks for being in the wrong place at the right time." Nora reached over and put her hand on Tunney's forearm. He felt a gentle squeeze.

"I must just be over tired," Nora said as she rolled onto her side. Her shirt gaped in a way that exposed the top of a breast. Tunney took it in with a deep breath. *Pink beauty.*

"How many times do I have to tell you, kid. You're pregnant. You won't have any extra energy for a few months. The baby's taking everything you got right now. That's why you're feeling wiped. You are wiped." Tunney seemed to be truly the voice of experience, Nora thought.

"Okay. I will just stay here and rest, I guess." Almost before Nora finished her sentence her eyes were closed and her sleepy breathing pattern was back.

"Tunney?" Nora's eyes twittered but didn't open all the way.

"Yeah?"

"Tell Hank sorry I'm a party pooper."

"I will, Nora."

"Thanks, Tun."

Nora's eyelids stopped fluttering and clamped shut. Tunney smiled and mumbled, "This is the type of woman I get messed up with." He pulled the covers higher up on Nora and tucked in the sides so that she would stay snug.

I'm such a fucking boy scout. Hammerhead would have certainly taken advantage of Nora in her weakened state. I'd better watch the Hammer. Then suddenly genius struck. Simple solution. Tunney would just tell the Hammer that Nora was pregnant. Then he'll stay away from her like she's got the clap.

As Tunney came down the stairs he could hear voices that he did not recognize.

"Hey, Tonnage, glad you decided to join us, man. Where's Nora? You wear her out or something?"

"Very funny, Hammersley."

"Man, these are my local buds, Krypto and his lady, Jane."

Tunney nodded and reached out to shake Krypto's hand.

"Hey, man. Good to know ya. Hammerman has told us about you, from Nam, you know." Krypto shook Tunney's hand. Jane kept her head down so Tunney did not bother reaching out his hand to her.

"You know, I really wanted to join you guys in Nam, but the doc said I had too many defects." Krypto looked truly saddened.

"Fucking right, Krypto. How many years have we all been telling you that you're fucking defective?" Hank stood up from his chair and kicked Krypto's leg.

"Hey, watch out for the merchandize, Hammersley." Krypto looked like his feelings were hurt, but Hank did not notice as he walked to the kitchen to get another beer.

"Grab one for me too, will ya Hammersley?" Tunney yelled after him.

"So what's up with you, man? Where are you coming from?" Krypto asked.

"Philly."

"What are you guys smokin' in Philly? I'm sure it's better than this shit that Hank smokes." Jane laughed a little bit at Krypto's comment and he leaned into her on the couch and whispered something in her ear. Jane giggled and rubbed Krypto's thigh.

"What about acid, man? You guys tripping in Philly on acid?"

"Yah, we got acid. Some good, some bad." Tunney suddenly got the overwhelming feeling of boredom. Of not wanting to be in a room with dull mid-westerners like Krypto and his greasy girlfriend.

Tunney knew he must be tired. His tolerance level was very low. He had just met Krypto and already he wanted the skinny country boy to leave.

"Tunney, I heard you got a real pretty girl traveling with you. Where's she at? She ain't afraid of strangers is she?" Krypto laughed and hit Hank on the leg as he returned to his chair.

"Yah, where's the Beauty, you Beast? I was looking forward to having Nora to look at all night versus your ugly mug." Hammersley lit a joint and handed it to Tunney.

"Nora's a bit under the weather you might say." Tunney took another hit and passed it to Jane. She looked Tunney right in the eyes as she took it, trying very hard to look sultry but only managing to look even cheaper than she already did.

Krypto was oblivious of his girlfriend's flirty eyes. He was working on pulling a plastic baggie out of his sock.

"Check this shit out, man. LSD for you and me!" Krypto let out a yelp and laughed loudly. "We're goin' trippin' tonight, my treat. Let's eat!" He whooped again and Hammersley knocked him upside his head.

"You're a fucking freak, man. Give me one of those tabs. Tonnage, you in, Bro?"

"Yah, I'm in."

Krypto handed everyone a tab of the acid, looking like a priest serving holy communion. Tunney wondered how anyone could be as skinny as Krypto and still have so much energy. It was hard to stay with Krypto because his body, his hands, his feet, his head and all his facial features were constantly in motion. Tunney realized that part of his exhaustion was caused by watching Krypto twitch and gyrate on the couch.

"This shit is good, my buddies. Not too strong, not too light, but just right. I got it from a very trusted source." Krypto looked extremely proud of himself. His back got suddenly straighter and he looked smug.

Tunney thought that Krypto looked like a bird. His long, skinny nose and small eyes gave him a distinctly beaky look. The way he moved his head when he was excited made him look like a chicken pecking around for a morsel of food. It hit Tunney that he did not trust Krypto. There was no way he was eating this acid.

As Krypto, Hank and Jane each swallowed their tab with a gulp of beer, Tunney pretended to do the same but slipped the tab into his jeans pocket. He thought it a better idea to see how the three of them reacted and then see whether it was worth saving the tab for another time. Maybe until California where the weather would be warm and he could trip under the stars next to a lake, or watch a sunset.

The sorrowful wail of Savoy Brown's guitar work broke his sunshine reverie. *Train to Nowhere* was a haunting tune. The rhythmic monotony of the train, the whining whistle and an immense feeling of loneliness all came through to Tunney, sending him to another place.

Tonight he felt like the train to nowhere. Sometimes his "plans" felt so right. He had to keep moving, had to keep exploring, searching for whatever it was that would provide the guidance, or even just a clue, to what he was supposed to be doing. Tunney was interested in what really mattered. But how did he get there? Tonight he felt like his train had no conductor. He was racing along with his pregnant female side kick, simply headed west. Westbound without a clue. Clueless and blue.

Tunney was not sure what had put him in his current blue funk. This was supposed to be a fun part of the trip, seeing Hammersley and doing the buddy thing.

But both he and Hammersley had barely mentioned Nam. It was not in the room. They had not said, "remember when" once. Not verbally anyway. Tunney had seen Hammersley's eyes start to dart around whenever the conversation had more than a few seconds lull. That was Hammersley's signal not to go back to Nam through any stories. Talking about what they had done since they got back, or seeing another buddy, or even boot camp, but not Nam. All that tension and fear bounced back and forth in Hammersley's eyes. Tunney had connected to that because he felt the same way. He did not want to go back there either. The stories were still too fresh in their minds to be the past. The stories were still the present. But a present that took place a world away, a world apart while only really hours away. That was why Tunney and Hammersley could not talk about Nam with anyone yet, not even each other. The gut ache, the numbness, the madness was just beginning to subside, or so they hoped. Why awaken that? Why when there was California ahead, answers ahead, more trips, more chicks, more life ahead that would help him rush away from the unexplainable, beautiful, dichotomous hell of Nam.

Tunney pulled his small stash of pot out of his knapsack and rolled a joint. Hammersley had his head in a stack of albums, picking through them carefully as though they were a card catalog and he was doing research.

"Yes, I found it!" Hank held the album above his head and spun it around.

"What is it?" Tunney stood up and walked to where Hank was sitting near the stereo. He lit the joint and handed it to his friend.

"Love."

"Love?"

"Love, the band, man. Haven't you heard of them?" Hank slipped the record out of its white sheath and set it up on the turntable.

"Yeah, but I don't really know their music."

"Oh, it's a trip, Tonnage. This guy Arthur Lee can really mix it up. Rock, blues, classical and his words are so cool." Hank smiled. It was nice seeing him feel so happy about the music. Tunney smiled too as he took the joint Hank handed back to him. It was time for smiles and good times. Nam could just stay back there where it was.

"Listen to this cut, man. I don't even know what it all means, but I shiver whenever I hear it. It's called Alone Again Or.

"Or what, I wonder?" Tunney asked.

"Just listen, dumb shit. Don't start acting like Krypto on me. One of him is enough."

"Okay, I'll listen. Where are Tarzan and Jane, anyway?" Tunney looked around the room vaguely.

"I heard the back door open. Krypto's probably tripping on the stars or something. Every time he's high he thinks he's discovered a new planet or seen a Martian space ship." They both laughed.

Alone Again Or began. Arthur Lee's voice played with the melodic strains of a full orchestra at times, then Spanish guitars, then the song went all folksy.

...and I will be alone again, tonight with you. Yeah, I heard a funny thing somebody said to me...that I could be in love with almost everyone. I think that people are the greatest fun.

Tunney closed his eyes as the Spanish guitars picked a rhythm so evocative that he could clearly see the singer's intent. Let go, suspend judgment, don't be alone when you're with others. Be here, be now.

When he opened his eyes the song was over and he was alone in the living room. Tunney suddenly felt like the day needed to be over. The long days of driving and trying so hard to move ahead crashed down on him so suddenly that his only reaction was to stand and head upstairs.

As he passed by the kitchen he could hear Krypto and Hammersley outside yelling up at the dark sky. Jane's laughter spiked their shouts of awe. So far the acid seemed like the happy kind. Tunney was even too tired to say goodnight. Not that the star trippers would care.

Tunney opened the door to the bedroom. A scar of light cut across Nora on the bed. Conveniently she had moved to the far side of the double bed. Tunney did not hesitate but slipped out of his clothes and into the right side of the bed. He had originally planned on sleeping on the floor or the couch downstairs, but the soft mattress beckoned. Nora would not mind. Before Tunney could give it a second thought he was asleep.

Vines were everywhere. Wrapped around tree trunks and

branches strangling bark until it disappeared behind its brilliant green tendrils. Hiding ancient temples, hiding Viet Cong.

Clinging, the vines were clinging to him now, pulling him towards the temple. Monks in orange robes stared at him and through him. He was not there for them. They were seeking enlightenment and he was not that.

Where was his machine gun? Damn, he had left it under the tree. Had to get back to that tree again. What if he was attacked and did not have a weapon? But the mud. He could not get through the mud. It held his feet and sucked at them. Black, oozing mud.

The monks were gone now. He would follow them to escape. Monks did not kill, he remembered that. They would not even kill a fly. But his feet would not move. He panicked. Machine gun fire. They had his weapon and now he would be killed by it. He could feel the sweat rolling down his face. Still his feet would not move.

Voices shouting. Wait, his name being called. A woman, old woman coming towards him. Shouting his name. She smiles and holds out her hand. Grenade. The smile disappears. She yells his name and pulls the pin. Her arm pulls back to throw.

"Tunney, Tunnee-eee..."

"Tunney, please wake up," Nora was shaking his arm, hard enough to wake him up, she hoped, but not to scare him.

Tunney's eyes popped open.

"What, what's wrong..." Tunney sprang up, his hands clawing the air and trying to protect his face. His vision focused and Nora and Jane materialized in front of him. They were staring at him and looked frightened. Jane looked completely freaked out, Tunney thought. Not a good sign.

"Get up, man, Hank needs you!" It was Jane. She sounded scared, weirded out.

"Tunney, something's wrong with Krypto. Hank needs your help. Now." Nora did not seem scared like Jane did. But in her eyes was the anxiety and confusion that he had seen earlier in the night when her mind had finally let her body disclose the life growing inside her. The unexpected life, the secret life that was now waking up and waking Nora up with it.

Tunney followed the women downstairs, pulling on his jeans as he tried to navigate the room, hopping from one foot to the other. It seemed like a dream. But he only dreamed about Viet Nam, so Tunney knew it was real. A headache began worming its way from the back of his head to the front. Tunney was still so asleep that his mind could not fully focus on why he was being dragged out of bed to help Hammersley and Krypto. He followed Nora and Jane to the dining room.

Krypto's bare legs were sticking out from under the dining room table, the rest of him not visible. Hammersley was standing in the corner, only half visible in the light that shone into the dark room from the kitchen.

"Tunney, man, what the fuck? What's going on with him?" Hank pointed down at the floor next to the table. There was a whitish fluid pooled on the hardwood floor, moving out from underneath the table where Krypto was. Tunney switched on the light and looked under the table.

There was Krypto, naked and talking in low moan. One hand was on his cock, which was pulsing red, cum spurting out and adding to the growing pool.

"Holy shit, is that all cum?" Tunney knew it was and he involuntarily moved backwards, away from the clotting mass.

"He won't stop cuming." It was Jane. The fear was apparent in her voice. "We was fuckin' but then he didn't stop cuming. And he was repeating 'I love everyone in the world' over and over," Jane looked down at Krypto's legs and shuddered. "Is he gonna die?" Jane's voice became shrill suddenly.

Tunney looked down under the table again and could now see that the words Krypto was repeating were the same ones Jane had heard. Krypto's skinny white body belied his large, throbbing cock.

"Has anyone ever cumed to death?" Although Tunney said it seriously, Hank started laughing. Nora let out one quick guffaw, abruptly stopped herself, and left the room.

"It's not fuckin' funny, you guys! It's like he's bleeding to death, and you don't even give a shit!" Jane started crying and kneeled down on the floor behind Krypto's head.

Tunney and Hank looked at each other. Hank shrugged his

shoulders but did not say anything.

Nora was back with a stack of towels and began tossing them on top of the cum pool. "That's all I do, guys. I can't clean that up." She looked at Hank and Tunney and then down at Jane. She was still whimpering and touching Krypto's head.

"I say let's throw him in the bath tub, cold water. I'd like to see Krypto's hard on survive that." Looking at Hank for affirmation, Tunney saw that his friend's eyes were glossy from the LSD, and not registering the whole scene as he would have if sober. Tunney wished he were not so sober.

"Jane, you gotta clean this mess up, honey. We'll carry him to the bath tub." Tunney looked at Hank, but he was staring at the white pool, mesmerized by its shine and volume.

Grabbing Hank by the arm, Tunney dragged him through the kitchen and into the backyard. When he opened the door the cold air slapped Hank towards sober.

"How do you like this country air, Hammerhead? Nice and fresh, huh?" Tunney still had not let go of Hank's forearm.

"We gotta go in, Tun. I'm fuckin' freezing, man!" Hank tried to pry himself loose from Tunney's grip but he was still too uncoordinated and weak from his high.

"Take one big, fucking inhale and I'll think about letting you back inside. You gotta be able to help me, Hammerman. Krypto is your friend and we gotta stop the love king from cuming himself to death or disability."

Hank started laughing and then raised his face to the sky and howled like a wolf. Tunney laughed too and pulled Hank by the sleeve back into the house. The smell of coffee hit their noses simultaneously and they said, 'Ah' in unison.

"It'll be done in five minutes. Right after you've given Krypto a bath." Nora looked tired but she was awake enough to know it might be a good idea to try the bath strategy to get Krypto to stop loving the universe and the dining room floor.

Tunney nodded. "Back in a few. Thanks, Nora."

# # #

Despite the welcome coffee from Nora, Tunney was still tired and his headache was worse than ever. He held the steaming mug in two hands, its warmth having a calming effect that he hoped might eventually temper his headache.

A rosy light was beginning to fill the kitchen as the early spring dawn cracked the plane of the horizon. It was even an effort to blink, so Tunney stared out the kitchen window, hypnotized by the dried grasses blowing in the rose-colored wind.

It was one of those rare times that Tunney's mind was purposefully unfocused. There was only the grasses and the dawn, the wind tumbling a tin can in the yard. Little frost crystals around the edges of the windowpane blinked against the early light. Soon they would melt.

"Hey, Tunney." Hank stood in the kitchen doorway, car keys in his hand. Tunney's eyes met Hank's. There had always been a lot of things that they did not need to say to one another.

"I gotta take Krypto and Jane back to town, man. Jane can't drive a stick and she's still freaked out." Hank whispered the last part so Tunney knew that the happy couple could not be far away.

"Okay, man. You need any help getting your boy out to the car?"

"Naw, he can walk that far. I'll help him."

Hank seemed at a loss for what to say next. Tunney helped him.

"Alright. So, I'll see you then."

The friends exchanged the look again. Hank just nodded then turned and left.

Tunney stared at the empty spot where Hammersley had been. He could hear Hank getting Krypto and Jane into their coats and out the door. Krypto was still mumbling, but he was walking at least. Tunney heard the bumps and crashes as Krypto weaved across the porch. A minute later the gravel in the driveway crackled loudly as Hammersley backed out Krypto's truck too fast. Jane followed him slowly out, driving Hammersley's Impala, her stunned eyes staring straight ahead of her.

Tunney stood up. It was time to move on again.

# # #

Chapter 17: Cardboard Hill

Botswana

April 1969

As Tom stepped noiselessly onto the bungalow's verandah he could hear Willa's voice through the screen door and the open window. There was no reason to let anyone know that he was outside. He could not be with anyone yet. He could not see that working.

So he would just listen to Willa's voice. Yet it was not her voice. She was definitely someone else. Then he realized she was reading aloud. Tom knew that Johnny and Dr. Jan would be in the room too. Sometimes Mma Cookie sat in on the readings, working on her sewing and seeming to savor all the words that were read.

...still I like that in him polite to old women like that and waiters and beggars too he's not proud out of nothing but not always...

How many years was it, he was trying to remember. It was so hard for him to focus. Johnny had mentioned it to him about a month ago.

"We've been reading *Ulysses* for almost four years now," Johnny had announced when Tom had shared a meal with him, Dr. Jan and Willa. There had been a mini-rainy season. A week and a half of good rains had brought the grasses back to the veldt and all the babies born had seemed plumper and shinier. And Johnny had started talking about Willa and Molly.

"Willa's old enough now that she can read Molly." Johnny had made the statement in a definitive way as though no one would think otherwise. Tom had noticed that Jan's head had lifted quickly, instantly shifting her attention from the meal to Johnny's eyes and then to Willa's.

"She's a grown woman now, Jan. Willa can read Molly Bloom." Again, it was a statement not something to be discussed.

"Of course Willa can read Molly." Jan's eyes flashed at Johnny and then met Willa's. "Molly has a lot to teach all of us. Willa will know how to read Molly." Jan winked at Willa as she stood up and started clearing the dishes.

"You're bloomin' right she knows how to read Molly!" Johnny slapped his hand on the table, making Tom jump in his seat. Johnny laughed loudly as only the Irish know how and Willa joined in, then Jan, as they both got his play on words.

Tom had sat in on a few of the *Ulysses* readings but mostly felt confused by the language and lack of a story line with any continuity. Johnny had told him to suspend his desire to understand it all and to just meet the flow of the words and let his mind travel along the streets of Dublin, allowing the characters to do the heavy lifting.

That was hard for Tom. He was an engineer. His natural tendency was to sort, categorize, analyze, measure, detect, and translate into movement everything that he experienced. James Joyce was not required reading in engineering programs. *Ulysses* would give scientists a nervous twitch if they tried to pin down the characters and action that rambled through Dublin during Bloom's infamous Day.

So now, weeks after that dinner table conversation, Tom sat on the stoop, his presence unknown, and listened to Willa's Molly float out the open window. His neck muscles suddenly gave way and his chin fell to his chest.

...love it's not or he'd be off his feed thinking of her so either it was one of those night women if it was down there he was really and the hotel story he made up a pack of lies to hide it...

Tom stood up, his chin still to his chest, and walked away from the house. His eyes burned from tears unshed and his gullet burned from the confusion of shame and hate. He could hear Willa's Molly-voice getting louder for a moment and then receding as he moved slowly away from the house.

...not that I care two straws who he does it with or knew before that way though Id like to find out so long as I don't have the two of them under my nose all the time like that slut that Mary...

It was pitch black in Mother Mercy compound. Tom stumbled over stones and bushes as he sought the open veld beyond the clinic borders. If he just kept walking straight the desert's edge would soon meet him. Dangerous animals might catch his scent. Maybe one would kill him or at least maim him. The thought almost comforted Tom. That would be his escape. But escape for a coward.

No, dammit. His father was a coward. He would not be that.

Suddenly Tom's knees collapsed and he hit the hard ground of the Kalahari. He thought he might be choking but it was all the tears. The sobs he finally let come. Rushing out now, tears from the last few days and tears from his past that were never allowed to form or fall from his eyes. He had never let his pain materialize. Until now.

Too much had happened too quickly and the control he always had over his actions and words was forced aside. When did it all start? It could not have been only a few days ago, but it was.

Mma Lilli had a kerosene heater that she used on the chilly fall mornings and in the evenings to warm up her sleeping hut before she went to bed. It was an ancient device that had seen better times and had finally given out. Mma Lilli expected that Tom could fix anything. She had dragged the heater out and set it in front of him early last Saturday as he sat drinking a cup of milky, sweet tea in front of the cook fire.

"Tommiwe, you must fix. I'm too cold to do my chores." Mma Lilli showed Tom her fingers that were stiff from arthritis and the harsh morning cold. Her knobby fingers were gnarled and shook like a thick-legged spider startled by a disturbance in its web.

Mma Lilli was looking at him in that way he dreaded. His manhood was at stake if he did not at least attempt to fix the ancient clunker of a heater.

Tom set to work, testing the heating unit, examining the moving and reactive parts and cleaning out years of neglect that had sealed up the fuel line and mantels. Mma Lilli brought him the container of kerosene and Tom refilled the tank. After an hour of this primping and priming Tom thought the old heater just might work.

“Say a prayer, Mmawe, so that this thing will spark.”

Mma Lilli took him literally and began reciting the Lord’s Prayer in English.

The mantel lit and popping wisps of heat brought a delighted laugh from Mma Lilli.

“Oh, Tommiwe! This is too nice. Too nice. *Ke itumetse*!

Just as Mma Lilli began singing Tom a praise song, the rumbling sound of a lorry began to drown her out. Vehicle noises were cause for curiosity. Tom stood up and saw a powder blue Land Rover round the corner at the kgotla and head towards their compound.

He knew right away that it was the Peace Corps vehicle. He had never seen any other Land Rover in Botswana painted this distinctive blue color. A second later the Peace Corps logo on the Rover’s door became visible.

It was not usually good news when the blue truck came to a volunteer’s village. It could just be the Peace Corps doctor making his routine rounds, Tom thought. Once in a while Doc Jones would venture out of Gaborone and make sure the rural-stationed volunteers were physically and mentally healthy. Tom had not been very good about getting his gamma globulin shots on time. Had he missed two already?

“Shit,” he mumbled under his breath. He hated those shots. His ass hurt for two days last time he was slammed with a GG shot. It had about four times the fluid as any other inoculation. And Doc’s less than gentle method of shooting it all in as fast as he could would break all the blood vessels in Tom’s ass cheek and leave him with a painful, ugly purple bruise the size of a small roast.

Tom moaned involuntarily at the thought and an achy twinge reverberated through his ass.

“Shit.”

“What, Tommi? Peese Corpse?”

“Yah. And they probably want to hurt me.”

Mma Lilli looked worried. Tom laughed.

“Hey, I’m just kidding. Peese Corpse humor.” Tom’s smile reassured Mma Lilli and she clucked at him.

"Humor, humor, Mister humor. Hey, you are not always funny without much explaining."

Tom stared at Mma Lilli quizzically and cocked his head. "*Ga ke ultwa*, Mma Lilli."

"You do understand me, Tommi." Mma Lilli clucked at him and walked to the compound wall as the Land Rover stopped outside of the entry gate.

It was Jim Sachs, the Assistant Peace Corps Director. Tom had met him a few times during training in Molepolole and at his group's swearing in ceremony at the American ambassador's residence in Gaborone. After the ambassador's party was over, Jim Sachs had invited the volunteers who were not quite done celebrating over to his bungalow a few blocks away. Jim needed little excuse to convene a party at his house, all in the name of helping volunteers cope with the deprivation and loneliness of living in Africa.

Being in the company of all those lovely Peace Corps women was likely Jim's strongest incentive for arranging so many ad hoc parties. He knew that he would always start looking attractive to the female most lonely, most liquored and most recently the recipient of a Dear Jane letter from a disloyal boyfriend back in the states. The intended woman would feel special and appreciated as Jim poured on his charm and kept her glass filled. Tom had heard other male volunteers' comments that Jim generally scored, but how they could never figure out. They all considered themselves younger, better looking and better conversationalists than Jim. Damn if he did not have some secret weapon that they knew nothing about.

"Hey, Tom, *Dumela Mme*." Jim walked towards Tom and nodded at Mma Lilli. She greeted him back and noticed that he was not smiling. Tom noticed that too.

"Hey, Jim. How goes it"? Tom reached out to shake Jim's hand.

"Hey, Tom. Good. Well, not so good." Jim seemed extremely uncomfortable, even a bit pale around the edges.

"What's up, man? You want to sit?" Tom gestured toward the stools near the fire.

"No, Tom, no, I'm good." Jim bent his head for a second. "Tom, no easy way to say this. Jeesuz...Tom, your father, he was in an accident. I'm sorry, Tom, he didn't make it. Yesterday. It happened yesterday, no, two days ago, I guess. Jeesuz..." Jim bent his head again then remembered that he should be supporting Tom.

"Hey, Tom. Let me help get you a seat." Jim tried to lead Tom to the seats by the fire but Tom shook him off.

"You mean a car accident or what?" Tom's voice was quiet and tense, but steady. Jim seemed a little surprised for a second. He expected something different.

"Um, it was a car accident."

"Anyone else get hurt."

"Oh, I don't know. I'm not sure. That information was not wired to us. I'm sorry, Tom."

"Drunk driving I presume."

"Jeesuz, Tom, I don't know." Jim seemed at a complete loss. He looked over at Mma Lilli, hoping she might help him out.

"*Wa reng, monna*? What you say to Tommi?"

Jim walked towards Mma Lilli.

"Tom's father was in an accident. He is late now."

A loud moan rose out of Mma Lilli and she ran to Tom.

"Tommiwe, no Tommiwe." Mma Lilli grabbed his hands and brought them up to her eyes.

"Tommiwe, oh, we are sorry, sorry." She let go of his hands and backed towards her hut. Suddenly she started singing a mournful song, the death song. It was necessary to ensure that the dead would go swiftly to heaven with great blessing for those left behind. Without such a song, the dead person's spirit might linger too long on earth and become evil or at the very least, annoying when it haunted its relatives' lives, always stuck between earth and the afterlife.

"Tom, I know this is a shock and that you'll want to go home to be with your family. I'm here to take you back to Gaborone. There's a flight we can get you on tonight if we hurry. You'll be in New York tomorrow night." Jim took a deep breath. Tom was staring straight ahead out towards the fields behind Mma Lilli's compound.

"Let me help you pack a few things, Tom. In fact, you just sit and I'll do it for you." Jim could not figure out what to do with his hands and kept over gesturing as he attempted to talk to Tom. Jim had tried to practice in his head all the way from Gaborone how he would tell Tom about his father. He thought he had it down and then as soon as he saw Tom, the rehearsing failed him and it all came out wrong. Why did he always get these jobs?

"I'm gonna go in your hut now, Tom. I'll just get a few things and we can leave." Jim was backing towards the hut as he spoke, and then turned and moved quickly to the door.

Tom could not hear Jim. The buzz in his ears and the pounding in his chest were too loud. But he could still hear Mma Lilli moan-singing. That would certainly attract other villagers. Within a matter of minutes the compound would be a wailing mess of Batswana.

What was Jim saying? Leaving now? Leaving? For his father?

"No!" Tom shouted loud enough to stop Jim in his tracks and shut down Mma Lilli's requiem. Jim turned and Mma Lilli walked towards him.

"Don't pack anything." Tom's voice seemed almost amplified to Jim.

"I'm just trying to give you a hand, buddy."

"Buddy? I'm not a mental patient, Jim."

"Jeesuz, Tom. I know, man. Hey, this is rough. I've been through it too. Let me help, Tom." Jim was pleading and pitying. Tom felt the heat rising on his face. His tongue felt swollen and heavy.

"I don't need help, Jim. You can go back to Gabs now."

"Go back? Tom..." Jim stopped, exasperated. "Tom, I need to take you with me. You need to go home for a few weeks and be with your mother, your family."

"I'm not going back." Tom turned and began walking towards the rear compound gate.

"What?! Tom..." Jim threw his hands up and looked at Mma Lilli, as though she could explain Tom's behavior.

Jim started after Tom, yelling behind him. "Tom, this is a

shock. I know how you feel. Hey, slow down, man. You've got to slow down." Mma Lilli began following behind Jim, the caboose on his pity train.

Tom started up the kopje behind their compound. But he stopped abruptly and turned around. Jim stopped suddenly too, not giving Mma Lilli enough notice to stop. She plowed into Jim's back, her girth knocking him to his knees.

A yell of shock and pain erupted as Jim's bony knees connected with the hard, rocky soil.

"Ooh-we, *ga o itse Modimo*, so sorry, *ntshwarele*, excuse myself, Rra!" Mma Lilli made an ungraceful attempt to lift Jim up from under his arms. Suddenly Tom was there and Mma Lilli backed off to give him room. He lifted Jim up easily as though he were a child.

Jim was breathing hard, his gasps punctuated by groans and curse words. The dusty patches on his knees made him look like a little boy who had been pushed down in the schoolyard by bullies. Tom held on to Jim as he regained his balance.

"You okay, man?"

Jim stopped brushing the dust from his pant legs.

"No, I'm not okay." He stood up straight and put a hand on his hips. "I was told to bring you back to Gabs and you're walking away from me. Tom, help me here. I'm at a loss, quite frankly."

"That makes two of us, Jim."

"Jeesuz, this is..." Jim stopped. "Please Tom. It'll be okay once you get home. You gotta go home, Tom."

"Jim, I don't gotta." Tom looked down at the ancient path where they stood. So many feet and hooves had worn away at it. Now his joined theirs.

"Help me here, Tom. What am I supposed to tell Director Beatty? What about your mother, Tom?"

"My mother will be fine now, Jim. It's over."

"I bet she needs you, Tom."

"No."

"You're so far away, how do you know?"

"I know my mother."

"Have you known her through something like this, Tom?"

Tom looked up from the ground.

"About five times a week."

"Five times a week?"

"The frequency of his knuckles meeting my mother's face or mine. You could almost set your clock to it."

Jim opened his mouth but closed it again. He could see in Tom's eyes that he would not be going back to the states.

"I need to be here, Jim. I don't mean to be rude. Thanks for driving up."

Mma Lilli put her hands gently on Tom's shoulders. "Tommiwe, was your father a bad man?"

"Eh, Mmewe."

Mma Lilli looked at Jim. "Tommi stays here. He's not being rude. You can't chase evil. It needs to leave on its own, Rra," Mma Lilli held out her hand to Jim. He took it and seemed grateful.

Tom's eyes met Mma Lilli's. "*Ke itumetse, Mma Lilli. Ke thla tsamaya, janong.*" *I will walk now, yes, walk now.*

"*Tsamaya sentle, Tommiwe.* Go well. The fish eagle will mind your walking and lead you back."

"Thank you. *Ke itumetse.*"

As Tom turned to walk up the kopje, Mma Lilli led Jim back to the compound. She held on to his hand and talked quietly in Setswana. Jim could not understand much Setswana, but his mind was elsewhere already. Trying to explain why he came back alone to Peace Corps Director Beatty was his next challenge. Beatty would have to call Tom's mother. Jim moaned again. Mma Lilli looked up at him.

"You are lucky, Rra Peese Corpse. Only your knees hurt. Hey, but Tommiwe. His heart hurts too much. I can see his father was a bad man. That is a shadow on his face. Now I know the shadow. Hey, my Tommi." Mma Lilli clucked sadly.

Jim mumbled a goodbye and headed to his truck. The six-hour drive was long enough to come up with his speech for Director Beatty.

But maybe he would just stay over in Francistown and face the drive tomorrow. Jim weighed that for ten seconds. All he had to do was radio the Gabs office from the Francistown Police station that there was a delay. Didn't the Tati Hotel have a pretty good steak? And waiters who wore white jackets? The jackets did show their age close up. Likely remnants of the heyday of the British Protectorate era, not so long past and still a habit not yet extinct.

Jim turned the truck around and gave a quick toot on the horn. Mma Lilli raised her hand. Francistown it would be, Jim had decided. A radio, a steak, a few nips of Jameson and face tomorrow, tomorrow.

"Damn." Jim shook his head as he turned past the kgotla. " I don't get that kid," he said aloud. But only forty minutes to town, and the steak.

# # #

There had been no awareness of time all day. Not since Tom had learned about his father. The world had moved away from him as the death words had formed on Jim's lips. It was just like a camera shot in a Hitchcock film where the present quickly recedes into the distance and the seer can no longer touch it.

Walking became the only thing he could do then. He had to move, keep moving so it would not start. No direction was consciously chosen. He just walked.

By mid-afternoon Tom was passing through the cattle posts area. Herd boys offered him water and he drank it. They could see he needed it. That was Tom's fuel. And the distance ahead and the past that was refusing to leave him alone, threatening to move into his present.

Tom saw his mother's head hitting the floor, his fingers touching the blood, his mother's empty eyes. She was exhausted by her own pain, drained of hope.

Then he saw his father's head hitting the windshield. Glass breaking out from the circle of impact, shards shredding his eyes, filling his nostrils. Metal crushing his legs, piercing his left side. Opening his father up, exposing him, cutting him. Ridding him of his twisted mind, of his last breath. A fist flies out of the shattered window, hits a tree trunk and fractures apart.

His mind played the scene over and over again. Tom had

always imagined how sweet revenge would taste when his father finally got his due.

But it was not sweet. It only felt empty. Sick.

When his father beat him and his mother, Tom made himself feel empty to survive. It was allowing any emotion to surface that made everything hurt so bad. She would not leave. Tom could not stay.

The batterer was gone. It would feel good to him soon.

Every step was emptiness. The vacant fullness of the veldt matched Tom's steps and helped blur the visions running through his mind. He understood that a new certainty had emerged.

He had been so unprepared for it. Tom had assumed that he would not see his mother for many years. Now he could see her again. Just not right now.

Tom could feel no grief. If his mother did, that was something he could not see. That could only bring an ugly anger, igniting the resentment that Tom had trained himself to stifle. His mother's weakness was unbearable for them both. "I can't see that," Tom said out loud to no one.

Tom knew that his mother would understand why he did not come home. They had shared a million unspoken conversations when their eyes had met in the bathroom mirror as one was cleaning up the other after a beating. His father always left the scene of the crime. That gave Tom and his mother a chance to clean up the blood, ice the welts, butterfly the cuts, pick up the furniture, sweep up broken dishes, hide the gun, bury the bullets in the back yard. Act like it did not happen and it would not be repeated as quickly. It was their covenant.

Suddenly the sounds of a struggle made Tom stop. A young rock rabbit raced out of a bush followed in close pursuit by a Cape Fox, jaws snapping and closing in fast. Just as suddenly Tom's anger flared up and exploded like a leopard jumping its prey, a heat rash of resentment and hatred.

"Why? Goddammit. Why?" Tom shouted out across the veldt. His feet stomped down on the sandy earth. Exasperation pounded a barrel drum in his chest.

"You mother fucker! Fuck you!" Tom spit on the ground. "I'm

not giving you the pleasure of seeing me cry, you useless asshole! Rot in hell, forever!"

Tom spit again. His dry eyes would not yield moisture for his father's violent time on earth. "Never for you, you dead fuck. Never waste another damn thought on you."

In the late afternoon Tom found a lorry track and began following it. Was this the western road to his village? Or was it the road to Maun? He could not place it. He could not find the context.

He did not care.

He was a little boy again. The big hill behind their plain, gray shingle house seemed to undulate in the wind as the flaxen grasses blew back and forth. His mother had taught him how to wax a large piece of cardboard with a paraffin bar and use it as a grass sled.

Tom felt pure joy his first trip down the hill. It was not cardboard he was riding on but a magic carpet. It was not his mother but a fairy queen who taught him tricks and whispered secrets to him.

Airy, swishing sounds surrounded Tom's magic carpet. Bumps caused by rocks became wind gusts in the clouds. His mother laughed with glee at the bottom of the hill and shouted, "Whee, Tommy!" again and again and kept standing up on her tiptoes as she clapped her hands.

Tom laughed too until his cardboard sled finally came to a stop at the base of the hill.

"Isn't it fun, Tommy? You were flying!" His mother stood with the sunlight behind her, framing her against the house. She really is a fairy queen, Tom thought for a second.

Then they both felt it at once.

He was watching. Waiting to pounce.

Tom's eyes met his mother's.

"Run up again Tommy. Hurry, run up again."

Tom hesitated.

"Go on, go on." Her voice sounded more urgent.

He picked up the paraffin bar and his cardboard sled and turned towards the path leading back up the hill.

A crash and the sound of breaking glass stopped him. Tom looked towards the kitchen window and could see his father in the house.

His mother stood very still, waiting like a little frozen bird on a fencepost in the winter. Not long now. The yelling, the fist, the crying, the I'm sorrys, the pain. It would all start, take its choreographed course, and then stop until the next time.

Tom quickened his pace. He was scared for his mother, but he was more scared for himself. His second grade teacher had already asked him about a bruise on his cheek, and the bandage on his head from where he hit the edge of the shower door when his father came after him in the bathroom. But to everyone else, they were caused by bike riding accidents that he could recount in whatever level of imaginative detail was required to be convincing.

His teacher had not seemed convinced and had sent a note home to his parents a few months before. Tom's father learned quickly. He started hitting him only in areas that were covered by clothes. But when his father was too drunk to remember the rule, Tom would work out a new reason for the visible injury on the way to school.

He got quite good at lying and almost convinced himself a few times that the bruises and cuts were from slipping when he cut wood, a fall in the creek bed, a tumble out of a tree, a cut while whittling. Tom created a collection of excuses for his welts and bruises.

When he got to the top of the hill, Tom looked down at the house. The yard was empty. The house was full of hate and violence. It would come crashing in on his mother now.

Suddenly, little Tommy felt so tired. He put the paraffin aside on a rock and sat down, the cardboard sled at his side.

He began untying his shoes. In his little boy's mind it was his only defense against his own cowardice. He could not run that far without shoes. He could not run at all. His mother needed him.

Little Tom took a deep breath and grabbed the paraffin wax and his cardboard sled. Holding the sled up against his leg, he waxed the bottom of it until the cardboard became shiny and milky white. This time Tom would not stop at the base of the hillock. This time he would keep on sailing, across the yard and in the back door, knocking his father's feet out from under him. His mother, smiling in gratitude would hug Tommy and take him out for ice cream.

Jumping on to the cardboard, Tom's head jerked backwards when it shot forward, jolting him backward and then forward. He could not believe the sled's quickness this time. Giving it the extra wax seemed to have doubled its speed.

Leaning to the left, Tom tried to adjust his landing point so that he would sail through the screen door. He bit his lip and wiggled back and forth until he was almost directly aligned with it.

When Tom hit the base of the hill the jolt knocked the wind out of him. The cardboard slid only another few feet. The screen door might as well have been a mile away. A cry of disappointment escaped Tom's throat. Now how would he save his mother?

A few days before a police officer had come to the school to tell the second graders all of the duties of his job. Tom remembered Officer Friendly telling him that he helped people who were in trouble or in danger. Certainly Tom's mother qualified as in danger.

It was only eight blocks to the police station. Tom knew exactly where it was because he rode his bike past it almost every day. It had always looked like a scary place until Officer Friendly had taught him that it was a safe place.

Tom jumped up and ran around the side of the house. He could hear his father yelling and knew he was hitting his mother. Her whimpering was softer but he heard it too. He always did.

As soon as Tom's feet hit the sidewalk, he remembered that he had taken his shoes off. That could not matter, though. As if to prove it, Tom pushed himself to run even faster. He did not ever remember covering all those blocks. Only the police officer who took him by the hand into a room once he got to the station.

"Officer Friendly said you could help people in danger. Please go and help my mom." Tom had seemed so old to the policeman when he said this. It was not a tone or sentiment that seven-year-olds usually possess.

"I'm Officer Joe. We'll try and help your mom, Tommy."

Tom gave the Officer his address when asked, and then just said, “My father.”

“Oh, you’re the O’Conner kid. Stay here. I’ll be right back.” The Officer got up quickly and left the room. Tom could see through the glass in the door that he was talking to another policeman who then left the building.

Suddenly Tom was scared. What would they do to his father when they got there? What would Tom’s father do to his mother and him after the policeman left?

“Wait!” Tom shouted as he jumped off the table he had been sitting on. He opened the door, his eyes searching for Officer Joe.

“Officer Joe!” Tom shouted across the station room. Every eye turned towards him. A man passed out on the bench scowled through his stupor.

Officer Joe came running in through a side door, a coke and a donut balanced precariously in one hand.

“Hey there, Tommy.” Officer Joe set the snacks down and knelt in front of the boy. “It’s okay, Buddy. You did the right thing coming here.” The policeman had seen this reaction before in young children who had turned in their parents for abuse. *Too bad innocent kids like this had to bear the brunt of a sicko father*, the officer thought.

“No. Don’t go over there.” Tom’s eyes brimmed over with tears.

“Hey, Tommy. You love your mom, right? Yah, so you are trying to protect her aren’t you, huh?”

Tom nodded his bent head, his tears falling onto the floor and hitting his now ragged socks.

“Oh, Tommy, guess what I found? Coke, donut and, tah dah, a genuine pair of police socks!” Office Joe had pulled the socks out of a pocket on the side of his trouser leg. Tom looked up.

“That’s a neat pocket in your leg.”

“I keep a lot of interesting things in this pocket.” Tom’s eyes went big as Joe described the odd things that had made their way into his pocket. As he recited a list of fictional and actual items, Joe peeled off what was left of Tom’s ragged socks, now just a few threads covering the bottoms. He quickly slipped on the new socks, rolling up the tops so that they would stay on his little feet.

"Can I go see my mom, now?"

"You eat that donut and drink the coke, and then I bet we'll be ready to go."

Tom went at the donut with relish. He had never had one like this before. It had chocolate on the top and was filled with sweet, yellowy custard. Remembering the coke, he took a big swig and hiccupped. Officer Joe laughed.

"You sit tight here for a few minutes, Buddy, and finish your donut. I'll be back in just a minute." Officer Joe rustled Tommy's hair and made the sad boy smile a little.

Tom raised his head and stared across the Kalahari veldt. The memory of Officer Joe rustling his hair made him smile a little again, just like it had twenty years before.

He had saved his mother's life that night. The policeman had found her unconscious. Tom's father had left minutes before. His last push before he left through the front door had knocked his wife against the brick fireplace.

Tom's mother stayed in the hospital for two weeks. He went to live with his aunt then. Every few days his aunt would take Tom to visit his mother. She looked frail and so tired, Tom thought, like she had walked across the whole United States with an uncomfortable pair of shoes. Tom's father did not resurface for a few months. When he did, they put him in jail for almost a year.

It had been so peaceful during that time. Tom's mother began smiling again and they had picnics on the beach and trail walks in the pine forest that edged part of the town. She started spending more time making her hair look nice. And she did not look tired any more.

So why did she let him come back?

Tom could not answer that then and he still could not. Her betrayal still stung. Why had she chosen his father and not him? A brute versus a little boy? Whimpers and scars, or picnics and laughter?

The dusk was starting to wrap itself around the bush. Kopjes in the distance were only outlines against the muddy orange sky. Smoke from the suppertime cooking fires laid a musky haze across the lorry track. Tom knew now that he was on the northern road into his village. Red Hill was directly in front of him. On the other side of it was the kgotla where only a few weeks before Willa had received her praise party from the chief.

Willa. She had not even been able to enter his thoughts. She seemed very far away now. It was another world and another time that Willa lived in. Could he go back to her world? Was he just kidding himself? Running away to Africa to escape his past and playing carefree Peace Corps boy.

Tom felt like a fraud. He did not belong here. The disingenuous should not be allowed. Africa was too sweet for that. Too proud and too genuine for someone like him.

He had taken advantage of Willa. He could see that now. She was so young, only nineteen. The way Willa looked at him like he could do no wrong had turned him into a fool. Willa had made him imagine for a few months that unconditional love could exist. She loved him. Tom had loved being with her. It had made him forget that he was damaged goods, poisoned by his father's hate and resentful of his mother's inability to leave, to protect them.

It was completely dark in Mma Lilli's compound when Tom passed through the gate. Usually there was candle or kerosene lamplight shining out of Mma Lilli's rondovel windows and in the cracks between the thatch roof and the mud walls.

Tom went to his rondovel and pushed open the door. He felt around for the matchbox and lit the kerosene lamp on the small table. Then he saw the note and the food.

I go to Francistown. Mma Lilli

She had left Tom something to eat in an enamel bowl with a plate cover. Lifting the lid his stomach growled as the smell of stringy beef, gravy and bogobe hit his nose. The bowl was still warm, so Mma Lilli must have left on the late afternoon bus into town.

Tom practically gulped down the food. All that walking and no food all day finally hit his appetite head on. Mma Lilli was so sweet to have left it for him. He would have to remember her favorite Cadbury bar next time he went to Gaborone or Bulawayo.

All he wanted now was respite. If Tom fell asleep, maybe when he woke up it would be like it was before his father invaded his life again.

Tom reached up into the rafters of his hut and felt around for his wallet. He needed some beer. White-man beer, not Chibuku. There was probably a *mosimane*, a small boy, nearby who would run for the beer for a very modest reward of a few *thebe* coins.

He could hear *basimane* voices in the distance. Tom stood outside his rondovel and shouted at the boys. They were used to running errands for Rra Peese Corpse and giggled and yelled at each other as they raced towards Tom.

Twenty minutes later they were back with ten white-man's beers. Each boy carried two. They all smiled wide at Tom, anticipating a reward of a few *thebe* for their fetching of beer from the shebeen. Instead, Tom counted out five, one-pula notes and gave one to each boy. They gasped in unison and looked at one another in disbelief.

"*Ke itumetse, Rra Peese Corpse*!"

"*Ke itumetse, basimane. Go siame.*" Tom put the beers in his hut on the small table as the boys ran off, chattering with excitement and sharing spending plans for their newfound wealth.

The snap of the tin as Tom cut into it with the opener sounded loud but welcoming. Wandering through the desert was hot work. Tom wondered whether ten cans of beer would be enough.

He was so thirsty that the first three disappeared within a few minutes. Then he slowed his pace. Reaching for his stash, Tom pulled out a joint that he had only taken a few hits off. A smoky perfume filled his head. Another tinny snap. A fresh beer enhanced the taste of the musky smoke. But now he needed *Love* too.

Glad that he had bought fresh batteries that week, Tom put *Love* on his turntable and sat back on his bed.

"Arthur Lee, where are you? What bad things happened in your life for you to produce this poetry for the damaged?"

Hadn't the witchdoctor seen it? *Yes, he had seen right through me.* The Dingaka was an expert at identifying damaged goods masquerading as normal people. Wonder why he didn't warn Willa? Maybe he had and she just refused to listen. Now he would have to be the one to push her away. It would be better to do it sooner rather than a few months down the road.

Most of the women he had known were prone to making serious long term plans after three months of continuous dating had passed. Tom was no fool. He knew that Willa loved him. She could hide nothing on that beautiful face of hers. Every emotion shone through bright and clear and willing, strangely both innocent and knowing.

It was funny how he had convinced himself that he loved Willa. When had he turned that corner? But it was natural to fall for Willa, he countered himself. There was no pretense about her. No airs about her, as his mother would say.

Yet she had done so much. She was already so much of a woman. A nurse, a medic who had literally saved lives and limbs. An African in a white girl's body, Willa could cross back and forth between the two cultures and languages. In fact, Tom thought, she actually seemed more comfortable and animated when speaking Setswana with her Batswana friends than she did conversing with her mother or Johnny, or him, for that matter.

Yes, often she was quiet with him too. She seemed to be studying him. Willa would listen so intently to him when he talked as though she were deciphering meaning beyond the words. Willa was trying to see what Tom saw in his head when he spoke about his hometown or the California beaches or a book he had just read. It was the way that she meandered her way into his soul, into understanding what he loved and why he loved it. That was what caring about someone must be like, Tom guessed. That was what being close meant.

But that was not possible now. Tom did not want Willa to have to feel any part of his anger. She would recoil anyway at a certain point when she realized that Tom could never love a hundred percent like she could. Love never works when there is an imbalance like that, he knew. Willa deserved better. Tom would live with less because he could only give less.

That did not mean he could forget her easily. Her sweet smell alone lingered for days after she would stay with him in his hut. Tom loved her hair, loved taking the pins out of her chignon after she returned from a shift as ward nurse. Her long brown hair would be set free, wavy and still slightly damp from her morning shower, smelling of fresh air and lemons.

For months Tom had known that Willa would be going to the states in June. It had seemingly been arranged for years, that Willa would do her pre-med at Harvard. June had seemed so far away when she first told him. And at the time Tom was not thinking about Willa at some point in the future. Futures were uncertain. Most of the time Tom preferred to live in the present.

Willa was beautifully present to him. And so far she had not pressed him on what the future held for them. For all her innocence, Willa was also a realist. She might love Tom, but that would not stop her from leaving in June to go to the states, go to her future in medicine.

Now Willa would be free too, Tom thought. I'll cut her loose and she'll go free into her Harvard future, and a new life with the father she barely knows, yet loves as though she had spent every day with him, not a few weeks years before. It would be a crime for her to go to the states in love with Tom when he could never give her his whole heart. He simply did not have one. His had been cut so deep that it could not heal.

Tom choked back a sob that he would not let out. "Damn it," he shouted to no one. He had almost made it out. Willa had opened a door for him and he almost made it through. "I felt it, I did." His voice sounded weak even to him. *Pathetic.*

There was his father's face, taunting him. "Yes, fuck you again, you broken fuck." Tom relit the joint.

He missed Willa.

Couldn't she be here with him now and then he could feel it again? She loved him and that felt good. She deserved his love. But his love was not healthy. His love shut down unexpectedly. His love hedged its bet. His love was a half-stepper. His love was a fucking joke.

So tired now. Need to sleep.

A list rattled itself off in his head. Love is a trip to the hospital. Love is tattered socks. Love is hiding the bruises. Love is taking *Him* back and never going on a picnic again.

In his dream his high school math teacher was knocking on

his hut door. She had come to tell Tom that his father was dead. Mrs. Oakley. Her ass shook when she erased problems off the board. Mrs. Oakley had come all the way from Cape Cod to tell him that his father was dead. He had better answer the door. She would not stop calling his name.

"Tom, Tom are you there?" It was not Mrs. Oakley.

"Tom?"

"Yah. I'm here. Hold on."

Tom slowly raised himself off the bed. His alarm clock showed that he had only slept an hour. He was still in the same damn day.

"It's me, Tom. Jill."

"Jill?"

"Yah, Jill." Tom heard her laugh a little. He opened the door.

"Hey stranger? How are you?" Jill walked forward and hugged Tom hard. He felt her breasts against his chest.

"Hey, Jill. Shit, I'm sorry. I dozed off and..." Tom looked around behind him as though the rondovel would finish his sentence for him. "Let me light the lantern. Hold on a sec."

In a moment the hut was filled with orange light.

"There. Sorry you didn't get the red carpet welcome. I don't get a lot of guests, as you can see."

"I'm just so glad you were here, Tom. I came up here on a fluke. I'm on teacher's holiday for a few weeks so I thought I'd hitchhike the country or at least as far as I can in two weeks. I've spent all day in the back of a very slow lorry from Gaborone. I don't know what I would have done if you weren't here."

Jill paused for a second and Tom watched her look around the rondovel. It reminded him of his mother inspecting his bedroom after he had been told to clean it up.

"Well, this is sort of it. Hut sweet hut."

"It's fine, Tom. You've made it real cozy."

"I was told by a realtor that cozy is a nice way of saying small and cramped." They both laughed.

"How about a warm beer or some cold tea?"

"Water would be good." Jill sat down on the rickety chair next to Tom's bed that he used at night for his windup alarm clock and reading lantern.

"Cool water coming up." Tom opened the top on his water storage jug. He loved the sound of empty becoming full as it ran into the enamel mug.

"So what's going on up here, Tom? Nobody ever hears from you. You never come down to Gabs. Are you going native, or what?" Jill laughed. It sounded forced and a little nervous. For Peace Corps women, the definition of a white guy going native was sleeping with Batswana girls.

The content and tone of Jill's words were a big part of the reason Tom did not go to Gabs. He would not and could not answer to anyone right now. So he was at the decision point: be an asshole and say nothing, just walk away; or act like a good Christian boy and keep his mouth shut. For his mother, he would do the latter.

"I guess I've just been busy. When you drill boreholes and fix water pumps in the desert there's never a dull moment, and you have pretty good job security." Tom reached for one of the now warm beers and cut into the top with the opener. Thick foam bubbled through the silver triangle.

"Is that as warm as it looks?"

"Eh, Mma."

"Would you be interested in something that is palatable when warm?" Jill looked at Tom conspiratorially.

"What do you have in mind, madam?"

Jill began searching through her knapsack and finally pulled out a bottle in a paper bag.

"I won it in a tennis tournament at the Club in Gabs. It's pretty good scotch, I'm told." Jill handed it to Tom.

It was a bottle of Dewars.

"This will do." Tom cracked open the bottle and smelled its contents.

"Holy mackerel, does that smell strong. Strong and sweet." Tom reached for his only two real glasses and poured a draught in each.

"Here's to spontaneous hitchhiking." Tom raised his glass and knocked back the scotch. Jill laughed at his raised eyebrows.

"Now I know what it takes to get a rise out of you!" Jill clinked her glass against Tom's and tossed back her scotch portion.

"Whew! That just erased eight hours in the back of a lorry!"

Tom refilled their glasses.

"Then here's to the next eight hours. May they surpass the first." Tom looked directly into Jill's eyes and then tossed back the next shot. This time his eyebrows did not raise up. Jill noticed that.

"You are one cool cucumber, Tom O'Conner." Jill took her second shot and shivered a little as it hit her.

Tom sat on the bed and patted the space next to him.

"You'd be wise to sit somewhere with a soft landing at the rate we're going."

"That's a new line I've not heard before to get me into bed." Jill smiled seductively. Tom grabbed her wrist and pulled her to him. His lips burned slightly from the scotch when he pressed them against Jill's mouth. The scotch made his lips feel more powerful, like he could make love with his lips.

Jill gave no resistance. She had waited months for this. Tom's lips were even more delicious than she had remembered from their time together in training. Maybe this time she would have more success at making herself memorable to Tom.

# # #

A rooster crowed in the night, probably confused by the full moon. Tom sat up and reached for his watch. It was three thirty-five.

He could feel the heat of another person in his bed. That it was not Willa made him suddenly sick. Swallowing back the bile in his throat, Tom moved his foot along the floor until he found his thongs. He was careful not to wake up Jill. *If he could just be clear again.*

The bright night pulled him towards his favorite hill. In a moment Mma Lilli's compound disappeared as Tom rounded the small kopje. Taking a deep breath he fully realized the variety of intoxicants he had imbibed in the last ten hours. His lungs felt tight and his gut gurgled and burned. It was something to pay attention to, he thought. Tom was fighting to pay attention to the mundane but kept getting pulled back to the places he did not want to see, could not see. How long could he push it away? As long as he could walk away, Tom guessed. *Tsamaya sentle.* Go well.

# # #

Mma Lilli had chattered away the whole trip back to her village, but Willa sensed that she was very worried about Tom.

Willa had not been surprised when Mma Lilli related the news that Tom's father had died and that he was not returning to America. On a few different occasions Tom had told her about the periods of abuse that he and his mother had endured at the hands of his father. Willa never pushed Tom to tell more. He struggled with the telling of it so he obviously struggled with it in his heart. That was what the Dingaka had told her the night she met Tom. Such advice was wise to follow, especially given her relative inexperience with men.

Willa had always just ignored Jan when she ranted and raved against the Dingaka. Mma Cookie had shown Willa that the Dingaka did know things about people that they did not even know about themselves. It was the Dingaka's job to warn people of their own foibles and those forced upon them by man, nature and circumstance.

Mma Cookie made it a practice to visit the Dingaka a few times a year just to check up on her spiritual and physical health. She always brought Willa with her on those visits. Willa was a child of two worlds, white and African, so Mma Cookie felt she needed to know about the power and the systems in each world so that she would not stumble. Mma Cookie spent much more time with Willa than Jan did as the little girl grew up. The African mother felt it her responsibility to school Willa's African side thoroughly. It was a job she took seriously. Willa was her white daughter.

Willa was surprised that Tom had not at least come to the clinic compound to tell her. Weren't they close enough at this point to share that serious of news?

A little ripple of fear rushed up from Willa's stomach. There was that darkness that showed up in Tom, behind his eyes or in the tone of his voice for a moment. A darkness that she had purposely slipped quickly past and ignored whenever it arose. A darkness that was only dormant, Willa realized, and now it had pushed its way out.

Just wait and see, Willa admonished herself. *Let stories reveal themselves.*

"Oh, someone is at my house," Mma Lilli said as she leaned her head out the window for clearer look. "It's a white girl with white hair too."

"Blond hair, Mma Cookie."

"Blond, *go siame*, okay. What is she doing here?"

Willa pulled the lorry onto the gravel spot behind Tom's rondovel.

As Mma Lilli got out of the lorry, the white girl came around the hut and greeted her.

"*Dumela, Mma.*"

"*Dumela, Mma. O tsogile, mosetsana*?"

"*Ke tsogile, Mma. Leina lame ke Jill. Ke Peace Corps.*"

"Oh, you friend of Tommi's," Mma Lilli spoke in English, so that she would not have to listen to Jill-white-girl's poor pronunciation of Setswana any more.

"Yes, yes I am." She seemed very relieved to speak English, as though she had expended her whole vocabulary. "He was kind enough to let me stay here last night. I got here late and luckily Tom was here."

Willa walked around the lorry.

"Hi, I'm Willa Dodge. I work at the health clinic."

"Hi, Jill Stockman. I live in Gabs but am on holiday. Just sort of traveling around."

Willa heard Mma Lilli calling Tom's name.

"Oh, Tom's not here, I guess. I haven't seen him all morning."

"Do you know where he went?" Willa's voice sounded small even to herself.

"No, I don't. I've been up for two hours and no sign of him. I was just thinking about walking out to the road and hitching into

Francistown."

Willa could hear an annoyance in Jill's voice, like Tom should have been there with her all morning.

"Is he okay? I mean with the news about his father and all..." Willa stopped when she read the confusion on Jill's face.

"What news?" Jill looked at Willa suspiciously.

"Tom's father died a few days ago."

"What?!" Jill's mouth fell open. "You're kidding? I can't believe he wouldn't tell me something like that." Jill paced back and forth with her hands on her hips. "I don't get this guy. Wouldn't you tell a friend that type of information?" Jill made a tisking noise that Willa found mean and annoying. She was glad that Tom hadn't told her. She must not have been that great of a friend.

Mma Lilli came out of her cooking hut and stood next to Willa.

"Tommiwe was too troubled when I saw him last. He had gone to *tsamaya*, just walking into the bush. He has gone again, I think."

Mma Lilli looked at Jill. She was pretty by lekgoa standards but too skinny. And the yellow hair! Ugh! Mma Lilli wondered where she had slept. She hoped Willa had not thought of that.

"Jill Peese Corpse, many lorries go to Francistown from the main road up there. And a bus leaves at ten o'clock too from the kgotla, that side." Mma Lilli pointed eastward.

Willa could tell that Mma Lilli was trying to get rid of Jill, who was looking even more annoyed than when they had arrived. It was a look that said, 'I've been stood up and Tom wasn't straight with me.'

"Okay, I'm going to head out." Mma Lilli and Willa both nodded at her. "If you see Tom..." she hesitated. "Oh, forget it. Thanks." Jill slipped a backpack over her shoulder and started towards the road. Suddenly she turned around, belatedly remembering her manners.

"It was nice meeting you. *Sala sentle.*"

"*Tsamaya sentle, mosetsana.*" Mma Lilli turned and waved. When she turned back, Willa was going into Tom's hut.

"Willawe, Tommi's not here. Come and take some tea with me now!"

But Willa was already inside. The hut looked the same as it always did, except the bed was made. Tom never made the bed. Mma Lilli had spoiled Tom, he admitted, and went into his hut every day and made it for him, also sweeping his floors and picking up his clothes. But Mma Lilli had not been there. She had been in Francistown.

"Come outside for tea, my daughter, it's getting cold."

Then she saw the note on Tom's table on a torn out page of a journal. It was not folded up, just flat on the table for anyone to read.

Tom – thanks I guess. Wasn't sure where you'd gone and never heard you leave. I'm heading into Francistown for a few days to see Jules and Mark. Come in to town too if you can. –Jill. PS, are you always running away from me, or am I just paranoid?

The words on the page began to blur. Willa's ears buzzed and burned hot. She could hear her heart pounding loudly in her ears like an army of drummers.

"Willa!" Mma Lilli walked into the hut and saw Willa's face. The old woman's heart sank. *She knew.*

"Come, my child." Taking Willa's hand Mma Lilli led her out to the courtyard and sat her on a stool. A minute later she handed her a hot cup of milky sweet tea.

Mma Lilli could see that she needed to talk to Willa. She spoke in Setswana.

"*Willawe, my daughter. Please, you must look at me, child.*"

Willa looked up and met Mma Lilli's eyes. The old woman smiled and took Willa's hands in hers.

"*Do you remember when I met you, huh? You treated my feet so nicely and got me the right medicine that I needed. You are really a fine young woman, Willawe. And Tommi is a good man, like a son to me. He does so many nice things for me, like fixing my water pipe and buying me meat all the time. No men do crazy things in my yard any more now that Tommi is here. No way. Tommi understands respect. Um. Yes.*

"That is why I came for you, Willa. Tommi was not himself after he heard about his father. He went dark." Mma Lilli saw a tear roll down Willa's cheek. *"Tommi's father was a very bad man and his poison is haunting Tommi. We need to help him."*

Willa squeezed her eyes shut. Three more tears fell into the dust, little puffs of sadness marking last moments. She stood up and wiped the tears off her face.

"How can I help him? I don't know him anymore."

"Yes, Willa, you know him. We both know him. He needs us, Willa. We cannot turn on him when he's in this dark time. He is not there now. We need to help find him." Suddenly Mma Lilli stood up.

"Let us go see the Dingaka. Tommi needs more help than we can provide."

"The Dingaka? How can he help Tommi? Tom is a lekgoa."

"Dingaka can free Tommi of the darkness. I know that for certain."

Willa looked in Mma Lilli's determined eyes. The old woman had seen Tommi in this state, she had not. *Give the story time to reveal itself.* The pain of betrayal made Willa want to push Tom away, not help him. *But he is sick. He is in the darkness. And I love him.*

"Let's go see the Dingaka." Willa headed for the lorry.

"Wait. We must bring something of Tommi's. His hat!"

Mma Lilli grabbed Tom's baseball cap from the hook on the back of his door. The hat was perfect. It had carried all his thoughts since before he left America, Mma Lilli realized.

She walked quickly to the lorry and closed the door, putting the hat on her lap.

"Willa. Let me tell you this, my daughter. Us women sometimes must take over life actions to bring good things back. Let the Dingaka aid us now. It is needed because of the darkness that has stolen Tommi. But know this so well, yes, it is women who bring back the smooth times. It is just how it is that we have to be the strong ones when darkness takes one of our mens." Mma Lilli smiled at Willa and touched her cheek. "But it is not an easy duty, my daughter."

Willa clucked her tongue in affirmation. She glanced in the rearview mirror, hoping for just a second that Tom might suddenly appear and the world would be as it was before the death. But it was only the village she saw growing smaller behind them.

# # #

Chapter 18: Hills and Windows

Haight Ashbury, San Francisco
April 1969

Windows could surely be considered friends. At least the window in Nora and Tunney's flat seemed to have earned that status. Looking down to the sidewalk from her perch in the window seat, Nora watched all the neighborhood characters walk by. She guessed at their stories and their lives. It usually stopped the loneliness from settling too deep in her bones.

Tunney would be back from work soon, fresh with new tales of the Haight's finest and most unusual inhabitants. Nora smiled. Leave it to Tunney to get a job the day they arrived in San Francisco. That was ten days ago and he had already cashed his first paycheck.

Everything hit Nora's senses hard on that first day. The Haight was a bomb burst of freedom and color and smells. Everyone dressed and talked and grooved however they wanted, with nothing considered too wrong or too strange. A no-judging policy permeated the district, allowing for experiments in living that were felonies in other neighborhoods.

It had been a long day of driving when Nora and Tunney yelped together, their goal finally met: they were in San Francisco! The loudness and length of Tunney's stomach growls had them looking for cheap takeout food in an area that seemed mostly occupied by clothing shops and hippy haberdashery selling everything from gauze Indian shirts to piñatas. Suddenly Nora spotted a sign in the window of a small unisex boutique.

"Tunney, look. HELP WANTED. Hey, they sell the same stuff that Max does." Nora smiled as she said Max's name. She missed his wise and always direct counsel.

"I'll flip you for it." Tunney reached in his pocket for a coin.

"Oh, no, Tunney. This is going to be your town for a while. I don't know what I'm doing yet. No, you take the job."

There was no doubt in either of their minds that whoever

walked in the door just then would have a job when they walked out. Tunney and Nora both knew that the other was a shoe-in for the job, if either wanted it.

"You sure?" Tunney looked Nora in the eyes to make sure she was not just being polite.

"Yes, I'm sure. Maybe Max's west coast cousin runs it. You'll own the place by next week!"

Tunney laughed. "Then wish me luck."

"Luck!"

"Thanks, kid." Tunney smiled his winning best, a prep for his spontaneous job interview.

"I'll meet you here in 15 minutes. I'm going to find us something to eat."

"And a couple of quarts of Bud or something too, please." With that Tunney went into the boutique.

An hour later they sat on a bench up the street from the boutique, eating turkey sandwiches and celebrating Tunney's new job with shared sips from a quart of beer wrapped in a paper bag.

Nora felt so good that night. She was satisfied. She did not feel the need to do or seek or ask or manage. It was so easy being around Tunney. Whether by proximity or need, they had become close friends in a short time. Tunney was someone she could rely on, and he could trust her too. That was such a wonderful, calm feeling, Nora thought.

After they left Hank Hammersley's house in Iowa, neither one of them spoke until they stopped four hours later for some lunch.

"Why didn't you or Hank stop when we passed him on the road on our way out? Didn't you want to say goodbye?"

"We'd said goodbye. Our eyes met and we said goodbye." Tunney pictured Hammersley's blue Impala coming toward them from the opposite direction. They both saw each other but neither slowed down. Each raised a palm as they passed, their eyes meeting and the familiar understanding passing between them, connecting them, and then letting them separate.

There were so many things that Tunney and Hammersley had shared that ranged from horrid to whoring. Watching Krypto practically fuck himself to death had fallen somewhere in between all the surreal scenes they had managed to live through in Nam. But the backdrop of Iowa was so tame in comparison to the mysterious terror of a night in Nam, that Krypto was merely a weird annoyance.

Nora never brought up the Krypto incident during the rest of their trip to California. Tunney read the look on her face as they were driving away from Hammersley's house as a mixture of puzzled and grossed out. Better to let that particular memory just fade away for her, Tunney thought. She had bigger fish to fry in the worry and weird categories.

How strange to feel so lonely when now I have a little person inside me, Nora thought as she continued to stare out the bay window. *Constant company who cannot leave the room when I'm silly or grumpy. A captive audience.* Part of me but not me, she realized as she rubbed her hand over her growing belly.

When Tunney was around Nora forgot her loneliness. He brought back stories and new friends to their flat every night. Sometimes they were interesting women who really knew about a given subject at intense levels, like the plight of migrant workers, DDT poisoning, or herbal remedies. The men were artists and activists, also with their specialties and stories, cures and chakra-talk.

Tunney was a nice looking guy, but Nora observed that women seemed to trust him first and then fall for his looks. Nora was not quite sure why she and Tunney had not slept together in all their close quarters since they left Philadelphia. Somewhere along the way they had developed an unspoken agreement to be more brother and sister than man and woman. *It's what we need right now from each other.*

That was good right now, Nora decided. Although she still seemed to get a little jealous when the women Tunney brought home were prettier and more accomplished than her. It was fun getting attention from Tunney. He could make her laugh and pull her out of the deep lonely times. Where was he anyway?

Tonight was cheese-steak night. Tunney had found a tiny storefront sub shop a few blocks from the boutique that made a "halfway decent" cheese-steak, according to his high standards. He had promised to pick up a couple of subs on his way home from work. Nora's stomach suddenly growled so loudly she startled herself and stood up. Just then she heard Tunney on the landing.

"Anybody hungry in there?" Tunney yelled through the door as he wiggled the key into place. Nora beat him to the lock and opened the door.

"I'm beyond hungry, Tun. I just scared away all the dogs in the neighborhood when my stomach growled." As Nora pulled the door fully open, she saw a woman standing off to the side.

"Hey, Nora, this is Bea. Bea, Nora. Bea is Joey's mom. Joey who works with me at the boutique."

"Hi, Bea. Come on in." Nora quickly walked to the couch and grabbed the newspapers from the cushions and a few dirty glasses off the coffee table. Bea was somebody's mother. A cleaner standard applied to visitors like her.

Tunney got Bea situated on the couch and made a spot for the cheese-steaks. Nora brought in a few bottles of beer and a couple cokes from the refrigerator.

As they all fell on the cheese-steaks, Bea asked Tunney and Nora to tell her about their trip west. In between bites, Tunney traced their drive across the country. He made it sound dramatic, as though they had ridden in a covered wagon across the plains and over the mountain ranges to reach San Francisco. Nora inserted truths in between Tunney's tall tales and also told Bea about Max and the boutique in Philly.

"And what about you, Nora. Tell me about you." Bea put her hand on Nora's back and she suddenly felt at ease. Bea's touch was what Nora imagined a mother's touch would feel like, soothing and secure.

"Oh, well, not much to tell. I'm from Boston. College drop out. My father's a doctor, a card-carrying member of the Establishment. My mother is a no show. I'm on the run, I guess, or on the seek maybe. I don't know." Nora finished abruptly and looked up from her lap where her eyes had been fixed and met Bea's intense gaze.

"And you're pregnant." Bea said it as a truth, a simple statement. Nora looked at Tunney. He cleared his throat.

"Nora, Bea's a midwife. When I found out I thought you might want to talk to her. About the baby and your options, you know."

Nora looked down at her hands again.

"Yes, Bea, I'm pregnant. Pretty dumb, huh?"

"No, honey, not dumb, just life." Bea put her hand on Nora's back again. "Have you seen a doctor, Nora. Had a pregnancy test?"

Nora shook her head.

"Do you want to talk a bit about your options at this point?"

Nora nodded. "I do. But..." Nora stopped. What she now had to say had been lying in wait in some far corner of her mind, tossing hints around so lightly that it had taken weeks to emerge clearly. It had only been Bea's questions that made Nora realize that she did know what she was going to do about the baby. Yes, the baby. She had finally called it that.

"...but, I don't think I see options here." Nora paused and looked at Tunney and then at Bea. Then the words just began falling out of her mouth in a flood of relief.

"I'm going to have this baby and stick with her or him. But I feel frozen. What do I do now? Am I supposed to automatically know this stuff?" Nora looked at Bea for an answer.

Tunney picked up the sandwich wrappers and his beer and went into the tiny kitchen. Nora heard him open the walkout window and jump out onto the fire escape that they used as a deck. *He is my brother.*

For the next hour Bea took Nora through a verbal journey of what the upcoming months would bring, first explaining what a doctor would be checking during different stages of her pregnancy. Then she went through what Nora should be eating, and that she should not smoke, take drugs, and work at not drinking very much.

"Everything that you do from now on affects two people. If you get high, your baby is getting high. If you eat well and keep active, your baby will be healthy and able to grow."

As she listened to everything that Bea had to say, Nora felt a weight lift off her shoulders. She had worried so much about being pregnant that it had stopped her from figuring out what she needed to do next. Bea offered her a roadmap to follow. Maybe she could really do this.

Tunney finally came in from the fire escape as Bea was setting up an appointment for Nora at the clinic where she worked.

"It's a beautiful night out there, ladies. Not to be missed." Tunney looked over at Nora and noticed a change. There was a growing certainty apparent in her eyes and the set of her mouth. The crease in the middle of her forehead that was often there from her constant questioning and worry had disappeared. *So it was the right thing to bring Bea here. Mama Nora is emerging.*

"Hey, Tun?"

"Nora?"

"Thanks for bringing Bea here." Nora walked up to Tunney and wrapped her arms around his neck.

"She should come here every day if I get good hugs like that." Bea joined in the laughter.

"Nora, I expect to see you in a few days, huh? Do you have a calendar where you can write down the appointment?"

"Oh, yes, the puppy calendar!" Nora and Tunney laughed as she ran to the kitchen and wrote in her appointment in the big box two days away.

"We inherited a puppy calendar from the last tenants, their only parting gift besides a nice family of well-behaved roaches." Bea laughed and cringed at the same time as she headed towards the door. Nora followed her out.

"Bea? Thank you. I'm starting to figure this out now. I do want this baby. And now I know where to start, where to focus. Thanks for getting me here." Nora hugged Bea on the landing. Bea squeezed her back hard.

"You would have gotten to this point on your own sooner or later. But sooner is always better. That's a good friend you have there in Tunney. I don't usually make house calls, but that boy is persuasively charming. He runs deep, that one."

"I know he does. Not sure where I'd be if Tunney hadn't needed a gas-paying partner on this trip."

"You're obviously more than a gas partner, Nora, if Tunney is bringing an old midwife around for you. Be good to that one."

"I will." Suddenly tears welled up in Nora's eyes.

"Oh, my. Did I tell you that your emotions are going to be haywire for the next year?" Nora nodded as a few tears fell from her eyes. Bea gave her another hug.

"Get some sleep, Nora. I'll see you in a couple days."

Nora bit her bottom lip and raised her hand in a silent goodbye. She waited until she could not hear the clip-clop of Bea's clogs and went back into the apartment with a smile on her face, still shiny from her tears.

"You okay, kid?" Tunney walked up to Nora, took her hand and led her to the couch.

"I don't deserve you, Tun. Why are you helping me so much?" Nora looked up at Tunney.

"Oh, kid. What you see is what you get." He shrugged his shoulders and pushed a lock of hair off her forehead. "We're journeyers, Nora. Sort of like Stanley and Livingston. Neither of us know the way, but we're trustworthy and good company, and we pull our own weight. Your weight happens to be increasing of course..."

"What! What are you saying?!" Nora grabbed a pillow and hit Tunney in the face.

"Low blow from the opponent in the blue corner! Just because you're somebody's mother now doesn't mean I won't retaliate accordingly."

Tunney stopped laughing when he saw that Nora's face had gone completely white.

"I'm going to be sick." She ran to the bathroom and Tunney could hear her heaving into the toilet. He gave her a few minutes and then brought in a warm towel. Nora wiped her face and then rinsed her mouth out in the sink. Her little body was shaking from the effort. Tunney put his hands on either side of her waist and held her steady next to the sink while Nora brushed her teeth.

"I guess cheese-steaks weren't the best choice, huh?"

"The cheese-steak was great, Tunney. It was your words that scared me. You called me somebody's mother. I'm going to be a mother."

Suddenly Nora was laughing and crying at the same time. Tunney felt helpless and confused. This was getting more emotional and complex than he signed up for.

Nora wiped her nose and eyes on her sleeve and sniffled. “I don’t know a damn thing about being a mother. I haven’t even had an example to follow. I’ve seen my mother once. Jesus, what do mothers do? What if I can’t figure it out?”

“Well, you know what a bad example is. Just try to be everything to Baby Dodge that your mother never was to you.”

“Baby Dodge.” Nora repeated the name and beamed.

“Better than calling the baby ‘it’.”

“Well, ‘it’ already loves you, Uncle Tunney. And so do I.” Nora wrapped her arms around Tunney’s neck and buried herself in his chest. Tunney closed his eyes and gently rocked Nora back and forth.

“Do you think my father would be happy about the baby?” Nora snuggled her head deeper into Tunney’ shirt as she asked the question.

“No.”

“Gee, thanks for the encouraging words.”

“Just being honest, kid. Dads like their daughters to get married before they have kids. Sorry, I was just giving you a Nam vet’s brutal honesty treatment. I’ll lie next time.”

Nora laughed. “No you won’t. I need some brutal honesty right now.” She lifted her head off Tunney’s chest and pulled back to look at him.

“If you keep hugging me like that I’ll assume we’re engaged and act accordingly.”

“Sorry, Tunney.” Nora stepped back away from him and sat down on the couch.

“No sorry, but we’d better figure out what we’re going to be to each other. Half the time you’re my annoying sister and the rest of the time I want to jump you.”

Nora laughed and blushed at the same time. “I guess I could say the same thing, Tunney. But I’m not squared away. I need to figure out who I can be on my own before I sleep with anyone again. You’re solid, Tunney. You deserve a solid woman.”

“Okay, sis.”

“That’s not to say I don’t think you have a great ass and that I have had unclean thoughts of you." Nora smirked and pulled the pillow up in front of her face.

"That's encouraging. Don't clean up your act on my account." They both laughed and Nora stood up.

"Good night, Bro." She leaned over and kissed him on the forehead. "I owe you, Tun." He watched her walk towards the bedroom.

"Your ass is definitely getting bigger, Mama." Nora turned her head around.

"Tunney, if I wasn't so tired I'd kick your butt."

"I'm scared."

"How did your sisters live with you?"

"They just decided to adore me and leave it at that."

"I'll consider their strategy. Goodnight Uncle Tun."

"Night, kids."

# # #

Chapter 19: Que Sera, Sera

Mother Mercy Clinic, Botswana
May 1969

Mma Cookie breathed in her beloved fall morning, still quiet out and just barely warm. Once Dr. Jan and Willa went to the clinic, Mma Cookie had the whole house to herself for a few hours. She reveled in the peace, drinking three cups of rooibos tea, thick with sweetened condensed milk, as she wrote up her provisions list for Sammie Po to purchase in town.

On days like this, with the birds singing the praises of the desert and the air sweet with jacaranda perfume, Mma Cookie made it a practice to contemplate the future.

Her own daughter, JoJo, was at the university in South Africa studying law and justice in an unjust country that had legalized its cruelty. Mma Cookie knew it was difficult for JoJo to accept the harsh treatment of Africans by the whites in South Africa, which made the prejudices of Botswana's former British protectors seem almost quaint. But JoJo was studying law, and she would be the tougher for it. Botswana needed Motswana lawyers for its new democracy who understood the traditions and ancient laws of the tribe as well as the laws of the whites. It was that balance that JoJo would bring back from South Africa, if she could survive the apartheid forces pressing against her and the other students.

Mma Cookie could see big changes in store for Botswana. Just a few years before Sir Seretse Khama had become Botswana's first president of their free republic. No more Bechuanaland. No more British rule. Now they ruled themselves again.

Mma Cookie stood on the veranda and looked north at the twin baobab trees on the clinic's upper border.

The baobab on the left was her daughter's choice to stay in South Africa and finish at the university. Only two years to go in pre-law, and then the potential of a bursary to study in the U.K. So much time away from my baby girl, Mma Cookie thought. But time away brings JoJo back as one of Botswana's new leaders. Sir

Seretse knows the power of women. His own wife, a British white woman, had the power of influence behind her eyes. Mma Cookie had seen it herself when Lady Khama visited Francistown a few months back. The First Lady was defiant. She stood tall and unapologetic. To be married to an African man had brought much hatred to Lady Khama's door. But she met it bravely and head-on. Mma Cookie respected bravery like that. But that kind of righteousness could get a black girl killed in South Africa.

Then there was the baobab on the right. That would be JoJo's choice to come back to Botswana. Mma Cookie did not see her daughter being able to live the village life now that she was highly educated. That would be an unhappy and restless life. But JoJo could live the town life in Francistown. Maybe she could be a law clerk in the district office. Mma Cookie would see her all the time then. JoJo could turn away from the white glare of South Africa. But could JoJo still be a leader if she just came home? How could a solicitor have many babies herself? Mma Cookie clucked her tongue in frustration.

It was too much to think about, too many possible futures. And of course it was not up to her to choose the future of her daughter. JoJo would choose what her spirit could accept. JoJo would choose right. *I see a leader coming and her skin is black and she is a Motswana. And she is my daughter.*

When JoJo and Willa were little girls, constantly laughing and playing in the free days before school was a thought, Mma Cookie used to look at the twin baobabs and think of them as the girls. One was black and African and would penetrate the white man's world of privilege, learn the rules, and then learn how to use them for Africa. The other was white and American but raised as an African, a confusing legacy for some maybe, but not Willa. She embraced all sides of herself and built bridges between her mother's war on traditional healing and the Batswana's skepticism of western medicine. She, too, would become a leader. Chief Tau had seen that when he recognized Willa.

That the quiet of fall punctuated with weaverbird song could conjure the future, Mma Cookie did not question. Change was just in the air. And change would take Willa away very soon. Education would carry her far away, just like it had done with her own daughter. Was that not a good reason to leave one's home village and one's own country? Soon Willa would be in America doing the book learning she needed to become a doctor and make Dr. Gakelape proud. *And make me so proud too.*

Having Willa around had made the pain of her own daughter's absence easier to bear. But now Willa was leaving and only the desert wind and the cleansing rain knew when she would return to them. Yes, Willa would certainly return, but Mma Cookie suspected that she would need to find her way in America before she could find her way back to Botswana.

In the distance little bells tinkled as a herd of goats moved to a new grazing ground. It reminded Mma Cookie that she had many tasks to complete, including bread to bake while it was still cool. Tonight Johnny would be in from his trip to Chobe with the German game hunter. That meant an extra special meal, which Mma Cookie was happy to make. There was no one who praised her cooking like Johnny did. There was a man who knew how to make a woman smile, even Dr. Jan. And that was some feat, Mma Cookie thought as she came in off the porch and gathered the bread ingredients on the drain-board.

Johnny had even made Willa smile when she was all soaked full of sad when Tommi went through his dark days. Mma Cookie had been worried sick, seeing Willa like she never had before. It was certainly love that had shaken Willa. Her heart was breaking for all to see because she just could not hide it. Willa had no capacity to mask her pain or her happiness. It all just leaked out for the world to see. Thank goodness we all love her and shield her, Mma Cookie thought. She clucked her tongue and shook her head. An openness like Willa's was a thing that someone with bad intentions might take advantage of. *I will have to counsel her on that before she goes to America.*

Mma Cookie felt herself somewhat of an expert on the potential evils in America. Watching films at the Catholic mission had taught her just how it can be in America. Gangsters with guns who did not take no for an answer. And forward boys with racecars could prove even more dangerous. Mma Cookie clucked at the many hazards. Yes, she would have to speak with Willa at length about those American dangers.

But for now Willa was smiling. Tommi was okay again since receiving treatment from the Dingaka some weeks back. Mma Cookie had heard the story of Tommi's dark days and his healing at the Dingaka's from both Willa and Mma Lilly. She had never known anything about Tommi's childhood and how he and his mother had suffered at the hands of a very bad father. Facing those memories was indeed like evil knocking on the front door again. And Tommi had not wanted to answer it. But he did not realize that it would not go away until he faced it and knocked it down.

Punching down the dough, Mma Cookie thought back on her own family evil. It was an uncle who thought nothing of rape and thievery. More than once he had cornered Mma Cookie but she had fought him off. If he did not have such a hard head he would be dead from the cooking pot that Mma Cookie had thrown at the back of his skull. She still could see him dropping fast and flat on the mud and dung surface of the compound courtyard. Certainly she had killed him, Mma Cookie thought at the time, because he was so very still.

That was the last time she had seen the evil uncle, as Mma Cookie's father banned him and his caved in head from the family compound until he converted to being a good Motswana. A few years later they heard that he had been killed in Johannesburg by a vengeful father whose daughter had been defiled by Uncle.

No tears were shed by Mma Cookie or anyone in the family, although there was sadness at the thought of a lost cause. No one liked it when there was a violent conclusion to a family or village matter. There was much bone throwing and singing of protection songs and enlisting of the Dingaka to wash away the scars that evil Uncle had left on the family.

A low rumble grew steadily louder and Mma Cookie knew that Willa had returned from her visit to Shashe to check on recovering patients. Dr. Gakelape had actually given Willa some increased responsibilities since Chief Tau had honored her daughter at the kgotla ceremony. Of course, Willa rose up to meet her new duties and already there were many requests from former patients, mainly the *basadi ba golo*, the elderly women, for home visits from Willa. They loved receiving "Dr. Willa" in their homes, and quite often made tea and served biscuits despite not feeling well. There were young people in every village who were recognized as the special ones, the ones that everyone wanted to take credit for. Willa had a way of spreading around well-being. That was a gift. Yes, Willa would be missed *thata thota*, by so many. What will the days be like when she is here no longer, Mma Cookie wondered?

"*Dumela, Mme. Le kae*?"

"*Ke teng*, my daughter. So you are back from your circles."

Willa smiled. "You mean my rounds, Mma Cookie."

"Oh, yes. I knew it was a shape word."

Willa took Mma Cookie's hand and kissed it. "It smells too good in here, *Mme*. Many people will accidentally stop by this morning." They both laughed.

"That is good because I have many chores, and many hands make work light. My bread will trap the workers like bees to honey." Mma Cookie smiled in a proud way.

"Can I be your first bee? What can I do to help?"

"No, no. You are not a housemaid, Willawe. I have heard many call you Dr. Willa now. Do you want me to be disrespected if people think I am making you clean floors? Your hands are for healing, so go to the clinic and heal. Here, take this." Mma Cookie handed Willa a thick slice of warm bread.

"I can only listen to you, my mother. But who is helping you today?" Willa took a spoonful of green fig jam and spread it on the bread.

"My useless nieces are supposed to come just now. It takes two of them to do the work of one." Clucking impatiently Mma Cookie pulled out a chair and joined Willa at the table.

"Where is Tommiwe? Is he coming tonight? You know that Mr. Johnny is coming from Chobe?"

"Tom is coming. He's over in Tsamaya today fixing a borehole pump, so he's popping in on his way back to Bodiba."

Mma Cookie studied Willa as she talked about Tom. Her eyes still shone with love for him, but now there was a shading of uncertainty that outlined her face.

"I'll add another kg of meat then. That *mosimane* can eat, I'm telling you. The cattle shiver when he walks by."

Willa laughed. "They grow them big in America, Mme. Tom is known as an all-American boy."

"Except he's not a boy is he? And you're not a girl." Mma Cookie smiled conspiratorially.

"Hey, you are so bad, Mme. I have to pinch you!"

Willa reached over playfully for Mma Cookie's waist but the old woman grabbed her wrist and suddenly looked serious.

"How is he treating you, my daughter? Are you feeling settled with Tommi?" Mma Cookie put both of her hands on Willa's forearm.

"Yes, Mme, I'm fine. Tom is respectful. I am almost fully settled. It must be mother's influence that still makes me cautious." Willa paused and pulled a crust off her bread. "That's good, I guess. Sammie Po told me that I always make a full investment up front and sometimes I need to hold back so that when I fall there's always a cushion there."

"Hum, yes, Sammie knows falling. Many cushions are flat from his heavy falling. But he does give good advice."

"You are too tough on Sammie Po, Mme."

"I am not, Willa. I'm an old woman. I have seen more than you. The past rests in here." Mma Cookie tapped on her forehead.

Willa sighed heavily and pushed her chair back. She suddenly looked very tired, Mma Cookie noticed, and a worry line creased her forehead.

"Where are you going, child?"

"I need to go and help Dr. Jan for a while. There were many ill people waiting outside the clinic today when I drove past."

"As your mother, I must say no."

Willa let out a surprised chortle and looked up at Mma Cookie. "Now what?"

"Ah, you are cheeky today, Willawe. And you are tired. I'm telling you to go upstairs and take a rest for just a short time. Your patients will benefit, I'm telling you."

The young woman went to protest but then stopped. As usual,

Mma Cookie was right. She was over tired. The thought of laying her head on a pillow was too comforting to resist.

"*Ke itumetse, Mme.*" Willa thanked Mma Cookie as she stood up. "If I don't come down within an hour will you please come and shake me?"

"Oh, yes, my child. I will not let you lose the day. No worries."

"All right. I hope Dr. Jan doesn't come looking for me."

"And if she does, I will tell her that you are flying to America."

Willa laughed. "Thanks, Mmago. I'll be down shortly."

"Be down long-ly, eh. *Robala sentle.* Don't let the biting bugs in bed."

"*Danke, Mme.*"

Willa plodded up the stairs and fell onto her bed. As she kicked her shoes off, she thought of Tom. He always liked touching her feet and often took Willa's shoes off for her. At first she was embarrassed, as many women are of their feet, perceived as not their most attractive asset. But Tom's romantic touching on her always-tired feet made her embarrassment stop. *If Tom loves my feet then they must be okay.*

A sharp wave of fear ran through Willa suddenly. It was thinking of the bad time that did it to her. Would that sudden pain in her gut ever go away when she thought about Tom's dark period? Was it true, as Mma Cookie had said, that soon those old fear pains would disappear as the memory moved further away and eventually let her move on too.

Willa rolled onto her stomach and buried her face in the cool pillow. *Stop it!* She admonished herself. Tom was fine now. He was healed. *Why can't I be healed permanently?*

A good Motswana would forgive and forget past indiscretions. *Why can't I just drop it,* Willa wondered. Tom was ill when he slept with the Peace Corps girl. *Why do I want to call her a slut?* It was only one night. It was the act of a man in the throes of a nervous breakdown. Willa knew all this. What she did not know was how to stop all the noise in her head.

"I love him," she whispered into her pillow, already damp from the tears. "Stop it, fool!" Willa admonished herself.

I'm just tired, so tired. I just love, just love him.

It was what she had said to the Dingaka when she and Mma Lilly had sought out the traditional doctor to help Tom.

Willa remembered clearly what the Dingaka had said in his ancient Setswana as the two women approached him.

"Eh, Willawe, eh, Mme Lilli. I can help the young man find his soul."

Mma Lilli seemed dazed and had nodded as Willa's jaw dropped. How did he know why they were there? But of course he did. That was the power of the Dingaka. He knew well the goings on in the surrounding villages and who needed his aid. But he needed someone to approach him and seek his help before he could begin to heal.

Handing the Dingaka an envelope enclosing a twenty pula note, Willa met the traditional doctor's eyes as he began to speak.

"Yes, my child, I know where your young man is and I can help him. His soul is trying to run away with the dead but it has not yet crossed into the madness. Go home now and in two days your man will reappear in your lives."

With this, the Dingaka turned and ducked through the entryway of his hut. Mma Lilli and Willa looked at each other and then silently returned to the lorry. Neither spoke on the bumpy ride back to Bodiba and Mma Lilli's compound.

Later that night Johnny had flown in from a safari in Maun. He was animated at dinner, having earned a large bonus from shuttling around a wealthy landowner from Virginia and his two spoiled sons. It was *Ulysses* night and Johnny would not take no for an answer when it came time for Willa to read. For years, it seemed, Johnny had been waiting for Willa to be able to read Molly Bloom's soliloquy. And finally Jan had begrudgingly agreed.

As Jan nodded her acquiescence she had the sudden recognition that Willa was a grown woman, and that time had passed far too quickly without her noticing it. The skinny girl who followed Jan around the clinic naturally translating all the Setswana for her was gone. Now there stood a woman who had experienced love, felt the pain of it, and who was now recovering from its blows.

Willa was Molly Bloom that night.

In all the nights of their reading of *Ulysses* out loud, there would never be another like that one, Johnny supposed. As Willa began reading as Molly, her voice and physical demeanor changed dramatically. Willa was Molly with her sharp tongue and clawing descriptions of the men in her life and their confused, sloppy, amorous wanderings. Johnny, Jan and Mma Cookie were locked onto her every word, fully hit with the impact of Molly's emotions rolling off Willa's tongue and sparking from her eyes.

Johnny was transported back to Ireland. Silent tears rolled down his cheeks as Molly spoke for his mother and aunts, his sisters and sisters-in-law, women he had carelessly tarried with, and old spinsters he had scorned.

After reading four pages, Willa suddenly stopped. Her face shone with perspiration and her eyes flashed with a powerful misery.

Willa had simply closed the book and walked out on to the porch. No one said anything. The screen door banged against the jamb.

Night sounds of crickets and a distant radio in the nurses' quarters drowned out another sound that Willa would have heard.

Tom had not been far away, just outside the compound's border, choking out tears, confused and hateful, and providing a beacon of pain that led the Dingaka right to him.

It had not made sense to Tom at first. Two dusty feet in tattered leather sandals stood before him and seemed to loom over him. Tom froze. He felt a hand on the top of his head then the growing pressure of it.

He coughed suddenly, fear and phlegm rising in his throat.

"Another power is trying to take you. It is time for you to dismiss it, Tommi Peese Corpse."

The Dingaka spoke slowly in Setswana. His words were a simple statement, a fact. Tom understood the Dingaka's words and looked up at him.

"Stand now and come with me. You need a guide because you are so young, and your hands are tied tightly by the boy you once were."

As Tom stood the Dingaka took a dark powder out of a leather pouch and rubbed it between his fingers. The traditional doctor pressed his palm in the middle of Tom's chest, leaving black smudges on his tee shirt. Instantly Tom felt lighter and somehow safe.

He had no idea why the Dingaka had appeared out of nowhere and was now leading him out into the desert. It just felt right to follow him. Tom had reached the end and he knew it. There was nothing left to lose.

How long they had walked that night Tom could not recall. It could have been one hour or five, there was no way for him to tell. Walking behind the Dingaka it seemed that he was out of time's normal flow, moving outside of the night that his body walked within. Did he walk one mile or ten? It did not matter.

At some point the two men reached a hut that stood alone at the base of a kopje. Holding aside an animal skin flap the Dingaka motioned for Tom to enter. It was pitch black inside. A match was struck and the Dingaka lit a tiny candle, giving off the barest of light. Odors similar to those Tom had smelled in the Dingaka's Shashe village hut enveloped him. But this time Willa was not with him.

Later when Tom had tried to tell Willa about his night with the Dingaka, he found that he could not remember anything in real detail after entering the medicine hut. Hands on his head, a deep chanting, moaning, burning smells, sweet smells, then acrid. Shapes and shadows on the mud walls, pulling at him, pulling away memories, showing him how to remember without the pain.

Gone now. Pain was dead. Embrace the mother who was so battered she could no longer make any decisions and split her world between the before and after. Both of you are victims. Embrace the mother. Embrace the little boy who could not protect her from a monster. Let the monster leave now.

None of the memories were very clear. And trying to remember the sequence of events only made them slip further away, made it all seem more like a dream.

Tom had awoken in his own bed, in his hut in Mma Lilli's compound the next morning. He had no idea how he had gotten there. All he knew was that he had never felt so rested in his life.

And that he loved Willa. And that he needed to call his mother.

As he pulled on his shorts, Mma Lilli's broom began its daily ritual of sweeping the dirt compound.

"*Dumela, Mme. O dira eng*?"

Mma Lily laughed with glee and walked towards Tom.

"I am being a diligent Motswana and keeping my compound in order. And I can see you are back. Good." Mma Lily handed the broom to Tom.

"I was just thinking how nice it would be to have my tea while a gentleman swept my compound."

"The gentleman is back and sweeps your compound with pleasure." Tom bowed deeply and began dancing with the broom across the compound, sweeping and humming.

"What is this song you are pushing?"

Tom began singing in the best Broadway voice he could muster. "I could have danced all night, I could have danced all night, and still have begged for more..."

Mma Lily began laughing so hard at Tom's singing and broom dancing that she had to sit down on a stool and hold her head.

"...I could have spread my wings and done a thousand things I've never done before..."

"Oh, joy. Oh, my *Modimo* on high. Tommi, you are breaking my throat. Just stop."

Tom abruptly shut his mouth in mid phrase.

"Seriously, Mme, I need to go to Francistown. I need to call my mother."

Mma Lilli clapped her hands together. "Oh, yes, Tommi. Your mother is waiting. And don't forget Dr. Willa, too." Mma Lilli bent her head down and rolled her eyes up at Tom.

"Willa I will never forget." The two grinned at each other in mutual understanding. Grabbing Tom's hands in hers, Mma Lilli pressed them to her forehead.

"Ke itumetse, Rra. Ke boitumela go go bona."

"Thanks, Mma Lilli. I'm really happy to see you too. And I'm starving. Any tea left? Any bread today?"

Mma Lilli clucked. "Peese Corpse's eat too much bread."

"That is because it reminds us of home, Mma."

"Home in Amerika?"

"Yes. American's worship bread. It's our mealie meal."

"Okay, Tommi. But don't pray for bread when Mma Seakgosing walks by."

"Why not?"

"She will lecture you *thata thota* on praying to false eye-dolls."

Tom laughed. "Bread is never false, it is the staff of life. Does Mma Seakgosing often lecture you on false idols," he asked as he walked toward the cooking hut.

"Yes, Tommi. Don't you remember how she clucked at my fertility statue and said I was blast-filming."

"Okay. Eh, now I recall. She wanted you to burn it."

"Hey, imagine the holy cheek of it, Tommi! She's another one, she is."

Tom clucked in agreement then focused on the two thick slices of bread and the milky sweet tea. *Damn, it feels good to feel good again.*

Two hours later he was actually talking to his mother from the phone in the American doctor's house in Francistown. At first Tom's mother could not stop crying, so he just kept talking to her through the tears. Eventually she stopped and told him about the events of the last few weeks starting with his father showing up after an absence of six months, and the subsequent drunken bender he went on. His mother had stayed away from their home, hiding out with her sister and a few loyal friends. It was when his father did not find his wife at home one night that he drove off in a rage and hit the tree on Cape Shore road.

Tom's mother spoke of the incident as though it had happened a long time ago. There was a strength coming into her voice again that Tom could hear. The same strength that would always come back whenever his father was away from them for long periods of time in jail or working on a fishing boat. Squeezing his eyes shut Tom apologized for not coming home.

"I'm sorry, Ma. I just couldn't. I know you needed me and for that I'm so sorry. I was just too angry at him. I thought my head was gonna blow off, Ma. But I should have come. I know that now and I'm just sorry, Ma."

"Dear, Tom, there are more sorrys that need to go around this family than we can count. I knew why you couldn't come, Tom. I know." His mother's voice choked up and she stopped talking.

"I gotta go now, Ma. I'll see you at Christmas. I'm coming home at Christmas. And Ma, you won't believe it, but I'm in love. Her name is Willa and you'd just love her. I love you, Ma."

Suddenly the line clicked dead just as his mother was replying. Typical overseas telephone call, Tom thought. The voice delay was so long that callers had to clearly stop at the end of their remarks and wait quietly for a response. If both people talked at once or interrupted, both voices were cut out.

Tom felt dazed but at peace when he left the American doctor's house. He felt almost selfish for feeling so good. *Now to see Willa.*

When he arrived in the Mother Mercy compound, the usual line of patients was there. Men and women of all ages formed a black line of pain that wound its way out of the waiting room and under the line of lemon trees that separated the outpatient clinic and the hospital. And there was Willa. Kneeling in front of a Motswana and her baby, Willa was asking the woman questions as she smiled at the little girl and touched her forehead with the back of her hand. Tom remembered that Dr. Jan had developed a triage approach to helping people in the waiting line. Willa and the other nurses interviewed those waiting and determined who the patient needed to see and when, depending on the extent of the illness or injury.

Tom parked the jeep under a mopane tree at the edge of the compound. He realized then that he had not thought this through real well. He could not interrupt Willa at work. That would not be a good place to start. Maybe he should see if Mma Cookie was in and she would know when Willa would be freed up.

Tom admonished himself. He was stalling.

Just then as he stared at Willa across the large compound expanse, she looked up and their eyes met and held. Willa's shoulders straightened. Tom saw her saying something to one of the Motswana nurses. She was walking towards him.

Tom straightened his shoulders and started walking towards

Willa. As they got closer, Tom could see a smile on Willa's face. He grinned.

She took his hands as they met and smiled but did not say anything.

"Dumela, Mma. O tsogile?" Tom squeezed her hands.

"Ke tsogile, Rra. Le kae."

"*Ke teng, Willawe.* Now I am anyway."

"You've always been fine, Tom. You just had a shock." Willa's smile quivered and turned down on itself.

"No, don't be sad, Willa. You're the one who made me so happy that I forgot what it was like to stew about my old man. That was my favorite pastime before I met you."

"I can't help it, Tom. I thought you were gone from me. You've changed me. Now it hurts when you're not here." Willa said it matter-of-fact, as though the whole world was aware of it.

Wrapping his arms around her, Tom pulled Willa tight, nuzzling into her neck and hair.

"You've changed *me*, Willa. Now I know what love is." He pulled back from her and looked into her brown eyes that glistened from their reunion. "I love you, Willa. I've never said that to anyone before."

Laughing, Willa pulled Tom in close and they kissed. Tom breathed her in and knew then that somehow their futures would be tied together.

"I love you too, Tom. And I haven't said that to a man before either." Willa paused and then smiled. "I think the Dingaka would have something meaningful to say about these firsts."

"Ah, my friend the Dingaka." Tom bowed his head and looked at his dusty shoes. Willa had on her white nurses shoes. They were ugly shoes and Tom loved them. "He really helped me, you know? I'll have to tell you about last night some time." Tom looked up.

"And then I'll tell you about my last night." Willa's voice was quiet and she looked past Tom toward the stoic line of patients. Her eyes reflected the pain Tom had brought to her, sad yet hopeful, a Willa dichotomy. Tom took her hands in his again.

"Willa, I'm so sorry. I know I hurt you. I was an idiot. You're so important to me." Tom stopped and cleared his throat. The lump in it was growing. He had a bridge to cross.

"Willa, we're connected now. When I cut myself off from you I didn't care what happened to me or anyone else, or what I did. I could only think that I wasn't a guy who would ever know real love because I'm damaged goods. I thought I didn't deserve love, deserve you."

"No, Tom."

"Wait, wait a second. I know I was wrong. I know that now. I still don't know if I deserve you, but I know that I won't shut myself off from you like that again." Tom took her mouth again, remembering the joy of stealing her breath.

"I love you, Willa Dodge. Can we start over again?"

Willa nodded, her brown eyes flashing mischief already.

"When's our first date?" She put her hands on her hips and cocked her head.

"How about now?"

"Can't. Have to finish working."

"How about tonight. Dinner in Francistown at the Tati Hotel. Steak and thou. We'll drink two bottles of wine and have to stay over at the Tati."

Willa dropped her arms and laughed. "Pick me up at six?"

"It's a date."

"A first date."

Now, as Willa flipped restlessly on the bed in her room, the reunion between Tom and her seemed so far away. She smeared the tears with her palms, the competing thoughts that all was well and all was not well were impossible to sort, to turn off.

I love Tom. What's wrong with me? Why am I suddenly uncertain again about him? We started over gain. Just stop. Stop second-guessing everything. \

Their relationship had been wonderful again since that "first date" at the Tati Hotel. That was what was so strange about the feelings that were overtaking Willa. *When everything is so good, why am I questioning and worrying about our relationship? What happened to letting the relationship guide itself along on its own momentum? Wasn't that their unspoken rule?*

Then Willa heard the voice that she had been trying not to

hear. *Because you're leaving this time. You're going to America in a month and where does that leave you?*

Willa startled herself and sat up. The dialogue in her head was getting louder. *I love Tom but I have to go to Boston.* There's no room there for any change of plans, Willa acknowledged. Plans that had been in the works for three years and on which her whole future in medicine rested.

Was she trying to spoil things so that it would be easier to leave? *Don't do it. Make the days last. Fill them up with love. Make them last so I can hold Tom close to me when I'm in Boston living with a father and a sister and a stepmother I don't know in a world a million light years from Mother Mercy and Dr. Jan and Mma Cookie and my whole everything.*

Trying to sleep was definitely not going to work. Willa got up and went to the open window. She leaned on the sill letting the afternoon breeze cool her forehead. Cicadas buzzed in the heat, a noisy monotony that absorbed the breaths and pants and pulses of the Kalahari and spit it back out again in a droning desert dirge.

Then a different sound made its way up the stair well. Mma Cookie would occasionally put a record on the old turntable in their living room. Only a few of them passed her high standards for musical entertainment, like Nat King Cole, and the original cast recording of *West Side Story*, especially the *Amerika* song.

But today it was Doris Day. *Que sera, sera. Whatever will be, will be. The future's not ours to see. Que sera, sera.*

Willa shook her head. Leave it to her African mother, she thought, to put a band aid on my latest wound. It was not like Mma Cookie to do anything accidentally. It was as though she was Willa's birth mother they had such a telepathic connection. Mma Cookie knew when it was time for a Doris Day reminder.

I guess this is love, Willa thought. Nothing else seemed to matter to her when Tom was with her. When she wrapped her arms around him, she could not imagine that any other woman he had known had loved Tom as much as she did. And she wanted to believe that he had never loved as deeply with anyone but her.

Tom had told her that. She believed him.

But it was a lot easier to believe him when he was standing in the room. When Willa looked into Tom's eyes and watched them absorb her, there was a security in that. Love was like two links in a chain, connecting two people intimately but causing a great stress when they are pulled in opposite directions.

Heat raced to her head and flushed her face. *Why did he have to sleep with the Peace Corps girl? Was that act so inconsequential that it could be done and then dismissed?*

Stop it, Willa admonished herself again as she slipped her shoes on. She suddenly felt like running. Pumping her legs and pushing off the oppression of that incomprehensible thought: *Tom had been with someone else.*

Willa jumped up and ran to the stairwell. Taking two steps at a time she landed at the bottom with a loud thud. Mma Cookie ran out of the kitchen.

"*Wa reng*?" What is the clatter?"

Willa looked guiltily at Mma Cookie, her face flushed.

"What is this, Willa? Are you a child again?"

"*Nna, Mma. Ke mosadi.* I just need to run somewhere. I'll be right back," she yelled back as she opened the screen door and jumped off the porch.

Mma Cookie clucked in annoyance, wondering what was going on with Willa to make her so moody. It had to be some form of love, the old woman thought. That was the only thing that could knock a woman outside of her steadiness. That Tommi had better be good to Willa, Mma Cookie noted silently. There were many friends of Willa's who would make life miserable for him if he did not treat her with respect.

The fall air felt cool against Willa's face as she ran toward Tsebe Hill. So many times as a child she had run to Tsebe, marveling at how it grew larger the closer she got until she could no longer see the top.

She found the old trail that goats had worn into the hillside over the years, the same one she had raced up a million times as a child. Thorns from the low bushes grabbed at her legs and snagged her nurse's uniform at the hemline.

But Willa did not slow down.

She could feel her power growing again, her confidence. *What is wrong with me? I am a Motswana. I am loved and I love.*

A voice in her head kept saying, 'Shake it off, shake it off,' to the rhythm of her feet hitting the dirt trail.

As she reached the top, the landscape opened up to a vista that included Mother Mercy in the distance and the vastness of the desert towards the west. A dust cloud on the horizon marked the passage of a herd of cattle moving to new grazing land. Willa knew that there were probably two young boys managing the entire herd. A huge responsibility for boys who still played the games of childhood but were expected not to lose a single head. She always made a point to show respect to Batswana herd-boys. Besides managing the cattle they also prepared their own meals and snagged small animals such as rabbit and guinea hen for their cooking pots. They were brother and mother to one another, united in their solitude and duties.

Won't see that in America, Willa thought. Boys there rode their bikes and played baseball. She had seen them racing up and down the street where her father lived in Boston, the only time she had gone to visit the other Dr. Dodge. Her sister Nora had seemed more annoyed than pleased to have her around. Even at eight, Willa realized that Nora resented the attention that their father paid to his "African" daughter.

Several times when Nora pulled toys from Willa's hands or shut the door of her bedroom when she saw her "African" sister coming towards it, Willa had said, "But I'll be leaving soon, you know."

Dr. Dodge spent long hours in surgery and meeting with patients, so most days Willa had been left on her own with Mary, the housekeeper cook who lived in Roxbury but spent almost every day, all day, looking after Nora and now Willa. Mary was also there to make sure Dr. Dodge had good meals and a smart home.

Willa could still hear Mary's laugh in her head. It was a wonderful laugh and seemed amplified from her throat the way it was so deep and beautiful.

During the six weeks that Willa was in Boston, she and Mary became close companions. When Nora went to one of her friend's homes to play or spend the night, Willa and Mary would bake snickerdoodles and exchange songs they enjoyed sharing with one another. Mary taught her gospel songs that she sang every Sunday at the African Methodist Episcopal Church in Roxbury, or the AME as Mary called it. Willa loved the cadence of Mary's songs and all the stories of Jesus that filled each verse. Dr. Jan had not cultivated Willa's spiritual nature, so Willa never spent a lot of time in church. To her, Jesus was a folk hero, almost like the Daniel Boone man she read about in a book her father had sent her.

When Willa asked Mary if Jesus had a skin hat like Daniel Boone, the black woman had laughed so hard that she knocked over a pitcher of milk. Willa was sworn to secrecy about the milk being wasted. Mary had been yelled at enough in her life as a black woman by whites who shrugged off the mistakes they made, the same ones they would scream at a black woman for making. Mary had never seen Dr. Dodge scream, but she could not take the chance. At this point in her life her tolerance for being berated for being black was so low that she would lose her job before she would take it again from rich-ass white folk, or poor ones for that matter.

As a reward for not telling Dr. Dodge about the milk, Mary came and got Willa on a Sunday and took her to the AME Church. Dr. Dodge had two surgeries that day and was grateful that Willa was being looked after. Nora could always stay with one of their many family friends, which she preferred to being stuck at home with a sister she did not want to waste her time getting to know.

Willa was surprised when one of the AME Church songs was the same as one she had heard Mma Cookie singing quite often. After the service, Mary and Willa joined the other members for coffee and sweet cakes in the hall attached to the church. Willa told everyone she met that she knew the song they had called We Shall Overcome, but in Setswana, not English. When one of the elders, Mr. Homer, finally understood the little white girl's accent and heard what she said, Willa sang it without hesitation at his request. The old man smiled at the beauty of the African words to this song that had run through his veins for seventy years, deflecting a thousand insults and ugly stares, and letting him feel and embrace his dignity.

Mary smiled proudly, as though Willa were her kin. Smartly dressed ladies patted her cheek and shook their heads about the white girl "singing African." Most everyone did not want or need a white girl being the center of attention at the AME Church. But Willa had no pretense about her, so the ladies could not complain but instead just laughed with Mary when she told them of Willa's origins and her home in Africa. Yes, she was one of a kind, they all agreed, as they wrapped up little after-service cakes for Willa to take home with her.

That evening when Dr. Dodge came home and Nora had returned from her friend's house, Willa asked both of them to come upstairs. Nora tisked at being asked to do anything by Willa, but her curiosity was stronger than her annoyance, and their father had begged her with his eyes to just "be nice." In the corner of her bedroom, Willa had set up a very fancy tea party with an old tea set that Nora had tucked away in a closet when she outgrew tea parties for transistor radios and experimenting with eye shadow. The extra cakes that the AME Church ladies had given her were laid out with great care on paper doilies.

"Please join me for tea. You'll see that the cakes are really quite delicious."

Dr. Dodge smiled at Willa and took her hand as she led him to the tiny chair. Nora pulled up the chair closest to her father and looked over at the fourth place setting.

"Who's that seat for?"

Willa looked at her sister. It was one of the rare times that Nora had directed a question to her. "That's Mother's chair."

"But she's not here, stupid."

"Nora, please, behave yourself." Dr. Dodge looked pained. Nora folded her arms across her chest.

"I know Mother is not here. But we're remembering her."

Nora unfolded her arms and stared across the table at Willa. "I don't remember her, Willa." Nora's voice was thin and angry and she clutched the edge of the table in front of her.

"I'll remember her for you and father. And, Nora, you can eat Mother's cake, because of course she can't."

Although he was at a complete loss, Dr. Dodge knew he had to say something or Nora would probably flip over the table. Her clenched jaw and grip on the table looked like it had a purpose behind it.

"Thank you, Willa. And Nora, you can remember that your sister is far from home and she misses your mother." Dr. Dodge opened his mouth as though he were going to say more but then closed it.

"Does our mother remember me, Willa? Does she ever say my name?" Nora's voice had a hardness to it that startled Dr. Dodge. It belonged to someone older, not a 12-year-old.

"Yes, she says your name. And so does Mma Cookie."

"Who's Mma Cookie."

Willa seemed surprised by the question, as though Nora would know all about their life at Mother Mercy. "Mma Cookie is our African mother."

"You mean *your* African mother."

"Oh, no. She is your mother too. She asks me to think about what you are doing at certain times of the day and tells me when it is your birthday."

"You're such a liar!" Nora shouted and stood up. The teacups clattered against the saucers and Willa grabbed for the teapot. Hot tea sloshed up, flipping off the lid and spilling over the lip onto her fingers. She held the pot up over the table like a priest offering up the blessed sacrament over the altar during mass. Willa was not certain that Nora was done jostling the table yet.

"Nora Dodge, my heavens, what a poor show you're putting on!"

His oldest daughter let out an exasperated sob. "But Daddy, she's lying! I don't know Mma Cookie and she doesn't know me or my birthday."

Still holding the teapot up, Willa said, "But she does remember your birthday. It's on the calendar. Mother always puts it on the calendar."

Nora sank back down into the little chair, becoming little again herself, a child wanting a mother who did not want her. She stared at the cakes and reached for one that had slipped off the plate.

"Tea?" Willa skillfully poured tea into the tiny cup for Nora. Dr. Dodge fell in love with her right at that moment, the daughter he knew only through little girl's drawings and simple letters a few times a year. She *was* his daughter. He wanted her to be his own so badly, and not just Jan's second child. Willa was his daughter too, and he meant to claim her back. Of course, that would take some time.

Nora did not look up but picked up her teacup and sipped the warm liquid.

"Father, tea?"

"Thank you, Willa. I've never had tea with both of my daughters."

Nora raised her head in resignation. She would have to share her father with Willa. That meant he would have less love for Nora, less time for her. *Then I will also have less love for him,* Nora reasoned with her pre-teen logic. Let him see how he likes that, she thought.

"Where'd you get these cakes, anyway, Willa. They look weird." As Nora took the last bite of her piece she turned up her nose.

"Ladies at Mary's church gave them to me."

"Mary's church? Mary the maid?" Nora looked at her father in disbelief. "You went to church with Mary?"

Willa nodded. She was realizing that no matter what she said it was not sitting right with her sister.

"You let her go to church with Mary?" Nora looked incredulously at Dr. Dodge. "That's a black church, you know?"

"Yes, Nora, I'm aware of that. Willa expressed an interest in going with Mary. I gave her permission to do so."

"We rode the "T". That's the train, you know." Willa added to her father's admonition.

Dr. Dodge was glad that Willa seemed oblivious to the animosity and blame shooting out of Nora's eyes. *She's just a kid,* he thought. Nora's already a young woman, he realized now, already adept at training her anger at the guilty and innocent in retribution for a motherless childhood.

"I know what the "T" is. I live here, you know. I'm not a visitor like you." Nora reached for another cake and took a noisy bite.

"Sister, would you like more tea?" Willa would not give up, Dr. Dodge realized with awe. She was going to dog Nora until she cracked. He held his face still to hide a smile that was threatening to break.

Nora just looked at the younger girl in disbelief. Willa had called her 'sister'. How many times had she wandered around the house alone wishing for a sister to play with but instead ending up only playing make believe family with her dolls and stuffed animals. Maybe Willa was her sister but she would never feel like they had that type of connection. Willa was too far away. What was the point of being sisters when the distance of continents and oceans between them belied any connection?

After the night of the tea party Nora's resistance to Willa slowly began to weaken. Nora also realized that Willa had a lot of information about their mother that she wanted to learn. Soon a bartering system of sorts began between the girls. Nora would take Willa up to the attic and show her "old" photos of their mother when she was young and first married. Willa had never seen these views of her mother's medical school days and she marveled at the changes that had occurred over the years. As Willa stared at each photo, Nora would ask her questions about their mother. Is she fat, thin; does she smoke cigarettes; does she have a boyfriend; what is her favorite dessert, and other questions that a pre-teen would ask to build a profile of a person.

Willa patiently and honestly answered each question. It was starting to be fun being around Nora and being sisters, the younger girl thought. And Nora was smart. She knew what was going to happen on all the television shows they watched before the program even ended. Nora knew what their father's answer to her questions would be before he answered. Driving to Cape Cod one weekend Willa also learned that Nora knew all the names of the towns on the way to Truro before the signs gave away the answers. Nora was what their mother would call sophisticated. Willa suddenly realized that, unlike Nora, she was not at all sophisticated, and had no idea how a girl trained for that.

Just about the time Willa was scheduled to go back to Botswana, Nora realized that she was an older sister and she liked it. It was easy to snow Willa and she would pretty much go along with anything that Nora suggested, whether snitching cookies or helping her older sister clean up her room.

The last weekend before Willa left, Dr. Dodge took both girls to the Harvard Club for dinner. Willa was fascinated with the dark hallways and broad stairwells. Old men read *The Boston Globe* and smoked cigars or drank golden colored drinks that clinked with ice cubes when they sipped. Just as they sat down in an upstairs dining room, an attractive woman approached the table.

"Carol, I'm so glad you could make it. Please sit down." Dr. Dodge stood up and held Carol's delicate hands as he kissed her cheek.

Willa could see that her father became very happy as soon as Carol arrived. *He loves her*, she thought, or really, really likes her, anyway.

Eying Carol carefully, Nora tried to decipher her father's relationship with the attractive blond. Suddenly Nora realized that the two of them looked very serious, even in love. Her stomach gurgled, making her eye twitch.

Willa noticed Nora's movement and flashed a look at her sister: Don't ruin father's evening. Too many times in Willa's six weeks in Boston she had seen Nora's moods upset their father. Tonight Dr. Dodge was happy. And he was so handsome when he smiled. Willa was growing protective of her father whom she had grown to love and admire in their short time together.

"Girls, this is my good friend Carol. Carol these are my daughters, Nora and Willa." Michael Dodge smiled his handsomest grin, proudly introducing his little girls.

"Oh, it's so great to meet you girls. I've heard so much about you, and you're every bit as cute and smart as your father brags about." Carol and Michael were both smiling so wide now that Willa could not help but match theirs with her best. Nora was not giving in so easily to the mood. Her eyes slanted in suspicion. Why had father brought this woman to meet them on one of Willa's last nights in town? Something serious was going on and Nora meant to get to the bottom of it.

Willa remembered what she should say in Setswana in such a

situation and translated it in her head before she spoke.

"Good evening, Miss Carol. It's very nice to meet you."

Carol laughed, delighted at Willa's words and her unusual accent. "Willa, thank you, sweetheart. I'm so glad to meet you before you go back to Butchaland."

"It's Bechuanaland, not Butchaland." It was Nora. She was fishing for imperfection in Carol and had found a strategic opening. In a way, the older sister thought, she was supporting Willa, something her father kept telling her she needed to do.

"Oh, my, that's a complicated name. I'm sorry, it's Becha-what?" Carol laughed nervously.

"Bech-u-an-a-land." Nora pronounced it slowly, as though she were talking to a four-year-old. But in fact it was the same way that Willa had finally taught her how to pronounce the name of the African country.

"Okay, Bechuanaland. How's that?"

"That's very good, Miss Carol." It was Willa who answered quickly. She was afraid that Nora was going to be mean to Carol, and that would upset their father.

Nora glowered at Willa, her eyes expressing disgust at her little sister's easy acceptance of Carol. It would be good when Willa left, Nora thought. Willa knew nothing about their father, and yet she presumed knowledge by her acceptance of anything that Dr. Dodge said or did. Nora could feel her father moving farther out of her grasp as she was forced to share his attentions with Willa, and now with this Carol woman. Yes, it was good that Willa was leaving, Nora stated definitively to herself. It was hard enough getting her way without the distraction of a sister and a, what, girlfriend? Nora realized that she would have to raise her profile with her father. That would take some serious thought and planning, Nora reasoned as she tried to assess the extent of her father's and Carol's relationship as he told Carol about the house specialties.

"Nora loves the roasted chicken, don't you honey?"

A spoon hit the floor loudly when Nora started at the sound of her name.

"Daddy, that was when I was younger, when I was Willa's age.

I prefer the filet mignon now." Nora looked directly at Carol as she spoke. The blond woman glanced quickly at Dr. Dodge, and then met Nora's stare.

"My, what sophisticated tastes you have, Nora. I didn't even taste my first filet until I was in my twenties." Carol shook her head in disbelief and leaned closer into Dr. Dodge.

"Not so much sophistication as habit," Dr. Dodge said to Carol. "Nora practically grew up at the Harvard Club, we eat here so often."

Inside Nora began to fume. She was sophisticated, even Carol recognized that. How dare he say she wasn't.

"Women don't have food habits, Michael, we have tastes and preferences, right Nora?" Carol had recognized an opportunity to pull Nora in and she took it. She had already realized that Nora would be a major challenge in her relationship with Michael Dodge. A relationship that looked more and more like it would evolve into marriage soon.

Willa giggled and put her hand over her mouth. Nora looked back and forth from Carol to her father. But her anger against Dr. Dodge and her ego won out and she took Carol's bait.

"That's right, Carol. Sophisticated taste." Nora met her father's eyes, and then looked down at her menu again.

"I'm not sophisticated," Willa announced. "I eat goat and cow tongue and Mary told me that's poor folk food."

Dr. Dodge and Carol looked at one another and both began laughing.

"I can see that I'm outnumbered and overpowered, so I surrender. Let's eat and then I'll exchange ice creams for a kiss from each of my three sophisticated ladies!"

The rest of the meal and the evening went surprisingly well. Nora forgot to dislike Carol for a while and forgave her father by the time appetizers arrived. When Willa took Nora's hand to cross Massachusetts Avenue, the older sister did not shake her off like she had several times in the past six weeks.

Willa thought that she had never had such a sophisticated evening, and she could not wait to tell Mma Cookie about how much she had "grown up" in Boston.

Now, ten years later, Willa looked out across the Kalahari bush from her perch on Tsebe Hill. She had not thought about those weeks in Boston for several years, and the memories felt good. It was time that Nora and her reconnected and tried at being sisters again, this time for longer than a few weeks. She thought that if there was one thing that she and Nora shared it was the desire for a permanent sibling.

Suddenly Willa felt a presence behind her. In case it was an animal, she forced herself to turn her head around very slowly.

"*Dumela mosetsana Mmawe. Ke o go bona.*" It was the Dingaka.

Willa stood up from her rock perch and went to the Dingaka, her head bowed and her palms together in respect, pointing towards the traditional healer.

"*Dumela, Rre. Ke itumela go go bona.* I am happy to see you my father."

The Dingaka wore a leopard skin hat and it shone in the autumn sun as though it still had the life of a predator in its seams.

"*You are giving me no sleep, my daughter.*" Willa looked up at the Dingaka in surprise as he spoke the Setswana words.

"*I am sorry, my father, I do not mean to bother your great healing powers.*" Willa looked down at the ground as the Dingaka let go of her hands.

"*You must remember your Motswana self. You are worrying uselessly like a white woman.*" Willa looked up at the Dingaka not knowing how to respond or if the traditional doctor wanted her to.

"*Don't let your white side hide the wisdom of your Motswana side.*"

"*Yes, my father.*"

"*You must go to Amerika now because that is where your destiny lies. If you free the eagle he will fly back to you if it is destined. Your white family in Amerika needs you now. Your father needs your loyalty and respect, your sister is lost and you will help her find home again.*"

"*Back from where, my father? Where is my sister lost? Do you really mean lost?*"

The Dingaka looked into Willa's eyes and held them without

speaking for several minutes. It seemed like an eternity to Willa, but she knew better than to speak again. When he was ready, the healer would reveal much, or nothing.

Pointing towards the northwest the Dingaka finally spoke as he looked out past Willa and across the veldt. "*You will honor your father in Amerika with your respect and your African side will un-break his heart.*" He looked now at Willa and touched her forehead with two fingers. Willa's eyes closed and the darkness behind her lids brightened. She could see a blue sky with perfect white clouds meeting the white surf of a blue ocean. It was beautiful and calming, the sound of the waves rolling onto the sand more melodic than the most brilliant orchestra.

But then the vision disappeared.

Willa opened her eyes. The Dingaka was gone. She quickly scanned the tree growth on the top of the hill as she listened for the clue of a snapping twig. There was no sign of the healer.

Suddenly the cicadas high pitched buzzing broke the silence on the hilltop, but then just as abruptly stopped in unison moments later. Willa knew now what she must do. Instantly she felt lighter, unloading the uncertainty that had let doubt and distrust confuse her heart.

She was ready now to go to Boston and be part of her other family there, whatever that held.

A fish eagle screeched above her head and Willa looked up. Its wings cut a graceful, powerful pattern across the sky that created an elusive shadow on the veldt below.

And I'm ready just to love Tom, Willa thought as she watched the fish eagle circle back towards the waters of the pan. "My beautiful eagle, Tom," Willa said out loud as she started down the goat path and back to the rest of her life.

# # #

Chapter 20: Hope Creek

Oregon Coast
May 1969

For the thousandth time that morning, Nora was questioning her decision to leave. It had not even been a day and already she missed Tunney. Losing Bea's daily counsel was not going to be easy either. Nora had come to rely on both of these friends to help her get through the last few months. And now they were gone.

A fear gurgle made the baby kick. Nora smiled. *At least I've got you little one, little partner*, Nora whispered silently in her head to the baby.

Just then the bus driver announced over the microphone, "We just crossed over the border into Oregon, folks. Welcome to the beautiful Pacific Northwest!"

He was a kind man, Nora thought, and had been especially helpful and cheerful taking her sparse luggage that morning and directing her pregnant self to the right seat.

"Congratulations, young lady. Off to visit your mother, I bet." He was so genuine that Nora could not bring herself to burst his happy bubble.

"Yes, that's right. Thank you." Nora put her hand on her belly, signaling to the driver that the baby thanked him too.

"Your first baby, huh? Bet your husband is happy, eh?"

"Oh, yes. He's excited."

"Must be working, huh? And couldn't come with?"

Nora thought of Tunney. He wasn't the father of course, but she would use him to tell stories if she needed to. "He's in Viet Nam actually." Nora put her head down and acted sad, hoping bus driver man might move on and help someone else for a while.

"Well, God bless him, ma'am. He'll be home before you know it." He smiled and touched his cap. A minute later he was helping an elderly woman with many complaints settle into her seat.

Nora did not like lying, but telling the truth only brought scorn or pity, and she did not want or deserve either. At first, she did feel alarmed and uneasy, not wanting anyone to know she was pregnant. That was before Tunney brought Bea home to meet her and help her figure out what she really wanted to do about the baby.

With Bea, Nora never felt like she was being judged, as she did with most other women. Bea was only interested in a healthy, happy baby, and to her that meant a healthy, happy mama.

Since that first night when Tunney brought Bea back to their apartment, Nora's life had changed dramatically. That was the night she made the decision: she wanted to keep the baby. Suddenly she just knew. From a place where it didn't seem she ever could, her eyes opened and there was the way, clear and open. It was right.

Bea did her job as counselor and nurse, making sure that Nora understood her options and the implications of her choice. At her first clinic appointment, Bea made arrangements for Nora to talk to a few mothers who had children from three months to three years old. Bea always wanted the women she counseled to understand how much their lives would be changing, and to be ready and hungry for it. Too many abused, neglected children had passed through Bea's life over her years in clinics. A mother had to be able to love her child and care for it. All else that was good for the baby would follow from that.

Nora's visits with the other mothers were definitely a reality check for her. But it did not change her mind. Having and loving the baby was a certainty that simply was. For almost the first time in her life, Nora had absolute certainty about something. And she was simply in awe.

Every week brought with it new physical change or some crazy emotional swing that defied her own will and took over her body. After a while Nora submitted completely to whatever her body told her to do. This ranged from cravings for Zagnut candy bars at 2 a.m. to crying binges while watching comedies.

Throughout it all, Tunney seemed barely fazed. Nora's mood swings from tears to guffaws were routine for Tunney, his sisters having provided a full education on the multiple personalities of pregnant women. He even humored Nora when he patiently nodded agreement and made the right affirming noises on the nights that she would list all of her favorite baby names for that week. One day he even brought home a knitted baby blanket that he bought from an elderly woman who sold handmade afghans in her brother's used book store.

Nora had been touched by the gift and went on one of her crying jags. Tunney eventually retired to the fire escape with a beer and a joint, resurfacing only after Nora called him in to eat a plate of spaghetti.

The most interesting change, Nora thought, was that she did not feel at all embarrassed by her crying or laughing jags. She did not control it, so why act as though she could? Anyway, Tunney was a trooper and took her tidal emotions all in stride. Although some of the women that he brought home did not always appreciate a tornado of a pregnant woman distracting Tunney from their attentions.

Tunney and Nora had finally come to complete agreement that they would remain friends who loved each other rather than lovers. They both needed a trusted friend right now in their lives, and one who would not run out after a lover's spat or complicate one another's lives with the emotional teeter-totter of a sexual relationship.

While Nora and Tunney were absolutely clear about their relationship, his girlfriends usually were not.

"They're not girlfriends, Nora."

"Well, what should I call them, then? Your women? Your lovers?"

"Oh, please." Tunney scowled at Nora. "Why do they need classification, Nora. Why not try referring to each person by her name? That must be how you process information or something. You always try to categorize and box up. Is that how all the girls from Chestnut Hill are?"

Nora's bottom lip protruded and she truly looked hurt. "I'm not just another girl from Chestnut Hill, Tunney. They don't run away from their father's and get knocked up. See now. I'm quite unique." The pregnant runaway looked up defiantly and met Tunney's guilty eyes.

"Jeez, Nora. I'm sorry, kid. It was a long day at the office, right?"

"I'm sorry too. I asked that in a bitchy way and I deserved it. I guess I'm just a little jealous, in a sisterly way, and I want them all to fail to captivate you. Is that silly, or what?" Nora forced a chuckle and Tunney reached for her hand.

"Damn, it's easy to forgive you. You always claim guilt in the second round and we never need to fight until one of us gets KO'd."

"That hurts too much, Tunney. I've done that."

"Good. Now that that's settled, I'm going to fetch one of my lovers, Sally be her name, and I may or may not see you later." Tunney stood grinning and kissed the top of Nora's head. She could not help but laugh.

"Okay, lover boy. Be careful so we aren't walking our kids to school together in ten years."

"Ouch, but good, yes, good reminder there, sis. Very visual. What a boy like me needs."

After grabbing a beer from the fridge, Tunney wrapped a short paper bag around it as he walked to the front door.

"Want me to bring you back anything? A Zagnut?"

"No, Tunn. I'm going to curl up with a couple file boxes that I promised Bea I'd sort out for her by tomorrow. Go and have fun."

"Thanks, kiddo. I'll see you in the a.m."

As the scenery of the Oregon coast blinked past her window, missing Tunney was the seat partner she was stuck with for the time being. *My best friend*, she thought. But this was the part that she had to do on her own. Having the baby was her decision and she felt strongly that it should not be imposed on others, especially Tunney. He had only bought into a gas-sharing partner back in February when their adventure had started. Tunney did not buy into foster fatherhood. And anyway, he had his own way to find, his country's war and his own past to forgive and forget. Vietnam had always been a third passenger in the car and in their apartment, just as Nora's pregnancy had become yet a fourth passenger on their journey.

While Tunney always worked really hard to be up, he would

get very silent sometimes and drink for hours alone on their fire escape ledge. Nora had learned to leave him be when he went into shut-out mode. Tunney needed time alone to process his past and all his daily interactions with people he would meet at the boutique and in his wanderings in the Haight. In between he would find book stores where the owners helped him discover the works of the mystics and great minds of past ages and older worlds who asked the questions that most left to men of God and academics.

Although he was not college educated, Nora thought that Tunney was more of an intellectual than some of the professors and most of the students she had met at Boston University. Philosophical questions were real to Tunney, they were not just academic exercises held at arm's length from the real world. For Tunney, answering questions about the existence of God, man's relationship to the universe, whether time was a human-created or universal principle were the stuff of his everyday worries.

Half the time Nora had no idea what Tunney was talking about and why answering those obscure questions was so important to him. And then she would start to wonder whether those were the real questions that she should be focusing on too. But then thoughts of the baby would knock out every other thought, and make wondering about whether or not man's spirit is eternal seem irrelevant.

As though it read Nora's internal dialogue, the baby kicked her hard in the ribs. She closed her eyes and pressed her hand against her baby bulge. *I love you, Baby Dodge. And I don't even mind that I can't think about anything but you.*

Bea had laughed at Nora the week before when, lost in her own thoughts about the baby, she had not heard Bea ask a question.

"Yoo-hoo, Nora. Earth to Nora. Hello!?" Bea had stood with her hands on her hips, waiting for Nora to notice her existence.

"Sorry, Bea."

"You were thinking about the baby, weren't you?"

"How did you know?"

"You had that awed, glazed-over look in your eyes that I've seen thousands of times in other expectant moms who can't stop thinking about their babies."

"It's true, Bea. I'm useless at anything else right now but thinking about Baby Dodge."

"You've been doing a great job organizing my whole filing system, lady. That took a bit of thought, huh?"

"I guess so. But organizing is easy for me. Tunney says I categorize everything, and he's probably right."

"It's called systems organization, Nora. You're great at it. A natural. I'd still be sorting through files from 1959 for a patient profile if it weren't for you."

Bea was right. Nora had taken up her job offer to create a filing and organization system for all the clinic records to earn some money for her and Tunney's household. All of Nora's savings had finally dried up and it was very hard for a pregnant woman to get a job, even in the Haight. Bea was badly in need of someone to organize her files but did not want to pay for an expensive temp. One day she had asked Nora to help with a few boxes as a barter exchange for her clinic visits. After seeing the results, Bea hired Nora to get her organized once and for all, and set up a system she could live with and that was easy enough to work on autopilot as needed.

It was a confidence booster for Nora to learn that she did have some natural skills that could be applied to a job. She could be self-sustaining, earn a living and support the baby. If nothing else, her time in college would help her get a good secretarial job, or a management job in a small business.

Nora's greatest fear was that she and the baby would become destitute, with nothing to fall back on except her father. And she had fully convinced herself that Michael Dodge would slam the door in her face if she showed up with her love-child. Nora could not face the chance of a door closing on her right now.

Although it was warm in the bus, Nora shivered and Baby Dodge kicked in response. *That's right, my baby. We need to make it on our own. And we will.*

When Bea had first mentioned Hope Creek Farm for Expectant Moms near Tillamook on the Oregon coast, Nora could only picture a woman's prison camp she had seen in a news clip.

Women dressed in mauve housecoats smoking cigarettes and staring straight ahead like wild, captured animals, angry yet contained.

But after Bea explained how Hope Creek Farm actually operated and its history, Nora slowly realized that it might be the best place to spend her last trimester, and to stay until she was ready to venture back into the world as a woman and a mother. *Somebody's mother.*

Hope Creek Farm was started by a couple who had lost their daughter and only child after her botched abortion in a filthy motel room left them childless and asking why. Marge and Billy Gray realized that it was fear of their judgment that had pushed Ginny to the abortionist rather than telling them that she was pregnant.

Over and over again, Marge and Billy asked themselves how they would have reacted to Ginny's dilemma if she had told them. They would have sent her away, they concluded, and Ginny probably had realized that too. Sending a pregnant teen away generally meant to a religiously-run institution that forced repentance and shame on the young women. That type of environment was not one that Ginny could have tolerated. She was a free spirit who could not sit in one spot for more than a few minutes and thrived through movement, dance and the beautiful paintings into which she put her heart and soul. High school had been difficult for Ginny because it held little to capture her interest or sustain her already limited attention span for academic subjects. She had started skipping school a few days a week to hang out with artists and musicians and poets who took over part of an aging brewery district on the edge of downtown Portland.

Ginny's openness and trust eventually put her into the bed of a painter who had been the first to acknowledge her as a fellow artist. Falling hard, Ginny never let the possibility that sex could eventually mean pregnancy enter her seventeen-year-old head.

After almost two years of guilt and pain, and a million if-onlys, Marge realized that the only way they would ever heal was to not let what happened to their daughter happen again to another Ginny. Pregnant young women needed a safe place to retreat to where they would not be judged or pitied. A peaceful place where they could make a contribution while deciding whether they would be mothers or would give their children up for adoption. Again, no judgments. Each young woman was treated the same at Hope Creek Farm. Each would share in the many chores and responsibilities of making the dairy farm operate smoothly and efficiently, making enough money to support up to forty women at a time. The young, expectant mothers were each provided with prenatal health care and social services, a readjustment grant, and help getting a job and housing once they left the Farm.

Marge's family had owned the dairy for three generations, but none of her brothers had wanted to work it once their father could no longer manage the daily operations. When Marge asked her father if she and Billy could run the dairy as a means to support expectant single mothers, he simply nodded and said, "We'll have to start building a big dorm, huh?" And he turned and faced the wind coming off the coastal plain so his daughter would not see the tear that fell for Ginny, his lovely grand-daughter whose laughter was gone forever.

Billy had gladly quit his job at the phone company and applied his management skills to revitalizing the Farm, and adapting its operations to a workforce of soon-to-be moms. At first, it had been a real eye-opener for Billy. He had not anticipated details such as morning sickness coinciding with the time when the cows needed milking, or that the smell of sour milk would induce vomiting in some of the young women during the second trimester.

So even though there were generally forty women on the Farm, Billy made the operations work with a revolving crew of twenty-five. That level of operation produced enough fresh milk, butter, cheese curds and yogurt to sell at the local co-op at a fairly good margin and supply Hope Creek Farm.

Marge's job focused on keeping the women active, informed and healthy. Through her connections in the nursing community, Marge brought in midwives, social workers, job search specialists, psychiatrists, adoption agencies and doctors for "her girls" to meet with. Bea had gone to nursing school with Marge and they had somehow managed to stay in touch over the years. When Marge called Bea to help her set up comprehensive health and social support services at Hope Creek, the San Francisco clinic manager jumped at the chance, and helped the Farm secure grant support as well. Bea had seen too many girls and young women make the wrong choices about pregnancy because they did not have the information or available resources to know what the right path was for them; not for their parents, or their priests, or their boyfriends, but for them. Abortion was not one of the choices at Hope Creek Farm, only whether a woman would leave the farm with or without her baby. And no judgment.

It was the no judgment philosophy that had finally made Nora think that Hope Creek Farm was the place she needed to be right now. She thought it was funny that as soon as she was visibly pregnant, everyone she had contact with, including strangers in grocery store lines, thought they had a piece of her. Either through reaching out and touching Nora's stomach or eyeballing her and zapping a judgment with their readable stares, her pregnancy elicited physical and emotional reactions from many people.

It was so tiring, Nora thought, to be constantly at the ready to react to both the well-wishers and those sending negative vibes and pressing judgments on her. The openness and freedom of the Haight was great if a woman was single and had the right look or groove on to get a job or experiment with commune living. Nora was pregnant, and the Haight stopped being as cool. Her growing belly became a barrier, eliciting judgments from those who felt she became less able as she grew more pregnant. Less able to be a "chick," less able to be an employee, less able to be hip. Less able.

It was so easy to get pregnant and yet the severe judgments people made about her condition, pregnant and single, made it seem like she had purposefully schemed to be a woman of no morals or values. Nora wondered what it would be like if men could get pregnant. A wry smile formed as she pictured a drive-through gas station where men could get an abortion while they had their oil changed. Men certainly would not put up with the inconvenience of pregnancy unless they really wanted a baby. Convenient, legal abortion would be a community standard if the tables were turned. What was it about women that made it so easy for men to write all the rules and decide all the fates of their lives and futures?

She looked down at her belly. *Well, you won't be like that, will you Baby Dodge? If you're a girl, I'll teach you to stand up for yourself and be independent. If you're a boy, I'll teach you to respect women and take full responsibility for your actions.*

Shaking her head, Nora again realized the enormity of the responsibility facing her. She was going to be a mother. A category she knew little about since her own mother felt no compunction to be one. *I'll be different. I'm not my mother. I have no piece of her in me. I'll be different.*

Tunney and Nora's next-door neighbor in their apartment building had taught her about mantras. Nora thought that hers would be '*I'll be different.*' That might be the only defense she had against shutting out her own child like her mother had shut her out.

When Nora had talked to Bea one night after work about her mother, the older woman could feel the younger's resentment sucking all the air out of the room.

"You should seriously think about talking to someone about your mother. You can't hold on to all that anger, Nora. It's not good for you or the baby." Bea had taken Nora's hand in hers then and cocked her head slightly as she always did when she wanted a response.

Nora looked up at Bea in surprise. She had not realized that her anger was so apparent when she talked of her mother.

"What do you mean, talk to someone? Like a priest or something?"

"No, dear, like a shrink. A psychiatrist."

"I'm not crazy, Bea. I just hate my mother."

"Psychiatrists are not just for those with mental illness, Nora. They are for anyone and everyone who needs an objective source to talk to, about their fears, concerns, family issues, and you name it. You don't want Baby Dodge to inherit that anger, do you?" Nora shook her head. "Then you need to let it go, Nora. But it's real hard to do that alone usually."

Bea had written down the name and address of a woman psychiatrist she knew and trusted. Nora folded the paper and thanked Bea, but knew she would not talk to anyone about Jan Dodge right now. Her mother was the last person on earth who she wanted to focus any thought or energy on. *She doesn't deserve it*, Nora repeated in her head over and over, until Jan floated away again.

Suddenly the bus driver's voice pulled Nora out of her reverie. "Next stop Tillamook. We'll be at the bus station in about ten minutes." The driver's voice cracked over the ancient microphone, with every third or fourth word cut out by static. But Nora still understood.

She had landed.

Now the next phase of her life with Baby Dodge would begin. *Here we go little one. You'll be safe. I'll be safe.*

The Greyhound bus station was small-town small. Old wooden benches, shiny from years of wear, were empty except for an old woman clutching a small valise and a lonely soldier smoking a cigarette and thumbing through a comic book.

Nora was the only person who got off in Tillamook. The driver wished her well as he pulled her suitcases from the storage compartment.

"We're real proud of your husband, young lady. You tell your soldier that, will ya?"

"Yes, sir, thank you, sir." Nora turned away quickly, feeling terrible suddenly for making up a life that she was not part of. She wondered what the locals thought of all the pregnant girls milking cows at Hope Creek Farm.

Then suddenly she heard her name.

"Nora. Nora Dodge?" Turning, Nora saw an elderly man in baggy pants, suspenders and a well-worn flannel work shirt that had once been red.

"Yes, I'm Nora."

"Miss Nora, I'm Harry. I'll be taking you to Hope Creek Farm."

"Thank you, Harry. Thank you." Nora swallowed hard as her throat seized up. No other words could get out. She was so happy to be rescued from the bus station. The very air, every bench and faded wall schedule fumed with loneliness and the false promise of a better place somewhere else.

But this was her better place.

"I'll take your things. You shouldn't be liftin'." Harry bent down and took a suitcase handle in each hand. It looked so heavy to bear that Nora suddenly wished she had not accepted all the baby clothes, blanket and suitcases from Bea.

"Please, Harry, I can take one of those."

He stopped abruptly but did not put the bags down. Harry could not take his eyes off Nora. She shifted her weight and looked down at her feet. "Harry, can I..."

"No, Miss, no." The old man shook his head like he was shaking off an unwanted thought. "Sorry, Miss. You just reminded me of someone for a second."

Harry turned and headed towards the door to the parking lot. He mumbled something twice that Nora thought she caught the end of. It sounded like he said, *My Ginny*.

# # #

Chapter 21: Revelations

Boston

June 1969

Willa's memory worked on the faint, musty smell of old pews and prayer books as she passed a church on Tremont Street, bringing back the entire day she had spent with Mary ten years before. It was one of her favorite memories from her only other Boston summer.

On that day ten or so years before, Willa had for the first time felt a sense of belonging and family with her father and Nora. It didn't have the deep connections yet that she felt in Botswana, but a separateness that before had sat heavy in the air of her father's house and his life had now floated away. That was the day that the Boston house of Dr. Dodge began to emerge as a home for her. It was another place to belong, to love and be loved. Mary had seen the lonely look in Willa's little girl eyes as she roamed around her father's huge house. Being a woman with a talent for sensing what troubled folks, Mary could see Willa struggling to get her bearings and ground herself in her father's large and often lonely home.

Willa was lost. Botswana was as clear in its distance from her as Boston was obtuse in its presence.

"You've got an open spirit, girl. You need to exercise it a bit I think." Mary's voice carried the same tone of truth as Mma Cookie's did.

Willa nodded as Mary pulled a stool up next to her at the breakfast bar, her child's eyes full of unshed tears. She missed Mma Cookie and Sammie Po. And she missed being with her mother in the surgery and telling her what the Batswana patients were saying. Mary knew just the adventure that Willa needed.

From the moment she stepped on the subway with Mary for the visit to the AME church, Willa embraced the city of her father and sister. She reveled in the glory of the Black women singing in the choir, their heads a bounty of color in elegant hats, some feathered and others beribboned, weaving and rolling with the rhythms of gospel. Willa began to feel her heart again that morning. *So maybe I do belong here with my father, even if only a little bit,* she chanted in her head as the choir's united voice delivered a homey comfort, a sense of belonging.

Mary had kept smiling at Willa all the way back to her father's house, and squeezing her hand. Willa wondered if there was any way that Mary could be related to Mma Cookie. Both of them taught her things and comforted her, always knowing when she needed encouragement and when she needed a hug.

Willa broke out of her reverie of that long ago summer, walking away from the smells and rustles of God's printed words and the painted windows of Trinity church. It was almost noon and her father was expecting her at the Harvard Club for lunch. He had left her a note on the kitchen table as back-to-back emergency surgeries had kept them from having a chance to really catch up since she arrived in Boston.

It was just a week ago that she said goodbye to her whole life in Botswana. Goodbye to Jan, to Mma Cookie, Sammie Po and Mma Lilli, and to Chief Tau. Goodbye to familiarity and easy conversations, to desert winds and the infinite blue of the African sky.

And goodbye to Tom. Tommiwe of Botswana. Tom of Cape Cod, Massachusetts. Her Tom.

Willa was trying hard to ignore the hollowness that she felt in her chest and head. It was the spot that Tom had occupied in all his physicality. Gone was his smell and the touch of his fingers on the back of her neck, the beautiful spot right below his belly button, the way he took a sip of beer, his chest against hers and the rhythm of his heart as her ear kissed his skin. All gone. Now only a hollow spot. And not even the comfort of Mother Mercy's routines to provide ballast, or a stabilizing glance from Sammie Po to reset the fulcrum on the important and the real.

Tom's letter had been such a surprise. It had arrived just two days after Willa got to Boston. She smiled at his forethought and planning. It was the engineer shining through, calculating the variables that would produce the intended results.

Carol had brought the letter into Willa as she was finishing a bowl of soup and catching up with Mary. Carol had been very attentive to Willa and had all kinds of plans laid out for her stepdaughter. From that first day in her father's home Willa realized that the best response to Carol was just to smile and nod in agreement at all her suggestions. Usually they were good ones, and it precluded Willa from having to make any decisions while feeling so ungrounded. Mma Cookie would say she was homesick. Willa simply felt lost, the Mother Mercy context no longer lending its comfort and balance. But then the letter came.

"Well, here's a letter already for you, Willa. And it has African stamps on it."

"What? From Botswana?" Willa took the letter from Carol and examined the envelope.

"It's from Tom!" Willa looked up at Carol but realized that she could not understand the significance of a letter from Tom.

"Tom, huh. Is he your sweetie?" Carol asked conspiratorially and looked to Mary with a wry smile.

Smiling back, Willa excused herself and went to the stone bench in the back yard. Taking a deep breath she used her finger as a letter opener and took out the tissue-thin blue paper.

His hands have touched this paper and now I'm touching his words. What will he say?

The letter was dated ten days before she left Botswana.

Dear Willa,

First of all, I already miss you and you haven't even left yet. As I write this you're just a few villages to the east and I'm in a pup tent next to a sick borehole pump. But in real time, you're a few continents away, reading this letter under a Boston summer sky.

And aren't they beautiful there, those Boston skies? Endless blue in the summer with a few white, puffy clouds thrown in for perspective. Can you tell that I'm jealous that I'm not there with you, sharing a hard bench and a hotdog at Fenway on a summer evening?

But, alas, my far away Love, the light by which I pine for you is a paraffin lamp that is also serving as an effective heater in the tent. Remember that some of us, those inhabiting the southern hemisphere, are just beginning our winter.

I'm having a hard time figuring out how I'll keep my heart from breaking when you leave, and I haven't come up with any real effective strategies yet.

There's always the collection of 19th century books by British authors in the Francistown Library that could help me ignore the fact that you're no longer around. In fact, I could have a fantasy affair with Jane Eyre, or Elizabeth Barrett Browning, Georges Sand even. I figure it will be easier being in a fantasy England than being here alone in Botswana without you.

But enough of the whining and pining.

Did I mention that I love you?

Your father by now has certainly taken you to the most posh Boston eateries and introduced you to the most eligible bachelors in the City of Brahmins. But, alas, don't be fooled by doctors with large bank accounts. They only love your body, I mean your mind, I mean, can you tell I'm already jealous?

It's hard not to be because you are so exquisitely beautiful, and that's just your mind. Don't get me started on your body because there's not a cold shower anywhere within 100 kilometers of here.

Anyway, the fact is, things just won't be the same here without you, my Willa. I know that's taking liberties to call you "My Willa", but that's what's in my head.

Jan has already cornered me to work on a new plumbing system for the compound, she said, "After Willa leaves, of course." She has already imagined me wandering around aimlessly, mumbling your name, and wants to divert a potentially embarrassing situation before it starts. I think I agree that it will be hard to think of you as I wrestle with cold, hard copper pipes.

Without getting too sentimental, I just need to say, for the record, that you, Willa Dodge, have had a life changing effect on me. I can say with utmost certainty that I'm a better person for knowing you. And I know what love is. I've tasted love in you and through you and with you. What a treat you are!

The paraffin lamp is beginning to sputter and so time to finish this and grab a few winks. Please enjoy yourself to the fullest, enjoy being with your father and sister, and learning the streets of Boston and Cambridge. If you haven't fallen for a handsome intern at Mass General, an itinerant Gloucester fisherman, or a Brookline Democrat, I'll see you at Christmas. No strings attached, Willa. Find you and be you.

Love, Me (aka Tommiwe)

Willa read the letter only once as she sat there in the yard. Closing her eyes she could picture Tom and what he must be doing just then in Botswana. It was amazing how his words alone, written in his cursive scrawl, could build a bridge all the way from Botswana to Boston. She could feel him in the flutter of her belly.

Picking up her pace as she neared the Harvard Club, Willa half hoped her father would be late. Then she would have time to read the letter again.

How many times would she read it before Tom's face would no longer be clear, the sound of his voice no longer able to be heard? Would this happen at a certain point? It had happened before when she was a little girl, after she left Boston. All the way home on the plane she could visualize her father and Nora and Mary. But even before her mother picked her up at the train station in Francistown, all their images were getting blurry, their voices muffled.

As Willa approached the front of the Harvard Club, a doorman opened the heavy wood and glass doors, greeting her in a voice that reminded her of Johnny. Inside was just as dark and male as she had remembered it.

"Good afternoon. Might you be Miss Dodge?" a male receptionist asked, still withholding a full smile until he had confirmed her legitimacy to be there.

"Good afternoon. Yes, I am Willa Dodge."

"Miss Dodge, your father just called and he is on his way. Shouldn't be more than ten minutes."

"Thank you." Willa looked around for a place to sit near a lamp so she could read Tom's letter again.

"Pardon, Miss Dodge. Your father asked me to seat you

upstairs in the family dining room. Please follow me."

"If you point me in the right direction I can go myself, so you won't have to get up."

"Oh, no, Miss Dodge, you must be escorted. That is a firm rule for unattended young ladies."

"Okay, then lead me on, *Rra*."

"What? My name's not Rob, Miss. I'm Patrick."

Willa smiled. "Thank you, Patrick. I accidentally spoke another language."

Rra Patrick glanced over his shoulder as he led Willa up the broad stairway that consumed the main room of the first floor. It was a look meant to remind her that she knew nothing about the rules here, and to just obey. Thick Persian rugs covered most of the hard wood stairs and the hallway that led to the dining room.

Small sitting areas were formed in nooks and landings along the way. Most had an older man in residence in an ancient leather chair, reading the *Wall Street Journal* or a book under the dim light of a marble-based lamp.

Off the corridor that led to the dining area, two gated doors opened to a small ballroom. This was it!

This was the memory that Willa often recalled in the years following her visit to Boston. But the details blurred more and more each year until all she remembered was the floor.

Large black and white tiles formed a chessboard floor, made all the more apparent because the room was empty, save a few chairs by a window.

Now the memory came back in all its original detail. It was the end of Willa's first Boston summer, the night before she returned to Botswana. Her father had taken her and Nora to the Harvard Club, where they met Carol for the first time. Willa had never seen her father so happy and animated. Even Nora laughed at his teasing and jokes that night.

On their way out after dinner Willa had seen the chessboard floor in the empty ballroom. It had drawn her in, magnetic in its geometry and contrast. Nora followed her little sister into the large, silent room.

"Giant dead chessmen come in here after midnight and play on the floor." Nora looked directly at Willa, her eyes wide and serious. The younger sister stood stock still and unblinking.

"Have you seen them?" Willa whispered so as not to wake the chessmen.

"One night I saw them moving past the window at midnight when father and I were walking back from Symphony Hall," Nora answered in a fake-frightened voice.

"Girls, what are you doing? We need to head home now." Michael Dodge walked towards his daughters and held out his arms to round them up.

"I'm a Queen and I can move in any direction," Nora spoke to no one in particular and stiffened up her body, standing tall and still.

"I'm a Knight and I'll guard you, Mma Queen." Willa looked up at Nora, happy to have a sister, and thinking that Nora would be a queen when she grew up. Copying her sister, Willa also put her arms at her side and stiffened up.

Dr. Dodge laughed, finally understanding the girls' fascination with the ballroom. He walked over to Willa and lifted her from behind.

"I move this Knight up two and over two. No, up four and over five!" Dr. Dodge moved Willa around the black and white tiles, picking her up and setting her down like a chess piece. Then he walked over to Nora.

"I move this Queen all the way across the board." Michael Dodge then lifted up Nora and swung her around and danced to the other side of the room. Willa and Carol's laughter was drowned out by Nora's, who laughed in the great joy of being the special one in her father's arms.

When they reached the far side of the ballroom, Michael stopped. Nora wrapped her arms tightly around his neck.

"I love you, Daddy."

"Oh, Pumpkin. I love you too. You're my special girl."

Willa was happy for Nora, whom she thought of as lonely and often out of sorts. This night was a special one. They had all became a real family and were happy all at the same time.

"Miss, this way to the dining room." Willa's reverie was

interrupted by Patrick the efficient receptionist.

"Oh, yes, just going down memory lane for a second." Willa followed Patrick's heels so as not to get chided again. He led her to the very table where they had all sat that night when the girls were chess pieces, when they met the lovely Carol, and her father could not stop smiling.

"This is the table your father requested, Miss Dodge. He'll be joining you momentarily, I'm sure."

Willa thanked Patrick and was glad to see him rushing unobtrusively back to his post on the first floor.

Just outside of the dining room area an elderly man got up and walked towards Willa's table. She had noticed him looking intently at her when she had passed a minute before. And still his eyes did not leave her face.

"Excuse me young lady. But are you Michael Dodge's daughter?"

"Yes, I am. I'm Willa Dodge."

"So, you're Jan's daughter." Willa nodded at the old man as a faraway look crossed his face and turned into a smile.

"You look so much like her, you know. At least what she used to look like when I knew her 20 some years ago. Heavens, has it been that long?"

"You knew my mother." It was more a statement than a question.

"Yes, my dear. Jan was one of my best surgical students at Harvard, and one of the hardest working. She put most of the men to shame with her skills, except your father, of course. He's one of the best of all time."

"Please do sit down, Dr. ..."

"Oh, pardon my poor manners. I'm Lawrence Peters. Retired surgeon and doctor emeritus of surgical training at Harvard Medical School."

"Dr. Peters, please have a seat. I know that my father will want to greet you."

"Thank you, Willa, for being so kind to an old man. You didn't get that from your mother. Hah! Not a sentimental bone in her body, that one." Dr. Peters laughed and shook his head. Willa joined him.

"Well, my mother hasn't changed. Her patients in Botswana call her Dr. Gakelape, which means Doctor who never gets tired."

Together the old doctor and the doctor's daughter laughed.

"Tell me about Jan's work, will you?"

Willa smiled and nodded. "Mother Mercy Clinic is my mother's life. It's all she has focused on for 20 years." Willa told Dr. Peters how the clinic had grown over time and the way Jan had trained and mentored so many Batswana nurses and doctors from all over the world. Describing the compound in detail to Dr. Peters, Willa also transported herself back to Botswana for a moment. Her steady place.

"I'm so glad that Jan is happy and has been so successful. That was her dream all along, to go to Africa. We all listened to her talk about it. We all were a little or a lot in love with her. I'm sure she's told you that."

Willa's eyebrows shot up. "Oh, no, my mother never talks about that. Did she even notice that men loved her, or pay attention to any of you?"

Dr. Peters laughed as he took off his glasses and rubbed his watery eyes. "You are right, young lady. Jan did not notice all her admirers. She had a different end goal than marriage. Except marriage to her field I suppose."

"You could say that she's married to the Clinic. It is her life."

"But you must be part of her life too?"

Hesitating a moment, Willa weighed her answer. "I am because I'm part of the clinic."

Willa described how she had created a spot for herself at Jan's side by becoming her translator and then eventually nurse's aide.

"Tell me about what you did as an aide," the old man asked, enthralled by this unusual daughter of his former students with her intriguing accent and gift for storytelling.

"I interview patients and make a first assessment of what level of care they need, such as critical or simple care. I treat minor wounds and rashes, assist in surgery with the instruments, and diagnose the common and obvious ailments like ring worm and infected wounds, and can help with certain pregnancy conditions."

"My word. How old are you?"

"I'll be twenty in October."

"You should be in medical school. It's more than in your blood, dear."

"I start pre-med in August, Doctor, at Harvard."

"Sounds like you've had pre-med your whole life. We'll have to see that you get to accelerate through that."

"Oh, but there's so much I don't know, Dr. Peters."

"Nonsense. Sounds like you could teach a triage class."

"Willa can do just about anything, I'm convinced." It was Michael Dodge.

"Father!" Willa stood up and Michael kissed her on the cheek and then held out his hand to the old man.

"Doc Peters, how are you? We missed you last month at the Harvard graduation. Don't tell me you're getting tired of wearing your sash and robes?" Michael Dodge smiled and Dr. Peters laughed.

"I'm too damn old to stand so long anymore, Michael, and that thought keeps me at home watering my flower beds from my chaise lounge."

Both of the men laughed in the comfortable way of old friends.

"Michael, you have quite a young lady here. Why didn't you tell me that the second generation of Dodges was going to wow Harvard Medical all over again!"

"I guess I didn't want to jinx myself and have Willa decide not to come." Michael looked very uncertain for a moment and his daughter caught a flash of sadness and regret in his eyes. *Why does he hurt so bad*?

The two doctors exchanged information on old colleagues for another few minutes before Dr. Peters excused himself.

"Willa, it was delightful to meet you. I'm sure I'll see you in the fall. They still let me intimidate the tenderfoots every year, so I do my part to start weeding the wheat from the chaff."

"Well, Willa will see you on the wheat side." Michael put his arm around his youngest daughter and smiled down at her.

"I'll try to live up to that, Dr. Peters."

"You will, dear. Good day, Michael. And Willa, please send my best to your mother." Willa nodded and smiled. One day she would have to hear more from Dr. Peters about her mother's time in medical school. There was so much about Jan that Willa was realizing she knew nothing about. Doc Peters was right, Jan did not have a sentimental bone in her body. Telling stories of her youth was not something Jan ever spent any time on.

Michael Dodge and Willa watched Dr. Peters move slowly across the room and then descend the broad staircase to the main floor.

"You look really nice, Willa. All dressed up!" Dr. Dodge paused. "You look like your mother today. That's probably why Doc Peters knew you were a Dodge."

"Thank you, father. Or, thank Carol. She bought this entire outfit for me. I guess I didn't bring what you could consider an up-to-date wardrobe." Willa smiled, a little embarrassed but also resigned to the fact that she did not arrive in Boston as a fashionable young woman. "I did see Dr. Peters looking at me like he knew me."

"He probably won't be the only one. Just wait until the party on Saturday. We can both get tired of people saying that you look like your mother."

"I always thought that I looked like you and that Nora looked like mother?"

A shadow crossed Michael's face and curved into a sad smile.

"Father?" Willa knew immediately that something was not right. A grayness of despair drew the happiness from his face. The fear that had hidden behind his eyes now fought its way out, exposing the father to his observant daughter. He could wait no longer.

"Willa..." He looked into his daughter's eyes. How could he tell her this? Why had he waited so long?

"Honey, it's your sister, Nora."

Suddenly the words of the Dingaka on top of Tsebe Hill rushed back to her. *Your sister is lost...*Before Dr. Dodge could continue, Willa cut in.

"What's wrong, father? Did something happen?" A fear ripple cut across Willa's spine. She knew the answer.

"Willa, the fact is, we don't know where Nora is." Michael looked away from Willa's eyes and stared at his hands.

"What do you mean? You said she was traveling?"

"I was scared to tell you." Dr. Dodge pulled a hanky out of his pocket and rubbed his eyes. "I feel like such a failure."

"How could you be a failure, father? Did you ask her to leave?" Willa's eyes widened as she realized the extent of her father's guilt and hurt.

"No, I didn't ask her. She just left one day. She just left a note."

Michael described the last time he had seen Nora before Christmas, and how she had seemed so far away, so not like the Nora he knew. How she had talked about being in love with a musician.

"She said I wouldn't understand why she had chosen him. His name is Pete. And I didn't, I don't. But I shouldn't have pushed her so hard. Now I haven't seen her for months and months and God knows whether she's dead or alive." Michael's voice cracked at the end and he rubbed his eyes again.

He is like an elephant, Willa thought. He cries with no tears, only a sorrowful voice.

Willa put her hand on top of her father's. "Nora is fine, father. I can feel that she is fine." Dr. Dodge looked skeptical, then surprised.

"She's fine, you think?"

"That's what I'm feeling, and it's stronger than the sadness of her not being here." Dr. Dodge looked quizzically at Willa. But he wanted so badly to believe her words.

"Of course, we must find her, father."

Michael's mouth opened to speak but a waiter interrupted. He was relieved. How was he to respond to Willa?

He reached for his bourbon and gulped down the last sip, cringing as the ice cubes rattled against the glass.

# # #

Whenever Willa encountered the strange and opulent in Boston, she would picture what Mma Cookie's reaction would be and that would make her smile. It was Willa's way of keeping her African mother at her side. It was her way of staying protected until she could figure out how she fit in, what she should say, how she should act, and how to react to a culture that was unfamiliar and not always patient or friendly.

The Country Club was clean and green, an orderly groomed veldt of light-footed people. They seemed to float on top of the lawns, hovering amid their shared murmurs and smiles, basking in one another's general satisfaction. It was a world inverted from the dust and heat and spontaneity of Botswana. But it was beautiful and seemingly perfect, like a golden bowl Willa had seen in a glass display case in a Rhodesian museum.

Carol had again taken it upon herself to dress Willa in appropriate clothing suited for her welcome party at the Country Club. Never paying that much attention to what she wore, Willa had let Carol dress her since her arrival in Boston. Her stepmother had impeccable taste and knew all the rules. And, indeed, to Willa it seemed that Boston came with a lot of rules.

Carol was tentative and wary the first time she presented clothes to Willa on the morning after her arrival.

"If you don't like these we can go out later to Filenes or Neiman Marcus and let you try some things on." Carol said as she shifted her weight back and forth balancing several large white boxes. "I know that you didn't have a lot of shopping options in Botswana, and I just wanted you to have some nice things."

Willa laughed but then saw Carol's bottom lip quiver.

"Oh, Carol, thank you. You're right. I had to laugh because the nearest dress shop to me was about 200 kilometers. Most of my clothes are things that Johnny brought back from his trips to Jo'burg and Cape Town. So his taste in women's clothes and ability to get my size right have led to some unfashionable and awkward outfits."

Carol smiled and seemed relieved. "I know you'll look wonderful in these, Willa. Thank you for..." Carol stopped and set the boxes on Willa's bed.

"Carol?" Willa watched the older woman suck in her breath and then look up uncertainly.

"I guess, thank you for being nice to me. For being polite."

"You're my father's wife and you have been so kind to me. Thank you for letting me invade your life here with my father."

"Please, Willa, you're a joy." Carol paused, deciding whether to continue. "Somehow Nora and I never got along that well. To her, I stole Michael away. I've been in this house almost ten years but whenever Nora looks at me it's as though I'm still an unwanted visitor."

A sad smile lingered for a moment before Carol roused herself and stood up. Willa reached out to Carol and took her hand in hers.

"I'm so glad that my father found you. I remember how sad he seemed when I visited ten years ago. That was until he saw you and the light and happiness returned to his eyes. You are not an unwanted visitor. I'm sure that Nora doesn't mean to show that. She just never had a mother so she doesn't know what to do with one. She only had our father and then only part of him because the hospital owned the rest."

"My heavens, you probably have it right, Willa." Yes, she had it right because Willa had experienced the same sporadic parent in her mother.

"And you have it right with these clothes. They're beautiful, Carol. Please help me fit in so I don't embarrass you and father."

Carol smiled a bit guiltily as Willa had sensed her concern about her stepdaughter standing out as strange and quirky. As Dr. Dodge's second wife she had been forced to hear or had eavesdropped on enough talk about the beautiful, talented and quirky Jan Dodge that Carol did not want Willa to spur all that talk again. That was the kind of talk that would lead to one of her migraines. And she had not had a migraine since Nora had left the house.

Now at the Country Club, Willa stood out for the light in her eyes and her brown, elegant hair that hung long to the middle of her back, but not for having quirky clothes. Carol had dressed her in a peach knit mini dress that showed off Willa's curves and her long legs. Michael's jaw had literally dropped when she appeared in the kitchen before they left for the club.

"Holy mackerel!"

Carol laughed and put her hands together under her chin, studying her newest creation.

"You look fabulous, Willa! I knew that peach would suit you."

"But so little peach. Isn't it a bit short?" Michael Dodge asked as he took a step back to see if that would lengthen the dress.

"Oh, Michael. This is all the rage. Willa wants to fit in and this is what all the young girls are wearing."

"Well, just stick close to me, Willa," her father said as he wagged his finger at his daughter.

"Ah, Michael, shush. This is a dress that a girl gets swept away in," Carol almost sang as she slipped her arm through her husband's arm.

Willa's head moved back and forth following her father and Carol's repartee like a tennis match.

"Like I said, stick close to me, Willa."

Scowling a bit, Michael Dodge grabbed his keys off the kitchen hook and drove his women to the Country Club.

Pure white open tents stood in contrast to the greenest grass Willa had ever seen. Only the thought of seeing Carol cringe kept her from immediately taking her sandals off.

Long tables covered with mauve tablecloths held platters of hors' d'oeuvres and hot trays, bottles of wine and bouquets of flowers amid shining rows of glasses.

Suddenly a glass of champagne was in Willa's hand and her father was introducing her to what seemed like a hundred people. At first she tried to focus and remember everyone's name. But soon the ladies with polka dot sundresses and the men in golf shirts all merged into one. Then younger people, close to her age, began appearing and Willa tried again to remember their names.

Her champagne glass kept being magically refilled. Again and again she heard, "*Oh, so pretty. She looks so much like Nora, she looks so much like Jan, she looks so much like Michael. She's so pretty, so polite, so unlike Jan. So open, so sociable, so unlike Michael.*"

After an hour, Willa excused herself from her father's table and sought out the refuge of the Ladies Room. It smelled of roses and lipstick and had gold speckled mirrors lining the walls.

The champagne had slowed down her internal time clock. How long had she been sitting on the toilet? Two minutes or twenty? Willa squeezed her eyes shut as she stood in front of the sink and dried her hands. *Time to face the crowd again. A different crowd then the usual crowd.* No lines of proud Batswana standing stoically and ill in line outside the clinic. Now a sea of white faces and pink lips, cool and prosperous and appropriately spaced across the lawn.

What would Mma Cookie be doing right now? Probably making morning tea and bread for Sammie Po and the nurses. And Johnny would be reading *Ulysses* still and maybe making Jan read Molly Bloom, if she would have the patience for it.

But Willa's reverie was interrupted by a voice, someone saying her name as she floated in her personal champagne cloud towards her father's table.

"Willa? You're Willa aren't you?"

As her eyes focused towards the voice, a young man walked confidently towards her.

"I am Willa." She stopped and let him close the space between them.

"I'm Jay. Jay Rogers. I know your sister, Nora. We went to school together." Jay held out his hand to Willa and she met it with hers and smiled. *Someone who knows Nora!*

"You knew Nora at secondary school?" Willa asked moving a little closer to him.

Jay laughed a little and Willa realized how attractive he was. It was the kind of handsome that wealthy men were: good genes, good skin, lean body, great hair, tussled yet put together.

"No, we went to B.U. together until last fall. And then we'd see each other here at the Club or at parties sometimes. Nora is a good friend of my sister, Joan. They did go to high school together."

Willa stood very still and the look on her face made Jay take a half step back. He cocked his head and waited for Willa to say what was so clear in her expression.

"Jay, I don't know you well, but can I ask you something?"

He shrugged. "Sure."

Willa took a deep breath. "Do you know where Nora is? Did you know that my father doesn't know where she is and hasn't seen her since Christmas?"

"Yah. Hey, I'm sorry for Doc Dodge. That's tough when someone just splits like that."

"But do you know where she is? Or would your sister know, or anyone?" Willa could hear her own voice rising.

"You know, I think Joan did hear from Nora sometime last winter. But I can't recall what she said."

"Do you mean she wrote to her or called her?" Willa was fully sober now, the effect of the champagne having been burned off by the heat that was radiating from her racing heart.

"Oh, man, I really don't remember."

Jay saw Willa's face suddenly fall and her shoulders slump.

"Hey, Willa, don't be sad." Jay shifted his weight back and forth and put his hands in his pockets. "How about a drink? I'll get you a drink, huh?"

Willa kept her head down and squeezed her eyes shut so the tears would not fall. *Where is Nora? It's time for us to be sisters again, and as adults now. Nora probably doesn't even know I'm in Boston. Or does she and is staying away because of that?*

Shifting his feet, Jay looked around for a champagne waiter and raised his hand to get the bubbly bearer's attention.

"Hey, Willa. Here's an idea. Joan's going to be home later and in fact is having a bit of a party tonight, just a few close friends. Why don't you come over to our house later and you can ask Joan about Nora."

Willa's face transformed. Gone were the sad eyes, replaced with a tentative smile.

"Really? That would be wonderful. Thank you so much. But will your sister mind if I just pop in like that?"

"Oh, forget it. It will be a trip for Joan to meet you. Why don't you come with me after your soiree here is over. I can take you home later tonight."

"You're sure that's not too much trouble, Jay?" While in Botswana it was a usual and welcome occurrence to have unexpected guests, Willa remembered that it was not the customary practice in Boston. Carol had just reminded her of that two days prior when Willa had wanted to stop by and visit Mary without calling first when they had passed near her house after shopping downtown.

"It's no trouble at all. And we don't live that far from your father's house."

"I'll have to take your word for it. I'm so completely lost here in Boston."

"But you got found today, huh? Your father throwing this party for you, all his friends showing up. He knows a lot of people, your father." Jay smiled as he picked off two glasses of champagne from a passing waiter. He handed a flute to Willa and clicked his glass against hers.

"Cheers, Willa. Welcome to civilization. Boston will be the better for ya," he mocked in an Irish brogue.

He took a large drink and looked over the glass at this beautiful girl in the peach dress.

"Where *did* you get that accent? I just can't place it. Sort of British, but not..." Jay asked as he rolled out his best flirtatious smile.

Willa blurted out a laugh and then covered her mouth. "I guess it could be considered a mongrel accent, just a little bit of a lot of influences. Probably Mma Cookie has had the most influence. She's my Motswana mother. And then my mother, Jan, managed to keep her Boston accent even after twenty years away, so a portion from that. I went to secondary school in both Rhodesia and Botswana, with teachers from Britain, Rhodesia, India, the States, and different African countries."

Willa stopped abruptly. "Oh, I'm sorry, Jay. I'm babbling. The champagne..."

"No, please, keep going. You're the most interesting babbler I've listened to in a while."

They both laughed and Willa suddenly felt a little lighter. She was actually relaxing here at a party with 100 people she did not know.

A movement caught her eye. It was Carol waving her over to her father's table.

"I have to rejoin my father and Carol. Would you like to sit with us?"

"Let me check in with a few people first. If you don't see me before, I'll stop by when I head out to see if you still want to come to the house and meet my sister Joan."

Jay looked at Willa in a way that made her stomach flutter. If she had not drank so much champagne she would certainly have blushed. But now she felt emboldened and met his eyes.

"Thanks, Jay. You're actually the first person I've met who is close to my age since I've been in Boston. I'm feeling more comfortable here now. I guess I'm starting to find my balance," Willa said, just as she tilted slightly from the champagne.

He smiled with his eyes and took the empty champagne glass out of her hand. "I'm glad, Willa. I'll see you in a bit."

Nearing her father's table, Willa could see him smiling from ear to ear, his glance locked on her. She matched his grin and could not help laughing.

"Willa, sit next to your old man for a while. I can see now how hard it will be to compete for your time with your male admirers." Dr. Dodge smiled wryly. He too had been indulging in the champagne.

Carol moved over one chair and patted the seat she had been in. "Sit next to your father, Willa. He's not done showing you off." Carol smiled and then looked over at Michael Dodge conspiratorially. The doctor nodded and stood up. That was when Willa noticed a microphone in a stand next to him.

"Good afternoon everyone. Thank you for joining Carol and me here today to welcome my beautiful, not to mention very intelligent daughter, Willa, to Boston."

Suddenly there was clapping, and a few calls of 'here-here'. Willa beamed, reacting to Michael's joy as it wrapped around her and pulled her closer. *I have a father!*

How different he is from Jan, Willa thought. It felt good to be acknowledged, to be paid attention to. Willa felt spoiled and wonderful.

Her father continued. "As most of you know, I'm not much of a conversationalist. I never have been, which is probably why I became a surgeon. I let my hands do the talking." Guests laughed lightly and smiled widely.

"But today I want to acknowledge Willa's arrival in Boston and the start of her new life here." Dr. Dodge met Willa's eyes and she looked up at him, in awe that she would now have a father in the flesh.

"Most of you know that Willa has grown up in Botswana, in Africa, with her mother. And during those nineteen years that I missed her so badly, she was learning how to speak in three or four languages, administering to the sick as a nurse's aide, and putting up with her mother." Guests laughed heartily, whispering old gossip in each other's ears. Willa broke out in a noisy guffaw, the accurate characterization of her mother ringing only too true.

"So keep your eyes on Willa Dodge. She'll be the only pre-med student at Harvard who did her internship before she took old Doc Able's anatomy class." Michael met his daughter's eyes again.

Willa stood up and went to her father. Wrapping her arms around his neck she kissed his cheek, and he squeezed her hard in return. Willa turned her face to the microphone.

"Father, I want to thank you and Carol for such a wonderful welcome to Boston. And I'd like to ask everyone's forgiveness in advance for the dumb questions I'll be asking and the faux pas I'm likely to make. In Botswana we would say, *Ke motho, fela*, I'm only a human being. So forgive my naivety, my mispronunciations, and my utter lack of any fashion sense – thank god for Carol." Willa unconsciously pulled on her dress hem as chuckles and oh-nos came from the guests.

"You could certainly say that I've been isolated. But with all of your help, I know I'll be able to find my way in Boston."

Willa and Michael Dodge beamed at one another. Could it really be true, she thought? I have a father, an engaged parent, Willa kept saying to herself over and over again. It was something she had tasted only briefly when she had been with her father for part of a summer ten years before.

Michael Dodge was equally in awe. *I have a daughter who isn't trying to push me away or run away*. But would it stay that way? Would Willa get to know him better and then also turn away from him as Nora had done?

Nora. His heart ached for her in between his anger and underneath his guilt and disappointment. But the ache won out over all his other confused emotions. Nora was his baby girl. He had raised her, nursed her through the mumps, oohed and ahhed at how pretty she was in her first prom dress, and worried whenever she was out with boys. Being beautiful and being from an old Brookline family with old money could attract the wrong kind of boy. Carol and Michael had tried hard to ensure that Nora mingled with an acceptable crowd and was protected.

But then she had changed. All of a sudden nothing he did was right with Nora. Going with Carol and him to the Club stopped, as did meeting him at the Harvard Club for lunch. Nora would not go to Nantucket with them anymore during the summer, and she had always loved the island so much, and their time there, until a few years ago.

In fact, now that Michael thought about it, Nora had slowly cut him out of her life. They seemed to cross paths with only a few words passing between them, never spending more than a few minutes together. And Nora had been downright rude to Carol, forcing his wife to purposely stay out of her stepdaughter's way.

Had he gone too far in spoiling Nora? Had he left her raising too much to Mary because of his schedule at the hospital? Did she resent his absences? Had she never forgiven him for leaving her mother in Africa?

What was it, damn it, he wanted to scream across the perfectly manicured lawn and over the head of his perfectly manicured friends.

And what would Willa be thinking of him? She seemed surprised and disappointed that he had not even tried to find Nora.

Why hadn't he tried? He could have even hired a private detective to locate her. It certainly was not a money issue.

Dr. Dodge looked across the grounds and to the tree line in the distance. He knew why.

It was relief.

Ever since Nora had left there was an air of relief in their home. Carol was certainly calmer and less on edge, not having to face Nora's scowls and disapproval. Michael had begun to enjoy his evenings at home, not worrying about who Nora was out with, or when she was getting home, or whether she was studying hard enough, or whether she was trying drugs as a lot of the kids her age were.

Michael loved Nora. But he realized that he had not enjoyed being around her for the last two years that she had been in the house. Maybe he should have agreed to let her go to the Sorbonne like she had wanted. Now he could not even remember why he had been so adamant that she not go to Paris. Was it only because it seemed like something that Jan would do?

Michael thought about Willa's words at the Harvard Club earlier in the week. She had seemed so certain that Nora was okay and would want to see them. Poor Willa, sweet Willa. She would never acknowledge when Nora was mean to her when they had spent that summer together years before. And now she also refused to acknowledge that Nora might not be found, might not want to be found.

Maybe she would just forget about wanting to find Nora, Michael thought as he looked over at his youngest daughter again. *God, please let me hold on to her. And please let Nora be okay, wherever she is.*

# # #

Willa couldn't help control her gaping mouth when Jay pulled up to his family's house.

"This is your house?" Willa asked, in awe of the scope of the Tudor mansion.

Jay laughed at her expression and open awe.

"Well, it's my father's house. But it's more Joan's and my house, really. My parents are usually in Europe or the Caribbean. They come home at Christmas, most years." There was a hint of sarcasm in Jay's voice. "It's actually not the biggest house in the neighborhood, although I can see you're impressed with the size."

"When I tell people back in Botswana about homes this size it will only reinforce their notions that all Americans are rich and live in mansions." Willa noted with a smile as she took Jay's hand as he helped her out of the MG.

"You could tell them that size isn't everything. A large home is not necessarily a happy one." Willa heard a touch of sarcasm in Jay's voice again. It seemed that Nora and her father were not the only family having a hard time getting along.

Several other cars were parked around the circular drive, mostly sports cars, the type that younger, rich kids drove.

Willa's jaw dropped again when she saw the inside of the house. If only she could take a picture with her eyes and transmit it to Mma Cookie. But her African mother would not believe that only one family lived in such a place. Nor would she understand why a single family needed this much room.

'*I am not believing that a mother would not want to be closer to her children. A child could be lost or hurt and a mother would never know!*' Willa could hear Mma Cookie's voice clearly in her head.

Jay led her to the back of the first floor where there was a large family room off of the kitchen. The Moody Blues filled the room with soothing poetry that floated above everyone's heads along with thick marijuana smoke. A dozen people sat around on couches and puffy cushions on the floor, with a few couples nuzzling in corners.

"Hey everybody, this is Willa of Africa," Jay called out as he scanned the room for his sister Joan. There was a quick round of "hi and hey" and looks of interest and scrutiny from the young men and women whose attention was drawn by the arrival of the striking newcomer.

A head popped around the open refrigerator door in the adjoining kitchen.

"Jay! So glad you're back!" It was Joan, Willa surmised. She could see the family resemblance between the brother and sister.

Jay took Willa's hand and led her into the kitchen.

"Nora? No, what?" Joan walked towards Willa with a wine bottle in her hand.

"No, Joan, it's Willa, Nora's sister. Isn't that a trip! She's from

Africa and she just got here." Jay took the bottle from his sister's hand. "Let me get some glasses." Jay gave her a sideways look that Willa interpreted as, 'Haven't you had enough already?'

"Hi, Joan. I hope you don't mind that I dropped in. Jay thought you might be able to help me."

"Help you? Do you need drugs or something? I do have those, and if you're a friend of Jay's then you're my friend too, and all that." Joan laughed and walked back over to the refrigerator.

"Come here, Nora's sister." Willa followed Joan.

"This is what I got right now." Joan opened the refrigerator door and waved her hand along the inside of it, as though she were a showroom model. Across three shelves on the door, packed neatly in clear bottles, were rows of pills in various combinations of color: red and white, green and blue, purple and yellow.

Suddenly the door slammed. Jay was behind it.

"Jesus, Joanie. Willa doesn't want any of that shit. She just wants to talk to you. About Nora."

"Talk about Nora? What about?" Joan looked bewildered, her pupils so dilated that she resembled a rag doll with black button eyes.

Willa realized then that she had better talk quickly or she might lose Joan's heavily medicated attention. "Joan, we don't know where Nora is. I just got here from where I live in Botswana, in Africa, and I found out that my father doesn't know where Nora is and hasn't seen her since Christmas." Willa paused and looked to Jay. Joan's head was cocked, a look of rapt confusion on her face.

"Jay thought that Nora had contacted you a few months back. I thought that you might have an address where I could reach her." Jay could hear a strain in Willa's voice. *Please let Joanie have something*, he wished silently.

"Wait a second," Joan mumbled. "A postcard. Yah, I remember. I got a postcard." Joan reached for a full glass of wine from her brother and took a large swig.

Willa's heart skipped a beat.

"From Philadelphia. Yes. It was in the winter. Like January or something. Maybe February." With each sip of wine Joan seemed to remember another detail. Willa grabbed the wine bottle from the counter and refilled Joan's glass.

"Would you still have the postcard? Could I see it? Do you remember if she gave you an address to write to her?" Willa could hear her own voice rising with the hope that maybe, just maybe, Joan would have a clue to Nora's whereabouts.

"That funny card. It's where?" Joan took another sip. "It's in the mirror! I can see it in my head in the mirror." Joan seemed astonished at her own ability to recollect.

"What mirror, Joan? Your bedroom?" Jay said as he put his hand on Joan's shoulder.

Willa and Jay exchanged glances and he held his hand out to her.

"Follow me." Jay took Willa's hand and towed her behind him as he made his way through the hallway and to the staircase that led to the second floor. The music began to fade as they moved further down the hall until it was almost quiet by the time they reached Joan's bedroom, the last one along the corridor.

Jay led Willa into the bedroom with the familiarity and contempt that brothers have for sister's rooms. He walked straight to a French provincial vanity in the corner.

Willa spotted it before Jay did. Tucked into the edge of the mirror frame was a postcard of the Liberty Bell. Willa carefully wiggled the card free and turned it over. She began reading it out loud as Jay leaned over her shoulder.

"*Dear Joanie, so here I am in Philly. Pete's doing great and has a steady gig in town. You won't believe it but I got a job in a boutique for gay guys, and stranger yet, I love it, and all the guys have adopted me! It's great to be out of Boston and free. I'm not too far from Rittenhouse Square. More soon, Nora.*"

Willa kept flipping the postcard over but there was no return address. The postmark read *January 15, 1969*.

Plopping down on the vanity seat, Willa felt defeated.

"Hey, lady. Why the long face? You know where she is now."

"I do?" Willa registered skepticism.

"How many gay men's boutiques could there be around Rittenhouse Square in Philadelphia?"

Biting her lip, Willa looked up at Jay with hope. She suddenly had a lump in her throat.

"Do you think I could find that place?"

Jay heard Willa's voice catch and he wanted only to wrap his arms around her. It was a beautiful, real vulnerability that most young women he knew had already trained themselves not to show.

"Hey, lady..." Jay lifted Willa up from the vanity stool and hugged her. She smelled of fresh air and lemons. A sob escaped Willa's throat, the gentle hug releasing all the emotions she had tried so hard to keep in check since she had arrived in Boston. Jay hugged her harder as more tears fell.

"It will be fun, Willa. You can be a detective. Philly's just a train ride away."

Jay pulled out a tissue from a gilt edged box on the vanity and handed it to Willa.

"Just a train ride away," Willa repeated the words to make them real. It was a place to start. *The first step toward finding her sister.*

Finding Nora had become more than a wish. It was an entry point for Willa's new life. A portal through which she could begin to be a part of her family in Boston, and understand the world of her own origins. What was all of the *stuff* that she was made of? It was a lot more than what she had thought it was growing up in Botswana in the small, protective world of Mother Mercy, amid the pain and the joy of the sick and the cured and the brand new to the world.

With Nora gone there was something distinctly missing from her father's home. It was a clear and palpable void that Willa was afraid she would never breach until Nora came back. Only then could she begin to understand what it means to have a sister, and be one. To be a family.

"How about I take you home, Willa. As my grandmother used to say, you've had a big day, kid."

Willa looked up into Jay's green eyes. "Thank you," was all she could mutter or more tears would come. He had been so kind to her, so patient. She felt the same sense of trust that she did in

Botswana when the village rallies around to save the home or the farm or the marriage of an unfortunate family.

"You've been so nice to me, Jay. Thank you. You're not at all like my mother warned me about."

Jay laughed and took a step back.

"Your mother knows me? I didn't know that my reputation had made it all the way to Africa."

"Not you in particular. Just Boston men in general," Willa answered with a wry smile.

"And in general we are supposed to be exactly what according to the infamous Mrs. Dr. Dodge?"

"In the order in which it was dictated to me by my mother, you're shallow, fast talkers, use women as handmaidens and show pieces, and love hanging out with other men in dark clubs and on the golf course. And that pretty much sums up Dr. Jan's 'objective' warning."

A smirk grew on Jay's face. "Very astute, your mother. But she left Boston twenty years ago. She is only describing a certain segment of Boston male society. There are all kinds of new categories that she doesn't have a clue about."

"Well, today you fit only in your own category, as the understanding, patient new friend." Willa looked up at Jay. "I feel like we are friends and I just met you a few hours ago. Funny, huh?"

"Funny and cool, Willa." She was so open and innocent. Should he warn her that she must be more careful? Beware of the jackals?

On the drive back to her father's house, Willa answered Jay's questions about her home in Botswana. She told him about Dr. Jan and how she had started the clinic, about Mma Cookie and Sammie Po, about the Dingaka, the desert, and drought, and the patients at the clinic.

She told him nothing of Tom. That was still too intimate, too close to her heart to bring out into this foreign place with someone who had been a stranger only hours earlier.

The unique relationship that was her and Tom's belonged to them, alone. To tell Jay about it seemed like it would lessen it, make it seem like a silly schoolgirl's crush on an adventurous, charismatic Peace Corps volunteer who lived 7,000 miles away in a thatched hut.

Willa suddenly understood that only the two people in a relationship can understand it, know it fully. It cannot be described just as the taste of air cannot, or the scent of the wind cannot, or the touch of love's fingers cannot be described adequately with words alone.

Tom was hers, was of her senses. She was not willing to take him out and share him because his essence, who he was, could not be shared through words or anecdotes.

Tom was hers.

As Jay helped her out of his car when they reached Dr. Dodge's, Willa was suddenly hit with a great fatigue. Jay felt her strength flutter and he wrapped an arm around her waist as he led her to the back door.

"Jay, all I can say is thank you. You went beyond the call of duty, as my Uncle Sammi Po would say." Willa smiled, but it turned into an involuntary yawn.

"And I've been told I'm a compelling conversationalist," Jay admonished jokingly.

"I'm sorry. I'm overwhelmed. You're wonderful. Thank you." Willa reached for the screen door that led into the kitchen.

"You'll find her, Willa. I can tell."

Willa turned and faced Jay, then leaned toward him and kissed his lips softly. They both smiled the same smile at each other. Neither said a word.

The screen door clicked shut at the same moment that the door of Jay's car shut behind him. Crickets that had stopped chirping under the porch resumed their high-pitched twittering.

A world away the cicadas on the Kalahari veldt answered in their monotone, electric whine. Tom looked up from his cup of bush tea just as Mma Lilli did.

Neither said a word. Cicadas were telling tales that could not be spoken.

# # #

Chapter 22: Floats and Bellies

Tillamook, Oregon
July 1969

Nora loved these early morning trips to Cape Lookout more than anything else since she had arrived at Hope Creek Farm. Harry had asked her once if she wanted to go with him. The old man combed the beaches near the Cape for the rare whole sand dollars that had not been crushed by the beaks of scavenging seagulls, desperately seeking the shell's inner delicacy.

The Cape exuded peace. Nora inhaled it. During the week it was especially so as the weekend campers were not around to spoil the solitude with their loud trucks and trailers. Only the sound of the blue-green waves pressing new patterns in the sand, and an occasional gull cry, or a gust of wind hitting the catchments in the jagged cliffs.

"My Ginny loved this place best of all." It was Harry, his voice almost carried off by the wind.

Nora smiled at the old man. "I think it's become my favorite too, Harry. I feel like it's mine when I'm here. My special place."

"Yeah, same with Ginny. She'd run around the beach finding as many sand dollars as would fit in her sweatshirt pockets." Harry laughed and shook his head. "Her tummy would be bulging when we got back to the truck and she'd waddle and then wiggle into the cab so none of them would break."

Nora could see that Harry was far away now. He was back with Ginny and being a grandfather, building memories and dreams with his sweet granddaughter. Afraid to disturb his reverie, Nora said nothing. Her eyes scanned the beach ahead of them for the telltale white dots that marked a potential whole sand dollar.

Then a different colored object suddenly rolled up the wet sand, pushed by a large foamy wave.

Nora ran towards it. Harry was right when he said that she would catch the beachcomber bug.

A round, sea-green glass ball sat in its own puddle of salt

water. It was exquisite. Nora picked it up quickly before the next wave could lift it out of its pocket and pull it back into the surf. Rolling it in her hands she then held it up to the sky. A swirl of thicker glass at the top of the ball formed an opaque, flattened nipple. Maybe a mermaid's play top or a pirate's crystal ball. Today she felt childish, like she was little Ginny, discovering treasures on the secluded beach.

Harry walked up beside her. "That's a Japanese float. Keeps their fishing nets from sinking."

"It's beautiful." Nora twirled it again in her hands, mesmerized by the contours in the glass ball. "Did Ginny find these too?"

"Oh, yeah, once in a while. She found one once the size of the big globe in the county library." Harry made a big circle with his arms to demonstrate the size. "I still got that one. I'll show ya some time."

His voice faded out, as though the memory of Ginny had drained his will to speak any more.

Nora smiled at Harry and put her hand in his coat pocket, covering his bony, wrinkled fist, warm and strong with age.

"We best be getting back. I betcha that Billy is checking his watch wondering where his best worker girl is."

"I doubt I'm the best, Harry. My milking skills still leave a lot to be desired."

"But you've organized the farm books so well that everything seems to be working a bit better."

"Thanks, Harry. Sweet of you to say."

"Just talkin' the truth."

The old man and the pregnant young woman walked back to the ancient truck in silence. Nora wondered if she really had helped Hope Creek Farm as much as Harry had said, or whether he just liked her because she reminded him of Ginny.

Marge and Billy Gray ran a pretty tight ship, but Nora had noticed how the paperwork side of things seemed to suffocate them both. Their tendency to put off the bookwork resulted in production at the farm always being a bit behind. Bills sat too long without being paid, orders lagged behind a few days more than they should, and invoices piled up faster than the Grays could process.

Sensing Billy and Marge's stress about managing the books, Nora had volunteered to help organize the bills and the incoming revenue. When she noticed that the optimal times for delivering the milk to the cheese factory did not coincide with the girls' schedules for working, she asked Billy if she could rewrite the schedule. He seemed confused as to why it needed rearranging, but Marge saw that Nora was right. Simply moving the group therapy sessions to later in the afternoon opened up the morning to complete the milk processing and get the product to the cheese factory right when it was needed.

Billy saw the impact right away when the factory increased his quality rating as spoilage rates lowered. He wondered why he had not figured it out himself. But then he was always reluctant to make any changes that would affect the girls' schedules. That was Marge's department.

Within a month, Nora had caught the Farm up on its bill paying and collecting, and she'd straightened out the books so that there were more expense categories than they had previously recorded. Over use of the miscellaneous category had gotten to the point that it was hard to see where the money was going. Nora could see why Marge put it off. It was almost impossible to reconcile.

Billy did not talk with Nora much. She reminded him too much of Ginny, so that even making eye contact was painful. Yet he marveled at how Nora had organized the Farm's books, and saw the subsequent lessening of Marge's workload reduce the dark circles under his wife's eyes.

Marge was careful not to show favoritism among the girls, but that was hard after Nora came. So many of her facial expressions matched Ginny's that sometimes Marge almost felt her daughter had come back through Nora. But being a practical and generally unsuperstitious woman, she would chide herself and shake her head. Whatever the resemblances, Nora had really helped to straighten out the Farm's scheduling and the books, and for that she was thankful.

Being a bit older than the other girls had made Nora their

natural leader. Most of the girls were under 18. With Nora almost 23, it became routine for the other young women to come to her for advice, and to talk about their situations and future plans.

Yet, Marge could also see that Nora was inexperienced in the ways of the world, almost sheltered, often unable to fit in. When the girls would talk about their upbringing, Nora was frequently silent. These girls had seen their share of abusive fathers and boyfriends, poverty and dirty trailer parks, and parents who shunned them when they got pregnant. Most of the girls would give their babies up for adoption, the memories linked to the child too painful to carry with them.

But with Nora, her background belied her stay at Hope Creek Farm. Marge had learned through talks over coffee that Nora's father was a doctor in Boston and quite well off. Whatever had chased the young woman out of that lifestyle and all the way across the country, Marge had not figured out yet. While Nora was friendly and a cooperative team member, she also held back. Marge sometimes saw doors close in Nora's eyes that would reveal more about her than she wanted to the other girls and even to Marge.

"You know those are rare now."

Nora straightened her back up in the seat of the old Ford and looked over at Harry.

"What's rare?"

"The Japanese floats. They're all plastic now."

"Plastic?"

"The floats. Plastic is cheaper and easier to tie on to the fishing nets."

Nora looked out the window at the bogs dotted with shiny, green lily pads, and moats of skunk cabbage resembling Christmas wreaths encircling the small ocean lakes. Closing her eyes, she pictured a beach covered with white plastic floats, incongruous and stark on the wet sand.

"That's a shame."

"That's progress marching on."

"Isn't it funny that plastic is progress."

"It is. Imagine the work that went into making the glass ball."

"And the art of it. It's poetry, really."

"Rare poetry now." Harry slowed down as he approached the few blocks that made up downtown Tillamook.

Every time Nora came to town it seemed to her that time had stopped there ten years before and was just starting to catch up. Clothing store windows held the styles of several years past, never knowing that bellbottoms were the fashion or daring to hang a tie-dyed shirt in the window. Girls still wore pink in Tillamook, and shiny white shoes on Sunday with eyelet anklets that praised God with their simple beauty.

Yet while an unfashionable bunch, Nora thought the townies were what Harry would call neighborly. Tillamook was not an easy place to live much of the year. It rained more in the coastal hamlet than anywhere in the state of Oregon, with the sun an infrequent and shy guest. Cold winds and pellet hard rain would beat an ordinary person down. Throw in the ambient smell of cow manure and acrid piss, and only those in the dairy or timber business and the weathered fishermen could really handle a Tillamook winter.

That was what Nora was told by Harry, anyway. And yet he seemed to revel in the smells and the rain and the sturdy folk who lived in this wet world. 'If you can stick it out over a few winters then you are one of us,' Harry told her. It was how good neighbors were made. There was a shared pride that came with steadfastness.

Harry had a new story to tell Nora every time they took the old Ford out to Cape Lookout or into town for a tool or a new bucket. A story where a farmer was hospitalized after a stroke and all his neighbors formed an ad hoc co-op to keep his dairy afloat. Or the young girl who was a math genius but lived in a crab shack with her father on the bay. She was destined to a life of selling bait until a teacher convinced the town that she must go to college. Pooling the coins of a whole town got her to a state university, and now she was an auditor and a legislator.

Or all the times that folks gave boxes of food and clothes to Hope Creek Farm to help old Harry's family care for the poor, unfortunate girls.

"People in Tillamook, we know we're not perfect." It was one of those definitive Harry statements, Nora thought.

"Nobody's perfect, Harry."

"We know that. But how many people do you know who admit it?" Harry almost shouted it. There was pride in his voice.

"Not many, I guess. Most of the people I've known in my life seem to judge everyone against a perfect barometer. I always fell short." Nora's voice went very quiet.

"Well, we know we're not perfect and we don't expect anybody to be perfect either. We just help each other when the perfect goes by the wayside and all you got is your family and friends."

There was such surety in Harry's voice. *The truth rings true.*

Nora let her head fall against her chest as her eyes welled with tears. Her *perfect* had gone by the wayside a year ago, but family had only been there to point that out, not help her get through it. Her friends were, though. Where would she be without Tunney and Max, Bea and Harry? Most of the girls at Hope Creek Farm did not have that many good friends to help them navigate the trouble spots.

A jarring bump forced Nora to raise her head.

"Damn potholes. What does the county do with all those taxes we pay? Tell me that and you're today's big prize winner."

Nora laughed softly and shook off her teary hangover.

"I guess the government's not perfect either, Harry."

"But they'll never admit that. They'll just keep on raisin' our taxes." Harry pulled into the parking lot of Bayside Hardware.

"I'll just be a minute if you want to wait here."

"I'll walk down the block and back. Meet you back here."

Across the street was a clothing store for seemingly all ages and all styles from newborn to matron. Nora crossed over to the sidewalk, her eyes attracted to a window display of baby clothes and furniture.

I'm going to be a Mom! Even saying it in her head was still a shock.

Then suddenly, more shocking was her own reflection in the window. Nora gulped. There were not a lot of mirrors at Hope Creek and she had not seen herself in full view for many weeks. When did her belly get that huge? And her ass! My, god, if Tunney saw her now he would have some rare jokes to make.

Standing sideways, Nora pulled her shift down smooth across her belly. The very girth of it was impressive. Would all that really go away when she had Baby Dodge?

Inside the window display was a dainty, mint green bassinet with a whole baby trousseau laid out attractively around it. Pink and blue rattles and yellow bunnies and lambs gave it the look of an idyllic nursery. Nora thought that it was just the type of room that her father's wife Carol would create for a baby. Perfect and sweet.

Except, as Nora imagined, if she brought Baby Dodge home it would be considered perfectly indiscreet and unacceptable. Unless there was a husband, of course, to go with it. Not much likelihood of that.

"Yep, you're pregnant."

Nora dropped her hands down and looked up, startled by a woman's voice. A pregnant woman, seemingly the same girth as Nora, smiled back at her. Nora laughed.

"Did I look like I was questioning my condition?" Both women laughed together and both placed a hand on their bellies.

"Well, you just had this funny look on your face like you couldn't quite believe that belly belonged to you."

"That's exactly what I thought!" The two women exchanged knowing smiles.

"I'm Bobbie Jo, by the way."

"Nora, and the yet unrevealed Baby Dodge."

"We might be sharing a hospital room if you're having Baby Dodge at Tillamook General. We look about the same size, don't we?" Bobbie Jo turned sideways like Nora was angled and they glanced back and forth at each other's bellies.

"Wow, we are the same. What's your due date, Bobbie Jo?"

"Doc Linn says September 18."

"Mine's September 19!"

The two young women spontaneously reached out and clasped one another's hands. The size of their grins was of equally broad proportions.

"Nora, do you have time to get a cup of coffee at Penny's Grill?"

"I'd love to but I have to go back with Harry." Looking over her shoulder Nora saw Harry walking out the front door of the hardware store. "There he is now."

"Oh, Harry Gray. You must live at Hope Creek."

"Yes, I do." Nora looked at Bobbie Jo, thinking she might see the familiar look of discomfort and scorn that she had seen on the faces of those who frowned on her out-of-wedlock pregnancy. But Bobbie Jo still smiled.

She was a natural beauty, Nora thought. Long, honey brown hair framed her face and hazel eyes. Rosy cheeks from the sun added color to her clear, white skin. It was the real kind of beauty that only women who grew up near the sea wore, unaware of their loveliness.

"Well, I'll just pick you up there some time and we'll grab a bite or a cup, how about it, Nora?"

"I'd like that." Nora suddenly felt shy. The way she had in grade school when she met a new friend.

"I know the Grays. Harry's a sweetie, isn't he?" Bobbie Jo raised her hand and waved at Harry who suddenly noticed the two women. "Hey, Harry," Bobbie Jo shouted across the street.

He raised his hand in reply and started across the parking lot toward them. Both women clucked their tongues simultaneously in disapproval when Harry started across the street without even looking to see if any cars were coming.

"Harry, you're going to get yourself killed one of these days," Bobbie Jo reprimanded the old man as he stepped up on the curb.

"That's a fine hello, young lady." Harry pretended to scowl.

"Well, don't come crying to me when a semi hits you into next week 'cause you didn't look both ways before crossing the street!" All three of them laughed.

"Look at you girls, will ya? Matching bellies and all." Harry looked back and forth from belly to belly. "I heard you were expecting, Bobbie Jo, but I didn't know it would be so soon. When's that husband of yours coming home?"

A shadow of sadness briefly darkened Bobbie Jo's eyes.

"Not until after the baby's due." Bobbie Jo shrugged and gave her best attempt at a smile.

"Won't that be the day when he meets his new son," Harry said in the strong way of a grandfather.

"Harry, what makes you think it's a boy?" Bobbie Jo stood with her hands on her hips.

"I got my ways." A conspiratorial smile broke across Harry's face.

"Then what about me, Harry? Am I going to have a boy or a girl?" Nora put her hands on her hips, matching Bobbie Jo's stance, and they lined up hip to hip.

"Nora, it's a girl for you." Harry suddenly looked so certain and so serious that Nora gulped.

"It's a gift I have, young lady."

Nora wanted badly to believe the craggy old man.

"Why haven't you told all us girls at the Farm what we're having then?"

Harry suddenly looked serious. "Wouldn't be proper."

"But you told me?" Nora moved a step closer to Harry.

"But you're keeping your baby, right? The other girls aren't like you, Nora. They mostly want to have the baby, give it up for adoption, and move on, eh?"

Nora took in a sharp breath. "Sorry, I wasn't thinking," she said sheepishly, wondering what Bobbie Jo must be thinking about this conversation.

"Honey, you were thinking, you just weren't thinking like Harry," Bobbie Jo said as she pulled her purse strap up to her shoulder. "I gotta go, me and the boy, right Harry?"

Nora and Bobbie Jo exchanged glances and laughed as Harry tried his best to scowl.

"You'll see, you'll see!" Harry wagged his finger at Bobbie Jo. She touched his shoulder and their eyes met. "That boy will be saying his daddy's name in no time."

Bobbie Jo smiled sadly. "I'll tell Steve you said that in my next letter. Thanks Harry."

Nora and Bobbie Jo exchanged phone numbers and promised to meet soon. Harry looked impatient and he kept glancing across the street at his truck. He did not understand the bond that the two women already shared, in the special time before they alone would bring a new life into the world. It was powerful and daunting.

"Okay, we gotta go. Bye Bobbie Jo. Come on Nora." Harry was already half way across the street.

On the way back to Hope Creek both Harry and Nora were quiet. Harry telling her that Baby Dodge was a girl had changed things for her. It was more real now, more permanent. Suddenly the baby had a face, a beautiful glowing, pink girl face where before Baby Dodge was only an amorphous shadow, a future event that was fuzzy and uncertain.

I'm a mother. I have a daughter.

Just as she thought it, the same old shiver of fear spread from her belly down to her calves. This was uncharted territory she was entering. How could a woman who had not known her own mother know the first thing about being one? What had she been thinking?

"You gonna throw up?" Harry glanced over at Nora suspiciously.

"No, why?"

"You look sick all of a sudden. You're all pale."

Without warning, Nora's whole body began to shake as the sobs erupted. She did not even try to control the tears. They had needed to be released and there was no stopping the flood.

Shifting uneasily in his seat, Harry stepped harder on the accelerator and sped north on Route 101. Handling a crying pregnant girl was not his territory. This was a job for Marge.

# # #

The group counseling session was already underway when Harry dropped Nora off at the main house. She sat outside the old parlor door, listening to the girls discuss how to make good choices as she questioned her own. While she had stopped sobbing, silent tears continued to well in her eyes and spill over onto her cheeks.

Marge had glanced up when she heard Nora outside the parlor. The door was open as the room was otherwise intolerable, hot and stuffy with twenty pregnant girls in it. It was obvious to Marge that Nora was "having a spell" as her grandmother would have put it. She decided to give Nora some time before she made her join the rest of the group. Of course, Nora could always join Group B girls later in the afternoon. They would go through the same session as Group A was now. Marge learned early on that splitting up the girls was the only way to really achieve effective group counseling. Trying to get forty pregnant girls to sit cooperatively together in a little room was more difficult than giving birth.

"I don't think I have a choice. I know I can't raise a baby right now." Nora could tell that it was Susan speaking, her Alabama drawl still present, giving the teen's voice a sing-song quality.

"What do you girls think? Does Susan have a choice?" Marge asked as she glanced around at the young, tired faces. Some heads were nodding and others shaking.

"Dani, I see you nodding. Do you think Susan has a choice?" Marge stood up and walked over to Dani's side of the room.

"Yeah. She's chosen to not be a mother right now."

"Anything else, Dani?"

The seventeen-year-old looked up at the ceiling in thought, seeking an answer in the white swirls of plaster.

"She chose not to have an abortion."

"That's right, Dani, good. Thank you for that," Marge praised as she walked behind her and put a hand on the teen's shoulder.

"Now let's take a step back. What choice comes before abortion?"

Dani raised her eyes again to the ceiling, but no answer revealed itself this time.

"Not lettin' the man stick it in you." All the girls sniggered at Rachel's comment. She was considered the toughest girl in the group, a testament to having been raised in a traveling carnival by an illiterate father.

"Okay, quiet down girls. But, yes, Rachel's right. You have the option to say no next time. And you have the option to use birth control next time." Marge scanned the girls' eyes looking for acknowledgement, for some sign that they would not be back at Hope Creek Farm again.

"Rachel, why are you shaking your head? You just agreed that you do have a choice."

Carnival-girl let her head hang down and closed her eyes. "'Cause sometimes you don't." The hollow quiet in her voice made Nora's back straighten against the wall outside the parlor door.

"And when would that be, Rachel?" Marge cocked her head and waited for her answer.

"When the carney slime ball holds you down and rapes you." Rachel opened her eyes and looked up at the older woman.

Marge drew in a breath. This was Rachel's life. Her hard edge was honed on sharp realities.

"Yes, that is not a choice, Rachel," Marge responded quietly.

"Rachel, girl, you sayin' you was raped?" It was Susan again, her southern curiosity winning out over any propriety she might have once been taught.

"Susan, that's not an appropriate comment. Please apologize to Rachel." Susan hung her head and bit her lip. Marge knew she had to steer the conversation back to birth control quickly and give Rachel back her privacy. If she was raped, it was one-on-one counseling she needed, not a public airing.

"Miss Marge, I don't care," Rachel mumbled before Susan could offer her an apology. "I was raped. This baby in my belly is a crime. And I'm shamed for it. Daddy beat me up when he saw I was pregnant. It was no use tellin' him why."

Most girls would have been crying by now at the remembrance of the violence that had swollen her belly and kidnapped her childhood. Rachel sat stoically on an old ottoman, her eyes set and hollow, reflecting a resignation that was threatening to break Marge's heart. She recalled the state police bringing Rachel to the Farm. She had always assumed that Rachel was a runaway who had been caught stealing or was picked up for serial truancy.

Susan stood up and walked over to Rachel. Kneeling in front of her, Susan tentatively touched Rachel's knee.

"I'm real sorry, Rachel. Real sorry for askin' you that. And also sorry about, you know..." Susan stopped and looked up at Marge. The older woman nodded.

Rachel shrugged her shoulders. "It don't matter."

"Rachel, you matter very much. You're a special young woman. The violence done to you was a crime that I know hurt you badly. Thank you for sharing that so we all can learn." Marge put her hand on Rachel's shoulder. "Would you like to rest for a while in the dorm?"

Nodding almost imperceptibly, Rachel stood up. As she did, Nora stepped into the room.

"I'll walk her to the dorm, Miss Marge."

"Thanks, Nora. I'll be down soon."

Nora led Rachel out of the parlor and to the front door. She held it open for Rachel and followed her toward the dormitory.

As the two pregnant women maneuvered around mud puddles on the pathway, a gray cloud overhead moved aside to let a sun swatch bathe the pasture in orange.

The sudden return of the sun made Rachel stop abruptly.

"You okay, Rachel?"

Nora knew it was a dumb question. There had never been so obvious a reply hanging in the air.

Nodding, Rachel started walking again. Following the young girl, Nora's face became redder and hotter with each step. What a self-centered fool she had been, Nora admonished herself. To have cried in self-pity a half hour before because...why? She was going to be a mother and had no idea what that meant? *Who cares, you silly idiot*, Nora scolded herself. Having the baby is a great thing, the hell with knowing what that would mean every day of her life. Rachel had problems, real ones. Compared to what the carnival-girl had gone through, Nora's problems seemed small, overblown.

Had she been blowing her problems out of proportion since she quit college? Was that just the rash move of a self-centered Chestnut Hill girl? All of the girls at Hope Creek would laugh her out of the dorm if they only knew what she had considered problematic and confusing.

And what about her father? Was he really so bad, or just confused by the way she had changed so suddenly?

My god, he must be worried, Nora realized. Before, she had not cared whether Dr. Dodge was worried or not. Nora had blamed him for her feelings of confusion. He had no ability to see that the world was changing, that everything was not just all right. He could not see Nora any other way than his little porcelain doll. His daughter that spoke properly and dressed right and went to the right schools and dated the right boys and shopped at the right stores and would graduate from the right college and marry the right man.

But was she even right about that? Did she even know what her father understood or cared about?

Rachel started up the dorm's front porch steps, slick with rain and smears of mud. Just as she reached for the railing, her foot slipped on a stair.

As Nora watched, the atmosphere suddenly thickened and everything slowed down. Rachel's arms flew above her head before they dropped down to try and cushion her fall. A terrible rush of air and pain left Rachel, sounding like the wail of a wounded, wild animal. Rachel's seven-month belly hit the edge of one of the stairs, the concussion flipping her over on her back.

Then the slow motion stopped and real time returned. Rachel's eyelids fluttered and shut. Nora's scream of Rachel's name sounded muffled in her own ears.

But Harry heard it clearly at the barn and began running. This time he could help. Not like with his Ginny.

# # #

Rachel looked like a little girl, Marge thought, with her tiny face amid the pillows and blankets of the hospital bed. Now maybe she could be a little girl again.

When Marge had heard Nora's scream at the house her automatic thought was, 'Ginny's hurt.' But after a second, reality took over and she knew it must be Rachel.

It was just a freak accident, the doctor said; an unusual blow to the belly when Rachel hit the edge of the stair, fracturing the baby's skull with a terrible perfection.

At seven months, Rachel's baby was fully formed. Doctor Linn told Marge that it could have survived if the skull fracture had not been so severe. They removed it by performing a caesarian section.

A terrible scar would always remind Rachel of her baby, the child of dark memories.

Marge was doing her best to hold back her tears, but a few ran down her cheeks. Over the months that Rachel had been at Hope Creek, Marge had taken to her in a way that made the loss of the baby all the harder. While Rachel had always put on the tough act, Marge could see that she was a very sensitive and damaged young woman. Once Rachel had revealed the rape, it all began to make sense.

One thing was for sure, Marge knew. Rachel could stay at the Farm as long as she wanted. There was no spot on the earth better for her, Marge thought. The girl needed healing.

Other than recovery from the C-section, some bruises, and a sprained ankle, Rachel had no other injuries, at least on the outside. Her poor baby belly had taken the brunt of the fall. The child of violent conception had given its forced life to save its innocent mother from further injury.

A few more mother tears rolled down Marge's cheek.

"Don't cry, Miss Marge." The sound of Rachel's voice startled the older woman.

"Rachel. You're already awake. How do you feel, huh?"

"I'm fine Miss Marge." Rachel closed her eyes again and raised her chin up slightly. "The baby's gone, ain't it."

It was more of a statement than a question.

"Yes, the baby is gone."

# # #

Chapter 23: Sister Seeking

Philadelphia

July 1969

Philadelphia seemed darker than Boston. Between the height of the dirty-stone buildings and the narrow streets, the light struggled to reach the bottom of these city corridors. It made Willa walk faster along Walnut Street. She was a child of Africa who sought the sun.

One thing that both cities had in common was that no one would make eye contact with her. Willa was used to the constant eye communication and greetings between passersby in Botswana. Anything less was considered rude and unusual. People who would not look at their fellow citizens and acknowledge them were deemed to have mental problems, or possibly to be criminals or troublemakers of some kind. It seemed just the opposite in Philadelphia and Boston. Willa's greetings were met with incredulous stares and even annoyance. People's looks read, 'What does she want from me?'

Luckily an elderly man let down his guard and gave Willa directions to Rittenhouse Square from the train station. It would be the central point of her search for the boutique where Nora worked. While she had no address or shop name, Willa figured it was just a matter of starting at the square and following each of the streets down several blocks. A matter of search and deduction, eliminating one street at a time if it did not yield a men's boutique that fit Nora's description in the postcard.

Willa spread the map across a green metal bench and found Rittenhouse Square. Marking it with an X, she decided to begin at Locust Street, walk eight blocks and then move to the next street off the Square, moving clockwise, until she found Nora's shop.

"Are you lost, young lady?"

Willa looked up at a very tall, very broad policeman holding the reins of a horse. She smiled.

"Hello officer. I don't think I'm lost, but I don't know exactly where I'm going."

"Sounds like lost to me. You know it's not wise to spread that map out like that. It just signals criminals that you're an out-of-towner and an easy target."

"Target?"

"Yeah, for stealing your pocketbook or trying to lure you into an alleyway."

Willa's face fell as her smile turned into an embarrassed grimace.

"Now, don't worry about it. Just be careful. You don't want to be a victim."

"No, I don't." Willa started folding the map up, thinking that she would have to just mentally mark off each street as she searched for Nora's shop.

"Whatcha looking for anyway? The Liberty Bell? Constitution Hall?"

"No, sir. I'm looking for my sister."

"You're usin' a map to look for your sister?" The policeman scowled a bit, like Willa might be a kook that he had just wasted time on.

"Well, I know that Nora works in a boutique off Rittenhouse Square, but I don't know the name of it or the address." Willa pulled the postcard out of her knapsack and handed it to the officer.

Pulling his sunglasses down, he read the card, his lips moving slightly and his head cocked in concentration.

"Oh, this must be Max's shop. That's the only queer boutique in this area. Just head down 19th Street two blocks, and then turn left on Sansome, and it's up a few blocks on the left."

"Really?!" Willa's hand clasped over her mouth. "Wow, thank you so much. I'm so close." A grin broke out on Willa's face wider than the officer had seen directed at him in a long time from anyone her age.

"You're welcome, kid. Where are you from anyways? You have a funny accent." Adjusting the horse's reins the officer put his foot in the stirrup and pulled himself up onto the massive black-brown stallion.

"I'm from Botswana. In Africa."

"No kiddin'? How'd a white girl end up coming from Africa?"

"It's a long story, sir. But my mother's a doctor and she runs a hospital there. I was born there. That's why I have a funny accent."

"Makes sense. Well, good luck finding your sister. If you get lost just look for me or listen for the horse clops. And don't pull that map out again. And don't smile so much. It just makes you a target."

"Yes, sir, a target. Thank you again."

As the officer clopped away across the Square, Willa began to walk briskly towards Nora's shop, but her anxious legs took over and she broke into a run.

In her head she counted off the blocks: one, two, can I see anything yet? Three, four...there it was! *Max's Fine Men's Apparel.*

Willa stood outside the window for a moment to catch her breath. Mannequins stared back at her in silky shirts and pointy-toe shoes with spats. Her heart was pounding so loudly in her ears that it drowned out all the other street noise that had seemed so deafening a moment before.

Please remember me. Please want to see me. Please be my sister. Please need me like I need you to. It was a prayer that had run through Willa's head a thousand times since she had boarded the train to Philadelphia the day before at South Station. Dr. Dodge had reluctantly dropped her off after losing his tenth argument of the day with his single-minded daughter.

"Willa please wait for a few weeks and then I can go with you," he had pleaded, just before pulling onto Summer Street near the station.

"Father, please don't worry. I'll be fine, really I will." Willa looked towards the station entrance and then back at her father. "I need to go now to find Nora." Michael Dodge had rarely heard anyone sound so resolute.

"I know, you've said that, but I just don't get it, Willa. I'm sorry, but I just don't see the urgency. You just got here two weeks ago. What do you know about walking around alone in strange American cities? You'll stand out like a sore thumb!"

"I've survived several large cities, father. Johnny taught me city skills like how to be invisible by walking at oblique angles, and to look way ahead to anticipate any trouble. I've walked around Jo'burg and Cape Town and Salisbury on my own, and I was really much younger then."

Michael Dodge glanced at his daughter, a deep worry crease dividing his forehead into two equal parts. He pulled up next to the station in a drop off zone. "Alright. I can see that I'll never get past your stubbornness and get you to think this through longer. Here, take this."

Willa took a white envelope from him. "There's five hundred dollars in there and a credit card."

"Father, I..."

"No discussion, Willa. If you're intent on finding Nora you have to have the resources to do it. Just because the postcard came from Philadelphia doesn't mean Nora is still there. That was six months ago. A lot could have happened since then. If I know Nora, she's probably jumped to a few more places since then. It's always been hard for her to be focused. She's not like you, Willa."

Suddenly, Michael Dodge's voice cracked. His eyes held a plea for Willa to stay. The daughter put her hand on top of the doctor's. "I love you, father. I'll be back and I'll have Nora with me."

Willa's certainty disarmed the surgeon for a moment, but then his steadfast reason returned. "Willa, honey, don't set yourself up to be disappointed. Even if you find Nora it doesn't mean she'll come back. She was not happy here before she left."

"But now we have the chance to be a family, father. That's why it's important for me to go now. I can feel Nora in here." Willa put her hand on her heart.

Michael looked at her beautiful hand, wishing he could feel Nora in his heart the way that Willa could. Only the disappointment, fear, and guilt that a runaway daughter brings were there now.

"I'll find her father. We'll have a chance to be a family. We will."

Michael Dodge reached for his second daughter and held her close. There was that absoluteness again, the certainty that he wanted so much to feel.

"Be careful, then." He did not trust himself to say anything else. Tears not shed for many years were close to returning from exile.

Willa opened the door and stepped out. Leaning in she smiled at her father. "I love you. Don't worry. I'll call every few days or so, collect like you asked."

Her father nodded but failed at a smile. Then she was gone. He watched Willa walk through the revolving door of South Station. An errant tear escaped and dropped onto his shoulder.

Could Willa and Nora and he really be a family? Did that long-ago dream have a chance again? Willa almost made him believe that it could be true. He had felt it once before briefly when Willa was almost ten and had spent a few months in Boston. In that short time she had brightened the house up with all the love she had to give to him and Nora and Mary the housekeeper too. Mary had quickly adopted Willa and taken her to church and on other outings. She had never asked if Nora could go with her and Nora certainly would not have asked. She just was not that kind of a child. It was almost as if Nora felt that any affection she showed would be taken from her. So instead she held back, suspicious of too much affection, too broad a smile, or too loud a laugh.

They were a family for those few weeks almost a decade past. Maybe it was possible that it would happen again. Willa's surety had incubated a fragile optimism in Michael, already tested as he watched Willa disappear into the mauve hollows of South Station.

Now as Willa entered *Max's Fine Men's Apparel*, a little bell tinkled on the door. A sales clerk who was describing different type of belts to a customer briefly glanced up and smiled at Willa. She looked around quickly to see if Nora was there, but the store was empty save the two men by the belt rack.

A movement caught Willa's eye and she looked toward the back of the store. A tall, blond man had come out of the back room and suddenly saw her. His eyebrows rose and his mouth opened in surprise.

"Nora? Nora, is that you?" The blond man quickly made his way to Willa expertly dodging and weaving around the clothing racks. "Nora..." Suddenly he hesitated as if confused.

“I’m Willa, Nora’s sister.” Holding out her hand, she smiled at the blond man.

“The African sister.” Max’s voice revealed that he knew something of Willa’s history. That meant that Nora was close.

“Yes. I’ve come to the states and I’m trying to find my sister. Is Nora here?” Willa anxiously shifted her weight side to side and looked around again, hoping Nora would come through the door from the backroom.

“Willa, oh Willa, oh Pioneer! By the way, I’m Max, and this is my boutique.” He held his arms up and moved side to side like the door models on *Let’s Make a Deal.* “But you’re preoccupied, aren’t you dear?” Willa just looked at him. “Come upstairs with me. I’ll make you some tea and I’ll tell you all about Nora.”

“So, she is still here, still in Philadelphia?” There was so much hope in her voice that Max considered lying for a moment.

“Not exactly, dear. But come, come. Follow Max and all will be well.”

Max told the sales clerk to watch the till and he led Willa into the backroom and up the stairwell that led to his apartment. Willa followed him as if in a trance. It was apparent that Nora was not at Max’s or in Philadelphia any longer.

Everything on her body felt leaden all of a sudden. Willa grabbed the stair rail and sat down heavily, her chest heaving in and out as she tried to get a full breath.

Max heard the thump and turned around just as he was unlocking the door. Light from the apartment shone down on Willa; her chin was touching her chest.

“Oh, my. Are you sick, honey?” Max scooped her up easily and helped her up the last few stairs. After settling her in an overstuffed chair by the window he quickly put a teapot on the stove.

“Well, you and Nora certainly have one thing in common.” Willa looked up at Max waiting for the answer. “You both have very physical reactions to disappointing news.”

“Can you please tell me where Nora is. Is she okay?” Willa pleaded.

“Okay, I’ll cut to the chase and then give you the Max long

version. Nora's been gone since February. She went to San Francisco with Tunney after her boyfriend screwed around on her, because, in her opinion, what did she have to lose. And maybe, I hope maybe, she's found out who she is, why she's on this planet, what she wants to do when she grows up, and why she's so damn mad at your father. Why is she so mad at him?"

As usual, Max's answers turned into dramatic descriptions that raised more questions than they answered.

"You're sure she's in San Francisco?"

"Well, Tunney sent me a postcard in March with his and Nora's address on it so I could send their final pay out there. But that was the last I heard from them, the little shits. Why can't people write these days? Is it asking so much to verify that they got the money and tell Uncle Max what's up, huh?" Max clicked his tongue loudly and went to rescue the whistling teapot.

"Who's Tunney? Is that Nora's boyfriend?"

"Oh, no, well, at least not when they left. But being two lonely hearts with father phobia and Viet Nam thrown into the mix, and the fact that they're sharing an apartment, well, your guess is as good as mine, although their chemistry wouldn't automatically signal 'match' to me."

Max handed Willa a cup of tea. "I guessed you'd like it with milk and sugar. Nora told me that everyone drinks tea that way in Africa."

"Thank you. It's very nice." Willa's voice was quiet and deflated. "Do you still have the postcard they sent? Can I see it?" Max saw a little hope lighten up her eyes.

"I do. It's right here on the fridge still."

Despite the fact that the refrigerator had multiple layers of paper memories, Max easily pulled off the postcard from under a watermelon magnet.

"The Golden Gate Bridge." Studying the writing on the card, Willa felt somehow closer to Nora, even though it was Tunney who wrote it. She read it four times, looking for any nuances that might tell her more about her sister.

"Tunney says, 'Nora is feeling great.' Why would he mention that? Was she sick when she was here?"

Max hesitated for a moment. "No, not physically sick. But she was so mad at Pete, her boyfriend, and then sometimes at your father, that she would sort of be sick. Thinking or talking about your mother seemed to make her sick too. She was actually really angry, but also really confused. Such a good kid." Max sighed and sat down on the love seat.

Willa matched his sigh with a heavy one of her own. "My mother certainly can make people feel sick. I've felt that way around her, a good portion of my life, actually." Willa laughed and shook her head as though just discovering this now.

"She sounds like a real dream boat. Is that why you left Africa?"

Willa hesitated and took a slow sip of the tea before answering. "Dr. Jan is complicated. But she's gotten better lately. We went through a lot together over the last year. But yes, she can hurt your heart. But she has no capacity, really, for recognizing that. It makes it hard to stay angry with her. But she has been trying harder lately, since the Chief incident."

Max put his hands up. "Whoa, slow down sister. There were at least three juicy leads on subtext stories in there and I want to hear them all."

Willa laughed at Max. It was very apparent why Nora liked him so much and had found a place at his boutique.

"Hmm, where to begin...Did Nora tell you about our family history and how we got separated?"

"Oh, yes, well at least I know that your parents and Nora went to Africa, your father and Nora came back home to Boston, and mother bitch, knocked up again with little Willa, said ta-ta and had no qualms about never seeing her first born again."

"You've got that down. So about the Chief incident..." Willa started from the day that Tom brought the bloody Chief into the surgery, her visit to the Dingaka for medicines, her mother's blow up when she found out Willa had a witch doctor in the clinic. Then she finally got to the Chief's recovery ceremony where Willa and her mother were honored and a bridge was built between traditional and Western medicine in the villages surrounding Mother Mercy Hospital.

Max loved stories like this and said almost nothing during the hour that Willa slowly recapped those months, not that long before, but which now seemed like a lifetime ago and a world away to her.

"My, god, child, you must be almost like a doctor yourself! How old are you? And do tell, is Tom your boyfriend?"

"How did you figure that out," Willa laughed as she walked over to the window and looked down on the busy street.

"It's not hard, kid. You glow like a virgin bride whenever you say Tom's name. Do you miss him?" Max put his arm around Willa's waist. "You can't be more than twenty and you've done all those things, survived your mother, helped born African babies, and now you're Nancy Drew, Hunt for the Missing Sister, Part One. I can tell this is going to be at least a trilogy."

"Oh, no. I was hoping for a quick ending to a short story." Willa leaned into Max a bit, letting his quick friendship and strength soak into her skin and give her the energy for the next part of her search.

"You Dodge girls are good kids, you know? Your parents couldn't have been all that evil."

"No, not evil. In Botswana we have a saying, "*Ke motho, fela*, I'm only human. Recognizing that makes it easy for the Tswana to forgive each other and not dwell on human idiosyncrasies. They embrace the connections they have with one another, not the disconnections."

"Sounds like a bunch of hippies, those Tswana folk!"

Willa clapped her hands and laughed. "Or do hippies act like a bunch of Batswana?"

Now they were both laughing hard. "That's a question that only a bottle of red wine can fruitfully answer."

"I'll have to trust you on that one, Max." Willa's face turned suddenly serious. "But can I ask you something"?

Max nodded.

"Did Nora ever mention me or say anything about me? Did she remember me?" Willa paused. "Will she even want to see me?" There was such pleading in her voice. Max knew he would have lied if he did not have good news for this fragile and strong female dichotomy.

"Willa, Willa. Yes, sweetheart, Nora wants to see you. She probably won't be expecting you, but I would bet the store that she'll love having you in her life." Willa's smile got bigger and bigger as Max talked.

"You wouldn't have a picture of her, would you, that was taken while she was here?"

"Yes, I do have a picture. Hold on." Max scampered to the bedroom and returned with a cigar box.

"We had a kind of going away party for Nora and Tunney and one of my dearest friends took their picture. That's Tunney next to your sister." Max handed the photograph to Willa.

"This is Nora now. She's beautiful. She looks so much like my mother."

"And like you. Your father must be a cutie too if he contributed to you two."

Chuckling, Willa nodded. "Yes, I think he is considered a handsome man."

"And a doctor. What's not to love?"

"I don't know what's not to love. Including the last few weeks I've just spent with my father, we've been together about ninety days our whole lives. I need to find out more from Nora about her and father's conflicts. He just seems like a giving, caring man to me. But we're also both still walking on eggshells with one another, being polite, like new friends."

"He probably is very caring. You can't be a surgeon and not care about people. It's just that sometimes sheer vicinity breeds contempt between fathers and daughters. Having someone conveniently located in the same house to blame for everything, as needed, sort of happens, like osmosis. Top that off with Nora's recognition that she's had a sheltered life and needs to find out who she really is *sans* daddy's money, and her confusion leads her to lash out and blame the person located within eye and ear shot." Max took a deep breath and continued. "Nora can't lash out at your mother, who is probably the person that she is most angry with. As a former Psych major, it's textbook abandonment behavior."

Willa sighed heavily again. "I guess I never realized how Nora's separation from Dr. Jan affected her." She shook her head and bent it in disappointment at her lack of understanding of her sister's feelings. Nora had always seemed so far away. Not just oceans and continents away but they were all far away in their ability to connect as real family members. It seemed to be the storyline of their lives. All the disconnected Dodges made or found surrogate families because their own blood family did not represent their certain place, the place they went to when they needed comfort, help, trust.

How many times had Dr. Jan disappointed Willa and hurt her feelings, affecting their connection as mother and daughter? Willa realized that Nora must have faced these issues a hundred fold with an absentee mother, and a different type of disconnect with their father, also an absentee in his own way when the hospital kept him away for days at a time.

"Willa, dear, separation and the generation gap are America's big problems right now. Why do you think everybody either drinks too many Manhattans, or smokes too much weed, or drops acid? No one understands anybody else and they either don't want to or they just can't. But the ship is sailing and the older generation needs to get with it. We don't want to be like them. This is Stressville, USA, Willa. We're all dealing with it as we can."

"This world definitely moves at a much faster pace and with more pressures than in Botswana. I guess I'll either have to speed up or get everyone to slow down and take life the Tswana way."

"Don't count on anybody in Philly going-African. Maybe in California. They're more mellow on the west coast."

"More mellow. That sounds good." Willa's voice was far away again.

"Where did you go? You're scheming aren't you?"

Laughing, Willa walked over to a large globe on a pedestal in the corner of Max's living room and began turning it. "If Nora is in San Francisco that's where I need to go next." Her finger touched Pennsylvania and she dragged it across the mid-western states, over the Rockies, across the Nevada desert and into San Francisco.

"That sounds pretty final. Will it be by bus with the unwashed masses, or by plane with the smart set?" Max put his hands on his hips, smiling wryly.

"The unwashed masses sounds more like my way. And I'd get to see the whole United States."

"Not quite the whole thing. God, please don't judge America by the corn-belt states. You'll be on the first plane back to the Kalahari."

Willa contemplated the orange mass that made up the United States on the old globe. "I need to see as much of the space between Nora and me as I can. If I walk behind her in the path she took, I may know more about her when I find her. Or at least we will have shared a common experience. That ought to be worth something."

"It's worth a lot, Willa. And when Nora sees your face, she'll recognize that." Max put his hand on Willa's shoulder. The pressure of his fingers felt good, like a hug or a cluck from Mma Cookie always did. Willa looked out the window at the brick building across the street, wondering what Mma Cookie and Tom, Sammie Poe, Dr. Jan and Johnny were doing just at that very same moment.

It was the time of day in Botswana when the dusk teased the darkness into taking over. Patches of light trimmed purple-gray clouds that loitered still, wary of letting the darkness rule on its own. Lights on a few buildings came on tentatively, helping to push back the night.

Walking quickly and erect, there was Sammie Po, racing across the clinic compound towards the surgery, medicines in hand as directed by Dr. Jan. Johnny was there too, opening the door of his plane, and waving at her, his smile always steady and true.

And there was Tom. She saw his back and then he slowly turned around. His eyes fluttered shut and then opened again. Willa read his lips as they shaped her name. A beautiful smile made Tom's eyes squeeze down into tiny windows of blue love pointed directly at her.

On her shoulders and face Willa could feel the thick heat of Africa. It felt at once powerful and delicious, a familiar friend. She knew every inch of the compound so well, that her mind wandered among its walls and window wells, waiting benches and acacia trees.

Mma Cookie's laugh snuck into her head and Willa saw her, hands on her hips, cocking her head and clucking at her white daughter. Words of wisdom would follow that always rang true, and made Mma Cookie almost iconic.

Life was moving on at Mother Mercy, with or without her, Willa knew. An English doctor was due there soon, and two well-trained nurses had been promised by the Ministry of Health, to arrive within weeks. Dr. Jan had said how well it was all coming together. It made Willa wonder if her mother missed her even a tiny bit.

"Leaving is harder than staying." Willa stated it as a fact.

"Where did that come from?" Max asked exasperated and curious. "Oh, you're homesick, aren't you?"

"I must sound wretched."

"No, just lonely and a little sad." Max put a finger under Willa's chin and raised her face. "Come with me, sad sister. You need real nourishment before you embark on your Ameri-thon of travel. It's time you had your first cheese-steak."

"Cheese-steak? That sounds delicious and I don't even know what it is."

"Come, child, it's time for your baptism."

"I'm ready. My stomach has been calling for dinner for hours."

"God, I love your accent. If only I could show you off at a party. But alas, you'll be all but a memory by tomorrow night."

"You won't get rid of me permanently, though, Max. I already feel fully adopted, so it's a family issue now. I'm bringing Nora back here with me when I find her."

The two new friends walked out onto the street and headed north. Max told Willa about Perry's, a hoagie shop that made the best cheese-steaks in the area. It was about eight blocks away and Willa soaked in as much of Philadelphia as she could on the beautiful July night. Still hot, the air felt sticky against Willa's skin. It was a different heat than Botswana, oppressive and viscous and urban. The heat of her homeland was brittle and dry, snapping and singeing. But now it was winter in the southern hemisphere. Old Batswana women would be huddling over smoky cooking fires in big Sotho blankets, trying to keep their arthritic fingers from stiffening up to uselessness. School children would huddle outside their heatless classroom in any available sun patch until the last minute when the teacher would threaten them with a switch. With no heat or air conditioning in the buildings, everyone chased the sunny spots in winter and dodged them in summer. Either way the seasons were inescapable. Everyone accepted it. That was just how it was in Botswana.

There was a disembodiment about being in an unfamiliar place that held no markers of recollection. Willa had a strong sense that any minute this new world could vanish and she would be back on familiar ground, amidst the sands of Botswana's scrubby, high desert, in the compound of her upbringing, in the rondovel of her lover.

Flying north across Africa, Willa had spent hours of the two-day flight to Boston contemplating a million dots on the earth. Those dots were people, individual lives, each with their own story, their own homes and farms and babies and deaths and joys. How many lives! How many individual stories in how many villages in how many countries times a million. Millions of dots, millions of variations of life.

An elderly Greek man sitting next to Willa saw her staring out the airplane window and shaking her head in amazement as they flew over more lives than she could ever contemplate. "Are you scared, young Miss?" He had asked her, his Greek accent strong despite decades in Africa.

"Oh, no, sir. Just amazed at the many lives we're casually flying over. It's just so...vast." Willa shrugged her shoulders and smiled.

The old man nodded. "And us just a grain of salt, adding our own flavor to such a great and wonderful dish, this earth."

Willa had smiled at the old man's analogy. For the rest of the flight he said nothing, only tipping his felt hat to her as he deplaned in Athens.

And then the same feeling returned as the plane descended into Heathrow. A million lights reflected a million lives, some rushing to work at 5:00 a.m., the headlights of their cars marking the daily journey.

It was strange, connecting to a faceless driver thousands of feet below who knew nothing of the woman-girl from Africa tracking his morning commute and contemplating his life, his wife, a home, maybe in the countryside on a narrow lane behind a wisteria covered wall. And yet he thought nothing of her, not even realizing that a skyward spy, a remote voyeur was capturing a few moments of his life.

Now as Willa walked beside Max, again the many lives that drove past them or walked by them, or smoked a cigarette on a balcony above them, made her contemplate the tiny dots.

"Did you ever play with those books when you were young where you'd connect the numbered dots and a picture of something would emerge?"

"Willa, where the hell did that question come from? A shrink would probably pay you to analyze how your brain synapses spark." Max let out a questioning laugh. "But, yes, I did indeed play connect the dots and happen to hold the land speed record for fastest connecting in my age category. Of course I was twenty-two at the time."

Willa laughed and shrugged her shoulders. "I always think that whoever I'm with has been privy to all the machinations and surgeries taking place in my head." A rock that Willa kicked with her shoe pinged against the base of an *Inquirer* newspaper box. "I'm following the dots to get to Nora. When I get to the last one, there she'll be."

"But don't do what my little sister used to do. She would connect the dots but never color in the picture. Even when you find Nora, you'll still need to color the picture. And god knows what you'll use for crayons."

"We're sisters. We share parents, crazy as it's been with thousands of miles between us. My colors will have to be my stories and Nora's colors are her stories. I think we can connect and finish our page."

"Oh, my god!" Max stopped in his tracks and grabbed Willa's arm.

"What?!" Willa looked around quickly to see if a danger lurked.

"Look what we're standing in front of." Max swept his arm through the air, presenting the window in front of them. It was filled with vibrant paint palettes, thin tins of colored pencils, tubes of oil paint, and fancy French crayons. "Your colors! To finish your sister's page!" The two friends exchanged surprised looks as Max grabbed Willa's hand and pulled her into the shop.

Ten minutes later they were back on their cheese-steak trek, a bag of crayons and a sketchpad under Willa's arm.

This is one way of determining my future, Willa thought. *I'll just draw it myself.*

# # #

Chapter 24: The Dream

Mother Mercy Clinic

July 1969

It had happened again, and now Mma Cookie was truly frightened.

She had told Sammie Po about it, and he too became concerned. It was not normal to have the same dream again and again.

Mma Cookie described it finally to Sammie Po after the third time the dream had visited. He shifted around nervously on the kitchen stool. Such a dream about Willa was cause for concern. Certain people needed to be told. And of course the Dingaka had to be consulted.

Dr. Jan had not seemed concerned at all when Mma Cookie told her about the recurring dream.

"Dreams are just your worries transformed into senseless fiction," Jan had said to Mma Cookie. "You need to stop eating sweets before bedtime, Mma, and cut out all that sugar in your tea."

There was no retort that Mma Cookie could make to Jan that would have been polite, so she said nothing. Imagine not putting sugar in her tea! Dreams were not made from sugar, they were signals from the *Modimo* in the heavens and the ancestors about important events they wanted humans to know about. Dr. Jan did not know everything. Mma Cookie had determined that years ago.

Surely Tommi would be concerned and should be told. Mma Cookie had sent a note with one of the clansman from Tommi's village that he needed to come and see her on important business.

Two days later, Tom pulled into Mother Mercy compound, parking under his usual tree. While it was winter in the Kalahari, the days were still hot enough to cause his legs to stick to the seat and the cab to be stuffy and stale from its various uses over the years. The mottled shade from the acacia tree at least helped a little in lowering the temperature in the Land Rover.

Looking over at the main house, Tom saw Mma Cookie waiting on the porch for him, arms at her sides. Even from that distance he could tell that something was wrong.

Willa! Was Willa okay, Tom wondered as his stomach twisted? He suddenly felt sick.

Hold on, boy, he quickly said to himself. There is no reason to overreact.

He just missed her so much.

"*Dumela, Mme. O tsogile*?"

"*Ke tsogile, Tommiwe.* But my son, I am not really very fine. And I can see that you are not fine because you are missing our Willa too much, isn't it?"

By now Tom was used to the directness of some of the Tswana women, especially Mma Cookie. "Eh, Mma Cookie. I am missing her too much." It hurt to say Willa's name, so it was "her" instead.

"*Tsena*, Tommi. Come sit." Mma Cookie motioned for Tom to sit on the veranda. She called inside for tea and a moment later her niece, Tiny, brought it out on a tin tray along with Mma Cookie's favorite biscuits. Rather than cream and sugar, Mma Cookie preferred sweetened condensed milk and added two heaping tablespoons to her tea. Tom used about one quarter that amount in his cup. Today the milky tea tasted especially good to him.

"Tommi, what are you hearing from Willa?"

Tom looked up from his tea, trying to read the tone of Mma Cookie's voice. Was that a note of hesitation or was it fear that he heard?

"I haven't heard from her since the last letter I shared with you, Mme. Remember, she wrote that her father was planning a welcome party for her that she was looking forward to?" Tom paused for a moment. His eyes followed a bee-eater bird as it hopped along a branch on the jacaranda tree in front of the porch. "I was thinking that another letter would come this week. Or hoping, I guess."

Looking out across the compound, Tom saw a young mother walk towards the admitting office, a tiny baby pressed against her back with a red and black blanket-shawl tied under her breasts in a love package with its mother.

"And me, I have received no new letter either. But I have seen Willa, Tommiwe." Mma Cookie paused dramatically. "She has visited more than three times in the very same dream." Mma Cookie met Tom's questioning eyes.

"You had the same dream about Willa three times?" The old woman nodded solemnly. "What happens in it?"

"It is a strange dream, Tommiwe, and it has made me to become frightened."

As the Motswana matron began describing the dream, Tom suddenly felt as though he were hearing her through a filter, the words almost muffled, and stretched out, slowed down. Closing her eyes as if to remember better, Mma Cookie slowly described her repeating dream.

Willa is walking across a desert area, trying to find her way back somewhere, and then looking for water but always getting there too late. Suddenly she's in a field of maize, the stalks high above her head. Still she's searching, but then she's lost again, the endless maize stalks now battering her face and cutting her arms. Dr. Jan cannot be seen but her voice calls out to Willa, 'Where are you?' No matter how hard she tries Willa cannot shout back, her voice coming out a mere whisper so that only the Mokowe birds can hear her. They seem to laugh at her efforts. Then suddenly a pathway opens up in the maize field, but the light that shines through suddenly becomes foggy and Willa can't see anything.

"And just then, I awaken each time." Mma Cookie clucked in frustration, and looked at Tom.

"Mma, you say the dream is exactly the same each time, no changes?"

"Only little changes, but really I just notice more because I have been there before."

A man's voice called 'koko' at the side kitchen door. Knowing it was Sammie Po's voice, Mma Cookie yelled that he should come to the front porch.

Sammie and Tom had not seen each other for six weeks and they greeted one another fondly. There was mutual respect between the elder African man and the young Peace Corps engineer. To Tom, Sammie was the rock of reliability and care that he knew had influenced Willa and helped her grow up with love and an ever-present wall of protection and teaching. To Sammie, Tom was the man Willa chose to love, and he was reliable in helping all the villages get their old boreholes to work again. Some of the elders in the surrounding villages just called *him Rra Metsi*: Mr. Water.

"Mma Cookie, Tommi, I have spoken with the Dingaka about the dream. Yes, Mme, it is serious."

Mma Cookie gasp and grabbed Tom's hand. "Sammie Po, what am I to do?"

"It is time to see the Dingaka. Let us go now. Tommi will drive."

Of course Mma Cookie would want to consult with the Dingaka, Tom knew, but why did he have to drive? Knowing it would do no good to tell them he could actually get in trouble for using a government vehicle on private business, Tom decided it was simply easier to drive them to the Dingaka in the next village. He made a mental note to check the main well while he was there in order to justify his use of the Land Rover to visit a witch doctor.

Tom had another reason for not wanting to drive. He had not seen the Dingaka since his own cleansing in the healer's hut after his father's death. It was a very intense experience that still gave Tom the cold sweats whenever he thought about that night. The end result had been a good one, but how he got there was still difficult to think about.

Remembering the confusion and mental pain he was experiencing at the time, surprisingly, did not bother Tom that much. But it was frightening to consider how the Dingaka knew so much about him. The traditional doctor had helped him reconcile the past so that he could continue growing into a man who could live well among other men and women, and who could be a part of something. For an engineer who lived on absolutes and believed in a "right" answer, reconciling the Dingaka's powerful cures was not a straight-line equation. Willa had helped him understand that he did not always have to know how all the component parts worked to be able to trust the outcome.

Now without Willa, it made it all the harder for Tom to think that the Dingaka had the answers again. If indeed, Mma Cookie's persistent dream really had any merit at all, save for the worries of an almost mother for her almost daughter.

An hour later, Tom waited with Mma Cookie and Sammie Po in the cluttered courtyard of the Dingaka's compound. Had it been only months ago that he had driven Willa here the day of the leopard attack on the Chief? He remembered it like a dream, years in the past. Tom tried to put himself into that night again and remember what he had thought about Willa.

Mostly, he was impressed. Here was a nineteen-year-old with her head on straight enough to sew up a dying chief, and then negotiate his life with the Dingaka. Sure, she looked like she was going to lose it a few times, but she was decisive and took a major risk that night. It had threatened to destroy Willa's relationship with Dr. Jan. But ultimately it helped to bring them closer together. That was the power of the Chief. That was the power of the Dingaka.

A year ago, Tom would have been snickering under his breath if he had been told that the Dingaka was going to interpret Mma Cookie's dream. But now he judged nothing by his former cynicism and his Anglo-centric rationality. If he'd learned nothing else since the day the Chief was almost killed, he now knew that there were realities in Botswana that would not be realities in Cape Cod.

The air seemed to shift suddenly. All three of them looked towards the burlap covering the entrance of the hut.

A loud voice broke the silence. "Mma Cookie, Mother of Willa, Dreamer of the Dream, *tsena, janong. Ke batla go go bona."*

Mma Cookie sprang off the stool, and Sammie Po quickly followed. "He wants to see me now," Mma Cookie said nervously as she glanced from Sammie to Tom.

"We'll be here when you return," Sammie promised her.

Nodding, the old woman straightened her skirt and adjusted it so she could duck through the burlap door into the Dingaka's hut.

For the next hour, Tom and Sammie could hear the two voices in the hut and smell the smoke from the Dingaka's telling fire.

Chanting from the traditional doctor resonated through the mud walls and seemed to vibrate across the floor of the compound. Tom could feel it in his chest, a force he had felt before in the presence of the Dingaka.

A sudden, loud shout by the Dingaka must have marked the end of the session, as Mma Cookie emerged a few moments later. Moving unusually fast, the old woman went straight to Tom's Land Rover. Sammie and Tom exchanged glances but they both fell in behind her.

"A re tsamaya mo clinic-ong," was all Mma Cookie said, signaling that she wanted a speedy retreat. Tom quickly pulled out of the Dingaka's yard and headed back to Mother Mercy, just as Mma Cookie had ordered.

# # #

"Willa is searching for someone in her family. But she is running into obstacles." This was the beginning of what the Dingaka had told Mma Cookie about the repeating dream. Sammie held his hand over his mouth, knowing already that the interpretation would not sit well with him, as it would be frightening and involve the unknown.

"Do you mean actually searching like trying to find, or searching metaphorically?" Tom asked the old woman.

"Tommiwe, what is that, meta-what?"

"Oh..." Tom wondered how to explain what he meant. "Is Willa searching in her mind for someone, or really out searching across many miles."

"Dingaka said really searching, with walking and riding in lorries and such. It is like a honey badger in a trap. She keeps trying one way and it is a dead end but she keeps trying because the search is important." Taking a deep breath, Mma Cookie shut her eyes to recall all the Dingaka's words. "The searching will take her to big American cities and lots of tarred roads to cross. She meets new people who help her but still faces challenges and fearful times."

"What about the person Willa is searching for, did the Dingaka say anything else?"

"It is another woman Willa seeks. I say it must be Nora. What other woman is there in America that she knows?"

"Nora? Willa's sister?"

"Eh, Tommi."

"Does she find her? Is she safe?" All of Tom's American-trained instincts told him he was a fool to buy into the dream interpretation. But right then, to him it was the most real connection he had with Willa.

"The Dingaka only said that the searching would end, but did not say how."

"Is he saving the how until your next visit?" It was clear to Mma Cookie and Sammie that Tom was frustrated and afraid. Otherwise he would not ask such a disrespectful question.

"Tommi, the Dingaka can only tell us what he sees," Sammie reminded the white man. "It is not for him to invent an ending if one did not show itself."

Suddenly embarrassed, Tom put his hands up. "Sorry, Mma, sorry Sammie."

"Ga gona matata, Tommi. No problems, my son," Sammie said as he patted Tom on the shoulder.

"Oh, and something again." Mma Cookie raised her eyebrows as she remembered another detail. "The Dingaka sees a child." Mma Cookie looked at Tom.

"What child? Whose child?" Tom asked as he stood up and paced the veranda.

"Dingaka could not say."

Suddenly Tom laughed, mostly at himself. It was a dream! It was crazy for him to be emotionally invested in a dream, especially when it was not even his own dream.

A dung beetle moved awkwardly across the pressed-dirt patio behind the main house. Tom kicked it against the low wall encircling the compound. There was a sharp snapping sound as the beetle's hard shell hit the wall and cracked open.

"Okay, I can't believe I'm asking this, but why Nora? Why is Willa searching for Nora?"

"Oh, Tommiwe." Mma Cookie crossed her arms over her chest

and shook her head. “Willa loves Nora too much. When little Nora came to Botswana, Willawe followed her everywhere, and dragged her everywhere too, to all her favorite places at Mother Mercy and in the kopjes where they found flowers and pretty stones.”

“Oh, yes,” Sammie Po said in his remembering of that time. “Willa wanted to hold Nora’s hand too much and Nora did not understand that. She was frightened of everything here, and mostly of Dr. Jan. She only wanted to go home.”

Mma Cookie nodded in acknowledgement. “Nora was like a baby goat whose mother rejects it, and instead of nuzzling its baby it only eats the fresh sprouts off the thorn bushes. She knows nothing about her baby goat, so the baby only wishes it were the thorn trees.”

Tom listened as the old Africans talked about Willa’s efforts to make Nora her sister, and make her want to reciprocate the love the younger girl could give so easily. Willa had always wanted a sister. Once she found that she had one in Nora during the Boston visit, Willa would not give up extending herself when her sister came to Botswana a year later.

Willa was willing to do anything to make Nora like being at Mother Mercy. Before Nora arrived, she helped Mma Cookie fix up the guest bedroom with new sheets and a floral bed cover, and put her most special books ordered from England on the bed stand. Agates from Willa’s rock collection, shiny and smooth from Johnny’s rock polisher, lined the window sill, reflecting the light and becoming dancing fairies on the walls.

After Nora arrived, Willa took her on rounds with their mother. As Willa translated, Nora looked on in horror at the various injuries and illnesses of the patients. Something that Willa thought Nora would like to see had backfired instead. From then on, Nora stayed in her room or on the front porch during rounds.

An old gold mine a mile from Mother Mercy was one of Willa’s favorite places to explore. Besides old tools and an occasional coin or bead, the mine, which opened from within an old cave, yielded ancient paintings from earlier inhabitants of the Kalahari. Mma Cookie’s daughter, JoJo, and Willa had made up many tales about the artists and the meaning of the African frescos. Ochre elephants, zebra and kudu danced across the granite walls chased by little San men with black bows and arrows sticking out of long pouches.

Willa brought Nora to the caves to see the dancing San hunters chase their prey. Copying a phrase she had heard Johnny say, Willa told Nora, "you could count on one hand the girls who have been in this cave, and count on two fingers the American girls who have been in here."

But again, Willa had miscalculated Nora's ability to enjoy an outing of that type. It started off badly when a green mamba crossed their path. Nora screamed so loud that Willa was assured that no other creatures would bother them on the rest of the walk.

Then, of course, a bat flew near Nora's head once they got to the mine and that caused more screaming, and jumping up and down, which knocked the canteen out of Willa's hand. Almost all their water spilled out, and the two girls watched it soak instantly into the dry, sandy soil.

Nora came back dehydrated and with painful cuts from thorn bushes on her arms. With their water shortage, Willa had taken them back to Mother Mercy by a short cut. Her only mistake was underestimating Nora's ability to navigate a thorn bush field.

After a soak in a bush tea bath, Nora laid in bed almost a day and a half until Mma Cookie coxed her out with another soothing bath and warm bread and jam.

"So you see, Tommi, how much Willa loves her sister, but she could never tie the cord of love and family between them. Something always interrupted their sisterhood." Mma Cookie smiled sadly as she remembered the looks exchanged between Willa and Nora that showed their confusion and frustration.

Sisterhood did not come easy.

As an only child with a batterer for a father, Tom could not relate that well to the struggles of two sisters trying to forge a connection that they had only by birth, not by provenance.

Driving back to Bodiba that night, Tom tried to picture Willa in Boston, walking down Boylston Street or having coffee at a café in Harvard Square. How many times a day did he ask himself, what is she doing right now? What is she thinking, experiencing, talking about?

Is she thinking about me like I am her?

Boston seemed farther away from him right now than the moon. It should feel closer now that Willa's there. He had to bring it closer.

As he pulled into the graveled area where he parked the Land Rover, Mma Lilli walked out of the cooking hut. She smiled and waved. It was the way she did it that told Tom she had some news.

"Dumela, Mmawe."

"Dumela, white son."

"Mma Lilli, you look like the cat who swallowed the canary."

"Oh, Tommiwe, don't say I am a cat. Cats work for witches."

Tom laughed, making Mma Lilli scowl. "No, Mma, I mean it looks like you have a secret."

"A secret? Oh, yes, a secret but not for long." Mma Lilli reached into the folds of her skirt and pulled out a letter. "Look, Tommiwe. A letter for you. From Willawe."

Tom's pulse quickened. Taking the letter from the old woman, he held it gingerly, as though it were a sacred text or fragile parchment.

"I'll bring you some tea." Mma Lilli did not expect a response as Tom seemed to have folded in on himself. It had been a few weeks since he had received Willa's first letter sent from Boston. What would this one tell him?

Willa's first letter had thanked Tom for the one he wrote that arrived in Boston two days after she had. Hearing her impressions of Boston, her father and stepmother, the fondness still shared between her and Mary, Tom was both jealous and joyous about her new experiences. Nora had not been there to meet her because she was on an out-of-town trip. Willa's disappointment about Nora's absence filtered through the words she used in the letter. Even on paper, Willa's emotions were never hidden. She had little capacity to present herself other then as she really was. Tom thought that Willa would not know what posturing was if she tripped over it. In that way she was certainly naïve. Hopefully it would not lead her into harm in the sometimes unforgiving streets of Boston, where a tenderfoot stood out like a beacon for those with un-neighborly intent.

Using his pocketknife as a letter opener, Tom opened a slit in the top of the envelope and carefully pulled out the letter. A hundred winged birds fluttered in his stomach. *He was holding a piece of her in his hand.*

Taking a deep breath, Tom began reading the second letter from his Love.

July 15, 1969

Dear Tom,

How do I begin to describe my last few weeks in Boston and Philadelphia, and now many other states. Believe it or not, I'm writing this letter on a book in a Greyhound bus, somewhere in Nebraska...

Tom jerked his head up and a few pages of the letter fell from his hand. Fumbling, he quickly grabbed them before the wind did and then stood up.

The words of the Dingaka replayed in his head: *the searching will take her to big American cities and lots of tarred roads to cross...*

"Holy shit," he said aloud, and started reading again.

...so that this won't be a 20-page letter, I'll give you the short version. After I sent you the last letter my father finally admitted that he didn't know where Nora is. She's been gone since December and hasn't contacted father since then...

"Jesus Christ!" Tom said loudly.

"Tommi, what is it?" Mma Lilli asked as she walked quickly towards him with tea.

"It's just like the Dingaka said about Mma Cookie's dream!"

Willa is searching for someone, but she is running into obstacles.

"What did the Dingaka say, Tommi?"

"Wait, wait Mma. I just need to read this first." Tom continued to read the letter, sometimes shaking his head, sometimes smiling at Willa's beautiful naiveté, always wishing he were there on the Greyhound bus to protect her.

Willa described the party her father and Carol threw for her and how she met Nora's old friend who had the postcard clue that led her to Philadelphia.

"...Max was really great, providing a supportive 'shoulder' and telling me more about Nora, the all-grown-up Nora that I don't know. At the time it seemed like a good idea that I take a bus rather than fly to San Francisco. While I'm seeing a lot of the states, most of them so far are the flat states that are miles of farmlands and open range, really a lot like some parts of Botswana, and also of the Transvaal in South Africa. I've met lots of nice Americans, and a few strange ones too. An elderly woman told me all about her vocation in the Methodist church and asked me lots of questions about my faith and family. I was Tswana-polite for a while, but at some point I pretended to be asleep and eventually she went back to her bible reading.

A young Army guy was my seat companion for a few states worth of time after Bible-Lady. He had a hard time sitting still and smoked quite a bit. He had just gotten out of basic training and he was real scared about going to Viet Nam. I shared my box of donuts with him. It was hard not to feel uneasy about the soldier's future. It was almost as if he had foreseen his own fate and was walking head on into it. Frightened, yet also fully resigned..."

Damn, this woman has guts! Tom considered the courage it took for Willa to venture out into an America she knows nothing about to find a sister she knows little about and with no guarantee of success. He shook his head and chuckled. "That's my Willa. Damn, she's ballsy!"

"An old woman can only be patient for one cup of tea. My cup is empty, Tommiwe."

Tom deferred to Mma Lilli, describing the events earlier in the day, from learning about Mma Cookie's dream to the visit to the Dingaka, and now the confirming letter.

Mma Lilli clasped her hand over her mouth in amazement. She was realizing even more that the strength of Willa's spirit had remained in Botswana, connecting with those she loves in very deep ways. Her white skin belied the fact that she was an African girl, a true Motswana.

"Kamoso, you and me, Tommi, we shall go see Mma Cookie. You must read her Willa's letter." Mma Lilli had a stoic, faraway look on her face and she spoke quietly, as though a sacred thing had transpired.

Tom nodded. "Yes, tomorrow we'll go and see Mma Cookie and Sammie Po. Oh, and shouldn't we see the Dingaka too?"

Mma Lilli shook her head and clucked at Tom. "Not the Dingaka, Tommiwe. He already knew what would be in the letter, isn't it."

Tom met Mma Lilli's eyes. Her head was cocked waiting for his response. It was at that moment that it hit him dead center and clear: there was a reality other than the one that he believed in when he came to Botswana. It was possible for Mma Cookie to have a dream about Willa that represented the truth of what she was experiencing in the states. And it was possible for the Dingaka to interpret the old woman's dreams as if he were holding up a mirror to Willa's physical world ten thousand miles away.

"Of course, Mma, the Dingaka already knows. *Ke motho fela."*

"Yes, and I am only a human being too, Tommiwe. You are still learning our ways in Botswana, just like I am learning more about white men by you staying with me. You always use your bag of tools to measure and fix everything. But none of those tools can help you see the Dingaka and know of his ways. *O a itse?"* Isn't it true?

Nodding, Tom walked to the edge of the compound that faced west. Another winter sunset was painting the horizon with a palette of oranges and reds, igniting the desert brush to a beauty never realized in the light of day.

This is the sunset that will touch Willa's eyes in a few hours after it crosses the Atlantic and finds the windows of her Greyhound bus. It will find her face as it finds mine.

# # #

Chapter 25: The Sister

Haight-Ashbury, San Francisco
July 1969

As the sun set, the Haight would warble behind a smoky shroud, cool air from the bay meeting the heat vibrating off the streets, sidewalks and rooftops. It was a haze that Tunney loved. From the first time he walked through it, the Haight haze captured his artist-eyes, inspired his poet's-thoughts.

For some the haze distorted the street scenes and took the shine off the bay. For Tunney it clarified everything. Ugly, trash-filled alleys and Victorians decaying under a hundred years of peeling paint, became magical and beautiful in the haze. Now he could imagine a wise sage lived at the end of the mysterious alley and the Victorian was a regal beauty still in her prime.

All because of the haze. The great equalizer haze. The eternal optimist haze. The kind haze, transforming the world, or at least the Haight, into a tolerant and tolerable place.

Even the Artists Repertory Theatre looked good in the evening's haze. But hazy or clear, Tunney already felt a great fondness for the Theatre. Two months ago he thought he was doing the stage manager a favor by helping to build a few backdrops that were so far behind schedule that they risked a set-less show. Now he was working at the Theatre full time and quickly becoming a member of its eclectic family.

Tunney locked the basement door behind him and climbed the ancient stairwell up to street level. Full of a thousand nooks and crannies, secret rooms and incredibly steep stairways, the Theatre's chaotic architecture suited its actors and directors just fine. It had taken Tunney over a month to figure out the entire floor plan on each of the five stories and the basement. But it was worth it for the caches of old sets and lumber he found that everyone else had either forgotten about or never knew existed.

Exploring old buildings had been one of Tunney's "hobbies" since he had been a kid in Boy Scouts. His troop helped elderly widows and others in need in their parish clean out their basements, attics and garages, and then had a big garage sale with whatever the elderly folks did not want any longer. Tunney especially loved cleaning out the basements in these old homes. There were always hidden doorways and forgotten wooden trunks filled with old books and hatboxes piled on top of decades of memories. Not many of the scouts had the patience that Tunney did. He would sit with a widow and let her tell the story behind an old picture discovered under a box in a closet or in the bottom drawer of an old child's desk.

Decades would fall away as the stories brought eras past back to life for Tunney, and for the story-teller. These were stories of people who had lived hard lives, even harder than Nam. For they had mustard gas and trench warfare and influenza and lynching. They were happy with getting oranges for Christmas and watching silent movies. At Thanksgiving whatever fowl happened to be in the yard and ready to kill would be roasted. Tunney's love of stories and history must have started there. An old man's retelling of a battle against the Germans in North Africa relayed more history to him than did all the textbooks he slogged through in high school. Put history into a story and it became tangible. He could touch it and know it.

Working in the Theatre was proving to be a similar experience for Tunney. Plays that he could not comprehend when they were words on a page came to life for him through the actors' faces, hands and voices. Once Tunney heard the company doing a read through, it was easier for him to determine how the sets should be built to best complement the actors' words and movements. Granted, he still did the bidding of the set designer but Tunney's suggestions for changes to original designs were starting to be noticed and used.

Actors were a quirky bunch, Tunney realized quickly, but so was he. It worked. For once Tunney felt that he could be himself at a job, and not have to create a public face. It was a major realization for him that he could work in a job that he enjoyed, and that could be part of his life by choice, not necessity.

At this point, Tunney was not thinking that the theatre would be a long-term vocation for him. But he was relishing all his new experiences and friends. And he was learning a lot about what it took to run a successful playhouse. It was not work for the easily discouraged or the overly sensitive. Producers, directors and actors could all be brutal to one another when lines were not flowing right or the box office was down, or the lead actor had a coke hangover half the time. The old adage of 'The Show Must Go On,' remained the beacon that everyone looked to and believed in, whatever hardship presented itself.

Walking back to his apartment, Tunney felt satisfied and lighthearted. All of the sets had been completed before opening night, despite the producer's expressed doubts a few weeks back. Yet, opening night had come and gone the week before. Reviews were good and even mentioned the subtle power of the sets, complementing the acting and the story, not distracting from it.

Using his hands to create such an integral part of the play had given Tunney back some of the pride lost in the numbing sorrows and bloody realities of Nam's battlefields, and the cold welcome of his countrymen. It was funny in a way, the reactions he would get if someone found out he had been in Nam. Older folks welcomed him and praised him with patriotic pride. His peers were not as kind. They questioned his involvement in the war, either directly or indirectly branding him as a killer, stupid, obsolete, of another era. He didn't see himself in their words and he couldn't see himself in the boy he was before Nam.

At least in San Francisco most people took him at face value as they, too, had pasts that they would just as soon not want revealed or questioned. Tunney's long hair belied his service in the Marines. Now his work in the theatre just made him one of the crew, accepted, unquestioned, and expected to work his ass off every day for little pay. But the pride was coming back as he was reclaiming who he was, who he wanted to be.

A few blocks before he got to his apartment, Tunney stopped at the bodega on the corner for a few quarts of beer, bread, deli meat and cheese, enough to last for a few days. He was always so tired now when he finally left the theatre. Every day flew by quickly, the way he liked it. Focusing so intently on the sets made his old sense of time disappear, replaced by days that were measured in plywood, nails, paint and deadlines.

The current production of Shakespeare's *Measure for Measure* would last another three weeks so Tunney was experiencing his first break in the frenetic pace that had marked his short tenure at the theatre. The director had brought the play into contemporary times, mixing Old English tonalities with a modern context in language and history. Audiences and critics both had embraced it, and the producer was already talking with the backer about a possible extension. Tunney's colleagues made him aware that this was not something that happened all that often.

The little bell tinkled as always on the bodega's screen door as Tunney left with his provisions. It was almost dark, the streetlights making fairies dance in the bay haze. He could see his apartment on the top of the hill, the lights of his downstairs neighbor were welcoming yellow-orange eyes, watching his uphill climb.

As he approached the house, Tunney stopped abruptly. A woman sat on the front steps, obviously waiting for someone. *It couldn't be her*. His stomach flipped. *Was something wrong with the baby?*

"Nora?" His pace increased. The woman sitting on the front steps of his apartment house stood up. Back lit by the porch light she looked like an apparition, the haze softening the edges of her shape and face.

"Nora?" he said again when she did not answer.

"I'm Willa, I'm..."

Tunney interrupted. "The sister. The African sister."

Willa swallowed hard and nodded. "Yes, Nora's sister. You must be Tunney." Her voiced cracked slightly from the old, dormant words finally being used.

Tunney smiled and cocked his head. "For two people who don't know each other we still seem to know each other." Tunney paused, embarrassed. "That was sort of a dumb thing to say." For a second the two strangers just looked at one another. Tunney had the sudden realization that he could look at Willa's face for a long time.

"Tunney, I'm sorry to just appear on your doorstep, but I need your help? I'm trying to find Nora, and I just need to know if you know where she is?" Weariness spread across Willa's face. In it Tunney saw the hundred little towns she'd seen out the bus window, the hundred stories heard from seatmates old and young, and the naps that stood for sleep and produced dreams, vivid and surreal. He met her eyes and just nodded. Willa closed hers. A tear escaped, rolling slowly down her cheek and disappeared under her shirt collar.

"I know where she is Willa, and she's safe and well." Willa reached for a step to sit on. "Why don't you come upstairs, you look exhausted. I'll make you a sandwich and tell you all the details. Here, let me take your bag. It looks like it needs a solid floor to rest on."

Willa nodded. Tunney noticed the start of a hopeful smile that made Willa's bottom lip tremble.

When they entered the apartment Willa asked to use the bathroom. Tunney pointed the way and dug around for a clean towel in the musky linen closet. In the kitchen he poured two glasses of beer and made ham sandwiches. Surveying the contents of his cupboards he found a bag of potato chips and some Oreos. Just as he finished laying out the feast on the coffee table, Willa came out of the bathroom. She looked refreshed, still the edges of fatigue around her eyes and forehead, but wearing a new shirt, skin glowing. Willa sighed heavily and smiled at Tunney.

"Hey, that's the same sigh that Nora does. Must run in the family," Tunney said as he motioned for her to sit on the couch.

"Is it? You probably know much more about Nora than I do." There was both jealousy and desperation in her voice. "I'll try not to bother you too much asking for details but I beg you, any and all, please."

"On the bother scale, I'm guessing that you'd rank pretty low, Nora's Sister. Here, sustenance for the weary traveler."

Willa looked at Tunney with an intensity that startled him. "Thank you, Tunney. But before we eat, can you please tell me where Nora is? Is she here in San Francisco? Is she okay? I've been on a Greyhound bus for a week with nothing to do but worry about finding her. I'm afraid I've arrived here in quite a state, so please forgive me."

Tunney could hear the frustration and anxiety in Willa's voice. She looked so familiar, so much like Nora, he wanted to hug her, to calm her in his arms, the way he had done with Nora.

For the next half hour, Tunney described his and Nora's own cross-country journey, leaving out the details of the less pleasant incidents like the Hammersley visit, and their settling in San Francisco. Willa gasped when she learned that Nora was pregnant, and then beamed with excitement, sharing in the joy that Tunney said was fixed already in Nora's heart for her baby. *Nora can be the mother she never had,* Willa thought. *And the one I never had as well, not by proximity, but by Jan's nature.* How blessed Willa was to have Mma Cookie. Nora had never had mother love. She must be terrified.

Throughout his retelling, Tunney was able to take in all the beauty and emotion that Willa's face held. For the most part, Willa was quiet, only asking a question once in a while, giving Tunney a chance to take bites of his sandwich. Willa mostly asked about her sister's pregnancy, her health and whether she was getting good care. Tunney told her about Bea and the clinic, and arranging for Nora to go to Hope Creek Farm.

"Hope Creek in Oregon. That sounds like a beautiful place, Tunney. How far is it from here? Can I get there by bus?"

Tunney laughed. "Hey, kid, you need to slow down a bit. You've just traveled across this country and you're in one of the most beautiful cities we've got. Before you rush up to Oregon, you need to stop and smell the roses. Nora's not going anywhere. That's a guarantee."

Willa smiled wearily. "Dr. Jan used to say that too. It was a saying she got from her Aunt Dix. 'Stop and smell the roses or the thorns will reach out and prick you.'"

"I like the add on at the end," Tunney said as he stood up and carried their indoor picnic remnants into the kitchen. Willa stood up to help but Tunney stopped her. "You stay put. I won't have you passing out on me like your sister used to do when she was over tired."

Willa did not argue, her weariness pulling her back down. "*Ke itumetse, Rra.*"

"*Ke*, say what?" Willa laughed at Tunney's response.

"Thank you, kind sir, in Setswana."

"That sounds beautiful. That's a hell of an accent you've got there. You could read the tax code out loud and it would sound good." Tunney turned, giving Willa some privacy to get over her blushing. How could she not know how beautiful and compelling she is, Tunney wondered? He hurried in the kitchen, throwing the plates in the sink and grabbing the quart of beer from the fridge. Getting back in the living room and sitting next to Willa was his only thought right now.

But when Tunney came back into the living room, Willa's eyes were closed and her chest moved up and down in a way that told him she was already asleep. Instead of waking her, Tunney went out on his fire escape "deck" with his quart. He pulled a joint out of his wallet, the sweet aroma giving him the calming buzz he wanted after a long day of work, and now of his renewed connection with Nora through Willa's unexpected arrival. He felt a buzz of excitement, the kind he got when a great song resonated in his bones and became part of the memory of a night always recalled.

Tunney let out a laugh of surprise at himself. He felt like a school kid with a crush on the new girl in school. He did not even know Willa, but somehow he already felt fully acquainted, comfortable. Maybe it was just their common connection through Nora? But Tunney knew for sure that his stomach had not done flip-flops like that over a woman for a long time.

Back and forth he went, admonishing himself for his reaction to Willa. It was probably just his missing Nora and Willa's resemblance to her, as well as her sudden appearance, that was causing his usual guard to go down.

But it was more than that, he countered to himself. Willa was open, innocent. There was no fear in her, no agenda, no planning her next conversational step. Just a brilliant openness, a trust that made Tunney want to wrap himself around her, protect her in a city where innocence drew the wicked to take advantage.

When Tunney came in off the deck, Willa was fully stretched

out on the couch. He got a pillow and gently set her head on it, then turned out the light. Willa breathed heavily, the sign that she had not slept prone for many nights. Tunney had decided to offer her the bedroom earlier, but now did not want to wake her. She was fine, he thought. Probably dreaming about Africa and all the crazy people she had likely met on the bus trip.

Tomorrow it would be her turn. Tunney wanted to hear about her trip across the states, and how she had found her way to San Francisco and his apartment steps. Now he can ask some of the things he could not ask Nora. What was their father like to have pushed Nora away? And what about the mother in Africa whose connection with Nora was glaringly severed? For now, Tunney realized he needed to get some sleep. Keeping up with Willa and holding her in San Francisco for a few days would likely prove a daunting task if she was anything like her sister.

Looking at Willa's shape on the couch once more, Tunney shut off the hall light and padded quietly to his bedroom.

# # #

Willa was writing a letter on tissue thin pieces of blue paper when Tunney came out in the morning. He had awoken to the sound of the shower and of Willa's voice singing a rhythmic, lilting song. She was not being loud, but the shower stall acted as an amplifier into Tunney's room. It sounded like an African song, strange words and tonalities evoking vast villages and deserts and heat. It made it very clear that Willa was not of his world.

Tunney waited patiently until he heard Willa leave the bathroom and then he went in and took a shower. On most days he would have slept in until nine at least. It was seven-thirty but he knew he had to stop Willa from jumping on a Greyhound so that she could take some time to experience San Francisco. *And spend more time with me*, Tunney admitted to himself.

"Morning, Willa. Already busy, huh?"

Willa looked up and smiled. "My first time away from home, really. Everyone expects daily correspondence, but I'm having a hard time making it weekly."

"That still sounds pretty ambitious, particularly before you've had coffee. Are you up for breakfast at the diner down the street?"

"Mmhmm," Willa nodded vigorously and put the unfinished letter between the pages of her journal. "I'm famished again," she said as she stood up. "But this morning is on me, Tunney."

"In that case, we're to the Embarcadero. You need to see the waterfront, anyway." *Then you might stay longer.* "In fact, let's do the true tourist experience. We'll start at the cable cars."

It was easy to make Willa laugh and Tunney loved the sound of it. After a rumbling cable car ride that made Willa grin like a child, they ate a breakfast pancakes, bacon and eggs at a waterside diner frequented by a contrasting mix of fishermen, bankers and tourists.

Hardly able to keep his eyes off of her, Tunney observed Willa as she absorbed her new environment. She seemed as watchful as a lioness, taking in all the people, the wharf life, the place where the blue sky met the choppy waters of the bay. Interested in learning how the city worked, Willa asked about its commerce, biggest industries, schools and colleges, hospitals and clinics, and points of pride and shame.

Yet there was also a distance to Willa. She was not fully in San Francisco or even in America. Her eyes roamed back to where she had come from, part of her in California, but most of her in Africa. Willa was simply being the polite person she was by letting him lead her around as though she were just another tourist. Willa had an agenda. And it wasn't touring San Francisco or hanging out with Tunney. *Bingo, moron.*

"Willa, I know what we need to do. You need to meet Bea," Tunney realized. Willa didn't want to be a tourist. She wanted to be a sister again.

"Bea?"

"Nora's friend at the clinic who turned her on to Hope Creek Farm. You'll love her. She'll love you. Plus, she probably knows stuff about Nora that I don't. Girl stuff."

"I'd love to meet Bea," Willa said as she smiled at Tunney's reference to the language women share with one another. "And to see a clinic here in the states. We need a lot of help at Mother

Mercy. I'd like to see how they manage their patients and the operations side of things. My mother is an excellent doctor and surgeon, but she knows nothing about the other important things like ordering drugs and getting linens washed before they run out. We always feel like we're running behind. Always running behind."

There she went again, back to Botswana. Willa's eyes were focused so far inward that Tunney half expected them to roll back and show only white. She was here but not here. *Just keep talking and her eyes will meet mine again.*

"We'll go to Bea's clinic later this afternoon. But for now, I'm taking you to Chinatown, and by the time we get there, I want to know all about Mother Mercy and your life in Botswana. Is that how you say it?"

"Almost. Say 'boat' and then 'swana'. The way you said it, 'bought' and then 'swana' is Batswana, the name people call themselves. Like you say American."

Now it was time for Tunney to just listen as Willa described growing up at Mother Mercy. As she carried him through her youth, of following her mother around the surgery, and then later, her role as translator and nurse's aide, Tunney became even more amazed at this young woman who had come into his life the day before.

Tunney realized that the melodious ring in Willa's voice as she talked about Botswana was the sound of Africa. Willa was as much a part of the culture of Botswana as he was the United States. Soon he knew Mma Cookie, Sammie Po and Dr. Gakelape. He wished he had been there as Johnny read *Ulysses* out loud and when the Dingaka told Willa how to save Chief Tau after the leopard attack. She opened up her world to Tunney.

Willa found herself holding back when it came to talking about Tom. That was still too personal, too close to her heart to talk about with someone she had barely known for a day. And there was something about Tunney...something that made her not tell him that she was, or had been, attached to another. *Was she still attached to Tom? Attached in the way that they had been?* Did distance serve to stretch and weaken the attachment, or make it slowly fade away like the picture of his face when it visited her night dreams and daydreams?

Suddenly Willa realized that Tunney was talking to her.

"Knock, knock, Willa, is anybody home in there?" Tunney finally joked.

"I'm sorry, Tunney. I guess I'm a little overwhelmed and wandering in my mind a bit." Willa smiled sheepishly.

"Well, you wouldn't believe what you just agreed to while you were spacing out," Tunney admonished with a devilish look on his face.

"Uh oh. I plead temporary insanity." Willa's emerald eyes playfully begged.

"No such plea accepted, young lady. You'll have to come with me."

Willa laughed and took Tunney's outstretched arm. She felt so free again, free of burdens, just as she had when things were at their best between her and Tom. It was a release that occurred when two people connected in a way that created a mutual trust. *The Dingaka would tell me to just feel it, be with it, don't judge it.*

It felt so good feeling good again that she was not going to spoil it. Now she knew with certainty where Nora was. Their time together was near. Tunney had helped her get one step closer, the last step. *Or is it the first step?*

"Where are you taking me, Mr. Authority Figure?"

"Where every princess must go. To the tower, my dear, Coit Tower." Willa shrugged and sighed, play-offering her acquiescence.

For a few minutes the accidental couple walked in silence in the rhythm of each other's shoes clicking against the pavement. A bay breeze blew across a garden of roses and lilies, the fragrance prompting simultaneous smiles and matching deep breaths from Willa and Tunney. It was a perfume that would instantly conjure the day in future years, a scent memory that held the whole city, the whole day.

"Hey, Tunney, I'm not keeping you from your work, am I?" Willa looked apologetic that she had not thought to ask this earlier. Mma Cookie was scolding her in absentia for being so self-centered on her own agenda.

"Not for two days. The theatre where I work is closed Monday and Tuesday; so this is my weekend."

As they browsed the tiny shops and vegetable stalls in Chinatown, Willa asked Tunney about his job at the theatre. He brought her right into the playhouse with his vivid descriptions of the creation of the set designs and how these tied into the dialogue and mood of a play. Willa laughed in pure enjoyment at Tunney's descriptions of the spats between "the somewhat arrogant lead actor and the totally arrogant head writer and the nosey benefactor and the spastic director."

When he talked about his former boutique jobs, Willa had a chance to tell Tunney about her time with Max, and the postcard clue that led her to Philadelphia. Tunney's eyes lit up at the mention of his old boss in Philadelphia. Then he told a few stories of his own about the daily adventures at Max's boutique when he worked there with Nora. Willa learned a little about Nora's ex-boyfriend Pete, or at least as much as Tunney knew and could tell her without seeming like a gossip. *Pete was the father of Nora's baby.*

Willa surprised herself by feeling relieved. A small voice inside her head had already hoped that Tunney was not the father of Nora's baby. It confirmed what she had already guessed, that Nora and Tunney had been very close, but not lovers. At least that was what she interpreted through the way Tunney talked about Nora. Yet it also confirmed that there would be another child in the world who would be cheated of a father, who wouldn't or couldn't be there for his daughter. Girls imagine that their missing fathers are good and true, knight-like, and waiting to reunite and live happily ever after. Willa pictured Nora with a daughter who sat in a window box petting her cat and dreaming of a father who never was, but whose memory and history were as real as the kitten's warm body and soothing purrs.

At four in the afternoon on their way back from Coit Tower, the new friends got off a bus in front of Bea's clinic.

"She should be winding down about now," Tunney noted as they walked up the sidewalk to the front door of the clinic. "I think a night person comes at four or so, and Bea can usually take off."

For some reason, Bea turned around right when Tunney and Willa walked through the door. She stopped in her stride across the room and squinted her eyes, walking towards them.

"Bea, hey, this is Willa, Nora's sister from Africa," Tunney volunteered seeing Bea's questioning eyes.

Suddenly smiling, Bea cocked her head and then shook it. "My, Willa, you do look like your sister! Welcome!" Bea stepped through the opening of the reception desk and held her arms open to Willa. The African girl melted and fell into the motherly arms. Bea gave the tightest, most powerful hugs in San Francisco, and could pop anyone's anxiety right out of their body.

"I bet you want to know more about your sister, don't you? Let's all go to my place and I'll throw a few burgers on the grill and we'll catch up. How's that sound?" Bea beamed at her two visitors.

Tunney looked at Willa, who was nodding, her smile directed gratefully at Bea.

"Could I also come back tomorrow and get a tour of the clinic?" Willa asked Bea as they all headed out to the parking lot.

"It's not the most requested tourist spot, but sure, why don't you come over about two o'clock."

Willa explained her connection to Mother Mercy and her plans to go to medical school. Bea was delighted in the young woman's interest in the clinic operations and the types of cases that they handled.

By the time they got to Bea's, the two women might as well have been speaking another language for all that Tunney understood: names of medical procedures and illnesses, drug treatments and diagnostic machines. Every answer Bea provided led to three more questions from Willa. And Bea wanted to know everything about Mother Mercy and Dr. Jan.

"I only have Nora's pre-teen perspective on Mother Mercy, and on you and your mother, for that matter. None of it was real flattering, especially the parts about Dr. Jan and the long lines of patients waiting to be helped. And something about an abandoned mine," Bea remembered.

"Oh, god, the old gold mine. That was a terrible day. We're

probably lucky we made it back relatively unscathed. Except, of course, Nora's cuts and scratches from the thorn bush field."

Seeing that Willa and Bea would likely talk all night, Tunney volunteered to grill the burgers. It was a small backyard, San Francisco style, just big enough for a grill and a few lawn chairs. Knowing that Willa might want to ask some "female" questions about Nora, Tunney stayed in the kitchen for a while, molding the burgers, cutting cheese, lettuce and tomato, and heating up a can of baked beans.

Bea had just talked to Marge at Hope Creek the week before. She had learned that Nora was doing fine, was huge, and had become a leader to the other girls as well as an office manager for Marge. She could clearly see Willa's expression change as it reflected relief and happiness from the positive news of Nora. But then the impatience returned.

"Can I just go up there and see her? Should I call first? Do I need permission?" Willa's horizon was reuniting with Nora. She did not want to get that close and then be turned away at the gates of Hope Creek.

"It's not a prison, honey. The girls are free to come and go, as long as they fulfill their portion of the chores and duties, and participate fully in various group and one on one sessions. But given Nora's stage of pregnancy and her tendency to worry, I'd just show up if I were you. I can give Marge the heads up and ask her to keep it a surprise. I'll mention your healthcare background, but beware, Marge will have you giving birth control clinics before you get halfway up the driveway!" Bea chuckled at her friend's ability to get pro bono work for "her girls" out of anyone within her range of vision.

For the rest of the evening, Willa told stories about Dr. Jan. Bea carefully brought up Nora's hardened anger at her mother, and her sense of frustration about her relationship with their father. Nora's anger towards Dr. Jan was not difficult to understand, given the abandonment issues, but it was harder to pinpoint a cause for her anger at Michael Dodge, Bea commented during their talk. Listening intently, Willa further pieced together her sister's history, and Nora's new life that she was very soon going to enter.

Then Bea insisted that it was Willa's turn to talk, so she started at the beginning of the day that her world changed. Willa relayed the story of the leopard attack, her own response, and Jan's blowing up, but then their reconciliation over the use of traditional medicine to save the Chief. Bea listened in awe over the daily issues faced at this African version of her clinic, and the base of knowledge that Willa had acquired at such a young age. Then she clapped in glee over the telling of the Chief's recovery ceremony and how he had gifted the tribal land to Mother Mercy to honor the marriage of traditional and Western medicine.

"I'd love to meet that Chief someday, Willa. He sounds a lot wiser than most of the leaders we have running this city," Bea commented as the two women stood side by side washing the evening's dishes.

The sound of a baseball announcer and the cheering of fans wafted into the kitchen from the living room where Tunney was watching the Phillies and the Cubs sweat it out at Wrigley Field. An occasional groan from Tunney let them know who was winning.

At nine, Bea gave them a lift home in her old VW van. It sputtered and stalled the first few blocks, but managed to get them to Tunney's apartment ten minutes later.

"Thanks for the great meal, Bea, and the lift back. And for opening your home to me tonight," Willa spoke softly as she hugged Bea across the seat.

"You're welcome, hon. Get some rest, you look tired. And I'll see you tomorrow afternoon. Tunney can help you figure out the best bus to take."

"Or I'll just drive her there, Bea. I need to hit a few lumber and hardware stores tomorrow. We're already planning the fall play season and it sounds like the sets will be huge. I volunteered to do a little research on the best deals for bulk plywood and joinery." Bea could hear the pride in Tunney's voice as he talked about his work at the theatre. She was glad that he had found a niche for himself that was more creative and fulfilling than selling clothing. *And he seems extra happy tonight. Could it be Willa? Of course.*

As Bea drove off down the hill, Willa and Tunney watched the lights of San Francisco swallow up the van.

"This is a beautiful city, Tunney. You've been great to share it with me today. Thanks for slowing me down." Willa's smile made his legs feel shaky. *I have got to control that.*

"Oh, but just wait until you get the bill, sister. These custom tours are pretty expensive." Tunney turned away quickly on purpose, leading the way up the stairs. The urge to kiss Willa was too strong and seeing her smile at his joke might dissolve his wall of resistance all together.

By the time Tunney came out of the bathroom, Willa was, again, already asleep on the couch, the lights from the city illuminating her shape and giving a warm glow to her face.

It was at that moment that Tunney realized he could not let Willa take another Greyhound bus for the trip to Oregon. He would go with her as driver, companion, and possibly mediator, depending on Nora's reaction to Willa's arrival. But knowing both sisters now, Tunney was fairly certain that they would reunite in joy, their sisterhood given a new chance to gel, to mean something. But also knowing each of the sister's strong-willed nature, their complete reconciliation might not be immediate or simultaneous.

So Tunney would lead the way and stand out of the way as needed so he could see these sisters try and make a go of siblinghood. He had a stake in it now; he was going to be an uncle soon.

And he was not ready to let Willa go yet, even though he didn't know exactly what that meant.

# # #

Chapter 26: Reunion

Tillamook, Oregon
August 1969

Nora loved this time of day. The chores were done, the accounts at the Dairy balanced, and she was meeting Bobbie Jo for coffee.

Ever since the two pregnant women compared bellies in front of the baby clothing display in downtown Tillamook, Nora and Bobbie Jo had become fast friends. They met a few times a week either at Penny's Grill, where she was headed now, or at Hope Creek, to share coffee and stories.

Both women enjoyed the chance to compare the movements and twinges and aches of their expectant bodies. More than once their loud guffaws had turned heads at Penny's Grill. But when the other diners saw the two seemingly "twin" pregnant women, few could help but smile and join in the laughter.

Tillamook was small and Bobbie Jo knew everyone. Friends of all ages would stop by their table, asking how she felt and what she was hearing from her husband Steve over in Viet Nam. Bobbie Jo was always so polite, repeating the same answers again and again, and thanking them for asking. *Yes, I feel fine, Doc says baby's fine, Steve is fine, just got a letter last week, yes, he'd love it if you sent him some socks, and he'll be home at Christmas he says, yes, if it's a boy it will be Steve, Jr. and if it's a girl she'll be Eve.*

Bobbie Jo's patience and her obvious care for her many townie friends were traits that Nora knew she needed to learn from her friend. She began to relish the interruptions, learning more about the town folk and her new friend at the same time. Inadvertently, Nora was becoming an insider.

Another admirable trait of Bobbie Jo's was making Nora feel embraced. "This is my friend Nora from the East Coast. We're having our babies together!" Bobbie Jo would announce as she introduced Nora. Just the way she did it elicited automatic respect from those Nora met. No one ever asked about a husband. They just assumed that Nora had a husband in Viet Nam as well, and the two friends were together, supporting one another.

As Nora walked into Penny's, Bobbie Jo waved from their usual booth against the window.

"Sorry I'm late. I had to wait for Harry to get done unloading the feed from the truck," Nora said but Bobbie Jo just shrugged.

"I just got here too. Haven't even ordered yet."

Nora settled into the naugahyde booth. Ever since the manager had increased the space for their bellies, the pregnant duo always sat in the same place.

"The usual?" Bobbie Jo asked Nora, who nodded and smiled. "We'll have the usual, Blanche," Bobbie Jo spoke up so the waitress could get their order without having to come around the counter.

"Got it, ladies. Right up," Blanche called back as she opened the glass pie cabinet. Bobbie Jo always had lemon meringue and Nora had boysenberry pie, with hot coffee, lots of cream.

"This is my treat today, Bobbie Jo, no arguments," Nora said firmly to her friend as she pulled a five out of her wallet.

"No complaints from me, Nora. You come into some money or something?" she asked mischievously as she moved her arms so Blanche could set down the pie plates and coffees.

"I just have a few good friends who are watching out for me." Nora smiled as she thought about the Snoopy card from Tunney ten days ago with a twenty dollar bill and a single sentence: '*Thinking of ya, and Baby D – Tunney.*' There had been a playbill inside the envelope with Tunney's name circled under the *Set Design* category. Reading Tunney's letters were always more like deciphering code than anything else. She was happy for him. Finally Tunney had found a spot for himself that engaged his head and his heart, and paid the rent.

Not knowing whether it was a conspiracy, Bea had also sent a letter the week before with another twenty-dollar bill and a newspaper clipping on what mothers could expect in the first few weeks after giving birth. Nora had shared it with some of the girls during their group therapy session.

"Have you noticed an increase in your gas level?" Bobbie Jo

asked it very seriously, but Nora had to cover her mouth so she wouldn't spray coffee across the table.

"You are evil asking me that with a full mouth!" Nora admonished when she stopped laughing.

"Sorry, I didn't mean to be evil. I was just wondering if I was the only one burping and having, well, you know, the other kind of gas, all the time."

"You mean farting."

Bobbie Jo ducked her head. "Ssh, jeez Nora, tell the whole town about it!" Bobbie Jo giggled and Nora joined in until they were, again, drawing stares.

"The answer is yes. But I'm fortunate that I live with many other gaseous, pregnant girls so no one gives it a second thought."

"And I'm just glad Steve isn't around to experience this hopefully temporary state."

"What do you mean? He adores you. He would take you, farts and all." They giggled again in unison.

"I'm just glad that I don't have to test his tolerance right now. I don't want to ruin his overly glamorized impression of me."

"But haven't you two known each other from sandbox days? He knows you're not all sugar and spice."

"You'd think so, huh? But his letters from Nam are sometimes so complimentary of me that I think he sent them to the wrong woman." Bobbie Jo paused and looked into her cup. "That's how I know it's bad over there. It's like he's picturing a perfect alternative world that's nothing like Nam. It worries me."

Nora reached across the table and touched Bobbie Jo's hand. "Hey, the guy loves you. He needs to focus on the best things in his life in words when he can't have you next to him. My friend Tunney has told me a little bit about his time in Nam. Everything that means 'home' is worshipped. It's almost like a painkiller. It lets them forget where they are for a while."

"But what about when he comes back and I'm not all that he envisioned. In his mind I still have a waist and I never fart." Bobbie Jo started laughing after Nora's lead. "It would be sad if it wasn't so funny."

"It's sadly funny, Bobbie Jo. But you'll get your waist back and you won't be gassy anymore, not until you're really old, anyway, and then he'll be too old to leave you."

"Maybe we can do Jack LaLanne together after the babies are born. I only have until Christmas to mold myself back into his dream girl." A quick look of anxiety flashed across Bobbie Jo's face. "I just want him back."

"That makes two of you."

An old crabber entered the front door. Bobbie Jo stared past him at nothing, fixed on something deep inside herself.

"Nora, I'm so bad sometimes. I daydream about Steve getting hurt enough to come home but not hurt so bad that it will matter in the long run. Isn't that terrible? I haven't even told that to Father in the confessional. I'm so ashamed." Bobbie Jo cut her eyes down and she gazed, fixed on the slight movement of the coffee in her cup.

Nora got up from her side of the booth and slid in next to Bobbie Jo. "You have nothing to be ashamed of, Bobbie Girl. You miss him, you want him here. I'd be worried about you if you weren't scheming about ways to bring your man home sooner. I'm just jealous because I don't have a Steve. Go ahead and miss him, Bobbie Jo. You're having his baby while he's a million miles away in a war that's scary and dangerous, and... you gotta miss each other. It's the one thing you can share now."

Bobbie Jo hugged Nora hard and sniffled in her ear. "I'm sorry." She took a tissue out of her purse. "I should be buying you pie, Nora, not the opposite."

"Just remember, last week I was the one crying in my coffee and you pulled me out of my funk. We're conveniently taking turns."

"Thanks, friend. Now get over on your own side before we make the gossip section of the *Tillamook Headlight Herald*." They laughed, too loud again, but no one cared.

"I have to go anyway. I told Harry I'd have the truck back by four."

"I'd better go too. My parents are coming over for dinner and I haven't hid all the messes yet."

Hugging awkwardly around their baby bellies, the two women

said their goodbyes, agreeing that one day soon they would be having coffee in their shared room in the maternity ward.

It was a perfect summer day in Tillamook County. A blue, cloudless sky stretched forever out to sea and east over the coastal mountain range. It was rare for the thermometer to reach 80 degrees in Tillamook, but it was welcomed by all. A light breeze brought a cool touch of salt air up from the bay, making it a day for the history books, as Harry would say.

Nora did not even mind the smell of cow manure any more. She had realized a month ago that the smell of manure would always take her back to Hope Creek. For that she was grateful and no longer curled her nose at the often strong smell of manure at the Dairy, depending on the wind direction, of course. *I'm becoming such a farmer*, Nora admitted to herself. *What would my friends in Boston think*? That one piece of information alone could make her the subject of many a cocktail party gossip session, let alone if they found out she was pregnant, single, and planning to keep the baby.

The visual of her causing such a stir among the popular set of her old life made Nora smirk. What a joy to not have to pretend to care about that crowd any more.

Bets, her favorite cow, was munching away on purple clover as Nora drove up the dirt road to Hope Creek. She could swear that Bets nodded her head in acknowledgement of Nora's passing. *Who would have thought that Nora Dodge could love a cow*?

It was not unusual for a few visitors' cars to be in the gravel area in front of the main house; nurses and counselors visiting the girls, repairmen fixing the milking machines or the frequently broken toilets. Today there was only one visitor's car in the lot. As it came clearly into view, Nora suddenly slammed on the brakes. She would know that Mustang anywhere.

Tunney!

Gravel flew out noisily behind the wheels as Nora accelerated as fast as she had just braked.

Tunney's here!

Nora parked quickly and scooted herself out of the truck as fast as her baby bulk would allow.

There he was. Standing on the porch beaming at her and then laughing, his head falling back and then forward. Tunney whooped and jumped down the porch stairs, meeting Nora at the bottom. His strong arms wrapped her up in his brother bear hug that could have gone on forever if Nora had her way. *This feels so safe, so secure, so Tunney.*

Extending Nora out at the ends of his arms, Tunney looked her up and down.

"My god, Nora, you're so..."

"Big?" She finished his sentence and they both laughed. "It's okay to say it Tunney. Believe me, no one knows better than me that 'big' is the appropriate adjective."

They hugged again, Tunney successfully maneuvering around her belly.

"You've done this before."

"Five sisters, remember?"

Nora beamed. "I remember."

"Come up on the porch. I have a surprise for you."

"Aren't you surprise enough? How did you get here? What's going on? It's so great to see you, Tunney." Nora took his hand and squeezed it.

"Well, you certainly haven't lost your ability to ask twenty questions at once!" They both laughed, and Nora bent her head, pretending to be embarrassed. Then suddenly remembering she asked, "So what's my surprise? Oh, is Bea with you?" Nora looked around quickly for any sign of her mentor.

"No, better than that."

As if on cue, the screen door opened. Nora turned. Then she stood, her mind slowly verifying what she knew she saw.

"Willa," she whispered, but her sister heard it loud and clear.

"Nora. My sister!" Before she could even embrace her sister, Willa's tears began spilling, the years between them choking out in sobs that shook her in a hurricane of lost years and the hope of reconciliation.

Spreading her arms, Nora moved towards her little sister, her own tears now matching Willa's, and held her tight, the baby between them and of them.

Marge came out on the porch and spontaneously burst into tears. Tunney could only grin, his tears having transformed themselves into a pure joy that he knew was a rare gift that would not visit him often.

Running into the house, Tunney grabbed a few washcloths and ran cold water on them. When he came back to the porch, Willa and Nora had finally separated and were babbling incoherent questions at one another, then laughing and crying some more. They accepted the washcloths gratefully for their red eyes and let Tunney lead them both to the porch swing.

Marge shook her head as her own tears flowed, part from the obvious happy reunion, and part from Willa's close resemblance to her Ginny, even greater than Nora's. Suddenly realizing that she should warn her husband and Harry about Ginny's new look alike, Marge headed for the barns to find them.

"I can't believe you're here Willa! When did you leave Botswana? How did you get here? And how did you find Tunney?! Oh, and if you hadn't noticed, I'm pregnant!" This caused them all to start laughing again. Willa took a deep breath.

"I came to Boston in June to start pre-med in the fall. But no one had told me that you had gone away, and they didn't know where you were. I couldn't believe that, I guess." Nora squeezed her sister's hand. "It was finally my chance to be with my big sister and no one knew where you were."

"Oh, Willa. I'm so sorry. It's just that I had so many things to work out, and I thought I couldn't do that in Daddy's world. I needed to figure things out for myself. I was lost, I guess."

"But now you're found." Willa held tight again to Nora.

"But how *did* you find me? I thought I had done such a great job becoming an anonymous person."

"It all started with a postcard." Willa began to relate her welcoming party at the club, meeting Jay and Joan, and the postcard from Philly in the mirror.

Nora listened intently, in awe at her sister's ingenuity, and Willa's determination to find her, following a scant trail of clues across the county.

Willa told her sister about meeting Max and 'the guys' and the

San Francisco address he gave her that led to Tunney after a long, "educational" week on a Greyhound bus. Then sitting on Tunney's front porch until he came home and finally learning where she was. After an update on Bea and the clinic, Willa stopped.

"And now I want to know about your life and travels, Nora. What have you been doing since I last saw you at thirteen?" They both laughed.

"This is going to take a while, Willa."

"I've got a while, Nora. Of course I'll stay with you until the baby is born." Willa stated it as a fact. Nora opened her mouth to argue but then closed it again after catching a look from Tunney. It read, 'You can work out the details later, just enjoy your sister now.' Tunney was so wise in these kinds of matters. That was why Nora missed him so much. *An anchor*.

"Oh, here comes Harry and Billy. That's Marge's dad and husband. You'll love them. They're real people."

Taking Nora's arm, Willa helped her sister out of the porch swing, a challenge to escape even without eight months of baby added.

Marge held Billy's hand and led him to the sisters. Harry took his hat off and fidgeted with the rim. Both men looked at her strangely in a way that suggested they knew her. Marge looked from one to the other at her men, embarrassed that neither had spoken yet.

"Oh my, Willa, these two talkative guys are my husband Billy and my Dad, Harry."

Willa held out her hand and shook Harry's first and then Billy's. Still, they could say nothing.

"Forgive us all, Willa," Marge said apologetically. "You look so much like our daughter Ginny who passed away a few years back. The same thing happened to poor Nora when she got here. But you look even more like our Ginny." Marge smiled shakily. It was still painful to evoke Ginny's memory. Nora gave her a hug and then put her arm around Harry's shoulders.

"It's a sign, it is," Harry suddenly blurted out. "Ginny's happy with us. Happy about Hope Creek."

Billy's bottom lip was trembling badly. He mumbled

something and went into the house.

"I know that Billy thinks I'm crazy, and maybe I am. But I've been feelin' somethin' ever since Nora got here. It's Ginny tellin' us she's okay with it all, that she loves us still."

Marge leaned into her father and kissed his cheek. Then she went into the house to check on Billy. Sometimes Marge worried about her husband. He held onto his grief like an addiction, too guilty to embrace it, too guilty to shed it. Always in the purgatory of should haves and could haves when it came to handling Ginny's death.

"Harry, I'm glad to remind you of someone you hold so dear in your heart."

When Willa said this, Nora suddenly flashed back to her month in Botswana eight years before. She remembered that it was not unusual for Willa or Mma Cookie or Sammie Po to embrace and summarize grand emotional moments. It was the African in Willa that made her so unique, so special. *My sister*! Nora could see that now. In her brief weeks in Botswana the title "sister" had only served to confuse and annoy her: Nora wasn't one of them. She wasn't part of her mother or Willa or their African family. The dislocation of being in Botswana and the lack of emotional connection to her mother were the strongest feelings that Nora internalized when she left Botswana those many years before.

Now as Willa stood before her, the word "sister" became more than a word. There is a connection between Willa and me because we are sisters! Nora rubbed her eyes so that the tears would not fall. The very life growing inside her was acting translator and guide, helping locate Nora's place in the world: her motherhood and sisterhood, her place as a daughter, friend, lover...someday again.

Nora refocused her eyes on Harry's old, muddy boots and then looked up at him. Harry looked down at his shoes and flipped the brim of his hat back and forth.

"You'll be needin' a place to sleep. I'll fix up the guest house for ya." With that he nodded at Willa and snuck another brief glance at the face that brought his grand-daughter's memory back to him so vividly.

Tunney spoke up. "Can I help you with that, Harry? I'm pretty handy."

Shaking his head, Harry turned and walked back towards the barns.

Nora reached for the back of the porch swing and held it as she plopped back down into it. Willa and Tunney followed suit, sitting on either side of her. For a long time no one spoke. They just gently swung back and forth, watching the sun slip further down the horizon and dusk moving in to take its place.

# # #

Stars were funny, magical beacons of hope, Tunney thought. For thousands of years they had inspired men to wander and dream, find new worlds, write poetry that rang true across hundreds of years. It must be that infinite space elicited in humans, throughout the ages, an understanding of just how very finite they were. *We are,* Tunney thought. *Tiny nothings on earth for only a split second compared to the universe's infinite clock of time.*

He took the last hit on the joint and crushed the roach into a sandy spot behind the guesthouse. This was the first time all day that he had a chance to rewind the last 48 hours and start to sort through it. Some people could do that as they went along during the day. Getting input, acting, processing, making decisions, moving forward. Not Tunney. He needed to make a concerted effort to pause, stop the action, and rewind to figure out what it all meant and what his next move should be.

Tunney remembered Willa's reaction when he told her he would drive her up to Oregon to find Nora. It was one of the biggest smiles he had ever seen, growing larger as the realization hit her that she would not have to get on another Greyhound bus. Tunney hoped then that just a little of it was also that they would have a chance to spend more time together.

It had started out as a beautiful drive. Tunney headed north up Highway 1 out of San Francisco, hugging the coastline until they reached Rockport and joined 101, moving inland for a while until they rejoined the coast at Eureka. Willa gasped at the beauty of the rocky shoreline, her oohs and aahs making Tunney glad that he was giving Willa her first taste of this part of the country.

Viewpoints and waysides became their frequent stopping points. Willa had bought an Instamatic camera in Chinatown and had Tunney take pictures of her against awe-inspiring backdrops that she could send home to her Mother Mercy family.

At times she seemed such a child to Tunney, innocent in her glee at a rugged cliff meeting the Pacific or the taste of an ice cold Grape Fanta from a gas station vending machine.

Other times her womanhood distracted him to such an extent that he had to hold himself back from touching her face or leaning in to smell the back of her neck. If one of his sisters were with him, she would tease Tunney that he had a crush on Willa. He was afraid that it was true, despite his struggle to be independent and unaffected. Ties and commitments were not possible for him. Without the freedom to move on and out and over and up, Tunney felt he would never discover who he was meant to be or what the world held for him to unravel, to truly know.

That first night they stopped just north of Eureka to camp at a state park. Tunney pitched his pup tent, out of use since his cross-country drive with Nora several months before. He made a comfortable nest for Willa in it, and fashioned a bed under the stars for himself next to the fire with a foam pad and layered blankets. It was perfect weather for it, despite the fact that it reminded him of some less amiable nights on the hard, dangerous ground of Viet Nam.

It was late when Willa finally said goodnight and went to the pup tent. Earlier that night, after they had shared ham sandwiches, Willa had asked if Tunney would tell her what it was like in Viet Nam. Not having lived the war through the medium of television in Botswana, she had not seen the evolution and escalation that America was witnessing on the evening news each night. The first time she had seen news footage in her father's house a few days after her arrival she was shocked. Young men, bloodied and dazed from a firefight, tired, so tired, with a trace of fear in their eyes pushed back by the reality of what they had to do and keep doing. It was the type of courage that only those in war knew. The kind that created men who fought to keep their fellow Marines together and alive, the whole more important than the one.

Tunney had started out with some of the funny stories: the drill sergeants intimidating new recruits in boot camp; the creative use of condiments on C-rations after the tenth day in a row of lima beans and ham; and the surplus World War II cigarettes handed out liberally to a new generation of soldiers. He described the breathtaking beauty of the Viet Nam countryside, incongruous with the mortars and machine gun fire that pocked the earth and pierced the heart of his buddy who dropped, instantly, as they fought, shoulder to shoulder in the green, leech-infested muck of a swamp. *No need to stop for him, he was gone. Just keep going, keep going at them.*

Endless days and nights of patrols, with monsoon rains making rifles seize up and foul water spreading dysentery that made soldiers into shitting zombies, wishing for death and sometimes getting it in a matter of hours.

Willa's eyes shone with the tears that Tunney could not shed, and the agony that he could not yet reconcile. She stood up and went behind him, wrapping her arms around him and holding tight, hoping to squeeze out a little measure of the pain. Tunney bent his head forward and placed his hands over Willa's hands. Her head on his shoulder was warm and he could smell her hair and skin, sweet from ocean air and womanhood.

After a few minutes, Willa said simply, "Thank you, Tunney," and then went silently to the pup tent, closing the flap behind her.

Up with the sunrise, Tunney loaded his bedroll and the other camp supplies into the Mustang and walked down a short wooded path to the beach. Seagulls cawed at one another, fighting over the rights to the tiny sea morsels hiding in the sand dollars and hermit crabs that had already lost a claw and were unable to find their way back into the surf and safety.

One lone fisherman stood in his waders, surfcasting across the low morning waves. A brown wicker creel was the only object on the beach as far as the eye could see, waiting patiently for its owner's catch. Near the point where the sliding surf stopped and the wet sand began, Tunney spotted a whole sand dollar shell. He quickly snatched it up before a seagull could ruin it with a single crack of its beak.

When he arrived back in camp, Willa was up and carefully folding up the pup tent so it would fit into its narrow bag.

"*Dumela, Rra. O a robala sentle*?"

Tunney cocked his head. "Whatever you said it sounded beautiful and I'll just have to say 'yes'. Is that a good answer?"

"It is. I asked you if you slept well. Is this California soil as hard as it looks?" Willa asked as she stuffed the tent pegs and cord around the inside edges of the tote bag. "Next time you take the air mattress and I'll take the foam pad, deal?"

Tunney stretched, testing his back muscles and then cringed. "Hmm, didn't have that knot yesterday. Yes, the ground is suitably hard. But I slept okay. Lots of experience doing that."

Willa thought that Tunney seemed quieter than usual. She hoped her asking about Viet Nam had not taken him places that he had managed to forget. Admonishing herself silently she vowed to not be so insensitive with her questioning in the future.

"Tunney, I've got a great idea. How about a nice hot breakfast at the next diner we see, my treat." Willa still had a lot of the money that her father had given her. The two times she had actually got him on the phone, he had offered to wire more, which so far she had declined.

Two days before she had left a message with Mary for her father: she knew where Nora was and was heading up to Oregon. She told Mary about Nora being pregnant, but asked her not to tell Dr. Dodge yet. Willa thought that Nora should be the deliverer of her news, ideally in person. She hoped that Nora could be convinced to call their father. But how her sister would respond to that suggestion was as yet an unknown.

"Coffee is my master this morning, Willa. Lead on, no argument from this corner."

A half hour later Tunney was doing damage to a lumberjack's special of eggs, ham, hash browns, bacon and biscuits, while Willa had her first ever stack of blueberry pancakes and warm maple syrup.

"I think we were hungry," Tunney stated between mouthfuls of ham and eggs, watching Willa savor the pancakes and moan in pleasure.

"I'm ordering these from now on for breakfast. I've never had anything so good!"

Tunney smiled at her pleasure in small things, only wishing he were a blueberry pancake and discovering what Willa's tongue felt like.

"Oh, I almost forgot. Here, a gift for you from Poseidon." Tunney handed Willa the sand dollar.

"It's beautiful Tunney. It looks like someone carved it."

"You are from the desert. It's called a sand dollar. It's hard to find a whole one because the seagulls love the little critters that live inside of them."

"Thank you. It's a beautiful treasure."

When the waitress came back, Willa asked for extra napkins so that she could wrap up her sand dollar and keep it from breaking.

When they crossed the border into Oregon later that morning, Willa clapped and beamed at Tunney.

"Yeah, we're here, kid," and then he indulged himself and touched her face for just a moment, hoping his fingers would not tremble and betray him.

"Thank you, Tunney. I couldn't have come this far without you."

"Hey, we're a team, right? But don't get too excited. We still have a couple hundred miles before we get to Tillamook. And when it comes to beauty, you ain't seen nothin' yet. You're in for a treat today, my dear. This is one of the most stunning coastlines in the country."

They drove mostly in silence up 101, the majestic corridors of forest and the Pacific vistas evoking dreams and poetry and a sense of calm in both of them. Tunney found odd radio stations in open stretches along the coast. A few of his favorites came on and he had fun telling Willa about the San Francisco music scene and the summer festivals he had been to. Tunney loved that Willa was unpolluted by American culture and that everything was new to her. He felt like a teacher, schooling Willa on the "in" music, the latest slang, and some of his generation's more vivid experiences, such as what it was like to take LSD.

"But don't do it, kid. You don't need it. You're the clearest person I've ever met."

"What do you mean, clearest?" Willa asked, enjoying the chance to study Tunney's face as he focused straight ahead on the winding highway.

"You know where you're going, Willa. And you've already had enough real, important, life changing experiences that you don't need alternatives. There's no drug or yogi that's going to teach you anything you don't already know. And you don't have hang ups like some chicks, and you're just, I don't know, together, clear." Tunney glanced over at Willa. Their eyes met for a long moment before Tunney had to turn back to the road.

Willa was not sure how to respond, so she kept silent, thinking about Tunney's words. She did not want to say 'thank you' because then it would seem like she agreed with him about being clear and without baggage. And if she disputed him, it would be questioning his perceptions. A tiny tickle in her belly surprised her. It was the same tickle that Tom gave her when he would touch her hand or wave good-bye as he pulled away from Mother Mercy, headed to the bush to fix a borehole.

Tunney is giving me the tickle.

Just then a car passed them dangerously on a curve. Tunney swerved towards the cliff side and slowed down, cursing the driver.

"Sorry to swear, but what a fucking moron! Sorry." Tunney shook his head and sped up again, the errant driver already out of site around the next curve.

Willa fiddled with the radio dial at Tunney's request and found *Sail on Sailor* by the Beach Boys. Tunney knew all the words and sang along. His voice was good and true. It made Willa's tickle come back.

A few minutes later the station was out of range. Willa leaned over, moving the dial very slowly, trying to 'pull in' another station as Tunney had shown her.

"What the fu--..." Willa whipped her head up, hearing fear in Tunney's voice. He slowed down the car and pulled over on the shoulder.

"Oh my god," Willa choked out, her hand flying to cover her mouth. Ahead of them was the mangled wreckage of a car and semi-truck. Twisted pieces of metal were strewn everywhere. A bucket seat sat alone on the road, upright and seemingly unscathed. Dust and smoke mingled, a choking shroud that signaled to Tunney that the accident had occurred only moments earlier.

Popping his trunk, Tunney grabbed four flares and thrust them at Willa. "You know how to use these?" Willa nodded. "Run back a few hundred yards and put two in the road. Then on the southbound side." Willa was already running.

The car had flipped completely over, the roof crushed down so far there was little left of the sedan. Out of the corner of his eye, Tunney saw the door of the semi push open as though it had been kicked from the inside. He ran towards it, arriving just in time to catch the driver as he fell out of the cab.

The driver was gasping and crying through a mask of blood. Tunney held on to him, moving him away from the truck to a safe distance, just in case anything ignited.

"I couldn't do nothin'. Nothin'. Car come outta nowhere, my side. Nowhere to go." Sobs wracked the man's body and soul.

"I know man. It wasn't your fault. It wasn't your fault, man." Tunney pulled off his tee shirt and ripped it in half. Willa was suddenly there and took it out of his hands.

"I've got him Tunney. See about the others." Willa set to work, determining the origin of the head wound as she gently moved the driver to a prone position. Her voice had changed. It was now the soothing balm of a caregiver. A voice that would calm the injured man and give him hope: a qualified person was caring for him, assessing the damage, helping him not go into shock.

As Tunney approached the remains of the car, two more men had stopped behind the semi and were running up to the vehicles. Tunney yelled that the semi was empty and pointed to the car. One of the men yelled back that he had called the state police on his CB radio.

It was impossible to know if anyone remained in the flattened car. No windows had survived and the frame was crushed, making it unlikely that there was anyone still alive inside. A few more cars stopped and tried to help. An elderly woman pointed to a drainage ditch, locating the passenger who once rode in the bucket seat. It was a young man, probably about Willa's age. His neck was clearly broken. The old woman's husband put a windbreaker jacket over the body.

As Tunney and the other men talked about trying to turn the car over, a fire truck pulled up, escorted by the state police. The officers quickly took over at the scene and a medic saw to the semi driver. Willa gave her assessment of the man's wounds as the medic started an IV.

"You a nurse?" he asked as he snapped open a hypodermic needle already prepped with morphine.

"Nurse's aide and headed to med school."

"Thanks. You made my job easier."

The driver opened his eyes for a moment, his way of saying thanks. He was quiet now, the tears having given way to shocked silence.

For the next two hours Tunney and Willa watched the firemen peel open the car and extract another boy, this one barely sixteen. His body was so severely crushed that he did not resemble a person at all. One of the rookie cops had run to the ditch to throw up. His partner followed him and rubbed his back, remembering his own first bad accident call, as his young partner retched away the sight of the dead boy. Unfortunately, he was used to these by now. The coast highway was not a place to try and pass other cars, or take the turns wide. That was not survivable behavior.

When Tunney and Willa were done giving statements to the police, and the accident scene was cleared enough to pass, they headed north again. Tunney made sure to tell the officer that the boys had recklessly passed him minutes before the crash occurred, and related what the truck driver had said about the car being in his lane. The semi driver would have enough pain without the cops questioning his story about what happened. Regardless, Tunney knew that the guy would live with the vision of the boys hitting him head on, seeing the terror in their eyes before the windshield collapsed and the car went airborne fifteen feet before the crushing final moments as it met the unforgiving cement road.

Tunney drove ten miles north until he saw a picnic area on the coastal side and pulled into the parking area. When he stopped, he asked Willa if she was okay She looked at Tunney and nodded.

"What about you?" Tunney also nodded. That was all they said.

Wordlessly they changed out of their clothes, bloodied from the driver's head injury. They cleaned up as best they could at the water faucet and then used the outhouse.

As they got back in the car, Tunney looked over at Willa. In her eyes he read the same thing that was in his mind: *It could have been us.*

"You're sure you're okay?" Willa swallowed hard and then nodded.

Tunney started the car and turned back on to Highway 101. No longer was the drive scenic or calming or beautiful. The accident remained with them in the car, heavy and pervasive.

"Let's not try to get to Tillamook today." It was Willa, her beautiful African-British-American voice barely audible. "I don't want this to be the day I see Nora again."

"Okay, I'll find us a campground."

"No, let's stay in a cabin or a motel tonight, some place with walls. I've got the money for it. Please, Tunney." The plea in Willa's voice scared him a little. Then he realized it was the first time that he had seen her steadiness waver. She always seemed so strong. Innocent sometimes, yes, but always sure of herself, determined.

"Sure, Willa. Gold Beach is just ahead a few miles. I'll find us a place there."

"Okay." Her voice was that of a young child, suddenly soft and uncertain.

Tunney drove straight to the water's edge when they got to Gold Beach. There was nothing as healing as watching the waves crash on the shore. Willa needed a good dose of staring at the ocean, and probably a stiff drink besides.

Crestview Cabins offered an ocean view, soft beds, pullout sofas, a kitchenette, and “Free Color TV.” After he checked them in, Tunney found a grocery store in town and bought some bread, a cooked chicken, cheese, fruit, and beer for their dinner. On his way out of the shop he remembered Willa saying how much she liked powdered donuts, and he went back in and got her a large box.

Back at the cabin, Willa was fresh out of the shower and combing out her long brown hair on the sofa in front of the big picture window.

“You are a genius, Willa Dodge. This is a great little place. We needed it tonight.”

“Jan calls it my single-mindedness. I knew if I didn’t get a shower I would close in on myself. I was having a hard time picturing a night in the pup tent, my clothes and hands and hair...” Willa stopped.

“I know, kiddo. You feeling a little better?”

“Yes. I’m clean. Your turn. There’s soap and shampoo in there and a towel.”

“You don’t need to ask me twice. Hey, there’s some dinner supplies on the table. Could you throw those in the little fridge there? I’ll make you a Tunney Feast in a bit.”

Willa smiled. Tunney beamed. *Willa’s smile was back.*

“Oh, and I got you a whole box of powdered donuts.” Willa ooh-ed, her eyes meeting Tunney’s. “With me, kid, it’s ask and you shall receive.”

“I think *you’re* a genius, Tunney. Now go take a shower so I can devour my donuts in peace!”

Dinner that night was Tunney’s grilled cheese and chicken sandwiches, prepared artfully on the single burner stove in the room. Willa thought that no meal had ever tasted better to her. Tunney had moved the table in front of the window and they watched the sunset until the room disappeared into the dark around them.

Forcing a sense of normalcy back into their day was Tunney’s goal. He did his best to keep Willa talking, asking her lots of questions about growing up in Botswana, what her schooling was like, descriptions of her friends, and the airplane rides across southern Africa with Johnny. When Willa finally realized Tunney's ruse, she suddenly stopped talking.

"Hey, why am I doing all the talking. *One who speaks too much is tricking or being tricked.* No fair, Tunney."

"It's simple. You have a beautiful voice, complete with exotic African accent, and I? Well, I sprang from the bowels of Philadelphia, inheriting a less than melodious accent, and, frankly, I'm more than a little bored with my own stories."

"And I'm bored with mine." Willa pretended defiance.

"Then let's walk on the beach. It's perfect. No wind." Tunney stood and held out his hand to Willa.

It was perfect. A few spotlights from motels along the shore gave off just enough light for them to see their way down the stairs to the beach. The waves drew them to the waterside. Tunney took off his shoes and Willa followed suit. Cool water encircled their toes, the tide washing away the sand under their feet. Willa giggled at the sensation of the sandy earth disappearing beneath her, a desert girl embracing the ocean as it swept her off her feet.

"You've got a great laugh, kid." Tunney grabbed Willa's hands and began running into the surf as it receded, whooping and hollering at the sea gods. Willa laughed in glee the way a child does, free and unencumbered with the worries of adulthood.

Leaning over to catch her breath, hands on her knees, Willa felt Tunney's warm hand on her back. When she rose their faces were suddenly close, almost touching. He closed the space between them.

Tunney's kiss felt so right to her, as though their lips were old friends simply reunited after a long separation. His hands encircled her face, then pressed against her back, moving under her shirt, making her skin and every nerve aware of his strong hands, his lips pressed against hers, a kiss that stole her breath.

Tunney took Willa's hand and led her back to their cabin. No words were exchanged. They needed each other just as they needed to breathe and eat to survive. There were no thoughts of tomorrow, no plans or consequences.

Moonlight shone onto the bed illuminating Willa's skin, alabaster curves no longer unknown. Tunney moved slowly, caressing and feathering with his hands and lips and tongue across every inch of her body. It seemed like hours that they explored one another, until they finally joined, reaching and peaking together, the wait over. They were man and woman.

All night they lay entwined, their bodies a perfectly matched set. Both Willa and Tunney woke up several times in the night, the sound of the other's breathing and the rolling waves on the beach pulling them back to sleep each time.

When Tunney woke up in the morning, Willa was sitting up in bed next to him eating a sugared donut.

"Yum, would you like one?" Willa mumbled, her mouth full of donut and powdered sugar all over her lips.

Tunney laughed sleepily. "Put down that donut, you sugared beauty. I know what I want for breakfast.

Giggling, Willa dropped the donut to the floor and slid under the covers.

# # #

As Tunney stared up at the stars behind the Hope Creek Farm guesthouse, it seemed a lot longer ago than that morning that he had last made love to Willa. Between the rest of the drive up the coast, the tearful reunion between Willa and Nora, and then having dinner with forty pregnant girls, it seemed like a week's worth of time had been compressed into a single day.

Harry had made up two beds for them in the guesthouse. As far as anyone was concerned, Tunney was just Willa's ride to Oregon. He did not care if the whole world knew that Willa and he had slept together and probably would again. But Willa was afraid of loading too much onto Nora all at once. Reuniting after ten years would be enough for her sister to handle.

Tunney knew Willa was right when they talked about it in the car as they got close to Tillamook. Although Nora and Tunney had agreed to be brother and sister, that did not mean she would be thrilled that he had already taken up with Willa. Having grown up with five sisters, he knew well that the consequences of female jealousy were not to be taken lightly.

A screen door creaked. Willa was back. She had stayed behind in the main house with Nora and Marge talking in great detail about every stage of Nora's pregnancy. Tunney had feigned exhaustion. He wanted a joint and a beer. He hugged Nora hard, gave Marge a peck on the cheek, and glanced at Willa, saying he would leave the lights on for her.

As Tunney came in the back door of the guesthouse, Willa turned.

"Hi."

"Hi. How's your sis doing?"

"She's doing great. But I could use a hug."

"Come here, beautiful. I missed you today." Willa fell into his arms and they breathed each other in.

"I was with you all day. How could you miss me?"

"I missed touching you, angel. You are the sweetest thing I've ever met." Tunney's kisses covered her face and then he playfully pushed her up the ladder into the loft, nibbling on the back of her legs.

"We'll have to mess up the other bed downstairs so that they think we slept separately," Willa said very seriously as Tunney pulled her shirt over her head.

"Not a problem. I can easily defile you in both places." Willa laughed and they fell together on the bed, further exploring the treasures of one another's bodies that they had only briefly tasted the night before.

# # #

Chapter 27: Missives

Dear Daddy,

I hope that you and Carol are doing well. I think about you a lot.

I'm sorry I can't call yet. But I need to start here, on paper, where maybe I won't mess it up as bad.

First of all, I'm so sorry, Daddy. I didn't want to hurt you when I left. I guess I was pretty confused. But I should have let you know where I was, that I was okay.

I've figured out a lot of things over the last eight months that I think I'd still be struggling with if I had stayed in Boston. The experiences I've had and situations I've faced have made me grow a lot. You might not agree, especially when I tell you the big one.

I'm having a baby, Daddy. Please don't be upset, because I didn't decide to have the baby on a whim. I spent a lot of time figuring out what it would mean to have a baby and what it would mean to give it up. I tried to picture where my life would take me in both scenarios, and what I would be gaining and losing. Then I realized how much I did want to bring Baby Dodge into the world and love him or her and try my best to be a good mother.

I love it that Willa is here with me now. She helps me understand more about Jan and has had some of the same feelings I've had about "our" mother. Willa has also given me the courage and the encouragement to write to you. She wanted me to call you, and I will, but I needed to start here.

Baby Dodge and I are in a wonderful place called Hope Creek Farm. It's run by a couple, Marge and Billy, who you would really like. Hope Creek is a place where pregnant young women can live and work until they have their babies. The girls decide if they want to keep their babies or give them up for adoption. A wonderful clinician in San Francisco referred me here. I've even learned that I'm really good at something, and help Marge and Billy with organizing work schedules, managing accounts and supplies, and reorganizing their filing systems. I'm also the oldest one here, so the younger girls come to me for advice a lot. Imagine that!

I love my baby, Daddy. And Willa already loves Baby Dodge too. She told me that you'll love your grandchild and that I shouldn't have worried so much about contacting you.

Willa will call you about this but she is going to stay with me until Baby Dodge is born. The due date is mid-September. Everybody loves Willa here already. She is helping the girls with some of their basic medical needs so that they don't need to go into town as much for little stuff, like getting blood drawn or having their vitals checked. You must be very proud of her. I am too. But I have to admit that I'm also a little jealous of her. Please don't be mad at her for staying here with me. We're learning how to be sisters, how to be a family. It really feels good, Daddy.

You're probably curious about the father of Baby Dodge. It's Pete, and you were right about him. I left Pete and Philadelphia in February. I didn't know I was pregnant then. I've never contacted him about being the father and I won't.

I know this letter is a lot to handle and that maybe you can't support my decision to have Baby Dodge. But I love my baby so much already and I know with a certainty that I've never felt about anything else in my life that I can be a good mother. I have changed, Daddy.

Love,
Nora

# # #

Dear Willa,

It's been the strangest month here. While you may have thought we would all be surprised by your cross county trek to find Nora, thanks to Mma Cookie's dreams and the Dingaka's interpretations, we all knew before we got your letter. I'll fill you in more on this story at a later date.

Damn woman, I miss you.

If I had any doubt in the Dingaka before (which I did but it was small since he pulled me back from the edge, so to speak, a few months ago – well you know it all...), I don't any longer. I feel like maybe I should start making weekly trips to see him and I wouldn't have to waste any time planning out my next move.

Did I mention how much I miss you?

I try to keep as busy as possible so that the hole in my heart (that your presence used to keep whole) doesn't startle me so much every day. I think I mentioned that Dr. Jan has the mistaken impression that I'm the new handyman at Mother Mercy. She's better than the Dingaka at sensing when I'm within 20 clicks of the clinic and sends Sammie Po to fetch me for her latest project. By the way, the surgery is now properly insulated so that patients don't suffer in recovery from heat stroke. Some church group in South Africa donated a new generator – significantly quieter than the current circa-WWII model, and about 50 fans, so the spring, summer and fall this year should be more tolerable for patients and staff. Luckily the church group wasn't around when your mother called them "God-damned guilty Boers." Mma Cookie clucked at Jan and apologized to God, so hopefully the powers that be have been appeased appropriately.

Mma Lilli has been complaining almost daily that her feet hurt and she needs the special treatments "that only Willawe can provide." I think she wants me to massage her feet, but that's a frightening prospect to this engineer boy. I need to stick to inanimate objects that have logical, non-speaking parts. Just boreholes and ceiling insulation for me!

I'm sending this letter to your father's house because we

haven't heard yet if you've found Nora and whether you have an alternative address. Whenever you get this, just know that at that very second I'm thinking about you, your eyes, your mind, your beautiful skin. I reach for you in the night, hoping I only dreamed that you left Botswana.

Anyway, at the risk of being so sappy that even you will be embarrassed for me, I'd better sign off now. 'Nuff said.

Love you,
Tommiwe

# # #

Howard Pleasance, M.D., Ph.D.
Dean of Admissions
Harvard College
Cambridge, Mass.

Dear Dr. Pleasance,

As you know, my daughter, Willa Dodge, was to begin her pre-med studies this month at Harvard College. On her behalf, I respectfully seek an extension on her admission until spring semester, this coming January.

My other daughter, Nora, has had a medical emergency where she lives in Oregon, and Willa has gone out to the west coast to provide nursing care and aid until Nora is recovered.

As you know from meeting Willa in June, she is a highly responsible young woman, top in her College Boards, and already holding a medical background and experience despite her youth. This delay of a few months will not affect her studies in the long term. I am confident she will be an asset to Harvard in more ways than even I can imagine at this juncture.

Please do not refund or credit the first semester's tuition that I have already submitted. Rather, please use this letter as a directive to place those funds into the Harvard scholarship fund for international students from Africa.

If you should have any questions, please do not hesitate to call me at Mass General.

Respectfully yours,
Michael F. Dodge, M.D.

# # #

U.S. Department of Defense
Washington, D.C.

10 August, 1969

Dear Mrs. Barbara Jo Edwards,

We regret to inform you that your husband, U.S. Air Force Major Steven Francis Edwards of Tillamook, Oregon, has been classified as 'Missing in Action' after a mission commencing on July 30, 1969. Additional information will be forthcoming as it is determined.

Sincerely, Colonel Howard Biggs, USAF

# # #

Chapter 28: Rolling and Hoving

Hope Creek Farm

August 1969

Smells of cedar and ink resided in the Hope Creek office as much as the ledgers and files did. Nora was at home in this room, now an organized, logical version of its former self. It had taken her five weeks of daily commitment to both organize the current financial books and develop a historical filing system. She was proud of what the office had become, enjoying even more the cozy attic space that let in light from the tawny fields and cool salty-sweet ocean air.

Unlike other parts of the old farmhouse, it was quiet in the attic office. Although Nora had gotten used to the level of noise that a few dozen pregnant girls could make at any given time, she also cherished the solitude she found in this little comfortable room at the top of the rambling house.

Sometimes Nora had to share the office with Marge, Billy, or Rachel, but she never minded that. It gave her a chance to hear stories about the farm in the "old days" from Marge, or ask Billy about an old machinery receipt she was not sure where to file. Rachel had proven to be very well organized and had experience in bookkeeping from her years in the carnival with her father, a man who could not add two and two together. Nora was confident that Rachel could take over the management of the office after she had Baby Dodge and they left the Dairy. Marge had expressed how grateful she was that Rachel had wanted to stay after she lost the baby. Getting both Marge and Billy to recognize that they needed someone to help with the farm management had not taken too much effort on Nora's part. They both knew they needed help and that Harry could not and should not do any of the heavy labor or money management any longer. Gardening, running errands and little handyman jobs were all that Marge felt comfortable having her father handle. Despite his arguing that he could still manage certain jobs, Harry silently acknowledged the limits of his old bones. After a scare from a minor stroke and a broken wrist from a "fight" with a wooden beam, Harry had slowed down. He loved the Dairy, his Margie, and the girls. Adapting to his limitations meant he would be around longer to enjoy them all.

Heat from the August sun released the perfume from the cedar shingles. Nora breathed deep. She loved that smell, masculine and sweet all at once.

From across the field, Nora heard a shout and a laugh. She looked out the attic window and saw Willa walking towards the guest cottage from the path that led through the pasture and into the low hills north of the farm. In her hands were sprigs of pussy willows and orange poppies that grew wild at the edge of the meadow. Following the direction of Willa's wave, Nora saw Tunney behind the cottage, waving back. His wide smile was visible even from the attic.

Suddenly Tunney's words and moods and actions of the last few days made sense. *He's in love with Willa.*

Nora continued to watch them, following Tunney as he strode up the path, diminishing the distance between him and Willa. As they met, Tunney took the flowers out of her hands and then drew Willa to him, his arm encircling her waist. Their kiss was startling and compelling.

They were lovers.

I'm spying, Nora thought, but still she could not look away. *That's the way I want someone to kiss me someday.* There was care and passion in it. Nora felt a pang of jealousy. While she knew it was better that Tunney and she had never become lovers, she wanted to be that close to someone, to feel the heartbeat and the breath of a lover.

Then just as quickly, Nora admonished herself. *I am that close to somebody: Baby Dodge. He or she is my focus and where I'll direct my love. How could I fit in a man right now*? After her experience with Pete, a man who she mistakenly felt had truly loved and cherished her, it would need to be a very special man, indeed, to open her up again to the risk of being hurt. Betrayal was something that she would never set herself up for in the future.

Nora's new friendships since she had left Boston had taught

her how special and trusting friends could be. Tunney, Max, Bea, Marge, Billy, Harry, Bobbie Jo, Rachel, and now the love of her sister. These were people and friendships to be cherished and to learn from. Someday Nora knew that she would find someone to love and live with who would be a father to Baby Dodge. But she also knew it was not an effort that she wanted to expend any energy on for a long time. Baby Dodge was her world now. All her goals and decisions would revolve around what was best for her baby.

Tunney and Willa were both in the yard behind the cottage, the pussy willow and poppies on the old, gray bench in an overgrown patch of grass. Nora could see Willa talking to Tunney. He put his hands in his pockets. It was a gesture that Nora recognized. He always did it when he was not sure what to do next, or when he heard information that he could not immediately process.

Willa held out her hand for Tunney to take. One hand came out of his pocket and held Willa's. They walked that way, slowly, back on the path toward the low hills. Nora watched them until they went over a hillock and were out of sight.

Suddenly Baby Dodge kicked hard and Nora bent over, grabbing her belly. It took a minute to get her breathing back to normal. Lying down on the old couch in the corner of the attic, Nora focused on the rafters above her head, counting the nail heads with each deep breath.

"Are you trying to tell me to quit spying on my sister?" Nora whispered to Baby Dodge. Another strong kick caused her to groan and chuckle at the same time. "Okay, Baby Dodge. I'll stop eavesdropping and being jealous if you stop kicking."

It felt so comforting to be on the old over-stuffed sofa. Within minutes Nora was asleep, the bookkeeping and the lovers in the meadow now far away.

She was in a desert looking for her lost bicycle and then found a baby in a cave, the walls of which were covered by ancient paintings of hunters and strange beasts. The baby disappeared from its carriage, with only the glass Japanese float on its pillow, cool and green. Panic. But wait. The baby has not been born yet. So it's okay, Nora was telling Mary, her father's housekeeper who took her into the backyard that was suddenly a church. Black women in garden party hats and beautiful pastel dresses watched Nora walk down the center aisle, shaking their heads in disapproval. It was useless but Nora tried to cover up her pregnancy with her hands but nothing worked. A side door of the church opened and her father motioned for Nora to come to him. She wanted to, but her body and feet were suddenly so heavy that she could barely move an inch. Then her father was yelling, 'Hurry Nora the door is going to close.' But despite all her efforts her feet would not move her forward. Only half of her father's face was visible now. Right before the door closed all the way, Marge was suddenly there calling her name.

"Nora. Nora, honey, you okay?" Marge asked as she bent over her young charge on the couch. Nora awoke with a start and sat up.

"You feeling okay, Nora?" Marge asked, concern in her voice. It was not like Nora to take naps during the day when she was scheduled to work on the books.

"Oh, yes, I'm fine. The baby was kicking me so hard that I had to lie down for a minute. I must have dozed off." Nora swung her legs around and sat up.

"You're getting to the tired stage now, I guess. You're in the home stretch so it's not unusual that you're going to be tired. That's a lot of extra weight you're carrying around."

"Tell me about it." Nora stood up and Marge took her elbow to steady her.

"Doc Avery is coming here this afternoon to check on a few of the girls. Let's have him take a look at you as well. Sometimes babies have their own schedules. It wouldn't hurt for the Doc to check and see if you're dilated at all yet." Marge smiled reassuringly.

Nora nodded. "Alright. It was a major kick from little one. It was almost like she was protesting the womb." Nora laughed nervously.

"She? Do you know something that I don't?" Marge asked as she smiled and cocked her head.

"Oh, did I say she? Must be Freud at work, and of course,

Harry's predictions. I keep picturing an independent little girl in overalls when I see Baby Dodge in my head."

"Well, let's get you two headstrong girls downstairs for a cup of herbal tea before the Doc gets here. I'll even let you jump the line. How's that sound?"

"You spoil me, Marge. The other girls will be jealous."

"They already are, Nora, don't you know that? Half of them wish they were you, you being so sophisticated in their eyes, from Boston and all and a college girl. Most of these girls didn't finish high school. You're in another league than they are, Nora."

"Do I really seem so much different to them? I try so hard to fit in." Marge could hear the disappointment in Nora's voice.

"Hey, you're a lot older than they are. They look up to you, Nora, not down on you. Of course you fit in, but you're also different." Marge kissed Nora's cheek and then ushered her towards the stairs.

"Oh, but shouldn't I finish today's ledger first?" Nora said as she turned back towards the attic.

"No, girlie. You just need to listen to me and do what I say."

Laughing, Nora let herself be escorted to the kitchen. Tea and comfort, cookies and cinnamon smells. It was a wonder that any of the girls ever left Hope Creek Dairy.

# # #

As Tunney released Willa's waist he looked at her with an intensity that startled her.

"You are one beautiful lady, Willa."

"You make me beautiful because of the way that you look at me, the kind things you say to me."

"They're not kind, Willa. They're lecherous. I want to tear your clothes off right here."

"You are bad."

"No, I'm normal. You incite me to badness."

"No, I'm innocent."

"You can never be innocent with that voice of yours. Speak and I'll follow you anywhere." Tunney grabbed Willa from behind and buried his face in her auburn hair. It smelled fresh of the sea and scotch brush.

Willa turned around and brushed a wisp of hair off Tunney's forehead. "Will you walk with me up to the point? There's a beautiful view of the ocean from there."

Tunney cocked his head. But then he suddenly understood. It was funny how a slight change in the tone of someone's voice could tip off the listener to what the speaker really meant. He put his hands in his pockets and bent his head.

"I need to tell you about something, Tunney." Willa reached out her hand to her lover. "I need to tell you about Tom."

They walked in silence for ten minutes, holding hands even as a distance seemed to grow between them. Then Willa told Tunney about Tom, how they met, the closeness that happened between them so quickly, and the love that they had even as she left Botswana for the states. They stopped walking and Willa took both of Tunney's hands in hers.

"A few months ago the Dingaka helped me understand something." Willa brought Tunney's hand to her cheek and held it there. Closing her eyes, she continued.

"He helped me understand how important it is not to build a fence around my relationships. That can only stifle the growth and push the relationship into a corner, not allowing it to grow, or to perish, naturally. A relationship trapped in a pen cannot be healthy because there's nowhere for it to go.

"You and me, Tunney, somehow we made a connection and came together. We feel something for each other. It's real, but it can't be boxed or labeled. And it can't be defined by what will happen tomorrow. It's now. It's today." Willa opened her eyes and Tunney was there, close to her, absorbing her, holding her.

"I know. I've been pushing away the idea that I need to get into my car tomorrow and drive back to the Haight. And I also have been ignoring a strong hunch that there is another out there who found you before I did. I guess I kept thinking that something miraculous would happen and time would stand still or reverse its course. That I'd be able to capture you." Tunney drew Willa in and kissed her.

"But you're not capture-able, Willa Dodge, 'cause you're a wild, African gazelle who's got plans. They're good plans. And you need to see them through. Because you're going to be the best doctor that old, moldy Harvard ever produced." Tunney took Willa's hand this time and began leading her back down the path towards the Dairy. She willed a tear not to fall from her welling eyes because she knew it belonged to Tunney not to her.

"Oh, and by the way..." Tunney stopped and let go of Willa's hand.

"Yes?" There was apprehension in her voice, the timbre reflecting what had been lost.

"Just keeping today in mind and all, I have a new plan for this afternoon."

"Yes?"

"It involves you with no clothes on, me seducing you multiple times in multiple locations, and other vivid images that I'm better at showing you than telling you about."

Willa bent her head and grinned. "Consider me your intern."

"Then you'd better start running because I'm not waiting until we get back. You can't speak to me in that damn sexy voice and expect me to have any self-control, can you? I'll give you a head start. Okay, one, two, three..."

Willa broke into a run, only making it to a nearby meadow lined with scotch brush and sea grass.

A red-tail hawk surveyed the landscape, scoping in the two large creatures. It realized these were intruders but not competitors for prey and not prey either. Squawking with displeasure, the hawk flew on towards the meadow north of the hillock. Over there the white creatures would not be scaring away the prey of mice and rabbits with their rolling and hoving and noisy throats.

# # #

Chapter 29: Hope

Tillamook, Oregon
September 18, 1969

Although it had only been a two-hour drive from the Portland airport, Michael Dodge felt stiff and old when he got out of the rental car.

It was a warm afternoon so he had found a shady spot under a leafy tree and cracked the window a little bit. For a small hospital the parking lot seemed over large, as though they had extra room and were just filling space with all the neat, well-lined spots, hoping someday to grow into it.

Michael stood next to the car and stretched as he took in the hospital. It was a typical small-town, pre-WWII version, dominated by heavy arches and dark brick. He counted the floors, moving his lips as he said each one. Five floors. Original windows. Unusual chimneys. Overhead he heard a seagull screech.

I'm stalling. I'm scared.

A wave of nausea hit him suddenly and he held onto the car door to steady himself.

"Buck up, Dodge," he said aloud. These were not strangers he was seeing. *Or were they*? Would his little girls, his daughters and Jan's daughters, still want to know him? Could his once upon a time wife, the vaunted bush doctor, even claim Nora as hers? Could he claim Willa as his?

Michael felt suddenly vindictive. Why should he be standing in the parking lot of a small town hospital in the middle of nowhere, as scared as he had ever been, to reunite with his daughters, and yes, the bush doctor's daughters too. Where was Jan in all this? How could she not be here too when her daughters most needed a mother? Like it or not, Jan had raised Nora by not raising her, the power of her distance a constant reminder for Nora of not having a mother to run to with scraped knees and boyfriend woes. And Jan had raised Willa by employing her fully in her surgeon's life, joined by a common cause rather than an embracing mother-love.

Jan had broken Michael's life and his hope all those years ago when their dreams had met and clashed and fallen so far apart as to be unrecognizable as a marriage. Michael had been naïve, he admitted now. Jan was out of his league, a fully formed woman to his youthful maleness, the maturity of his surgical skills mistaken for a manhood that had not yet determined its own course, his best course.

Once Michael thought that Jan was his north star; that in following her it would make him a part of her great plan of saving Africans by changing the course of every life they touched. It was a burden he could not bear because it was only an adopted passion of his, not a real one as it was for Jan. If it had been enough to love only Jan's determination, he might have stayed and then seen his Willa born. Instead she became the bush doctor's daughter. And so by a cruel but inert abandonment did Nora also become the bush doctor's daughter.

Please be my daughters again.

Once inside the hospital, an orderly directed Michael to Room 423. As he passed by nurses and doctors in the hallways, he nodded and they nodded back. A few of the nurses smiled. It was strange being in a hospital where no one recognized him as Dr. Dodge; his special status non-existent here. He did not like that. More effort at being social was required when the cachet of being a surgeon in a surgeon's world disappeared. It had always been difficult for Michael to feel comfortable in situations where he had to meet new people outside of the language and world of the hospital. That world provided a common context that everyone understood. It was skill as a surgeon that mattered, not his conversational skills.

And then there it was: Room 423. It was a door like all the others, *except this one has the rest of my life behind it.*

Slightly ajar, Michael could hear voices inside the room, women's voices. His stomach flipped again and he took a deep breath to steady himself.

Open the door now. Your whole life is inside.

Pushing it open slowly, he saw his daughter there, but she was different. Still his beautiful Nora, but not his little girl any longer.

This was a woman. She turned her head to see who had come in.

Fear caught Michael Dodge again for only a moment, chased away by Nora's wide smile. *A smile for me! Her arms opening wide, welcoming me*!

"Daddy!" It was a happy sob from Nora. Michael dropped the package he carried to the floor and reached out to his oldest daughter.

"Nora, angel." That was all he trusted himself to say. The rest was choked back by tears.

The father and daughter just held each other, their tears and joy pushing away regrets and time apart. Only their special world existed for a moment. It had always been just the two of them as Nora grew up. Each had become a fulcrum for the other's happiness. They had raised each other, becoming father and daughter, friend and friend. Now the memory and strength of that raising and reliance enfolded them in the embrace of their new status as grandfather and mother.

Marge and Bobbie Jo looked at each other and quietly slipped out of the room. There would be time for introductions later. But this perfect time between father and daughter would never come again.

"I'm so sorry, Daddy. I'm so sorry..." Nora whispered to Michael through her tears.

"Ssh, Nora. No more sorrys now. I'm so happy to see you. You look glorious!"

Nora laughed through her tears. "You're a good liar, Daddy. After eight hours of labor, I doubt that glorious really describes me." They beamed at each other and embraced again.

"You are the most beautiful creature I've ever laid eyes on. You were the day you were born and you are today."

"The day my baby was born. You're a grandfather now, you know."

Michael looked shocked for a moment and then scratched his chin. Nora laughed at him.

"I guess I hadn't really been thinking about it in that way. But now that you say it, I kind of like the idea."

Taking his hand in hers, Nora looked at her father with the

same little girl eyes that she had many years before when she felt so happy she thought she might burst.

"I love you, Daddy. Please forgive me."

"No, baby. There's nothing to forgive. Let's just move on together from here. But please promise me you won't leave again without me knowing where. If you haven't noticed I'm a lot grayer and I slouch more since you left." Michael smiled and wiped away a tear from Nora's cheek.

"I promise I won't." The tears and regret stopped up Nora's throat, holding back the words she knew she needed to say. *But not now.*

Just then the door opened again. It was Marge holding a small bundle, with Bobbie Jo behind her, not willing to miss any more of the reunion.

"I thought you might want to introduce your father to his grand-daughter." Marge smiled and nodded at Michael as she carefully handed the baby to Nora. Cradling the baby against her chest, Nora moved the blanket away from her daughter's face.

"Daddy, meet Hope, my daughter...and your grand-daughter."

Nora handed the baby to Michael. He took her gingerly as though she were the finest, most breakable object he had ever touched. His elegant, skilled fingers touched Hope's head and hands and tiny feet. He was awe struck.

Shaking his head, he swallowed hard and a silent tear fell from his eye. "She looks so much like you did, Nora, when you were born. Just as beautiful as you were, just as precious. I never wanted to let you out of my arms."

Nora leaned against her father, her head on his arm. It was almost as though she could remember her father's touch and his love on the day she was born. The same eyes that were adoring her little Hope were the ones that adored her that day in Boston, twenty-some years before.

"What was it like for you, Daddy? How did my mother feel the day I was born?"

Closing his eyes for a moment, Michael took himself back to that day. It was still so clear.

"Well, despite your mother being a doctor, she was completely in awe that such a beautiful creature could have been created inside her." Michael laughed, shaking his head as that day replayed itself in his mind. "Of course she drove all the nurses crazy because she criticized the way they held you and took your temperature and handed you to her. But she loved you, Nora. You just seemed like an unexpected surprise to her. And that part didn't change."

"Do you really think she loved me?" Nora asked, the slightest amount of hope resonating in the timbre of her voice.

"Yes, baby, she did, and I know she still does. But Jan doesn't express love in the way that most people expect. She always held in and held back. Like she was afraid someone would take it away from her if she let on that she loved something."

Hope began scrunching up her face, likely working herself up to tears. Michael handed her back to Nora, not wanting to be the cause of his granddaughter's anguish on the first day of her life.

"Oh, Daddy, this is Marge. She runs Hope Creek Dairy. Marge, this is my father, Michael Dodge. And this is Bobbie Jo, my best girlfriend in Tillamook and pregnant twin."

Bobbie Jo held her belly with one hand and reached out the other to Michael Dodge. "It's now once-pregnant twin, Nora. Don't forget that you just beat me to the punch. It's so great to meet you, Mr. Dodge." Tears threatened to burst forth, so Bobbie Jo just smiled, her emotions at the high-water mark given her stage of pregnancy, Steve's MIA status, and the poignancy of Nora's reunion with her father.

Then Marge stepped forward and shook hands with Nora and Willa's father. There was something special about his hands, she noticed immediately. *The hands of a surgeon. Healing hands.* Michael asked a few questions about the Dairy and the girls. Marge described how the girls were cared for and the work they did on the Farm.

"And you'll have to ask Nora about how much she has helped us at Hope Creek. Thanks to her our books are in order, we have a schedule that runs like clockwork, and a filing system that is so organized that we can actually find what we're looking for." Marge looked proudly at Nora, who blushed but was obviously pleased by the compliments, and that her father was hearing them too.

"You hear that Daddy? All that tuition money wasn't wasted!" Although she said it jokingly, Nora wanted her father to think she was useful, that she was capable of being something other than a dependent daughter and student. That she had value.

Michael Dodge was suddenly serious. "I have always known that you would find what was right for you, Nora. I've just never been very good at expressing it. I'm sorry for that."

"Remember, Daddy? We agreed, no more sorrys."

"Okay, no more sorrys."

Just then Willa burst into the room and ran to her father. He met his second daughter's strong embrace and then held her at arm's length.

"You look older too, Willa. What am I going to do with you girls?"

"You'll probably have to stop calling us girls!" Willa chided.

"Never. You'll always be my little girls, no matter how old you are." Michael Dodge beamed. He could not believe that he was with both of his daughters again. And now a new lovely granddaughter to love and be loved by.

Willa handed two white bags to Nora.

"Mm, yum. Thank you, Willa. You're my favorite sister!" They all laughed as Nora dug into a cheeseburger and fries from A&W.

"Emergency rations," Willa said in explanation. "The hospital food just wasn't cutting it."

"That's probably the one commonality of every hospital in the world. The food is consistently bad," Michael agreed as he chuckled at Nora's voracious appetite. "Postpartum cravings are very common."

Two hours later Willa and her father were themselves eating in the local diner, having left to give Nora a chance to bathe and get some sleep. After the waitress took their order, Michael Dodge reached for Willa's hand.

"Thank you, Willa."

"For what?"

"For being you. For having the courage to go and find your sister when I was frozen and couldn't do anything. For making us a family again. But forgive me. I'm lousy at expressing how I feel. I'm clumsy or something. I think the current lingo is 'uptight'."

Willa squeezed Michael's hand. "We were always a family, father. There was just too much distance and too many circumstances between us. I always knew you loved me. And I've always loved you. With that, it doesn't matter whether we're near each other or not."

Michael looked at his daughter, surprised by the wisdom that belied her age. "Your mother did a good job with you, Willa. You're pretty smart for a freshman in college."

"Well, almost a freshman. I was and am very lucky. I had Mma Cookie and Sammie Po, not just Dr. Jan. It's different in Botswana. All of the adults in my life were parents in different ways, each passing on the lessons that they could and feeling responsible for me. I've always had a very big family caring for me."

"But Nora never did," Michael interjected. "She only had me, who was not around half the time. And Carol, who Nora would never consider as a mother. And then I would only get more frustrated and resentful when Nora wouldn't accept me and Carol and was always angry."

Michael stared out the diner window. Bright, sunlit reflections in the parking lot suddenly grayed as a large cloud formation paled the summer day. All of the scenes of him and Nora fighting over curfews, college classes she should or shouldn't take, weekends on Nantucket with other surgeon's families that she refused to attend, it all made sense. She had been angry. And Michael had never figured out why, or didn't want to.

Had he ever really gotten over his own anger at Jan, he thought? Or really asked himself why he had insisted so adamantly that Jan marry him and have his baby? It was probably his fault that Jan left him. She never wanted to be married in the first place. How stupid he was back then. He imagined that he could make Jan his by taming her, tamping down her spirit and independence and making her into a wife, his wife.

But thank goodness for his twenty-something naiveté. Without it he would not have his beautiful girls and the life and joy they had and would bring to him.

Willa watched her father and could see he was struggling with all the things that men worried about for their daughters, and always would.

"Father, you did a good job with Nora, too, you know."

Michael looked at first surprised and then a tentative smile formed. "Yes, despite my parenting skills or lack thereof, Nora has become a mature woman. And I know she'll be a wonderful mother. Have you seen how she looks at Hope?"

Willa nodded. "It's the same way you have always looked at Nora and me, father. When you know someone loves you that much, it gives you the grounding to become the person you were meant to be, no matter what else happens."

"I missed you so much, Willa."

"I'm coming home now, father, and so are Nora and Hope."

"We'll be a family again."

"We are a family already, father."

"We are a family, Willa."

# # #

Bobbie Jo was exhausted when she got back to her and Steve's small ranch house, nestled in a cove on the south side of Tillamook Bay. Her due date was that day, but the doctor told her it would likely be at least another week and possibly two before she would deliver.

Her belly that had seemed beautiful and alive to her only weeks ago, now seemed distended and annoying. The trip into the hospital to see Nora had taken all of her energy, emotional and physical. She could not even cry anymore for Steve. For days she had done nothing else, until she realized she was crying for herself, for her loss. It was Steve she should be crying for, and the baby who would probably never know its father. How could she be so selfish? How could she get herself to stop thinking that Steve was gone forever? If only she had not heard it so many times before: MIA's don't usually come home.

Why couldn't she feel him any longer? Was that because he

was dead, or because her faith and hope were now pushed so far inside of her that she couldn't touch them anymore?

A sarcastic laugh escaped her throat. Bobbie Jo remembered when she met Nora how smug and relieved she had felt, realizing that she had a husband and security, a future. Poor Nora was an unwed mother with no known path for her to follow.

Now she and Nora had more in common than not, given Bobbie Jo's new, uncertain status. What was her title now anyway? Potential-widow? MIA-wife? Pitied wife. Single mother?

Suddenly orange light bathed Bobbie Jo, the sunset illuminating her fair skin and wrapping her in its comfortable, nourishing stream. She sucked in a sharp breath. *Steve was with her*! There in her chest, layered in her skin, behind her eyes, she could feel him again. Bobbie Jo let her eyelids fall, let the weightless feeling overtake her, following it wherever it led, because she knew it took her to Steve. *The father of her child. He was still here!*

That was something Bobbie Jo could lean on, could count on. She would be Mrs. Steven Edwards of Tillamook, Oregon. There was strength in that, a power that Bobbie Jo knew she would need. She was more than one alone, because Steve was still here.

As she opened her eyes, the bay sparkled back at her, a confirmation of hope. *Steve is close. Thank you, father of my child. I see it now. You will always be here.*

# # #

The letter was on the entry table in the main house and was addressed to both of them. Willa turned it over in her hands, examining the thickness of the envelope, the stamp, the return address, the tape that secured the sealed flap. Since Nora was still in the hospital, Willa decided she should open it.

Inside was a folded up playbill from the theatre company that Tunney worked for. Vibrant in its multi-colors and paisley swirls, it announced *The Fantasticks*, listing all the actors and company members. Tunney had highlighted his name in yellow in two spots. *Assistant Set Designer* was one, and the role of *Roustabout* was another where his name appeared.

Willa let out a happy, “Oh!” but there was no one in the hall to share it with. Tunney was an actor! Turning over the playbill, Willa saw a short note from him.

Hey ladies,

Miss my Dodge girls and hope that Baby Dodge (a girl, I predict) has now joined you at Hope Creek.

I'm actually liking this theatre gig and accidentally ended up in the cast as well. Never knew it was so much fun getting to be someone else for a few hours a night! Everyone is crazy and egotistical, so I fit right in.

Just wanted to say 'thanks' for the fun and adventures, but 'no thanks' for setting the bar so high. There are few women who meet the high standards for beauty and smarts as my Dodge girls.

But, I'm having fun trying to find one!

Miss youse.

Peace,
Tunney

# # #

Chapter 30: Home is Close

Boston, Massachusetts
December 31, 1969

The clinic was almost empty now, even the ill and infirm leaving to celebrate New Year's Eve.

"Willa, please go home now. You're making me feel guilty," Dr. Berman shouted across the clinic so Willa could hear him in the examination room that she was cleaning and stocking.

"I'm leaving," she called back. "Just getting this exam room ready for tomorrow." Willa raised her head and Dr. Berman was behind her.

"There's no tomorrow, Willa. We're closed tomorrow. You need a day off anyway. Don't you have a party to go to or something?"

Willa shook her head as she picked up the garbage can.

"Amazing. It's New Year's Eve and a nice girl like you doesn't have a party to go to? I thought your father or at least Carol would have been introducing you to all the eligible bachelor's in town," Dr. Berman said in his wise, grandfatherly tone. He had known Michael Dodge for years, since the younger man had interned under him many years before.

"I think they've given up on me, Dr. Berman."

"What's that? Already you only have eyes for medicine and you haven't even started at Harvard yet?" The older doctor smiled and shook his head. "You'd better have some fun while you can, Willa. Your life won't be your own for many years."

"I'm prepared for that, Doctor."

"I know you are Willa. But you're the only twenty-year-old I know whose idea of a good time is working in a welfare clinic. You know I appreciate all the time you put in here. But I worry about your social life," Dr. Berman said jokingly.

"Don't. I don't have one."

"Well, go find one tonight. I'm locking the door and you need to be on the other side of it. Let me give you a lift to your father's. It's snowing, you know."

Willa set the garbage can next to all the others and then grabbed her coat off the staff rack, following the older doctor out the front door.

"Wait under the awning, you don't have a hat. I'll bring the car around."

Willa nodded, suddenly mesmerized by the endless, fluffy wall of snowflakes, illuminated by the streetlight and floating fast and steady to the sidewalk. 'L' Street in South Boston was empty now. In the distance a snowplow scraped across a manhole cover. Still Willa looked up, the magic and newness of snow capturing her as she stared up into the white infinity, mysterious and startlingly cold to the African girl.

"*Dumela, Mma. O a reng, Mosadi*?"

That voice! Willa snapped her head around, hoping she had heard correctly. *Please let my ears not be numb.*

And there he was. She had dreamed about it on so many nights. But there was his silhouette, his face, his shoulders, the arms and hands she had missed every night. *Was the dream real again*?

"Tom!" Her legs were suddenly frozen. If she moved would he disappear? Would he become something different than the Tom she fell in love with, and loved under the sun of a different continent?

"Willa. Willawe," was all Tom said before he wrapped himself around her, and all the months and nights and miles fell away. It was real and not real, electric and numbing.

He kissed the melted snowflakes off her face and she laughed for the joy of it.

Dr. Berman pulled up to the curb, illuminating Willa and Tom.

"Did I miss something, Willa?" He shouted out of the open car window.

"Oh, Dr. Berman. This is my friend Tom. Tom, Dr. Berman."

"Seems like maybe you don't need a lift now, Willa?"

"Yes, I'm fine. Tom will see me home. Thanks Doctor."

Dr. Berman laughed and rolled the window back up. He pulled gingerly out into the taxi-trail on the snow-covered street.

For a minute the two lovers just beamed at one another and

then started laughing so hard they both slipped, tried to save one another, and fell onto the sidewalk. Tom lifted Willa up and wiped her face with his scarf.

"This is the beautiful face that I've been waiting to see. God, you're a sight for these sore eyes, Willa. Let me look at you."

Tom held her at arm's length. She was Willa of Botswana and yet she wasn't. His African girl was gone. Not the beauty or the intellect. But the endearing innocence that made him want to protect her from all the cons and the meanness in the world.

She didn't need protection any more. Had she ever needed it, Tom wondered? Probably not. It was only because it made Tom feel more in charge, more like a man that he insisted on thinking her naïve and innocent, when it was Willa who was stronger and wiser than Tom could ever hope to be.

Tom laughed at Willa, all bundled up in layers of clothes and yet still shivering.

"Let's run down to the 'L' Street Café. You're freezing. We'll get a hot toddy in you, and my car is just around the corner from there."

"I've heard about American boys like you. You get a girl drunk and then go parking." Willa put a wry smile on her face.

"Damn, foiled again. You caught on to us American boys pretty fast, Willawe."

"I learned from the best when I was still an African girl."

"Well, one thing I know for sure. You're not a girl anymore." Before, Willa had always given all of herself to Tom, letting him take over her whole being, trusting him, deferring to his age and experience that put him automatically in charge. It was flattering and frightening. His maleness would win out and he would take her in fully as his, consuming her. But that wasn't the Willa he held now

"You're right, I'm not a girl any more. Now I'm a liberated American woman."

"And what exactly does that mean, Miss Willa?"

"Tonight it means that I want to liberate both of us of the last six months. I missed you so much, Tom." Tears fell from her eyes and she buried her face in Tom's heavy coat. He could sense that

Willa's tears were shed for more reasons than happiness at seeing him again. Each echoed the sadness and joy of journeys and reunions, disappointments and choices, dreams and could-have-beens. It was a real woman he held in his arms. *Please let me keep her. Please let me deserve to keep her.*

"Oh, Willawe, I missed you 'til it hurt. I've had more cold showers in the last six months than I can tell you about. I read your letters so many times that I can quote each one verbatim."

"I've got some new lines you can quote," Willa said huskily, her arms wrapped so tightly around him that they could hardly walk.

"Say that again and I'll be pulling you in that alley right there. You're killing me, Willa."

"Come home with me, Tom. That's all I want right now."

"Tell me home is close."

"Home is close."

# # #

Epilogue

Mother Mercy Clinic
November 5, 1973

Overhead, the unmistakable sound of the bush plane could suddenly be heard in the kitchen. The young girl jumped off her stool and squealed in delight.

"Johnny, Johnny's here!" She ran across the room and banged open the screen door before Mma Cookie could even raise her voice to stop her.

"*Tsholofelo*, you come back, little ostrich. You cannot run to the airfield!" Mma Cookie yelled as she heard her charge squeal again. She could not help herself and laughed at the energy of her little Tsholofelo.

Luckily Sammie Po was making his way across the compound and grabbed the excited four-year-old.

"Where are you flying to, *mosetsana*? Are you a girl or a fish eagle?" Sammie Po picked up Tsholofelo and tossed her into the air.

"I'm a fish eagle. Take me to Johnny. I will fly!"

Sammie Po laughed as he slung Tsholofelo over his shoulder like a bag of mealie meal.

"Mma Cookie, do you need this big old sack of mealies for our lunch today? I am so very hungry I think I will eat the whole sack myself." Tsholofelo squealed and giggled in mock terror.

"No, don't eat me, Sammie. I'm really a girl!"

"You are? How can I be sure? I'm too hungry to hear anything."

"I'm a girl. Mealies don't talk. And I taste so bad."

Sammie Po and Mma Cookie laughed together as he deposited Tsholofelo on the porch.

"You cannot run to the airfield, little ostrich. Johnny is coming here just now. You are too much curious. And you are frightening your mother too much. You'll be back in the corner if you are a bad girl, you see?" Mma Cookie used all her will power to look serious and force herself not to smile.

"No corner, Mma." Tsholofelo plopped down on the verandah steps, elbows on her knees and chin in her little restless hands.

The plane overhead had brought Dr. Jan out of the surgery and Nora out of the office, both into the inner compound.

"That has to be the new doctor," Jan said as she pulled off her latex gloves.

"What do you mean? I thought he wasn't expected until Friday?" Nora asked as she walked closer to her mother.

"Damn, I forgot to give this to you. It came this morning." Jan pulled a brown telegram envelope out of her smock and handed it to Nora.

DR KEANE ARRIVING M MERCY NOV 5

"That's all? No reason why he's early?"

Jan shook her head.

"Are we ready for him?" Nora asked, doubt clear in her voice.

Jan shrugged. "Could we ever be? He's been a Navy doctor. We'll never be ship shape enough for him, probably."

"Great. A doctor who's spent his whole career on the water coming to the desert. A real match made in heaven. Do you have a fall back in case he turns tail?"

Dr. Jan let out a sarcastic chortle and put her hands on her hips. "Now look who's being the cynical one. You always accuse me of seeing the glass half empty. Ha!"

Nora scowled at her mother but it quickly turned conciliatory. "I'm just trying to make sure we keep some semblance of order here. We can't keep losing doctors every few months."

"I know, I know. But it's not like we're offering a lot of perks here. We've always made do somehow."

"But I want us to do better than just make do."

Jan blinked at her daughter. Nora really believed in Mother Mercy. And she had made such a difference in the three years that she had been in Botswana. Jan used to wonder why hospitals needed administrators. But after Nora had taken over the operational management of the clinic, everything ran so smoothly now. They rarely ran out of medicine unless there was a regional shortage, and people were not asked to wait in the sun for five hours only to be told to come again the next day. Linens were cleaned daily, not once a week, and they always had a surplus. Nora had sent information on the clinic to aid agencies and foundations. Now Mother Mercy was a regular stop when organizations toured the region to assess health needs and determine who would get aid.

Nora and Jan both remembered their many battles in the beginning when Nora arrived at Mother Mercy. But the resentments eventually watered down as mother and daughter simply grew tired of always quarreling, and then realized how much they liked each other. Now they also shared a common love of the clinic.

Mma Cookie's wise words continued to play over and over in Nora's head: '*There is great power in forgiveness, Nora. Use the power. Forgive her. Free yourself.*' Her words, a gift she had given Nora at the end of her first week at Mother Mercy, were a guide stone that Nora found easier to understand and follow every day she was with her mother.

Jan put her arm around Nora's waist. "Dr. Keane will think we're doing very well. This is the new and improved Mother Mercy. You're making us look good, Nora."

"Whoa, you're being too nice to me. What do you want?" Nora stepped backed from Jan, a skeptical frown turning her smile upside down.

Jan put a fake look of hurt on her face. "Nothing," she said and turned to walk back into the surgery. "Oh, except I need you to go and welcome Dr. Keane at the airstrip." Jan shrugged and pointed to her blood-stained smock. "I'm a filthy mess! Please, Nora." Jan did not wait for Nora's response but headed back toward the surgery.

"Thanks for the advance notice, Mma."

"Don't call me Mma, Nora."

"Yes, Mma." Jan kept walking but shook her fist in the air.

"Scary, Mma, real scary."

"But I'm not scared, Mama." It was Tsholofelo, Nora's Hope,

standing at the compound entrance with Sammie Po.

"Of course you aren't, sweetheart. You're a Dodge woman. And we don't scare easily, do we?"

"No, Mama."

"Nora, we must collect the new doctor now, now." Sammie twirled his hat around on his hand, a clear sign that he was in a hurry.

"Oh, Sammie. Okay, let's go, doctor's orders."

"And little Hope wants to come too." Sammie and Mma Cookie only used the little girl's American name when they talked to Nora or Dr. Jan. Otherwise they called her Tsholofelo, the Setswana word for Hope.

"Please, Mama." Hope played the trump card that always worked with Nora. She made her beautiful brown eyes even bigger somehow, and filled them with a sad hopefulness that Nora could not stand to see.

"Okay. I know you love Papa Johnny."

"And his 'splane."

"Yes, his airplane."

"Eh-wah-plane."

"Good, Hope." The four-year-old beamed and then said something in Setswana that Nora did not understand. "What did she say, Sammie?"

He hesitated for a moment and then chuckled. "She say that Johnny is going to let her fly the plane and told her this."

"He did, did he?"

"She only talks about flying, my daughter. Her totem is a fish eagle, I believe."

"Hmm. We'll see about the flying part. Hope is still too young to do that." Nora looked in the side view mirror, watching the plume of dust and sand form a choking wake behind them. *Just what the doctor needs to see as his first vision of Mother Mercy,* Nora thought, as more doubts about the new doctor's tenure pushed their way into her head.

"Oh well," Nora said aloud.

"Oh well, what Mama?" Hope looked up at her mother.

"Oh, well, here we go to greet our new doctor. A new exciting adventure begins again!"

"Yippee!" Hope yelled out joyfully, and spontaneously began singing the Botswana National Anthem.

Sammie Po laughed aloud at little Tsholofelo, their little Hope, and then joined in. Nora sang the few words she knew and hummed enthusiastically the rest of the time. The rolling chorus finished the first verse just as they reached Johnny's plane.

"Look! The new doctor! He stands tall like a giraffe!" Hope called out. Nora loved her Hope's spontaneous outbursts. Most of the time they were the same thing Nora was thinking but would never say out loud and risk exposing herself.

Hope jumped out of the lorry and ran into Johnny's arms.

"My most Hopeful! Hello little leprechaun!"

"Johnny! I want to fly now!"

The bush pilot laughed and tossed Hope into the air. "Nora, dear. You look lovely as always." Johnny wrapped his arm around Nora's waist and she leaned into him. "Doc Keane, Nora Dodge, Dr. Jan's daughter and the one who really runs things around here. Nora, this is your new doctor. He's good. I can tell already."

Suddenly Nora felt shy and nervous. Dr. Keane's hand was cool and dry when she shook it.

"Welcome, Dr. Keane. This is Sammie Po, our ambulance driver and also everyone's father at Mother Mercy."

Sammie Po smiled broadly and shook the new doctor's hand as he held his hat in the other. "Thank you, Rra. Welcome, yes, you are welcome. And such a tall gentleman, you are," Sammie stated in his usual sure but quiet tone.

"How was your trip here, doctor? Not too bad, I hope?" Nora asked as Sammie and Johnny loaded his few belongings into the lorry.

Before he could even answer, Hope jumped in front of the doctor and did her version of an introduction.

"I'm Hope and Tsholofelo. That means Hope too. I'll teach you that." Hope sidled up to Dr. Keane and took his hand.

Nora looked embarrassed and was about to call Hope back when Dr. Keane beamed and gave Nora a look that signaled, 'It's okay, I'm enjoying this.'

"It's nice to meet you Hope and Tsholofelo. And Nora and Sammie. It was a great trip. Very clear all the way. At least I've seen Africa from the 30,000-foot level."

Nora smiled. She like the timbre of his voice.

"Where are you from, Dr. Keane? I can't place your accent."

"I have an accent?" Dr. Keane laughed. "Call me David, please."

"David please," Hope mimicked and then giggled at herself.

"You are on a roll, kiddo. Remember what you heard about sassy girls from Mma Cookie?" Nora did her best to look tough. Hope just smiled and did not answer, even as she gripped David's hand tighter. "Give the man some room, Hope!"

"I'm from all over, Nora. Navy brat then Navy myself." David picked up his black case with his free hand.

"It's a very nice all-over accent," Nora responded, and then cringed at the silly remark. It was something that Hope would have said. She silently admonished herself.

Nora motioned for David to sit in the front with Sammie Po. Before she could stop her daughter, lithe Hope dove over into the front seat and landed between Sammie and David.

"Hope Dodge, what were we just talking about? Get yourself back here and give the poor man some breathing room!" Nora reached her hand over the seat for Hope to grab.

Instead David lightly touched her hand.

"I'm good with her up here, Nora. I've been sitting on planes with strangers and generally poor conversationalists for two days now. Hope has made more sense than anyone yet, I'm sorry to say."

"Don't be sorry, Dr. David." Hope put her little hand on David's knee. "Mama said that you were our new exciting adventure."

"She did?" David exaggerated his reply. Nora groaned in the back seat and then they all started laughing.

Nora pushed down on Hope shoulders. "Don't worry, Dr. Keane, we lock her up at night and she's not allowed in the clinic."

Hope stood up in defiance and whispered loudly into David's ear, "But I go in there anyway. Don't tell."

Nora threw up her hands. “Hope Ginny Dodge, what am I going to do with you, Missy?”

Nora leaned over the seat and put her arms across Hope’s chest like a brace. Hope crossed her arms over her mother’s, her little fingers making pink indentations of love. The kind that daughters leave behind.

THE END

My respect and love to the people of Botswana. Thank you for the time, and the lessons, you shared with me. Ke a leboga.

ABOUT THE AUTHOR

D. Lou Raymond's six years in Botswana, Africa as a Peace Corps volunteer and later a development officer included travels to towns, villages, and remote areas in Botswana, Zimbabwe, Lesotho, and South Africa. Raymond won a writing competition from MacMillan Publishers (South Africa) for the short story, *Rain Woman,* and the award was presented by then President of Botswana, Dr. Quett Masire. *Rain Woman* was subsequently published in two anthologies by MacMillan, *Eyes on Africa* – stories by new writers – and *Patterns of Africa*, stories by well-known writers such as Chinua Achebe, Bessie Head, and Ngugi wa Thiong'o.

Raymond's focus on the relationships of sisters in *Dodging Africa* is borne from growing up in a large family of five sisters and one brother. Now living on the Oregon coast, Raymond is working on a second novel set in Europe during World War II (expected publication Fall 2021).

Made in the USA
Middletown, DE
06 January 2021